THE STREET OF A
THOUSAND BLOSSOMS

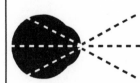

This Large Print Book carries the
Seal of Approval of N.A.V.H.

THE STREET OF A THOUSAND BLOSSOMS

GAIL TSUKIYAMA

THORNDIKE PRESS

A part of Gale, Cengage Learning

GALE
CENGAGE Learning

Detroit • New York • San Francisco • New Haven, Conn • Waterville, Maine • London

GALE
CENGAGE Learning

Copyright © 2007 by Gail Tsukiyama.
Thorndike Press, a part of Gale, Cengage Learning.

Thorndike Press® Large Print Basic.
The text of this Large Print edition is unabridged.
Other aspects of the book may vary from the original edition.
Set in 16 pt. Plantin.
Printed on permanent paper.

LIBRARY OF CONGRESS CATALOGING-IN-PUBLICATION DATA

Tsukiyama, Gail.
  The street of a thousand blossoms / by Gail Tsukiyama.
    p. cm.
  ISBN-13: 978-1-4104-0476-3 (hardcover : alk. paper)
  ISBN-10: 1-4104-0476-5 (hardcover : alk. paper)
  1. Tokyo (Japan) — Fiction. 2. Brothers — Fiction. 3. Large
type books. I. Title.
PS3570.S84S77 2008
813'.54—dc22   2007045366

Published in 2008 by arrangement with St. Martin's Press, LLC.

Printed in the United States of America
1 2 3 4 5 6 7 12 11 10 09 08

For Grace Yam Tsukiyama
In Loving Memory

Prologue
A Day of No Regrets
1966

A white light seeped through the shoji windows and into the room, along with the morning chill. Except for the futon he slept on and a teakwood desk, the pale, spacious room was empty. Hiroshi Matsumoto breathed in the grassy fragrance of the tatami mats, the sweet and stirring February air, his thoughts wandering to the cherry blossoms that would soon be poised like flakes of snow upon their branches. The trees that lined the streets of Yanaka would be in full bloom, and the labyrinth of narrow alleyways would swarm with tourists stopping to admire the Japanese quince, daffodils, and blue triplet lilies blossoming in flower boxes that crowded the teeming walkways. As boys, he and his brother, Kenji, had pushed single file past the old wood and stone houses to the park. Now, there were few of the old buildings left, long since having been replaced by brick and concrete ones. Despite the sharp edge of memories that stabbed him just below his rib cage, he still loved this season best, just as Aki always had — the doorway to spring with each morning gleaming with new possibilities.

Almost twenty years ago, his youthful agility had rekindled a national passion for sumo wrestling. In a country devastated by atomic bombs that flattened cities and scarred their spirits, Hiroshi's speed and strength had helped to revive the pride of his nation with every victory. He had barely been able to contain the joy he felt as he climbed the ranks. Not until he found courage enough to touch with two fingers the nape of his wife, Aki's, neck did any thrill ever match it.

Hiroshi pushed off his covers and stretched his body the full length of his extra-large futon, his muscular girth still impressive at his age. He had always valued strength and speed more than some other *rikishi,* sumo wrestlers who gained inordinate amounts of weight to dominate a match by their size. At thirty-seven, he was a good deal older and, at six feet one, more than a hundred pounds lighter than the heaviest wrestlers, who weighed in at four hundred pounds. Hiroshi sat up and fingered the faint rise of a scar that ran along his hairline and ended at his right temple, then rubbed his belly and pushed his rough feet to the edge of the futon, his calluses a souvenir of barefoot practice on dirt and wooden floors. *So many years,* he thought, and he touched for luck the soles of his feet, first the left, then the right, as he did every morning. As Hiroshi heaved himself up from the futon and reached for his kimono, he felt again that first step onto the *dohyo.* The smooth, sacred clay surface of the elevated straw ring was a blessing after years of discipline, training, and rituals. The scratching of his bare feet on the tatami mats made a sad insect sound, not unlike the swish of salt thrown down on the ring to drive out the evil spirits.

Competition had been a strong and potent drug. Everyone and everything disappeared as soon as he entered the ring, as if his life were narrowed to that very moment in time and nothing else mattered. Nothing and everything. He wondered once more if it had all been worthwhile — the sacrifice of family, friends, and lovers for a sport. And only now, too late, could he see the cost of it all as Aki's accusing stare flashed through his mind.

A sharp knock on the shoji door brought him out of his reverie. He quickly tightened the sash of his *yukata* kimono, and grunted permission to enter.

The door slid open. It was Haru, dressed in a dark blue padded kimono with a pattern of white cranes. It looked new, yet strangely

9

familiar to him, as if Aki had once worn one similar to it. It was Haru who had first introduced him to her sister, a lifetime ago. Aki was the most beautiful girl he'd ever seen — her clear, milky-white skin, the smooth, sharp curve of her chin, her hidden fragility.

Haru's movements were quick and sure, her dark eyes as intense and intelligent as they always were. Every morning, no matter the weather, she was out walking in the garden with his five-year-old daughter. And though Takara shared her mother's classic beauty, he saw Haru's strength emerging more and more in her each day.

Haru bowed. "We'll be leaving for the stadium soon," she said. "Kenji-san is coming for us after he picks up your *obachan*."

He watched Haru's poised figure and the same straight nose and thin, crescent-moon eyebrows that had also graced her sister, Aki. They would all be there at his retirement ceremony, his grandmother, brother, Haru, and Takara. *"Hai,"* he said, swallowing.

She moved across the room to slide open the shoji windows, admitting a cool breeze from the west. It filled the room with a sudden breath of promise. He cleared his throat but said nothing.

Instead, it was Haru who spoke, as she looked out at his acre of *sakura* trees. "A day of no regrets," she said, as if reading his thoughts.

And suddenly, something tender and inconsolable gripped his chest, an entire life boiled down to these last hours. He rubbed his eyes and nodded, always amazed at her astuteness. "What do you see?" he asked.

Haru turned to him again. "Such beauty . . . ," she began, without finishing her sentence.

■ ■ ■ ■

PART ONE

■ ■ ■ ■

When spring comes,
this world once more
calls to me —
in what other world
could I see such blossoms?
— Fujiwara no Shunzei

1
A CHILD OF GOOD
FORTUNE
1939

Late again, Hiroshi weaved in and out of the crowds near the Momiji teahouse. Sweat trickled down his neck and he pulled at the undershirt that was sticky against his back as he squeezed through the swarm of pedestrians clogging the labyrinth of narrow alleyways. They stopped to admire the deep blue and bright pink flowers blooming in the flower boxes — a heady fragrance drifting through the warm air. Eleven-year-old Hiroshi was already late to meet his grandfather and younger brother, Kenji, at the Keio-ji temple on the other side of Yanaka. He had dashed from the open, grassy field of the park where he and his classmates spent their afternoons practicing the wrestling techniques they learned in school — the *oshi,* hand push; the *tsuki,* thrust; and the *yori,* body push. "These are the fundamental moves of sumo wrestling," his coach at school, Masuda-san stressed, "the foundation on which we will build."

Once again, Hiroshi had lost track of time.

In the Yanaka district of northeastern Tokyo, the sloping streets were lined with traditional one- and two-story wooden houses. Despite the crowds, Hiroshi loved Yanaka for its familiar and quiet way of life, for the tantalizing smells of grilled fish kush-iyaki and the sweet chicken yakitori sold from wooden carts. When he wasn't in a hurry, he even loved the maze of winding alleyways with blooming gardens that hid the old wood houses and the small, unassuming shops with their cloth banners hanging outside, selling *hanakago,* or bamboo flower baskets, hand-made *washi* paper, and the soft silken tofu his grandmother loved to eat cold during the summer. The narrow streets offered a wealth of escape routes for the chase games he and the neighborhood children played — places you could get lost or hide in until you wanted to be found, or not found.

But now, it was impossible for him to navigate them quickly. Men his grandfather's age sat at battered wooden tables and played *shoji,* oblivious to the crowds as they pondered each chess move. Hiroshi squeezed by a woman in a kimono, a baby tied to her back; the round-faced girl with dark eyes followed his every move.

Once he neared the *ginza,* vendors lined the streets, selling everything from grilled

16

corn and sweet potatoes, to roasted *sembei* rice crackers and baked squid. The enticing aroma of the spicy shoyu crackers reminded Hiroshi of his empty stomach, but he didn't dare stop. The muscles pulled in his sore calves as he hurried up the hill. He wrinkled his nose at the pungent vinegary smell of *tsukudani,* a kind of Japanese chutney his grandparents ate over their rice, which came from a nearby store and hung heavy in the air. He was short of breath by the time he reached the Keio-ji temple to find his grandfather and Kenji waiting outside.

"Ah, the young master arrives," his grandfather teased. He sat on a stone bench in the shade of a ginkgo tree sucking on his pipe, his cane resting against his knee.

Hiroshi bowed low. "I'm sorry to be late, *ojichan,*" he said, pausing to catch his breath.

"Sumo, eh?"

Hiroshi nodded. At eleven, he was already the top wrestler in his class, perhaps the entire school. He'd grown taller and stronger in the year since he began taking the sport seriously.

Kenji pouted. "Why else would he be late?"

"I lost track of the time," Hiroshi confessed, trying to appease his brother. He'd already been late several times this month.

"Did you at least win the match?" His *ojichan* leaned forward on his cane and stood.

Hiroshi straightened up and answered,

"Hai," though it was just practice, not real competition.

His *ojichan* stepped toward the stone path and smiled. "Good, good. Hiroshi will be a champion one day. And you, Kenji, will find your place soon enough," he said gently. "Now, shall we take our walk?"

Yanaka was one of the few areas of Tokyo not devastated by the Great Kanto earthquake of 1923, a distinction their *ojichan* proudly repeated to Hiroshi and Kenji. He pointed his cane toward the same old temples that had once surrounded the Edo castle and had been moved to Yanaka after surviving a big fire, almost three hundred years ago.

"The temples withstood both disasters virtually unscathed," his *ojichan* said — the miracle of it emphasized in the rise of his voice. "And look there," he continued, directing their gaze to the lone smokestack of what was once the Okira bathhouse. "Not everything was spared. Okira-san never rebuilt after the quake, but he left the smokestack as a symbol of Yanaka's resilience. You boys must never forget."

Hiroshi wouldn't forget, not just because he couldn't walk thirty feet down any road without seeing an ancient temple, but also because his *ojichan* was the embodiment of that same fortitude. He looked into his grandfather's eyes. A cloudy film covered his dark pupils. Hiroshi wondered how much his grandfather could really see, and how much he saw from memory. He tried to imagine what it must feel like to slowly lose one's sight behind a thick, dense fog that left everything in blurry shadow. Hiroshi often wanted to take hold of his *ojichan*'s arm, afraid that he might stumble on an uneven path, or on the stone steps leading down to the Sumida River, but he once again refrained as his *ojichan* moved briskly down the road, not missing a step.

That night after dinner as Hiroshi sat bent over his schoolwork, his grandmother came into the dining room and sat on the tatami mat across from him, pouring each of them a cup of green tea. It was his grandparents, Yoshio and Fumiko Wada, who kept the spirit of his parents alive, long after three-year-old Hiroshi and his eighteen-month-old brother, Kenji, were orphaned. His *obachan* often stopped whatever she was doing, washing clothes or preparing his grandfather's favorite sticky rice, to tell Hiroshi stories of his parents and how they had saved his life. "You are a child of good fortune," his *obachan* whispered, so that the gods wouldn't hear her and return to take him away, too. "They loved you and your little brother more than life." She always sighed as if the ache of their deaths could be expelled.

When she began to speak, he looked up from his books, drank down his tea, and listened to his *obachan*'s story. *"Your mother and father were so happy to get away to Kyoto for their first overnight trip since you were born,"* she began, her voice clear but calm in the small dining room. *"And still, they wanted to take you with them. You were just three years old. Kenji was eighteen months and I insisted that he stay with your* ojichan *and me. It was the last evening of the Lantern Festival at Miyazu Bay. They wanted to show you the red lanterns glimmering on the dark water like fireflies, where the spirit ships welcomed ancestors back to the human world. It was a warm and still summer night and your mother wore her red-flowered summer kimono. Who could have known that the spirits would take your mother and father back into their world with them?"* His *obachan* swallowed. Her pause was like a sorrow she could never voice. *"Everyone felt festive in the calm, unusually dark night. The water gleamed the color of black pearl. Some men with a fishing boat offered to take spectators out into the bay to float among the lanterns. What possesses people to do what they do? Your mother and father stepped onto that boat, with you squirming in your father's arms. Too late they realized that the men steering the boat were drunk, that they'd been drinking sake all afternoon and should never have taken people out on that dark night. They went out too far, away from the shore, away from the lighted lanterns, away from all that was safe. In the blindness of that night, the boat struck rocks. The wood snapped and cracked. The boat ripped apart like shoji beneath their feet, separating your parents onto opposite halves of the deck. The boat sank in minutes — just enough time for your quick-thinking father to place you in an empty fish barrel. You floated on the waves, crying after him, while he dived into the dark waters in search of your mother, who had never been a strong swimmer. Just beyond them, a wall of floating lanterns blocked the view of what was happening; your screams were lost in the revelry. When the other boats came to the rescue, all eight passengers were found drowned that night in Miyazu Bay, all except you, Hiroshi, floating in your fish barrel, and the young captain of the boat. They told us that water had just begun to seep into the barrel."*

"What happened to the captain?" Hiroshi asked. He pushed his books aside and looked down at his grandmother's thin, blue-veined hands that never seemed to stop moving.

"His body was never found," his *obachan* answered. She sat for a moment in silence; Hiroshi felt bitterness cut through the air between them. "I prayed the spirits of the dead had taken him that night, forgetting to leave his body behind."

21

■ ■ ■ ■

At the end of his grandmother's story, Hiroshi stood and stretched. He took a deep breath, and went to study the black-and-white photograph of his parents, Kazuo and Misako, that sat on the *tokonoma,* the recessed shelf in his grandparents' living room. Misako had been their only daughter. He saw himself in his father's tall, heavyset build, his dark, almost brooding features, while Kenji was a daily reminder of his delicate mother with her liquid, faraway gaze. He wondered whether his parents might have lived if he hadn't been with them that night. Those precious moments given to him might have saved their lives. The thought stabbed at the side of his brain until his head ached. Which was worse, he asked himself — having them taken from him, or not remembering them at all, like Kenji? The answer tilted one way, then the other, never finding balance.

Where are they now? Hiroshi sometimes wondered, though he never said the words aloud. Were they watching from the heavens? Did they know when he and Kenji were bad? When he was a little boy, it all seemed too large and confusing. What he remembered felt less and less tangible.

As Hiroshi grew older, his own memories of that night blurred with the distance of a dream. He began to hear slight discrepancies in each version of his *obachan*'s story. He never asked how she could know so much. He never questioned any of the differences — the change in time, the shade of darkness in the night, the color of his mother's kimono or his father's shoes. He liked the way she reinvented his parents, brought them back to life. Bits and pieces of their existence returned to him, his father's arms holding him tightly, his mother's lovely, smiling eyes upon his face, the darkness of that night, the red lights, the slapping of water all around him as he floated light and ethereal. His *obachan* always began the story with a great burst of energy, her voice rising and falling like waves, lapping slowly to shore almost in a whisper as she came to the end. He sat back transfixed, wanting only to hear it again, while his younger brother, Kenji, covered his ears or left the room, preferring to be as far away as possible. But his *obachan,* tired and spent, always needed to lie down afterward.

Every August, during the Obon festival, when they went to the crowded Yanaka cemetery to honor the spirits of the dead, Hiroshi looked at the two stone slabs with his parents' names written in bold, black characters, but he refused to believe they could be there, buried in the hard, cold ground. They were floating, he thought, if not in water then in the air, all around them. The drifting fog of burning incense made his eyes water. His *obachan* placed bowls of rice, vegetables, fruits, and sweet cakes in front of the graves for the spirits to eat. At the sight of the gravestones, Kenji pursed his lips, jabbed at the dark earth with his foot, and remained silent throughout their *obachan*'s chanting prayers. It was the only time Kenji ever held Hiroshi's hand, squeezed tight in a sweaty grip. He never let go until they were back home.

THE STREET OF A THOUSAND BLOSSOMS

They lived on the street of a thousand blossoms, one of the narrow lanes not far from the Kyo-ou-ji temple, in a row of similar two-story wooden houses with a courtyard in front, a square of land in the backyard, slanting roofs, and jutting eaves. Though the houses were right next to each other, their wooden fences and blooming walls of thick bamboo provided each house with a separate intimacy. A string of wind chimes hung by Hiroshi's front gate next to a faded red metal mailbox, and when a brisk wind stirred the chimes, a chorus of tinkling filled the air like hurried voices.

What did set his grandparents' house apart from the rest in Yanaka was the soaring addition his *ojichan* had built after Hiroshi's parents drowned. The *tenshukaku* was added

24

onto the back of the house, off the kitchen, a wooden watchtower with a staircase that wound twelve feet above the surrounding rooftops to a deck at the top. It was covered with an identical slanting roof and jutting eaves.

As a little boy, Hiroshi remembered his *ojichan*, before he retired, returning from work as the *toji*, the brewery master at the Hanku Sake Factory. He changed his clothes and worked at building the tower board by board, fitting the wooden pegs in place — the rhythmic pounding a part of Hiroshi's childhood. He watched wide-eyed, as if it were a game his *ojichan* was playing, just like the building blocks he and Kenji stacked one atop another. But at the end of the day, their blocks came crashing down, while his *ojichan* slowly added to the tower's height like a child growing taller.

"Why?" he remembered his grandmother asking one night when his *ojichan* finally came in. It was dark and chilly and his grandfather's skin looked gray from the cold, his eyes half-closed as he sat in the warmth of the kitchen.

"It's to observe the life around us," he answered at last, and sipped from his hot tea.

"What life? What do you suppose you'll see up there, old man?" she muttered, a tenderness slipping in at the edge of her words.

"My eyes may be failing," he answered,

"but Hiroshi and Kenji have so much to see. Misako would have wanted that for them." His voice rose in strength at the mention of his only daughter's name.

Hiroshi thought about his mother every time he climbed the stairs up to the tower. Not only did it become a place for the boys to observe the world around them, but a space where they built imaginary worlds. The tower became the Himeji Castle, nicknamed the White Heron Castle, that soared into the sky. Other times it was a sailing vessel in the middle of an endless sea, but always it was a place of comfort and dreams. Perched high among the clouds, Hiroshi and Kenji could be gods or samurais, each finding his own kind of solace.

One night, when Hiroshi was eight years old, long after the boys were supposed to be asleep, he heard low murmurs and a girlish laughter coming from up in the tower. He might have mistaken the laughter for that of a stranger, if he hadn't heard it before, far away in the back of his memory. He stole out of bed and made his way quietly up the stairs, only to spy his grandparents together, watching the night sky, his *ojichan* leaning over and whispering something that made his *obachan* laugh again — high and girlish — a sound he suddenly recognized as his mother's laugh. She was there with them. And for a moment, Hiroshi felt a tingling sensation, his mother close by, hovering in the air just above them.

When neighbors complained or made a disparaging remark about the height of the tower and the obstruction of sunlight in their courtyards, his *ojichan* met their disapproving gaze with a smile and a bow of his head as if in apology. Then he leaned over and whispered to his grandsons, "Yes, but we are that much closer to the heavens."

CAT EYES

Kenji had been a frail and quiet baby. His grandparents always took great care to keep him from catching a cold or becoming too hot under the quilted comforters. He lay in his basket and always seemed to be searching for something with his dark, distant gaze. *Neko-no-me,* Cat-eyes, his *obachan* called him. "You are the small cat that will survive the fire," she whispered to him lovingly. "While your big brother, Hiroshi, will live by his head, you will live by your heart." It was something Kenji heard his grandmother say many times when he was growing up. But he wanted to know why he was the one who lived by his heart. Why couldn't he be more like Hiroshi? He put his hand over the left side of his chest, felt the dull thumping through his shirt, and smiled.

Whenever Kenji heard the low murmur of his *obachan* beginning another story about his parents, he would disappear into his room, or wait outside for his *ojichan* to return, or wander through the labyrinths of alleyways. At the age of nine, he couldn't bear to hear her story one more time. He used to make up his own stories, imagining his parents were secretly alive, living somewhere close by — memories of their earlier lives lost after swimming safely to shore. He felt this every time he saw a man or woman walking down the road who resembled the photo his *obachan* kept of his parents, and he was sure that like magic or wishful desire, they would recognize the baby they'd left behind. Eventually both his and his *obachan*'s stories began to hurt his stomach, giving him cramps that left his skin clammy and his head spinning. He couldn't breathe for the sorrow that hung on every word.

Sometimes, if it was still early, Kenji would walk toward the Yanaka *ginza*, lingering at the threshold of the small shops where repairmen patched bicycle tires, or craftsmen carved out *kime kome* dolls, covering their wood forms with red and purple brocaded cloth, painting their glistening white faces with a powdered seashell called *gofun*. Kenji stayed perfectly still and watched mesmerized as the inanimate object began taking on a life of its own. Soon the spinning motion of the bicycle tires would take people from one place to another, while a block of wood would be transformed into a graceful doll resembling a member of the imperial court. Knowing this gave Kenji a feeling of endless possibilities.

But nothing fascinated him more than the carved masks he discovered in a tiny shop, hidden away in one of the back alleyways. Kenji might have walked right by the shop if not for the sun's reflection off the gold trim of a mask in the window — a rope of light pulling at him. Kenji gazed into the small showcase where three masks stared back at him, hollow-eyed and powerful — an old man with long trailing whiskers, a beautifully austere, white-faced woman, and a red-faced devil, trimmed with gold. The masks captivated Kenji like nothing else, sent a shiver through his body as if he had a fever. He pressed closer to the window and saw through dirty glass into a small, cluttered room with two chairs and a table covered with papers. A tall shelf lined one wall with still other masks propped up on it. Toward the back of the shop a curtained doorway led to another room. No one seemed to be around. Suddenly, Kenji wanted desperately to see the other masks, a sharp longing that gave him courage. But before he could move, strange voices coming down the alley grew louder and he stepped back, half-hidden, to watch. One by one, two lavishly dressed people in dark Western clothing, and a woman in a bright silk kimono entered the battered, lopsided doorway of the shop. Kenji peeked inside to see them bowing low to a slight, bearded man who emerged from the back room, his long, disheveled hair covered with a fine dust.

Kenji's *obachan* later told him the shop belonged to a man named Akira Yoshiwara, who was well known throughout Japan as a master carver of Noh masks used in the theater. Rumors swirled around the eccentric artisan, who could pick and choose his clients, working for whom he wanted, when he wanted. Actors from all over vied for his masks, she said. Kenji daydreamed about being one of those clients, gliding into the tiny shop, holding each exquisite mask up to his face and breathing life into it.

When he heard his grandmother in the dining room telling Hiroshi yet another story, Kenji went outside through the courtyard to wait for his grandfather at the front gate. He heard stray voices echo through the alley, where oil lamps left an eerie yellowish glow. He turned when a gust of wind set the chimes tingling. Only when he heard the tap, tap, tap of his *ojichan*'s cane against the pavement did he feel the hard stone of sorrow melt inside of him, and an anxious, yet tender expectation take its place.

Even as his eyesight worsened, his *ojichan*

30

insisted on keeping his daily routine, walking alone to the bar down several blocks to sit with his friends around the table and talk of their younger days, of the growing war in China, and of the ongoing string of victories by a young sumo named Futabayama. Sometimes, Kenji went with him, sitting on a sticky chair in the corner to drink cold, sweetened tea, while his *ojichan* drank beer with the other men, lost in the cloud of smoke and laughter. In the small, closed room, he watched the rough and thickened hands of the men move through the air like clumsy birds, listened to their deep voices, and felt comforted. Often he fell asleep to the static hum of live sumo tournaments or the war news from China broadcast over the radio, only to be awakened from faceless dreams by the voices of the old men calling out his name.

"Kenji-san, are we boring you?" they said, laughing.

Then slowly he'd awaken, bleary-eyed until the smoke-filled room came into focus and he saw his *ojichan* sitting among the other men, his vague gaze cast over him like a net.

Now, Kenji stood up as his grandfather approached.

"What are you doing out here?" his *ojichan* asked, when he was close enough to see that

Kenji was there on the step right in front of him.

"Waiting for you," he answered.

Kenji looked into the old man's cloudy eyes. He loved the way the lines around them deepened and spread when his *ojichan* smiled, his cheekbones rising like the sun. As a young man, he was once known as the best dancer in Hakodate, his *obachan* told him, everyone watching his grandfather's light, seamless moves at the Bon Odori during Obon.

"Well, your *ojichan*'s home now," he said, rubbing his close-cropped gray hair and putting his arm around Kenji's slight and serious shoulders. "You could have come and fetched me," he added.

Kenji shrugged.

"Uncle Taiko asked me to give you this." His *ojichan* held out his hand.

Kenji smiled and reached for the piece of rice candy in his grandfather's palm, bowing quickly. *"Domo arigato gozaimasu,"* he said. "Please thank Uncle Taiko when you see him tomorrow."

"Perhaps you'd like to come with me to the bar tomorrow and thank him yourself," his *ojichan* said.

Kenji nodded his head, his black hair falling into his eyes. *"Hai,"* he answered, popping the rice candy into his mouth before his *obachan* found out.

He loved the weight of his *ojichan*'s arm on

his shoulders and the smell of his bittersweet pipe smoke. The rich, deep flavors that rose and curled up into the air made Kenji feel safe and at ease. Suddenly, the old man stepped back and danced a few unexpected circles around his grandson, extracting a wild, unrestrained burst of laughter from Kenji.

2
ANCIENT MATTERS
1940

Every evening after dinner, despite the winter cold, Yoshio Wada went up to the watchtower to listen to his neighbor's daughter practice her cello in the backyard next door. At sixteen, Mariko Yoshida had just been accepted into the Tokyo Conservatory of Music and was flourishing. The once quiet girl, who often babysat the boys when they were little, had found her calling. Before long, her music provided a soothing balm for the entire neighborhood. Yoshio lit his pipe and heard a door slide open like clockwork and close again, as she stepped out to the backyard carrying her cello.

Mariko began her practice with the same piece every evening, and once, when Yoshio asked her what the piece was and why she always began with it, Mariko grinned like a child and answered, "It's Bach's First Cello Suite. I always begin with it because it makes me realize why I play." And before he could ask why that was, she added shyly, "It makes me feel as if I'm taking the first lovely breath of life." He hadn't really understood what she meant at the time, but the more he heard the piece, the more he began to comprehend the power of it, how the notes themselves moved in and out like breath. And how the closest thing he might have felt to it in his life was dancing at the Bon Odori.

Yoshio turned when he heard his grandsons' heavy footsteps racing up the stairs to the watchtower. In the next moment, Hiroshi and Kenji filled the small, open deck with their exuberance, the planks beneath them vibrating. Mariko had just begun playing Bach's Second Cello Suite, the one she had confided to him was "the saddest of all the suites."

"*Ojichan, obachan* wants you to come back down now," Hiroshi said, the low crackle of his changing voice still startling to Yoshio. "She says it's too cold for you to be standing up here."

Yoshio felt another burst of winter air whistle through the tower. He knew Fumiko was right but he suddenly felt talkative. At twelve and ten, his grandsons were growing up and he wanted to keep them standing by his side, where he could still see the blurred shapes of their faces. "It feels like snow may come," he answered. "Your *obachan* loves it when it snows."

"I hope it does," Kenji said, leaning over

the side to see if it could be true. "Then we might be excused from classes tomorrow."

"I hope not," Hiroshi quickly said. "I have practice tomorrow."

Yoshio smiled. The increased food rationing due to the war effort hadn't affected their spirits or energy levels yet. Hiroshi had always been a strong and solid boy, almost a head taller than Kenji, who had grown in the past year but still remained thin and awkward. No two brothers could have been more different from birth. He cleared his throat, not ready to go inside just yet. "Listen to Mariko play, how sad this piece is." And then they stood silent, listening.

"Isn't she cold?" Kenji asked.

Hiroshi elbowed his brother, who returned the nudge and was pushed into his grandfather.

Yoshio stepped in between his grandsons. "Did you know that it's because of sumo that we're all here today?" he asked. It was a story he had told them many times, ever since they were little boys. He'd repeated it every time he wanted to gain their attention. "That the fate of the Japanese people was determined by a wrestling match?"

Watery lights coming from the surrounding houses illuminated the boys' faces as Mariko began playing another piece. Hiroshi turned toward him with eagerness, and Kenji stood still, his eyes widening with interest.

"Tell us again how a sumo match determined our fates?" Hiroshi asked.

He smiled at his grandsons, memorized their faces with a tender joy. "It is the legend that begins the history of our Japanese civilization, over two thousand years ago," Yoshio said, taking his time, knowing he had captured their attention once again, even the elusive Kenji.

"*Ojichan,* tell us," Kenji spoke up, his voice young and eager.

"It is written in the *Kojiki,*" Yoshio continued, "the *Records of Ancient Matters,* our earliest written Japanese history, that it was a sumo match, fought on the shores of Isumo, along the Japan seacoast, that determined the origins of the Japanese people. It was decided that there would be a great wrestling match between Takemikazuchi, a Shinto deity who wrestled for the Yamato clan, and Takeminakata, another deity, and the second son of the ruler of Isumo, over ownership of the land." He paused and listened for a moment to the garbled voices coming from a radio somewhere. "After a match that shook the earth to its very core, it was Takemikazuchi who finally won, and it is said that our imperial family can trace its ancestors back to him. There's a shrine that marks the place of the first sumo match in Shimane prefecture."

Hiroshi and Kenji listened attentively. The sharp, stinging cold didn't seem to deter their curiosity. Mariko's music provided a spirited accompaniment.

"But what if Takeminakata had won?" Hiroshi asked. "Would everything have been different?"

"I suppose so," he answered. "As much as each of us would see and do things differently."

"Can we visit the shrine one day?" Kenji asked.

"Of course." Yoshio smiled at the rare request from Kenji. "Can you imagine," he continued, "that our fate was determined by just the two gods?" He shook his head and sucked hard on his pipe. "If only the outcome of wars could be so easily determined now," he added.

"Why can't they be?" Hiroshi asked. "Why can't we have a great match between two men now to determine the winner of this war? Like with the grand champion Yokozuna Futabayama?"

Yes, why not? Yoshio thought. His own memories of the Russian-Japanese war in Mukden, some thirty-five years ago, were reduced to the blood-soaked earth littered with body parts, the now faded cries of men, the easy madness of pulling a trigger that could end a life, and the death of his older brother, Toshiro. And though Yoshio had been told he was fighting for his country, he really fought only to survive, to return to Fumiko,

38

who was waiting for him. Yet he could never reconcile that he had returned home unscathed, while Toshiro and so many others perished. He had suffered only a terrible bout of dysentery and a badly dislocated shoulder — the shoulder still a silent reminder that pulsated with a dull ache when the weather changed.

In the end, Yoshio knew that what wars really destroyed were families. His parents had never gotten over the loss of Toshiro in Mukden. And for what? Were all the lost lives worth a faraway port? A piece of land? Sometimes, in his dreams, Toshiro still came to him, as young and vital as the day they stepped onto the train together to leave for Tokyo. Their parents, and Fumiko, along with so many others, stood on the platform in the shimmering heat, waving frantically at bodies half-hanging out of open windows of the train, Toshiro's included. Yoshio had stepped back to let his brother get a clearer view of their vanishing parents. He didn't know it would be Toshiro's last. Two days later, they boarded the boat and sailed across the waters to a foreign land, whence so many would never return.

Yoshio swallowed his sorrow.

"It can't be, Hiro-chan, because great powers always want more," he answered. "Unlike the gods, mankind may never be able to settle on just two men and just one conquest."

The boys nodded. Yoshio knew Fumiko would be calling them in at any moment.

"I'd fight," Hiroshi added.

"Me, too," Kenji echoed, less certain.

Yoshio didn't doubt Hiroshi's idealism, nor that he would fight for Japan. Single-handedly. He was happy that his grandsons were too young to go to war. Not that he didn't love Japan and wasn't loyal to the emperor. He was just so weary of war, knowing that whoever won, too many lives would be lost. Yoshio put an arm around each of his grandsons. "Let's hope it never has to be."

But more and more, the war news screamed from the radio, how this war was *seisen,* a sacred war led by the divine emperor. Yoshio worried about what the conflict would lead to, and how it would affect his grandsons if it were to rage on for years. He was never quite happy to hear the broadcasts that boasted of the Japanese army's successes, of their advancing troops spreading through China, where victories came fast and furious — the capture of Nanking, then Shanghai, then Canton. And what next, the Imperial Army's push toward Hong Kong, then Singapore, the Philippines — faraway places that had nothing to do with their lives? More often than not, Yoshio snapped off the radio when a report came on.

Now, when he looked at his grandsons, he saw his gentle daughter, Misako, his son-in-law, Kazuo, and even Toshiro. He saw past and future before him in the fading light. And just as abruptly as Mariko's music had started, it suddenly stopped. "Just remember," Yoshio said quietly to them. "Every day of your lives, you must always be sure what you're fighting for."

KENJI THE GHOST

The icy winds threatened snow but it didn't fall that night. A few days later, Kenji hurried down the alleyway, clutching his left side, which ached with every cold breath. His jacket had been torn in the scuffle and his sleeve was stained where he had wiped the blood from his nose. His cheek throbbed beneath his right eye. He needed to stop, to rest for a moment and gather his strength before returning home to face his grandparents' concern and questions. He knew Hiroshi was still at practice and wouldn't be home until much later.

Leaning against the side of a building, Kenji closed his eyes until his breathing slowed and his dizziness passed. Underneath his torn jacket, a spreading bruise felt tender where he had been kicked. Kenji couldn't believe what had just happened. The first rush forward and wild swings belonged to him, but he wasn't certain he had hit anyone. He opened and closed his right fist, a swelling

41

and soreness around his knuckles proof that he'd made contact with something. The thought brought tears to his eyes, from happiness or sadness, he wasn't sure. After the name-calling and laughter, the rest was a blur, a barrage of hands and legs coming at him as he instinctively dropped to the ground and covered his head, rolling himself into what he imagined was a protective shell.

It was Hiroshi he thought of as he was being beaten, how disappointed he would be to know that Kenji had cowered on the ground like a *bebi.* But Kenji would always be the baby brother, and though he never said the words aloud, he loved Hiroshi for his innate strength, the lightness of his step, the way he always watched out for him when other children sensed his distant, tenuous nature. Growing up, he often heard his classmates chant "Kenji the ghost," as they surrounded him in the schoolyard before and after school:

Kenji the ghost,
watches, but never joins in.
Kenji the ghost,
listens, but never says a thing.
Kenji the ghost,
disappears within.

Their chanting stopped abruptly every time a teacher or Hiroshi came within hearing distance. Kenji would look at his older brother, standing there with his friends Takeo and Mako, feeling the tears push against his eyes, torn at that moment between running to Hiroshi and standing his ground. Not a word passed between them. The chanting echoed through his head, but the children had already scattered. He wished he were really Kenji the ghost, so he could simply disappear from sight.

Kenji took a deep breath, opened his eyes, and pushed away from the wall. The mask shop was just down the street. He hadn't stopped by in weeks and felt a twinge of nervousness now as he looked around. He didn't want anyone, especially the actors who came and went from the store, to see him like this, beaten and bloody. For almost two years, Kenji had gazed upon all the different masks displayed in the front window, never daring to enter the shop. Each time, he seemed to discover something more intricate and exciting in the carved features, the delicate paints, the gold dusting, the inlaid eyes, and teeth of brass. He read everything he could find concerning the Noh theater. Intrigued with the importance of the masks, Kenji learned that each subtle move of the actor's head and body projected a different emotion from the mask he wore. Kenji relished the idea that a piece of wood could be perceived as a living thing.

When he felt a hand on his shoulder, Kenji turned quickly and a pain shot through his ribs, as if he were being kicked all over again. Wincing, he looked up to see Akira Yoshiwara watching him, and not unkindly. Kenji wanted to run, wanted to die at the thought of his disgraceful appearance in front of the master artisan. He stumbled sideways but the hand only grasped his arm more tightly. Was this a dream? Without a word, Akira Yoshiwara slipped his arm under Kenji's, and holding him up, guided him down the street to his shop. Kenji was dizzy with the thought of finally entering the shop, but not as he had imagined so many times before. In his mind, he had often walked through the door with a great flourish. He never guessed his first steps into the tiny shop would be with the assistance of the master artisan, and in such dishonor.

Akira Yoshiwara unlocked the door. "Perhaps you'd like to come in and see the masks up close for a change?" he asked, his voice soft and teasing.

"You've seen me?" Kenji licked his lips, tasted the saltiness of blood and mucus, and wished for a sip of water.

"Once or twice. I take it you like the masks?"

"Very much," Kenji said.

Standing close, Akira Yoshiwara smiled for the first time, which made him look younger,

44

somewhere in his thirties. Without the layer of wood dust dulling his skin and hair, and dressed in a dark blue cotton *yukata* with a white lotus pattern, he looked like a different person. His dark, long hair fell over his slight shoulders and his closely trimmed beard gave him a defiant yet distinguished look.

Inside, Kenji breathed in the sharp and biting smell of paint, and the more subtle scent of cypress wood, which his *ojichan* sometimes carved. As the sun broke through the clouds, it filled the room with white light. Kenji saw that everything was covered with a fine powdery dust.

"Sit right here." Akira Yoshiwara helped him onto one of the low wooden chairs.

"Domo arigato gozaimasu." Kenji tried to bow low but grabbed his side in pain instead. "I should go home."

"Just sit," he said again, placing his hands firmly on his shoulders. "Let me help you first."

Akira Yoshiwara whistled as he disappeared into the back room. Kenji looked around to see there were no masks on the tall shelf against the wall. The room appeared desolate and bare, and in need of a good cleaning. It felt strange being on the inside of the window, looking out, as if he had stepped into another world and wasn't sure which was the lonelier. He ran a finger through the dust on the table and wrote his name in quick characters. He heard cabinets opening and closing in the other room, water being poured, and Yoshiwara's calm voice telling someone not to touch something. Kenji grew warm and his heart beat faster at the thought that someone else was there.

When Akira Yoshiwara returned, he carried a tray with a wet cloth, a bowl of water, and a clay cup of hot tea. He had tied his long hair back, and his dark eyes watched Kenji as he sipped from the steaming cup. "You don't appear to be the type of boy who likes to fight." With slender fingers he dabbed the towel lightly across Kenji's cheek, under his throbbing eye, wiping the dry blood from under his nose, then rinsed it in the bowl of water and wiped again with such gentleness Kenji wanted to close his eyes and sleep.

"It was an accident," Kenji said, flushed. "I tripped and fell." It was what he had rehearsed in his mind to tell his grandparents. He didn't dare look up and meet Akira Yoshiwara's gaze, knowing how hollow his lie sounded. Kenji wanted to say he wasn't the type to fight, that he didn't know what had come over him, but he heard something clatter in the back room and instead asked, "Is someone else here?"

Akira Yoshiwara laughed. "Yes, of course."

Kenji stood up abruptly, almost knocking over the bowl of water.

"Nazo," Yoshiwara called. "Come out and

meet —" He looked down at the characters written on the table. "Matsumoto, Kenji-san."

In the next moment, a black cat with white paws slipped into the room, tentative as he approached the table, stopping a moment to consider Kenji, then circling around their legs twice before leaping up to the table next to his master. "This is Nazo." The black cat brushed against Akira Yoshiwara's arm and arched his back until he was stroked. "As you can see, he's a very possessive cat."

Kenji sat back into the chair, at ease for the first time since entering the shop, and began to laugh. His ribs ached and he could barely breathe through his nose but he couldn't stop laughing. Nazo, which meant "mystery," looked at him as if he were the mystery. The cat watched Kenji closely at first, his eyes narrowing in scrutiny before he lost interest and set about licking the white mitten of his paw. For a moment, everything stopped hurting and Kenji felt something close to calm.

OMAMORI

Hiroshi bounded up the stairs after practice, slid open the shoji door, and stood in the doorway of his and Kenji's small room, across from the bedroom of their grandparents. When he was old enough to understand, his *obachan* had told him that it had been their mother's childhood room. Hiroshi remembered looking everywhere for some small relic that the young Misako might have left behind that hadn't been packed away — a doll, a trinket, or a book she had loved, but the room was clean and immaculate, and, over the years, the boys had made it comfortably their own. Or, at least, Hiroshi had. As he looked around, it appeared as if he had displaced his brother inch by inch, with his clothes, his stacks of sumo magazines, his sword collection, his sheer height and strength. Kenji never said a word, just seemed to occupy less and less space.

Hiroshi had promised his *obachan* he would clean up their room before dinner. His brother was late coming home and Hiroshi knew she was concerned. He gathered up his clothes, a seed of worry growing as he picked up his brother's book about Noh theater. During sumo tournament days, when he and his *ojichan* listened religiously to all the matches on the radio, Kenji always wandered away to a quiet corner to read his books. Sometimes he was a mystery, even to Hiroshi. He folded up his clothes, stacked his magazines into a neat pile, and tried to make more room for his brother. If Kenji hadn't returned by the time he cleaned up their room, he would go out and look for him.

Something shiny on the tatami caught his eye. Hiroshi stooped to see a yen coin wedged between the mats. As he dug for it, the coin slipped farther down. He wedged his fingers into the crack and pried up the corner of the mat to discover not only the yen coin, but also a red brocade *omamori bukuro* — a small, rectangular bag, no bigger than the palm of his hand, with a white-knotted cord. Embroidered on the bag in gold thread were the characters "great" and "to protect." His *obachan* had once bought such a bag from a temple they visited, explaining to Hiroshi that tucked inside each one was a prayer or blessing written on paper or a thin tablet of wood, sanctified by a priest from one of the temples. It warded off many evils, kept you safe, and protected from outside forces. He also remembered his grandmother saying that to open an *omamori* bag would undo the blessing. It was considered a lucky charm by most, just another superstition by others.

Hiroshi's first thought was that Kenji must have hidden the *omamori* beneath the two-inch-thick tatami. But when he lifted the mat higher, he found an old school writing tablet that had his mother's name, Misako Wada, written on it — the characters inside neatly lined up in precise columns. Could the *omamori* also have belonged to his mother? His grandmother often swept the mats but never lifted the tightly fitted tatami. Hiroshi pried up the other mats but lowered them back in place when he found nothing more.

49

His heart raced as he held the brocade bag in the palm of his hand, fingering the gold thread. Mesmerized by the thought that it had once belonged to his mother, he didn't move until he heard his grandmother's voice rise up the stairs, quick and excited.

Kenji had returned.

Hiroshi tucked the *omamori* safely into his pocket and hurried downstairs to see what had kept his brother out so late. He heard his *obachan*'s voice rising with anxiety and understood her concern when he was halfway down the stairs. Kenji stood just inside the front door with his head bowed. He looked up when he heard Hiroshi, his lips thin and serious, his misery apparent as he held his brother's gaze for a moment, before turning away. His jacket was bloodied and torn. A bruise under his right eye was darkening into the curve of a half-moon. Hiroshi paused for a moment, surprised to see that his brother had been fighting.

"What happened? Come, come sit down," his *obachan* urged, tugging Kenji's jacket sleeve and trying to lead him toward the reception room. "Your *ojichan* will be home any moment now."

"I'm fine," Kenji said softly. He tried to smile and shrug off their *obachan*'s concern by putting his hands reassuringly on her shoulders and holding her at arm's length. "It was an accident," he heard Kenji whisper.

"Are you all right?" Hiroshi asked. He hadn't realized Kenji was now taller than their *obachan*. In the past year, he had grown up and was entering that nebulous place between boy and man. Yet he could see hints of Kenji's trauma that gave him away — a thin smudge of dried blood right below his nose, the slight quiver in his voice, the way he winced as he lifted his arms, slow and deliberate.

Kenji looked up and nodded.

Hiroshi's mind raced, jumped from thought to maddening thought. He would get the names of the boys who had done this to Kenji and teach them all a lesson. He had no doubt that he alone could take care of all his brother's tormentors. At thirteen, Hiroshi's passion was still sumo wrestling. Wasn't he the school champion, two years in a row? Wrestling had been part of Hiroshi's life since elementary school physical education classes, and though he wasn't unusually big and tall, he had always been strong and solid.

Hiroshi tried and tried to teach Kenji to defend himself but his brother always shied away from fighting. On the rare occasions they wrestled together, he and Kenji took turns being Takemikazuchi-no-kami when they practiced. They imagined the earth shaking as the bodies of the two gods made impact, earthquakes originating from their great battle. Hiroshi often let Kenji win, happy to see the smile that spread across his younger brother's face. At other times, what began in fun turned quickly into something more, an uneven match, with Hiroshi the victor, leading to anger and tears. "Fight back," he yelled, pushing against his brother, wanting nothing more than for his brother to respond with added force. But it wasn't something Kenji did; he turned around and walked away, or closed his eyes when things became rough. "Fight back," he said again and again, irritated by his brother's passivity. He wanted Kenji to be able to take care of himself, but his brother resisted as if Hiroshi were making him take some bitter medicine.

After a while, they had stopped wrestling altogether and each pursued his own interests. In his everyday life, as in wrestling, Hiroshi was outgoing and expressive and filled each room with his presence, while Kenji kept to himself, shy and reserved, moving through each day as quietly as possible. Now, Hiroshi couldn't help but feel that he was responsible for Kenji's beating.

When their *ojichan* returned, he put down his pipe and leaned in closely to examine Kenji, not saying a word at first. He lifted Kenji's shirt and lightly touched the bruise on his side, tilted his chin to get a better look at his eye. Then he finally said lightly, "I'd hate to see the other boys," and went about his business as if nothing had happened.

Hiroshi could see the look of relief on Kenji's face.

After their *obachan* had attended to his brother's wounds, she patted Kenji's cheek and left the brothers alone in the reception room. Hiroshi stood in the doorway and watched Kenji, the dark bruise beneath his eye giving him the look of a young, helpless animal.

"What happened?" Hiroshi asked, his voice dry and tight.

Kenji stood up, filled with a sudden energy that Hiroshi had seen in other boys, just before a match, the split second before a wrestler was ready to bolt toward his opponent. "They were making fun of me at school."

"Who?"

"It doesn't matter," Kenji whispered. "All of them, all of the time."

"But what made you fight today?" Hiroshi asked. "Why now, after all this time?"

Kenji carefully touched his cheek and said, "I finally got tired of it all."

"So you started the fight?"

Kenji first shrugged, then nodded. "I deserved what I got."

Hiroshi heard the distress in Kenji's voice, and saw his eyes tearing. He moved closer and pulled from his pocket the *omamori* bag. "Does this belong to you?" he asked.

Kenji shook his head.

"I found it under the tatami in our room. I think it may have belonged to *okasan*." He swallowed. "Here, keep it."

Kenji looked up at him, his eye swollen shut. "Are you sure?"

Hiroshi put it in his brother's hand and smiled. "I think she would be happy to know it was protecting you."

Kenji barely looked up, whispered a thank-you. He glanced from Hiroshi to the photo of their parents, unable to meet their gaze for long, either. "They're dead. *Obachan*'s stories won't bring them back." Kenji's low voice sounded strangely distant and adult.

Hiroshi peered again at his younger brother, his spindly arms and thin legs. "No one ever said they would."

Kenji didn't reply, but rather than let the silence grow between them, Hiroshi reached out and gave his shoulder a warm squeeze, the way he did when Kenji was little and frightened. But this time Hiroshi held on until his brother relaxed and looked up at him.

"I didn't fight," Kenji whispered. "After I threw the first punch, I didn't fight like you taught me."

Hiroshi breathed in his brother's scent of stale sweat and something more sour and earthy — what he imagined fear must smell like. "It doesn't matter," he said, and made a silent vow to protect Kenji always. "Just don't ever think you deserve to be beaten."

3
THE BOOK OF MASKS
1941

Kenji hurried past Fukushima-san's *sembei* rice cracker store on the way to the mask shop, where he found Akira Yoshiwara intently working on a mask as if the world stood still around him. It had been almost a year since the afternoon of Kenji's fight, the first time he had set foot in the mask shop, hurt and miserable, only to find a soothing balm within the small rooms. Since then, he'd returned many times, shy and hesitant at first, yet always welcomed by Akira Yoshiwara, and even the cat, Nazo, who soon grew used to his presence.

It wasn't long before a visit every afternoon became part of Kenji's routine. His *obachan* agreed to let him go as long as he didn't bother the famous artisan. She smiled when he told her how he loved the dusty rooms that smelled of sweet wood and paint, where, isolated from life's disturbances, he watched each mask materialize before his eyes.

After Kenji swept the floors, he and Nazo

sat aside and watched Yoshiwara at work. When the cat became bored and stole away, chasing after some shadow, Kenji remained motionless, intrigued by the rough, grinding bursts of the saw that shaped the mask from a block of Japanese cypress. With a set of chisels, Yoshiwara sculpted out the eyes, nose, and mouth, the hairline and the high brow of what he said would be a *Ko-omote* mask. Kenji knew *ko* meant "youth," and that *omote* meant "face," and as Yoshiwara sanded with steady concentration, he saw the smooth, rounded features of a young girl emerge. He imagined it was like a face underwater slowly coming to the surface, the features becoming more defined. Yoshiwara then whitewashed the mask with a coat of *gofun,* or powdered seashell, and when it was dry, applied the first of six layers of paint to obtain the fleshy skin color. By the end of the week, Yoshiwara had brought the mask fully to life, painting in the finer details of the young girl's dark eyes, her eyebrows and black hair.

Week after week, Kenji watched as each different mask slowly took shape with the sure strokes of Yoshiwara's chisels against the wood. When he worked, he disappeared into his own world, oblivious, his dark hair covered in fine sawdust that gave him the appearance of an old man, just as when Kenji had first seen him through the window. The rhythmic scraping sound was hypnotic. Kenji loved the demon or spirit masks best, which were elaborately fitted with brass eyes or teeth, their horns dusted with gold. Simple masks took as little as a week or two, but the more elaborate ones required several months or more to bring to life.

In the beginning when Kenji was allowed to watch, he always grabbed a handful of the fragrant wood shavings from the floor and put them into his pocket. It made him feel close to the mask shop even when he wasn't there. When his *obachan* complained about the wood shavings still in his pocket on washing day, Kenji transferred them to his mother's *omamori* bag, which he always carried with him, careful not to look at the blessing inside.

One afternoon, Akira Yoshiwara suddenly broke his usual silence. "Gently," he said, his chisel never stopping. He didn't look up, and it was as if he were talking to himself, though Kenji knew that the words were directed at him. "Never force the chisel, let it glide against the wood."

After the features were sufficiently carved out, Yoshiwara took down a stack of sandpaper and taught Kenji how to sand the mask smooth without injuring the wood. He watched Yoshiwara, whom he suddenly saw as his sensei, the teacher who would show him how to create the masks he so loved.

"Here, now you try," Yoshiwara said. "Go gently or you'll leave scratches on the surface. Think of the wood as skin, as a living thing, smooth to the touch," he said, stroking the rough cheek of the mask. Then he handed the mask and sandpaper to Kenji.

The smoothness of skin. Like a living thing, Kenji repeated to himself. They worked side by side in a comfortable rhythm. He copied his sensei's every move until the sanded wood felt smooth against his fingertips. Finished, he waited, as his heart raced, while Yoshiwara examined the mask and nodded his approval.

With the exception of the week during Obon in August, Kenji spent most of his summer afternoons at the mask shop. When he arrived back at the shop the first morning after Obon, Kenji immediately felt something different, a stirring in the air that wasn't there the week before. Akira Yoshiwara was at his workbench, a slight smile on his lips as he looked up and waved Kenji in. "For Otomo Matsui," he said, looking down at the mask he was working on. Kenji knew that Yoshiwara was commissioned by individual actors to make their masks, including the great actor Otomo Matsui. He'd seen many actors come to the shop for their masks, but fewer now, Yoshiwara told him, as the war in China progressed. "Before all this foolishness," his sensei added, "they flocked to my shop like birds to their nest."

"Have they gone to fight in China?" Kenji had asked.

"Fight and die," Yoshiwara answered. "Did you know that hundreds of thousands of Japanese soldiers have already died in China?"

Kenji shook his head, anxious and confused. Weren't they winning the war in China?

"A real tragedy," his sensei muttered.

Then Yoshiwara lightened again. He stopped working long enough to explain that word had come that Otomo Matsui needed a new *Ayakashi,* a ghost-warrior mask, in only a few weeks' time. Otomo Matsui came from four generations of Noh actors, his sensei went on, and his father was the great actor Toshiko Matsui, who had performed for the emperor himself. Descendants of aristocracy, they had always performed the most difficult *shite* role, the principal character that remained onstage for almost the duration of a Noh play. Yoshiwara carefully chiseled and sanded the *Ayakashi* mask from start to finish by himself, while Kenji noted the extra care he took with every step.

Finally, just past *Shubun no hi,* Autumn Equinox Day in September, Matsui was scheduled to pick up the *Ayakashi* mask. Yoshiwara dusted himself off, changed to a fresh brown raw silk kimono with a gourd pattern on it, and tied his hair back. Kenji felt his nervousness as he glanced at the clock, picked up a block of cypress, and set it back down again, his usual calm demeanor rattled as he turned to speak.

"Otomo Matsui is coming himself to pick up the *Ayakashi* mask," Akira said. "Usually, he sends an assistant." He began to pace the floor. "Do you realize what honor he shows me?"

Kenji nodded. There was something frenzied about the way Akira was acting that made Kenji want to calm him.

"Maybe his assistant has been called to fight in the China war like so many others," he stammered. He hadn't thought to bring up the war just then, but it slipped from his lips.

Akira Yoshiwara stopped his pacing and looked at him. "Perhaps," he said, but no more.

Usually, Kenji stayed in the back room and out of sight whenever someone came into the shop. And it was no different when Otomo Matsui arrived that afternoon to pick up his mask. Instead of bringing a large entourage, he came alone, and Kenji stole quick glances between the curtains at the elegant figure that strode in wearing a formal black silk kimono, embroidered with four white diamond crests. Matsui carried a beautifully wrapped box in gold and black *washi* paper. The air seemed to shimmer with his presence, though he wasn't much taller than Yoshiwara. The actor studied the *Ayakashi* mask, his long fingers holding it up against his face, checking to see that all the dimensions were correct before he lowered the mask and praised Akira Yoshiwara's care and artistry.

"Yoshiwara-san, there is no finer artisan of the mask than you. I will wear it proudly."

Yoshiwara bowed low. "Matsui-sama, you honor me by wearing my masks," he answered.

When Otomo Matsui turned around, Kenji saw his dark, deep-set eyes, the high forehead and strong chin. He appeared to be in his early forties, a bit older than Yoshiwara-sensei. His face would have been truly perfect if it hadn't been for his slightly crooked nose. His voice was deep and resonant and Kenji imagined he was a wonderful *shite* onstage.

Still, it was not so much the appearance of Otomo Matsui that intrigued Kenji; rather, it was the first time he'd seen Akira Yoshiwara show such awe and respect toward anyone who came to his shop. This time his sensei was the one who bowed low to Matsui when he entered. He spoke in a soft, comforting tone, served him tea, and bowed again when Matsui handed him the gift he had brought. Kenji thought he was watching a different man. Yoshiwara's face appeared flushed as the actor left, carrying the carefully wrapped ghost-warrior mask in his hands.

The day after Otomo Matsui's visit, Yoshiwara was in an unusually talkative mood. His sensei always stopped working in the afternoon to serve tea accompanied by *sembei* crackers or English biscuits, which Kenji guiltily wished he could share with Hiroshi and his grandparents. Rice rationing of one cup a day had begun during the past year and he knew how his *obachan* worried. He longed to ask the artisan where he was able to get so much food when everyone else had so little. But then, he was one man, not an entire family, and from what Kenji observed of his furious work habits, the artisan rarely stopped to eat much at all. So when Yoshiwara turned around for some rags on the shelf, Kenji didn't hesitate to slip three biscuits into his pocket.

"I believe it's time for you to see a real Noh performance," Yoshiwara said, turning back again.

At first, Kenji thought he was teasing him. "When?" he asked.

Akira Yoshiwara laughed and fingered the small ivory cat Otomo Matsui had given him. "First you must go home and ask your grandparents. And tell them it is by invitation of the great actor Otomo Matsui."

Kenji stood awkwardly. "Yes, sensei."

"In order to be an artisan," Yoshiwara said,

glancing up from his table as he mixed some *gofun* powder into the first layer of whitewash, "it's important to experience the masks in performance, then to start at the beginning, just as I did when I was young."

Yoshiwara stopped mixing then crossed the room to pull a book down from one of the top shelves. "I have something I want you to study," he said, handing the large, leather-bound volume to Kenji. "Take this home and memorize it." Then Yoshiwara returned to his painting.

With the palm of his hand, Kenji brushed the handsome brown cover made of fine, soft calfskin, and carefully opened it, glancing down at the highest-quality *washi* paper. Turning to the title page, he read its flowing, gold characters: *The Book of Masks.*

THE GHOST WARRIOR

After Kenji had gone home, Akira sharpened his chisels and cleaned his paintbrushes. The boy was so much like him, so filled with wonder and fascination about the masks. And they were both orphans, though he knew no two stories were alike. He had walked away from his family, while Kenji had never known his parents, and sometimes Akira wished for the same — the luxury of invention, of believing in the family that might have been. Sometimes, without his knowing, he found himself re-creating the memory of their faces in a mask — the slight arch of an eyebrow that belonged to his mother, the sharp, turned-down mouth of his sister when she sulked, the dark, endless stare of his father. They came back to him at the most unexpected times. After more than twenty years, they weren't so far away, after all.

Akira looked up at the shelf where *The Book of Masks* had been, feeling suddenly bereft. It had been there on the top shelf since the day he opened the mask shop, twelve years ago. Now the vacant spot was a distraction, as he glanced up and then away again several times like a child, hoping it might magically reappear.

Just then, Nazo jumped up on the table. "Yes, Nazo, I'm all yours now," he said. As he stroked the cat, Akira relaxed. It had been a busy week. It seemed a dream to think the day had come that his masks would garner the highest price from the most important actor in the theater. And now he had perhaps found his heir apparent. Akira was as certain that Kenji would make a fine artisan as his own sensei, Wakayama-san, had been of him. It showed in his passionate concentration, as if gazing into each mask was like falling in love. He knew it was the right time for the boy to begin learning the craft from the bottom up. He glanced again at the empty spot on the shelf; the book he'd once received as a gift from Wakayama-san was a fine place for Kenji to start. In it were the detailed drawings of each of the eighty masks used in Noh. It would also give Kenji an introduction and brief description of the two hundred fifty plays written during Japan's feudal years, stories that Akira had come to know by heart and that had become a part of his life, though he had never set foot onstage. He smiled down at Nazo. After all, the drama of his own life was more than enough theater for him.

Akira Yoshiwara had been born in the port city of Yokohama, less than twenty miles from Tokyo; he was the eldest son of well-to-do parents. His father was not an educated man, but one whose business acumen had made him a great deal of money in the fish-canning industry. He had had high expectations for his eldest son to follow in his footsteps and take over the family business. But ever since Akira could remember, he had hated the factory — the constant noise of the machines, the slimy slip of his sandals against the wet wood floor, the rough, uneducated workers who teased him as he walked through the building to his father's office. "Ah, look who honors us with his presence," they called out. "It's about time to get those clean hands dirty!" they taunted when he stopped by after school at his father's insistence. But worst of all, he couldn't bear the stink that permeated everything, especially his father's clothes. Every night when he came home, the odor of whiskey and dead fish hung heavy in the air of their house. Even after his father had bathed and soaked in the *ofuro* every evening, the fish smell still seemed to course through his bloodstream and seep out of his pores. When his father was angry, his red-rimmed eyes grew wide and bulged so that Akira thought he was even beginning to resemble a fish. It wasn't a life he could ever imagine for himself.

His mother was no more sympathetic. "He is your father," she told him over and over, "and you must do as he says. The factory is yours to inherit as the eldest son, but instead of rejoicing, you find fault with a life that has brought our family such good fortune!"

"Give the factory to Shintaro," Akira said, "or Suki. I'd rather be penniless than spend my life working in that cannery every day."

The sharp sting of his mother's slap startled him, taught him to watch his words and keep silent, even though his feelings grew in strength and conviction over time. And as much as he loved his younger brother, Shintaro, and sister, Suki, he knew they didn't understand him any more than his parents did.

Akira knew he was different. He excelled in school and enjoyed art most, saw beauty in things most boys took for granted — the curve of a branch, the different shades of green in the grass, the shape and texture of stones. The life he imagined for himself had to do with beautiful things. He began taking the train to Tokyo, visiting galleries and then art studios, until one day he stumbled upon Yutaka Wakayama's masks. They were like nothing Akira had ever seen. As soon as he met his future sensei, he knew that he wanted to be a great mask artisan. At the time, Wakayama was near fifty and well known in the theater world. If Akira hadn't had the courage to leave his home and family at fifteen to become Wakayama-sensei's student in Tokyo, he might still be back in Yokohama, canning fish. He remembered boarding the train before his parents awoke to find him gone for good, feeling both exhilarated and frightened. As the train pulled away from the station at Yokohama, he began to laugh, which brought tears that didn't stop until he reached the Kawasaki station.

His father had disowned him twenty years ago. His parents were dead now, his brother and sister a long-ago memory from another life. But even now, whenever he passed a fish shop, the smell transported him right back to the hateful years of his youth.

Akira glanced at the ivory cat sitting on another shelf, the gift from Otomo Matsui, an acknowledgment of his talent and the success he had achieved in his art. Still, there was something he couldn't find in the book of masks, or the intricately carved cat, or in his beloved masks themselves. He missed the touch of another man. The first time Wakayama had stroked him tenderly across the cheek at seventeen, it was like a startling welcome through his body, and something, something Akira knew he had been searching for all his life, had finally come true. Since Wakayama-sensei had died ten years ago, there had been no lasting relationship in his life, only a series of mistakes, quick, empty encounters that had left him dazed and discouraged, and worst of all, the young writer Sato, who had left him heartbroken. Three years had passed since he'd left, and Akira still felt Sato's smooth body pressed against his back, his quickening breath, followed by the flicker of his tongue on his neck. Like a ghostly presence, it haunted him at the most unexpected times. It wasn't the close paternal comfort that he'd had with Wakayama, but a flash destined to burn itself out, leaving ashes.

Over the years, actors and artists came to his shop, revering him and hoping that he would consent to make them a famous Yoshiwara mask. If he let himself, he might find one who would return his affection, relieve his loneliness for just one evening as he'd done before. He thought of Otomo Matsui and felt as if all the air had been pulled out of him, then pushed the silly thought from his mind. Matsui had been linked to the most famous geisha in Kyoto, Hanae Mitsuhara. It was rumored he was her *danna,* her patron, and they had a child sent away to boarding school in Europe. Besides, Akira Yoshiwara knew it wasn't for himself that Otomo Matsui, or any of them, visited his shop. It was for the masks — the one thing he could hide behind.

A DEFINING MOMENT

Ever since he was a young boy, Hiroshi's *obachan* had told him that each person's life was made up of one defining moment, that instant when he would understand his *unmei* — his destiny and direction in life. "Whether you step toward it or not is up to you," his grandmother added. "Just remember, it will follow you no matter where you go."

But the more Hiroshi thought about what his grandmother had told him, the more he began to worry. What if he missed his moment? Would he have another opportunity?

"But how will I know it's my destiny?" he asked his *obachan.*

His grandmother laughed. He thought his *obachan* sounded very young, more like his mother than his grandmother. "Like love, it will possess you, Hiro-chan," she said. "You can't help but know."

Six weeks later, in late October, Kenji attended a Noh performance with Yoshiwara-sensei. He arrived early at the mask shop to find his teacher dressed in a formal black kimono, his hair tied back and beard neatly trimmed as he paced the floor, waiting. Kenji was dressed in his dark blue, double-breasted school blazer and shorts, the only formal clothes he had. He had thought about borrowing one of his *ojichan*'s kimonos but decided against it. Now, he wished he had, instead of looking like a twelve-year-old schoolboy.

Yoshiwara stopped abruptly. "Ah, you're finally here," he snapped.

"It's still early," Kenji answered. "We have plenty of time."

Yoshiwara-sensei smiled and disappeared into the back room. When he emerged again, he was carrying a blue silk kimono with a subtle white wave pattern on it. "Perhaps you might want to change into this. It will be much more comfortable."

Kenji hesitated.

"It's much too small for me," Yoshiwara added. "I was hoping you might honor me by wearing it. It would be a shame to waste such a good kimono."

Kenji eyed the kimono and bowed low to his sensei before receiving it. *"Domo arigato*

71

gozaimasu." The material felt smooth and cool to his touch.

"Go change then," he instructed. "And hurry, so we won't be late."

Moments later, Kenji had shed his blazer, white shirt, shorts, and pulled on the silk kimono, so light and fluid against his body. He tied the sash and glimpsed his reflection in the dirty window. For the first time he felt like an adult, no longer just the younger brother, the one left behind.

Yoshiwara locked the shop and they made their way toward the train station. Kenji's voice filled the quiet alley with excited questions. How long were the plays? Had he seen Otomo Matsui in this role before? What was the theater like?

"Time stops when you're watching Noh," Yoshiwara turned to him and said. "Life pauses. It's best seen if you clear your mind and let the performance take over."

As they approached the train station, Yoshiwara told him that they wouldn't be seeing a full-length program, beginning with the ceremonial *Okina,* the ritual dance of an old man. The *Okina* was usually followed by five Noh plays, with a short Kyogen, or comic play, performed in between. Instead, they would be seeing two Noh plays, separated by a Kyogen play, as ordered by the Home Ministry.

The train station was bustling and noisy; a

knot of people gathered around a young soldier who was leaving to fight in China, while the *kempeitai,* the military police, with rifles slung over their shoulders, lingered on the platform, and beggars and vendors pushed and shoved in front of people. Kenji could barely keep up with Yoshiwara's quick stride.

On the train, Kenji remained quiet the rest of the way into Tokyo center, secretly hoping everything would be as magical as his sensei made it sound. October was still very warm and the train crowded. He began to sweat with the excitement of visiting the theater and seeing Matsui perform. He raised his arms to the back of the wooden seat in front of him when he felt the dampness, and feared it would leave dark stains on the kimono Yoshiwara had given him.

When Kenji stepped from the train station and out into the afternoon sunlight, he paused to look around at what was once the bustling theater district of Tokyo. It looked tired and stripped of the glamour he imagined. The buildings stood in shadows, looking dark and dingy, the slip of blue sky above, mocking. Many of the shops and theaters had been boarded up and closed since the China war. People lingered in front of the station as if held captive, as if they had stopped and simply couldn't go on. Kenji felt something sink in the pit of his stomach.

"Kenji." Yoshiwara's voice startled him. "Come this way," he said, and touched his shoulder.

The moment they entered the dark coolness of the Jincho Theater, it was as if he'd entered another world. Time did stop for Kenji. They found their seats up front in the second row. Much to Kenji's surprise, the theater was almost filled. The soft chanting of the chorus onstage filled the room and mesmerized him. The curtainless stage was simple and bare, covered with a long sloping roof like that of a Shinto shrine. Kenji spied a lone pine tree painted on the back wall. He had read that it symbolized longevity and steadfastness, standing behind a wooden bridge from which the actors entered and departed. He heard drums, and a flute begin to play in the background. Yoshiwara explained that the chorus of eight, called the *jiutai,* sat to the side of the stage and narrated the story.

At first, Kenji was too excited to pay attention to the chanted words that hummed through the room, muted by the beating of his own heart. *Hagoromo* was the story of a heavenly maiden and a fisherman who finds her magical feather robe. Otomo Matsui would appear as the fisherman. When the players all came forward, filling the spare stage, Kenji saw that each step was like a dance. Each gesture meant something, and each word was recited like poetry. Matsui's every move animated his wooden mask and brought it to life. As he bowed his head, the fisherman appeared to smile, but with a slight upward tilt the fisherman stood defiant. Kenji studied every one of the great actor's shifts and moves, and marveled as the mask became part of Otomo Matsui's own body.

Afterward, he and Yoshiwara-sensei went backstage to congratulate and thank Matsui-sama. A small crowd had gathered around the actor, but he looked up and saw Yoshiwara-sensei immediately. "Come, come," he announced, "I want you all to know this is the man who creates each of our wondrous masks."

Yoshiwara hesitated, but Matsui urged him forward and bowed low to him, still clutching the fisherman's mask in his hand. Kenji had never seen his sensei so happy.

"And who is this with you?" Matsui asked, as he stood straight.

It took a moment for Kenji to realize that Matsui had focused his attention on him. Up close he appeared older, though no less commanding.

"This is the next great mask maker for the Noh." Yoshiwara turned to him. "Kenji Matsumoto."

Kenji bowed low to Matsui-sama. It was the first time Yoshiwara had said anything about his work. He felt the blood rush to his head with the suddenness of his sensei's praise.

"And how did you enjoy our performance?" Matsui asked.

Kenji felt his face burn and he quickly bowed again. For the entire performance, he had felt suspended above his real life — his troubles with the other boys at school, the seed of fear planted in the middle of his stomach since the China war began, even his hunger had suddenly subsided as if by magic. "I found it the most moving performance I've ever seen."

Matsui laughed. "Yoshiwara-san, I don't know what kind of mask maker this boy is, but he certainly knows how to praise the actor behind the mask!"

With that, the entire group laughed. Kenji swallowed with relief when he looked up to find that attention had shifted and Matsui was already greeting other admirers.

A month after seeing Matsui's performance, when Kenji entered the warm shop one November afternoon, Yoshiwara unexpectedly stopped working and asked, "What are the two categories of masks?"

Kenji put down his schoolbooks on the table, watched the wood dust rise into the air. It was like a test, he thought, but one he wanted to take. "The two categories of Noh masks are male and female."

76

"They are?" Yoshiwara glanced up, eyed him closely and waited.

Kenji wet his lips, pushed his hair away from his eyes. "The four categories of male masks are the Okina, human, ghost, and spirit and demon masks. The two categories of the female masks are the human and the ghost and spirit masks."

Yoshiwara nodded and smiled. "Good, you pass for today."

Then he was silent again.

And what if Kenji didn't know the answers to Yoshiwara's questions tomorrow? He took a deep breath, picked up the broom, and began to sweep away the wood shavings. Nazo suddenly jumped out in front of him, his body arching as he rubbed up against his legs, reassuring him that he would.

BATTLE MARCH

When Hiroshi arrived at practice on a chilly December morning, he found another man standing next to his coach, dressed in an expensive dark blue silk brocade kimono, rather than a cotton yukata. He was a big man, even taller than Masuda-san, though he was thinner and carried himself well. He watched Hiroshi at practice while casually chatting with Masuda-san. Ignoring the audience, Hiroshi concentrated on his match as he twisted his body to the right and moved quickly out of the way as his opponent charged at him, missing the tackle and stepping out of bounds.

For the past year his coach had taken a real interest in Hiroshi's skill and speed as a wrestler. Every day at practice, Masuda-san watched him intently and seemed to encourage him more than any other student. "Ah, you see," he told the other boys gathered around during physical education. "Hiroshi understands how to use his body — the power of it must be controlled, channeled seamlessly into the movements. Did you see how he used his opponent's weight and force against him?" The boys bowed their heads, stifling their laughter. Many of them thought Masuda-san strange; he was a large man and it was rumored he once hoped to be a *rikishi*, but hadn't skill enough to succeed and remain within a stable. His past was evident in his small office, crowded with his wrestling trophies and certificates, but most intriguing to Hiroshi were the photos of *sumotori* that lined the wall — their bulky, imposing bodies filling the space around them.

As Hiroshi continued to train, he began to see sumo as more than just a sport — it was deeply rooted in the Japanese culture, and he loved the dance of it all: the small expressions of tradition and ritual, the power water and cleansing salt Masuda-san always had at practice. Hiroshi had taken to it as if the holds that brought his opponent to the ground were as natural as walking. In his spare time Hiroshi studied moves and techniques, read sumo magazines with a gradual yearning to become a *sumotori*. The growing ambition was as subtle as swallowing. One day it was just a part of who he was.

Before Masuda-san, it was his *ojichan* who introduced him to sumo. "It's not about fighting," he stressed to Hiroshi from the time he was a boy. "It's about using your strength." His grandfather was an ardent fan who followed the histories and rankings of wrestlers as if they were family relations. He sucked on his pipe and embellished his stories with obscure sumo statistics and fragments of information — the one hundred bottles of beer a sumo supposedly drank at a sitting, the sumo who won despite having only four fingers on one hand and three on the other, and the *sumotori* who stretched his body from head to toe for months, so he could make the minimum height requirement of five feet six inches. Though the boys laughed at the last piece of information, Hiroshi was also thankful he was already two inches over the height requirement. But always in his *ojichan*'s mind, the greatest *rikishi* of all time was Yokozuna Futabayama from Tatsunami-beya. In 1936, at the age of twenty-four, he began a three-year winning streak of sixty-nine consecutive sumo match wins, more than any other wrestler.

Amid the ongoing war news, the rationing of rice and miso, and the formation of *tonari-gumi,* or neighborhood associations, comprised of five to ten households established to watch over each other, it was Futabayama's continuous presence in sumo that kept the nation enthralled. Hiroshi marveled when the announcer described Futabayama's strength as having the force of a train when he slammed into his opponent, ramming him completely out of the ring before he could regain his balance. He remembered his grandfather's story about two wrestlers fighting in place of the hundreds of thousands who might fall for their country.

"Hiroshi!" Masuda-san called out to him after practice.

"Hai, sensei." He bowed, and hurried across the room to his coach and the other man, who had eyed him all during practice.

Hiroshi bowed low to his coach.

"This is Tanaka-san. He is the esteemed *oyakata* from the Katsuyama-beya and he would like to meet with you and your grandparents."

Hiroshi bowed low to Tanaka-san and felt his heart racing. The *oyakata* had a reputation as a skilled stable master, and not just of any sumo stable. If he remembered correctly, the Katsuyama-beya in northeastern Tokyo had produced another champion, Kitoyama, and a host of other wrestlers in the top ranks of the Makuuchi Division, which included the five upper ranks of sumo. Tanaka recruited boys and trained them to become champion sumo wrestlers, guiding them up through each stage — *maegashira, komusubi, sekiwake, ozeki,* to the top rank of *yokozuna.* Even in all Hiroshi's nervousness, he couldn't help but ask, "The Katsuyama-beya of Yokozuna Kitoyama?"

Tanaka-san laughed loudly. "Yes, that Katsuyama-beya, but don't expect to see much of Kitoyama-sama as an apprentice. You'll only wish for sleep the first few years."

"More than a few years." Masuda-san laughed.

Hiroshi could hardly believe what he was hearing. The Katsuyama-beya, one of the most prestigious sumo stables, wanted him to join as an apprentice. It meant years of hardship and training, but it was the first step in becoming a *sumotori.* He glanced up at the faces of the two men, waiting for them to tell him that it was all a joke.

"Go home, Hiroshi, and tell your grandparents Tanaka-san and I wish to speak with them about your future, tomorrow after practice."

He bowed low to both men, but his mouth was so dry he could make no reply.

■ ■ ■ ■

As Hiroshi hurried home from practice, the morning air felt terribly thin and cold; the December sky was blue and cloudless. The fog that had hovered for the past few days had lifted, leaving Yanaka sharp and focused, the icicles like ghostly branches hanging from the edges of roofs. For a moment, Hiroshi felt like a little boy again, his breath like smoke rising, as he stole down the alleyways of Yanaka. The sharp wind that glazed his cheeks only made him feel more alive. He wondered if this was what his *obachan* meant by *unmei,* following his destiny.

Sudden shouting brought him out of his reverie, and he saw people spilling out of doors into the streets and alleyways, talking among themselves with slightly stunned, confused looks on their faces. He heard excited cries of "Victory, victory!" and snatches of conversations and foreign words that puzzled him more. He guessed it to be another war rally. Hiroshi rubbed his hands together for warmth and breathed in the cold air as he pushed forward through a group of people headed toward the *ginza.* He rounded the corner and hurried home.

When Hiroshi rushed inside, anxious to tell his grandparents about Tanaka-oyakata and the Katsuyama-beya, he found them huddled around the radio in the kitchen. The "Battleship March" blared through the room, followed by a high-pitched, static-punctuated voice on the radio repeating that the emperor's Imperial Air Force had bombed a place called Pearl Harbor in the Hawaiian Islands. A stern, worried look clouded his *ojichan*'s face. The joy that had borne Hiroshi home disappeared as he realized that war had begun between Japan and America. Suddenly, his news of the Katsuyama-beya seemed small and unimportant.

4
VICTORIES
1942

The war changed everything. Hiroshi couldn't understand why they had less and less at home, despite the Japanese imperial forces claiming one victory after another. By early 1942, Yanaka's alleyways were crowded with women and children who lined up and waited hours for meager rations of rice and salted fish. Each day more shops were closed and boarded up for lack of merchandise, while the streets were patrolled by the *kempeitai.* Everything familiar to Hiroshi diminished — the crowds of people who pushed along the narrow streets wore looks of bleak desperation; the fragrant smells of food, once so pervasive, were now only a thin memory as the war dragged on. But the most frightening thing to Hiroshi was the gradual disappearance of all the capable men from the neighborhood — husbands and sons, teachers and doctors. Even his coach was called to serve by the army.

At their last school assembly, Masuda-san,

along with three other male teachers, stood on the stage and bowed low to the students, each wearing a white sash with a red sun on it draped across his chest. After each man spoke of the great honor in serving his nation, Masuda-san added, "And when I return from our nation's victory, I will expect to see similar victories from all of you on the *dohyo*." His coach glanced in Hiroshi's direction before looking away again.

A month after the bombing of Pearl Harbor, Hiroshi finally told his grandparents about Tanaka-oyakata and the Katsuyama-beya. His dreams of becoming a *rikishi* had evaporated overnight, supplanted by the immediate needs of survival. Nevertheless, sumo matches with top-level champions were still being broadcast on the radio every week.

His *ojichan* shook his head and grasped his shoulder. "I'm proud of you, Hiro-chan. We can't control our fate but I have no doubt you will be a champion when all this is over."

Hiroshi looked away, swallowed the lump in his throat. At fourteen, he stood in that awkward space between the very young and very old men left in Yanaka. The loss of sumo practice felt like yet another defeat. Each day that his energy went unspent, he was left more agitated. Occasionally, Hiroshi still practiced his wrestling moves with his classmates Takeo and Mako at a nearby park after school, savoring the moments of pleasure, when the war felt far away and he concentrated all his energies in the corporal heat of the moment.

Classes were still in session, most now taught by women. The only man left teaching at his school was Hirano-sensei, whose withered right leg had kept him from being drafted, and who taught Hiroshi's class. He was thin and pale, serious and soft-spoken, in his mid-thirties and fiercely loyal to the emperor. One morning, just six months after the Pacific War began, Hirano-sensei pointed to an enormous map of what had become the Greater East Asia Co-Prosperity Sphere, littered with small Japanese flags marking the recent Japanese victories in Guam, Hong Kong, Wake, Manila, Singapore, Bataan, and Rangoon. He lifted his pointer and explained where soldiers had landed in Malaysia, the Philippines, and Burma. "Our imperial forces have driven away all Western dominance, allowing for a stronger, greater East Asia." He droned on excitedly about Japan's successes for the rest of the morning.

"I don't think he likes women," Mako leaned over and whispered to Hiroshi.

"How would you know?" Hiroshi stifled a laugh.

"Look at the way he moves, dragging that foot behind him, swinging his hips from side to side."

Hiroshi waited until Hirano-sensei turned

around again. "You don't need two good feet to like women," he whispered back.

"Just as long as something else down *there* works," Mako said, laughing.

Hiroshi shook his head at Mako and smiled. He hadn't paid much attention in the classroom since the war began. After a morning assembly, their days were filled with fire drills and marching in formation. His sensei's fervor for the war was carried over to their assignments of writing new slogans for each campaign. Their classroom walls were lined with phrases such as "Until victory is achieved, deny one's self" or "The invincible imperial forces will walk the path of victory." Most of the students made fun of Hirano-sensei behind his back, but Hiroshi understood how ashamed he must feel, teaching among women, unable to fight for his country. No wonder Hirano-sensei couldn't stop talking about the war; living his nation's victories made them his, if only through words.

FAMILY

As was his habit, forty-year-old Sho Tanaka rose early, careful not to wake his wife, Noriko, as he slipped quietly through the house. Down the hall, his daughters, five-year-old Aki and eight-year-old Haru, still slept. Not until he slid shut the door to their living quarters and walked across the court-yard did he resume his regular stride. His tight muscles awakened as he quickened his step, and he remembered how it felt to work his body beyond endurance. He breathed in the mildness of the early June morning.

Sometimes, in the thirty feet from his house to the sumo stable, he could almost make himself believe that the war hadn't changed anything. But when he entered the stable through the side door, he found the building eerily quiet. Six months after the bombing of Pearl Harbor, most sumo stables had closed. The fifteen- and sixteen-year-old boys were sent to work in munitions and aircraft facto-ries, and most of the low-level *rikishi* over eighteen were drafted to fight for their em-peror. But Yokozuna Futabayama was still the reigning champion, and with only a handful of top-ranked wrestlers left, including Ki-toyama, the Katsuyama-beya hadn't been completely shut down. And with Kitoyama's continual victories came the assurance that he wouldn't be called to fight.

Now, Sho Tanaka's main concern was Noriko and the girls, and keeping their lives as close to normal as he could. He had always dreamed of one day telling his own sons of the honor and greatness that came from sumo. Instead, Noriko had borne him two daughters, Haru and Aki, whose names meant "spring" and "fall"; and far from being discontent, he loved his daughters for their beauty and the lightness of their movements, so different from the sturdy rowdiness of the boys he worked with every day. It was true that at first they hadn't been the sons he had wished for, but he came to treasure them more.

Tanaka slid open the door to the now silent *keikoba* and stepped onto the dirt floor of the training area. It was already six in the morning, late by training standards. Ordinarily, it would have been a flurry of activity. The youngest and lowest-ranked wrestlers, wearing their dark-colored canvas *mawashi* belts, would already have been exercising for an hour and a half. Each boy came to the stable as young as thirteen with the unrealistic dream of becoming a *yokozuna*, but only a minuscule percentage of *sumotori* ever reached the status of grand champion. Most would never even reach the halfway mark, that of the Juryo Division, which meant they would finally graduate from the apprentice stage and be considered *sekitori*, or professional wrestlers, who received a monthly salary from the sumo association. Still, Tanaka hoped to provide the inspiration to make them work harder. By eight o'clock in the morning, the higher-ranked wrestlers in their white *mawashi* belts would enter the *keikoba* for practice.

Tanaka was careful not to disturb the *dohyo,* outlined in white. Many of the *rikishi* were just boys when they arrived at the stable, their first time away from home, just as he had been so many years ago. If he closed his eyes, he could conjure up the activity that once flourished every morning in the now quiet room — the smack of flesh against flesh, the low grunts of the *rikishi* at their morning stretches, and the sound of his irritated voice when a boy moved without thinking. "Not just your body. All your senses must be alert to your opponent. No move should ever be wasted!" Tanaka remembered the stinging blows of his own coach's bamboo stick across his back and legs when he was a young *rikishi*. No mistake went unrewarded, leaving a raised welt for days. As *oyakata,* he refused to beat his *rikishi,* hoping their pride and desire to win would be enough, knowing that sometimes it wasn't. Tanaka shook his head, remembering. It was a shame about the Matsumoto boy. Hiroshi — Matsuda-san's protégé — whom he was finally persuaded to visit at the school, never had the chance to enter the stable because of the war. His talent and speed were evident, and there was something about the lightness with which the boy moved that reminded Tanaka of all the best wrestlers. It didn't happen often; not once in the past few years had he felt in his bones that a boy's raw talent could be shaped into a champion.

"Otosan," a small voice rang out.

Tanaka turned to see his younger daughter, Aki, standing in the doorway. "What are you doing up so early, Aki-chan?"

"I heard you get up," she said.

He smiled and bent to pick her up. His older daughter, Haru, always more independent, was past the age of wanting to be carried. He was amazed at how light and fragile Aki felt in his arms, how soft and delicate her pale skin was against his fingers. She was the child they almost lost, sickly and small as a baby; twice she had soaring temperatures that made her skin turn a rosy pink, burning up from within. She was still so tiny. They held vigil at the hospital, and he and Noriko lit incense and prayed to the gods at a small temple down the street. Day and night, the murmuring chants had filled him with a heavy grief. Then days later, her fever broke and Aki had been healthy ever since, though always frail in his eyes. Even now, he couldn't smell the pungent, sweet incense or hear the low rumble of chanting without a shiver passing through his body.

"Where are the big boys?" she whispered into his ear, then pulled away and cupped her small palms against the scratchy black stubble on his cheeks.

"They've gone for a little while."

"Will they be back?" she asked.

The *rikishi* treated his family with the greatest respect, and Noriko had made a special effort to get to know each boy when he entered the stable. To Tanaka, sumo was more than sport and years of hard training. Sumo was family. Sumo was history. Sumo was community. That was what Tanaka missed most now.

"Hai," he whispered back in her ear. "They'll be back."

REFUGE

Since the Pacific War began, Kenji's world had grown frenzied. At school, he studied ethics and composition, listened to the increasing fervor of his teachers' lectures on militarism and nationalism, marched in step to martial music during physical education, and then hurried after school down the alleyways, his heart racing for fear of reaching the mask shop and finding it deserted. What if Akira Yoshiwara were no longer there? What if he'd been called up to fight, as so many of the younger men had already been?

The once quiet streets of Yanaka were now filled with tumult, from the *kempeitai*-organized rallies, to the slogans of national devotion plastered on walls — Kenji's favorite being "Luxury is the enemy." He thought America was. Women cheered at train stations as men left for the front, only to turn to tears once the train was out of sight. Newspapers and magazines were filled with victory reports. The capture of Singapore and Bali by the invincible imperial forces blared constantly from radios. A manic feeling seemed to speed the very pulse of the town.

Kenji stopped at the door of the *sembei* rice cracker store. Even Fukushima-san, the owner, who appeared much too old to fight, had been drafted. Women from the neighborhood associations were visiting his shop this afternoon, congratulating him on being able to serve his nation, and leaving him small sums of farewell money. Kenji watched as Fukushima bowed low, saying to them, "I am truly the fortunate one, to serve our emperor and country."

The only place Kenji heard any conflicting views about the war was at the corner bar with his *ojichan* and his friends. As the men huddled around the battered wooden table where they had met for thirty years, there was little room for secrets. His grandfather's brother had been killed years ago at Mukden, and Kenji could see that his *ojichan* disapproved of what his old friend Tokuda-san was saying.

"So, Yoshio, you don't agree this war will make Japan a world power?" Tokuda-san ran his hand through his gray hair and sat back on the wooden stool.

His grandfather smiled and looked right at his old friend, his cloudy eyes revealing nothing. "It saddens me to think that war must be the means to power," he answered.

"Would you rather we sit back and allow America and all the other Western nations to strangle our culture, and that of our neighbors, just as they've done for centuries?"

Kenji listened as their talk turned hard and serious, watched his *ojichan*'s face grow stern, as it did when he and Hiroshi were bad. The set stare reminded him of one of Akira Yoshiwara's masks.

"Is it worth the lives of so many?" his grandfather asked, his voice low.

Kenji watched Tokuda-san lean forward, his face inches away from his grandfather's. "It's what our divine emperor believes, and what we as a nation must also believe. Yoshio, you're beginning to sound like one of those young *hikokumin*."

Kenji held his breath. He didn't know how his *ojichan* would react to being called a traitor. He thought Tokuda-san a stupid, insensitive old man. It was widely known that the son of Uncle Taiko's cousin, the painter Wadao Miyami, had refused to paint propaganda art for the war effort and was imprisoned as a traitor. A month ago, the *kempeitai* came for him in the middle of the night and he remained in prison, awaiting trial.

Then Uncle Taiko cleared his throat and

said, "All this talk is making me thirsty. It's my turn to buy."

"There's nothing left to buy, no rice for sake," Tokuda-san then said, his voice lighter. "Isn't that right, Yoshio?"

Kenji saw his grandfather's slow smile as he took a breath and released it. "No, there's very little left."

By late fall, as the war intensified, the government allowed some theaters and movie houses to stay open, as long as they showed movies made by the Home Ministry. His *ojichan* called them propaganda films, false illusions of what was really happening. Kenji asked him what he meant, but his *obachan* shook her head and answered, "Don't listen to everything your *ojichan* says. He has a mind of his own." Yes, Kenji thought, with admiration at his singular strength, his *ojichan* never let anyone sway his thoughts. He spoke his mind at the bar; he built the wooden watchtower with his own hands, and bravely faced the loss of his sight.

Kenji began to pay closer attention to the life around him. He noticed that in the past few months, men who weren't customers had been coming to the mask shop to see Yoshiwara. He knew they weren't actors by their darting gazes, their soiled, thin cotton kimonos bought cheaply from small side-street shops off the *ginza,* the agitated movements of their hands. Mostly, they were abrupt and sullen, whispering to Yoshiwara and then leaving quickly.

"Who are they?" Kenji asked, the last time they'd come to the shop.

"Acquaintances," Akira Yoshiwara answered, without looking up from his work.

"Not actors?"

Yoshiwara laughed. "No, not actors," he said. "Other important characters in the theater of life. They've come to tell me that the *kempeitai* have been sending their military police to theater performances. If they see or hear something they don't like, anything deemed unpatriotic, the show is stopped." Yoshiwara shook his head. "They've been closing down more and more theaters."

"But the Noh plays are centuries old! The stories are classics."

"It makes no difference, the human condition doesn't change. They can read something into anything, if they want to."

Kenji nodded. So these men were agitators, the kind that he heard his *ojichan* and his friends speak about at the bar.

"They make you unhappy," Kenji said. He didn't like the way they looked, their bleak, serious stares. After visits from these men, Kenji saw Yoshiwara turn quiet, returning to his masks, saying little the rest of the afternoon.

Yoshiwara's gaze turned serious. "They're

96

art students. They remind me that there's a world outside of this room," he said, holding an unfinished mask in front of his face.

Kenji stared hard at him and asked, "Will you have to go fight soon?"

Yoshiwara lowered the mask. "It's nothing you need to worry about."

"But everyone is leaving."

"I won't." Yoshiwara smiled.

Kenji continued. "But sensei, my *ojichan* says everyone of age will be called up before this war ends."

Yoshiwara rose from his stool. "Kenji, like the men you've asked me about, I don't believe in this war."

Kenji was stunned. He knew his old *ojichan* wasn't happy with the war, but he'd never heard younger people speak such words aloud. He didn't understand. If it wasn't the right thing to do, why was the entire Japanese nation behind it? He remembered Yoshiwara receiving a letter one day, which he quickly read and tore up, mumbling angrily to himself that he would never leave his shop. Kenji started to ask what was wrong, but Yoshiwara turned away and began working on a new mask, putting an end to the subject.

From then on, Kenji worried. What if someone from the neighborhood associations heard Yoshiwara and told the *kempeitai?* He would be accused of being a *hikokumin* and taken away to prison like Uncle Taiko's nephew. Kenji never asked about the men again, and tried instead to concentrate on the masks.

Each evening before dinner he ran upstairs to his and Hiroshi's room, slid the door closed, and studied from the book of masks Yoshiwara had given him. He heard Hiroshi and his *ojichan* downstairs listening to a sumo match on the radio, his *obachan* in the kitchen taking bowls down from the shelf. Since the Pacific war had started, fewer and fewer matches were being played, though the remaining bouts were broadcast with bravado. Kenji read on. Tomorrow there would be another set of questions from his sensei. He always tried to imagine what they would be ahead of time. "How many Noh plays have been written?" About two hundred and fifty, he answered in his head. "What are the five categories they're grouped in?" Kenji was ready; they were God, man, woman, madness, and the demon. A roar of voices came from downstairs, cheers for Yokozuna Futabayama, who was still the undefeated champion. Even though Kenji didn't pay much attention to the sport, he was happy to hear Hiroshi and his *ojichan* find such pleasure amid the war. He turned from page to page with the greatest care, and marveled at the intricate drawings. He studied how the simple strokes of the chisel could add subtle frown lines to the forehead of a *Ko-omote,* a young girl's mask, changing it to an older female, a *Zo-onna* mask. Each drawing was masterfully done, not one detail forgotten. He turned the page and read on. "The Kyogen masks are mostly demons and trickster animals, like the raccoon dog, used in plays that offer comic relief between the drama of two Noh plays . . ."

He stopped reading and dreamed of the first mask he would complete on his own — a *Ko-omote,* like the one Yoshiwara-sensei had taken him through step by step. Her simpler, smooth features would be less complicated. The greater depth would be left to the actor behind the mask to bring alive. Yoshiwara-sensei wanted him to know everything about Noh before he was allowed to make a mask. The more Kenji read, the more he felt the need to begin. But what if he wasn't meant to be a mask artisan? It was one thing to want to do something, another to have the required skill. "A living thing," he whispered to himself and closed his eyes. That was how the wood felt in his hands, like something he was bringing to life. His hand closed around an imaginary chisel and he could feel it move through the wood in clean, confident strokes . . .

"Kenji-chan," his *obachan* called, breaking into his thoughts. "Come down to dinner!"

Kenji opened his eyes. *"Hai, obachan,"* he answered, closing the book and tucking it carefully under his futon. The sharp stab of hunger returned. He heard the roar of his grandfather's voice as Futabayama must have won yet another match, and followed it like happiness to the kitchen.

Fumiko Wada

Each morning since the Pacific War began nine months ago, Fumiko Wada waited in long lines just to obtain a cup of rice, a bit of tofu. She stood with all the other women hoping this was the morning there would be more food for them to purchase with their ration coupons. Sometimes, an unexpected shipment of dried fish or seaweed came in and the women pushed forward like a violent wave, eager to purchase some before the box was empty. Such difficult times made Fumiko creative, tucking small pieces of salted fish or pickled vegetables into the middle of rice balls. She watched the faces of Yoshio and her grandsons at dinner as they bit into the small surprise. But over time, the rice balls became smaller and smaller with nothing in the middle but a bit of red bean. Soon, she stopped making the rice balls and put the meager scoops of rice into bowls, hoping it might appear more, or she made *omoyu,* a rice porridge, which consisted mainly of a watery soup.

Later, when there wasn't any rice, sweet

potatoes became their mainstay, or an occasional *kasutera,* a thin, loaf-sized sponge cake, made of sugar, eggs, and cake flour. It was always Yoshio's favorite, and a luxury she brought home from her friend Ayako-san's bakery. Through barter and trade, Ayako's bakery stayed open and flourished. Long lines formed outside her bakery before dawn when the rich smells of baking bread and *kasutera* filled the neighborhood. Ayako set aside a cake or two for her every week. In return, Fumiko took apart several kimonos and sewed them into *monpes* for Ayako and for her daughter, Mikiko. As the war progressed, women were ordered to wear the wide-legged pants and a top instead of kimonos for more mobility. Most women wore khaki or muted-colored *monpes* now. Any clothing that had overly bright colors or a sense of frivolous elegance was prohibited. She also stitched together several of the cotton padded head coverings they were supposed to wear in case of air raids as protection from falling debris. Fumiko had been an expert seamstress since she was young, and was happy to have a way to repay Ayako for her kindness.

By late October, the mornings grew colder. After hours of waiting in ration lines, Fumiko visited the bakery, where she would sit with Ayako over a cup of hot tea, just as she had for the past forty years. Even the war couldn't change this ritual. Ayako felt the same and left Mikiko at the counter to sell whatever baked goods were left to the long line of women and children waiting.

Fumiko shook her head. "Maybe we should meet later," she said, seeing the length of the line. She knew how tempers flared when food ran out — women stealing from each other, pushing and shoving to get a share of the food, taking whatever they could in order to feed their families. And she couldn't blame them one bit.

"Don't worry," Ayako whispered. "Miki-chan knows how to gently turn them away when we run out of anything to sell."

Fumiko watched Mikiko bow respectfully to the next woman in line then followed her friend to the small kitchen in the back. On the stove a pot of soup boiled. She smelled seaweed and the sweet scent of miso, and her stomach clenched. On the floor, Mikiko's five-year-old son, Juzo, was playing with his metal trucks. When he saw Fumiko enter with his grandmother, he stood up and bowed low to her.

"Juzo, what a good boy you are." Fumiko smiled. She bent down and touched his cheek. With all the bad in the world, there was this child before her, a spark of joy for her dearest friend, who had lost so much in her life. Still, Ayako always saw the good in things. "Between us," she often said, "we have three boys."

Ayako Sugihara was Fumiko's first and oldest friend in Yanaka. She had told her grandsons they had met the moment she stepped off the train in Yanaka from Hakodate, newly married to Yoshio. "Ayako was standing on the platform, as if she were waiting for me," Fumiko remembered. "Actually, she was waiting for her new sister-in-law, whom she'd never met, and had mistaken me for her. You can imagine how surprised I was to have this young woman bowing to me with such respect. I bowed back low and we've been great friends ever since."

"Where was her sister-in-law?" Hiroshi asked.

Fumiko smiled. "Ayako later found her. But they've never gotten along well. I was the lucky one. I was the first one to receive her friendship. I don't think my life here would mean so much without it."

But the boys had already lost interest.

Besides, Fumiko knew that the strength of her friendship with Ayako was based on things she couldn't tell her grandsons. She found Ayako a remarkable woman, to have survived the deaths of two husbands, along with their shared pain of each having lost a child. She always believed the gods had them meet for a reason. While both of Ayako's husbands died before her, it was their mutual understanding and grief that came from the death of their children that bonded their hearts and spirits.

A year before Yoshio and Fumiko arrived in Tokyo, Ayako had come to Yanaka from a small village near Kobe to marry. By the age of twenty-four she was already a widow, and the arranged marriage with Masaru the baker was to be her second. While her family rejoiced that her fortune had changed, that Ayako would have another chance at love and a family, she felt numb to everything and everyone. Ayako's child with her first husband, Kyoshi — a son — had been stillborn. After his death and her marriage to Masaru, six years went by and she remained barren. They had long given up on having children when Mikiko was conceived.

Now, since the start of the Pacific War, Ayako spoke more of Kyoshi, who had been killed fighting at Mukden. His death, she told Fumiko, seemed like another life. "I was another person, just a girl. I don't know if he'll recognize me in the other world now," she said, pouring another cup of tea for Fumiko. "How will he know it's me looking so old?" Ayako asked, and then pulled out a worn sepia photo of her first husband, a thin, good-looking young man.

"I'd like to believe that we'll all meet again, that we'll see each other as we did during our best times," Fumiko said, sipping her tea.

"He didn't want to go," Ayako continued. "We were married less than a year when he was called to serve in the army. I remember he said to me, 'Aya-chan, I'm not a soldier; I'm a husband, a farmer. I want you always to remember me in that way.' I thought it would only invite bad spirits for Kyoshi to speak like that and I quickly made him stop. But it was too late. All these years, I have honored his wish. I will always remember him as my husband and a farmer."

Fumiko cleared her throat. She couldn't imagine what it would have been like to lose Yoshio in Mukden. "You have had the good fortune to have a family, to have such a fine daughter in Mikiko."

"Ah yes, but like a foolish old woman, I still think about the family I might have had with Kyoshi," Ayako said. "And what of Masaru, will he be waiting for me in the other world, also?"

Fumiko looked up and smiled but didn't have an answer for her friend. She never thought what it might be like for Ayako to have both of her husbands waiting for her in the other world. Would they know each other? Would they be standing side by side waiting for her?

Masaru was a mild-mannered man whose talent for baking cream cakes was known throughout Yanaka and beyond. He was already forty when they married, and had died in 1938, at the age of sixty-four. Since then, Ayako had run the bakery with her daughter, whose husband had left for the front two months ago. Mikiko and Juzo were the joy of her friend's life. Together, mother and daughter baked *kasutera* three times a week, or until they could no longer get enough sugar and eggs to continue.

Ayako took down bowls from the shelf above the sink. "Have some soup."

Fumiko shook her head. "No, it's for your lunch."

"There's more than enough."

She watched her friend ladle the soup into three bowls and place one in front of her. For a moment, Fumiko closed her eyes and wished she could share this with Yoshio and the boys. It felt somehow a betrayal that she should savor it when they had none. If she could pour it into her pocket and take it home with her, she would.

Then, as if Ayako knew what she was thinking, she said, "Yoshio and the boys will be fine. You need to keep up your strength to help care for them."

Fumiko smiled, sipped the fragrant soup, and felt the salty warmth slip down her throat. As a child, she had disliked soup. Her mother used to tell her how the broth held all the ingredients to make one strong in body and spirit. Fumiko would slowly sip her soup

106

as her mother told her the story of the woman who was so poor she collected stones off the Izu peninsula in order to make soup for her family. She would boil the stones in water for hours, and, magically, each night her family filled their stomachs with a soup tasting of salted fish and seaweed, or miso, or red bean — each night it would be different, yet no less filling. Fumiko had loved that story and couldn't wait to drink her soup each night afterward.

"Besides," Ayako said, breaking into her thoughts. "I have a little something else for you to take home." She opened a cabinet and pulled out a package wrapped in thin brown paper. "I've saved the last *kasutera* for you," she said, smiling.

Fumiko put down her bowl, and then, like Juzo, she stood up and bowed very low to her friend.

At dinner that night, Fumiko smiled sadly and said, "I'm afraid this will be the last of the *kasutera*. Ayako can't get any more fresh eggs, not even through the black market. She tried to bake with powdered eggs from Shanghai but the *kasutera* didn't taste the same. She hopes to start baking bread for sandwiches starting next week."

"Ayako will always find a way to stay in business," Yoshio said. "She has the strength of ten."

Fumiko nodded. She watched as they all ate their *kasutera* slowly, relishing each bite. Yoshio looked up and caught her eye, his smile a little sad as he swallowed his last bite of cake.

5
HUNGER
1942–1943

Every day after school, Hiroshi walked home through the Yanaka *ginza.* Even before he reached the Kyo-ou-ji temple, he heard the bells, the low moans of chanting that hummed through the neighborhood, and breathed in the sharp sting of incense. A funeral was being held. Since the war began, steady streams of the dead were returned to families in Yanaka. Hiroshi saw his *obachan* shake her head and lament all the spirits of the missing that would never find their way back to their loved ones. *"Obake,"* she whispered. Ghosts. The first person killed from Yanaka whom Hiroshi knew was the sixth-grade teacher's husband. He remembered the simple coffin draped with the Japanese flag that came off the train, the same red sun that blazed on the sash across his chest as he stood on the auditorium stage just before he left for the war. Whereas it seemed to glow with heat as he stood before the crowd to say goodbye, the same red sun now hid itself in shadows as the coffin was carried into the station.

While most of the able-bodied men had been drafted, women of all ages filled the streets. The poor became poorer and begged on the streets for scraps of food. Women stood on corners asking other women for stitches to be added to a family member's *sen'ninbari,* their thousand-stitch belts made from long pieces of woven cloth. His *obachan* explained that grandmothers, wives, even small daughters rallied around the popular talisman, which was thought to protect a soldier from harm. Each stitch embodied the woman who stitched it. When enough stitches were gathered, the cloth belts were distributed to troops to protect them from being killed. While the protective belt gave each soldier a renewed sense of courage, it also filled the women back home with the hope that their loved ones would return safely to them.

In the swarm of bodies standing outside the boarded-up Takahara dry-goods store, Hiroshi thought he saw Mariko and turned shyly away. He hadn't seen her in months. Ever since the bombing of Pearl Harbor, she'd stopped practicing her cello out in the backyard. Just before the start of the Pacific War she'd been accepted into the Tokyo Symphony, and it was rumored that she was engaged to marry another member of the symphony, a viola player, until he had been called up to fight. When Hiroshi turned back to search the faces for hers again, she was gone. He remembered his *obachan* saying that Mariko was one of the many single women working in factories to replace the men. He couldn't imagine the same long, thin fingers that played the cello so beautifully sorting oily aircraft parts, or packing munitions in an assembly line.

Hiroshi stopped abruptly when he heard the yelling, though raised voices were common enough on the streets these days. All too often, voices rose with a frantic edge, and he could usually distinguish the degree of trouble by how loud the voices were. Across the road he saw two women waiting in line, fighting over a piece of dried squid. It fell to the ground as they clawed at each other and a third woman snatched it from under their noses and ran. He heard the thud of boots, the clink of the swords against their legs, before he heard the breathless shouts of "Stop now!" from the *kempeitai,* as the crowd quickly scattered. But the desperate women paid little attention. Hiroshi knew this would anger the military policemen and move them to cruelty as they roughly pulled the women apart and slapped them hard across their faces. The blood rushed to Hiroshi's head as he backed up and turned away from the pleading women, their screams cut short by more slaps. His heart hammered in his chest, not so much from fear as from anger. He would have been arrested if he had interfered. Always, the same questions turned over in his mind. Who did they think they were? What made them change from regular men to the *kempeitai,* men who seemed just as bad as the enemy?

When the rationing began in 1940, it wasn't so difficult for Hiroshi's *obachan* to still put food on the table with sufficient rice to provide sustenance. But after the bombing of Pearl Harbor, the American embargoes stopped everything. Now, a full year later, Hiroshi couldn't remember the last time they had had any meat or fresh fish to eat. He and Kenji ate more and more slowly, trying to make what little they had in their bowls last longer. He'd never felt this way before, this hollow gnawing in the middle of his stomach, the dull throb of hunger. There'd never been a time when his grandparents hadn't kept them safe and well fed. Now, Hiroshi watched the pinched expressions on his grandparents' faces and felt everything was being rationed: even joy and happiness came to them in small doses now, while fear and dread of the war and their increasing hunger weighed heavily on everyone's minds.

Most mornings, while his *obachan* waited in ration lines, Hiroshi's *ojichan* procured whatever he could on the black market through friends at the bar. Sometimes, he would get lucky and return with a few real eggs or cans of marinated eel. Still, it never seemed enough, and when the Pacific War began, it had dwindled to next to nothing. Hiroshi could see that the failure had discouraged his grandfather, who appeared frail and lost; his eyes blank and lifeless. He spent more and more time up in the watchtower, alone.

But while his *ojichan* grew more remote, his grandmother couldn't stop moving. On one warm April morning, as Hiroshi hurried home to retrieve a forgotten schoolbook, he saw his *obachan* leaving the house carrying one of her favorite kimonos — the pale green silk with a flowing pattern of purple irises — which she quickly tucked into a *furoshiki.*

"Hiroshi, are you all right?" she asked, her voice rising with concern.

"I'm fine, *obachan.* I just forgot a book. Where are you going with your kimono?"

She paused and then asked, "Is a kimono's beauty more important than food on the table?"

It took Hiroshi a moment to realize what she was saying. One by one, she was selling her best kimonos — for more rice, canned food, powdered eggs, half a dozen sweet potatoes, and some precious salted fish and miso. He also knew there would be penalties if she were caught by the *kempeitai;* another woman's small rice ration was taken away when she was caught selling her kimonos on the black market. His grandmother's courage frightened him, made him want to hover over her and protect her. He glanced down at the *furoshiki* clutched tightly in her hand, and grieved for the soft touch of the kimono's silk, the vibrant colors and bold patterns of his grandmother's youth. He silently vowed to get them all back for her, each and every one.

If his *ojichan* had found solace in the stars, his *obachan* put her energy into the soil. By the spring of 1942, it became mandatory that each household in the neighborhood plant a vegetable garden to supplement the rationing. The neighborhood associations were given seeds to distribute to each of the households under their jurisdiction, while the *kempeitai* made rounds to make sure each family was doing its share, taking advantage of the opportunity to make off with the best vegetables. Every square foot of dirt was tilled and planted, with hopes of producing enough food for the neighborhood.

As the demand for food increased, Hiroshi watched his grandmother kneeling by the patch of earth in the front courtyard, while she hummed the folk songs that she sang to them as children.

"It reminds me of my childhood," she said, instructing Hiroshi to water each sprouting plant. "Not too much," she directed.

"I didn't know you were such a gardener."

"Your great-grandmother had the gardener's touch. I believe she could bury a pebble and something would bloom from it." She rubbed the dirt from her hands and pushed herself up from the ground.

Hiroshi helped her to her feet. "Just think what her daughter will grow with real seeds," he said.

She looked at him and smiled, then reached up and patted his cheek. "How did you grow so tall and strong? With so little to nourish . . ."

"Because of you," he said, laughing. "You have the gardener's touch."

Hiroshi liked working in the garden, digging down into the earth and dropping the small seeds, always amazed that with a bit of watering, the strong stems would rise from the plot of dirt no larger than a tatami mat. It gave him hope that miracles could still happen. Funny how he'd paid no attention to that patch of earth before, and now it produced vegetables that the *kempeitai* picked over, leaving only some spinach and the few turnips that graced their table. He felt overwhelmingly proud the first time they sat down to eat their own wilted leaves and soft turnips.

And while he and Kenji often helped their *obachan* in the garden, Hiroshi knew his *ojichan* was frustrated that he couldn't do more. His eyesight was failing, shadows now, Hiroshi thought. It seemed his *ojichan* was disappearing more and more into his own world. The last time his grandfather tried to help, he accidentally stepped on some newly sprouted shoots. He heard the distress in his grandmother's voice as she said, "No, Yoshio, no! Perhaps you should stand over here." She took his arm and led him away like a small child. Now every bright spring morning, when Hiroshi went up to the tower to fetch his grandfather down to help in the vegetable garden, his *ojichan* refused. He never ventured near it again.

By the warm summer evenings of 1942, they ate in silence. Hiroshi listened to the empty clink of the bowls and decided he had to do something to appease their hunger. He watched his *obachan* ladle a watery stew made of the last of the turnips and carrots on top of his half bowl of rice and felt whatever happiness he'd had slowly dissipate. His *obachan* placed the bowl in front of him, her gaze avoiding his. Hiroshi remembered her wide smile when he was a little boy, as she told him how each bite of food would make him bigger and stronger, filling his bowl with choice morsels of fish, chicken, and thin slices

116

of beef. He remembered the laughter, the buzz of all their voices humming through the kitchen. Now as his *obachan* hardly ate, he knew she was saving her little bit of rice for him and Kenji.

Like their grandparents, he and Kenji learned to battle their hunger in different ways. Lying on his futon at night, Hiroshi slowly came to see that the war and rationing were depleting not only their bodies but also their spirits. He saw that when there was so little, everything mattered, and even fantasies provided nourishment. While Kenji lost himself in his theater books, Hiroshi dreamed of sumo, of what it might have been like to enter the Katsuyama-beya and become a champion. Sometimes these small hopes and dreams helped to divert his thoughts from his empty stomach.

On other nights, he and Kenji lay on their futons in the dark and faced their hunger head-on; they would remember something they particularly loved to eat, describing it so vividly that Hiroshi's mouth watered and his stomach ached from the want of it. Kenji was especially good at description.

"Hiro," Kenji whispered from his futon. "Tonight, if there were no war, we would have eaten *obachan*'s sukiyaki. The bowl would be steaming hot with the shoyu, sweet rice wine, cabbage, rice noodles, carrots, and chunks of tender chicken still boiling to the top. You would have eaten three bowls of rice and *ojichan* would have teased you about leaving something for the rest of us."

"So then," Hiroshi added, "*obachan* would return to the kitchen and bring out a plate of pork cutlets, fried crunchy the way you like them."

"And more steaming rice, with layers of marinated eel on top. Red bean cake, for dessert."

"And *orenji*," Hiroshi added. Just saying the full, round word "oranges" made his mouth water. He tried to remember the last time a wedge of sweet juice exploded in his mouth. Then he groaned at the dearth of such food, and the hunger that clenched at his stomach. A sourness rose in his mouth and he covered his head with his comforter.

Persimmons

It began with persimmons. Afterward, the stealing became easier, though much more dangerous. Hiroshi had stolen a dozen rotting persimmons from the yard of their neighbors the Odas. The *kempeitai* had taken all the rest, leaving all the rotted fruit scattered on the ground. Such waste seemed careless and arrogant, even though his grandparents might have done the same thing prior to the war. By late 1942, nothing could be taken for granted and the idea of waste filled Hiroshi with anger. Before the Odas dared to come out, he climbed over the fence and took as many as he could carry, at least a dozen. Three for each of them. That's the way he thought now; it was always "how many were left?" and "how long would it last?" until the rice was gone, until the miso ran out, until they were reduced to eating turnip soup. He would make it up to Oda-san another day, he thought, as he ran with the decaying fruit in the pocket of his outstretched T-shirt, sticky and wet against his stomach, as the juice ran down his arms and hands, and the sickly sweet smell stayed with him for days after.

Long before the war, the tall persimmon tree with its large leaves bloomed brilliant shades of yellow, orange, and red in the Odas' yard every fall, the dangling fruit like shiny lanterns. The children in the neighborhood called it the *kurisumasu tsuri,* the Christmas tree. Now the real gift was the smile on his *obachan*'s face as she caressed each one of the rotting, sticky fruits. She then made a persimmon pudding out of them, never once asking where they came from.

After the persimmons, he stole a can of pickled vegetables, snatched from a black marketeer when he turned his back, a few carrots left in someone's vegetable garden, and a container of fresh tofu from Okata-san, their neighbor down the block, who was

119

rumored to be a puppet of the *kempeitai*. Early on, Okata volunteered to lead the neighborhood association. No one suspected he would betray his friends and neighbors for extra ration coupons, or a carton of cigarettes. It was said he had turned in a neighbor for having as little as a cup more of the allotted rice.

Hiroshi was exhilarated when he set the tofu in front of his grandmother. Stealing from Okata felt better than any wrestling match he'd ever won. His *obachan* watched him, a glint of fear in her eyes. "No more," she said softly. And Hiroshi nodded, because he knew it would put her mind at ease. But he wouldn't promise to stop stealing if it was the only way he could help them survive. So he told her a funny story, to tease her out of her seriousness. "You look as if I've come home with the lowest grade in the class," he said easily. Gradually, she smiled, but not before pleading with him again to be very careful.

108 Evil Thoughts

Every night as they lay on their futons, Hiroshi whispered a new story to Kenji. He had stolen from Okata again, and not just anything but a box of New Year's *mochi*, sticky rice with red bean in the middle, given to Okata by the military police for his exemplary service as head of the neighborhood association. "I heard everything," Hiroshi said. "I was waiting just outside his kitchen window. When Okata showed them out, I took the box of *mochi* off the table and walked right out." Hiroshi snickered and spread his body full length on his futon. "He shouldn't leave his back door open."

Kenji could feel his brother smiling in the dark. With Hiroshi next to him in their small room, it felt like the safest place in the world. How could everything change so quickly? The once vibrant streets of Yanaka had turned gray and drab, the bright-colored cloth banners hanging from shops torn down, replaced with blackout curtains or black inked-out windows. Everyone walked around like hungry ghosts, while he moved carefully down the alleyways to the mask shop. But what Kenji hated most of all was the noise — the air-raid sirens that blasted in the early hours of the morning and brought them outside, shivering as they squeezed into a makeshift air-raid shelter, the high, scratchy voices that came over the radio, the whimpering ones begging for food in the streets, and the low, worried whispers between his grandparents that hummed through the house like persistent flies.

Just yesterday, Kenji had turned down a quiet alleyway, away from the noise and crowds, lost in his thoughts. A sudden, high-pitched shriek made him glance up; two *kempeitai* stood not ten feet away, watching something on the ground and laughing. A terrible burning smell rose through the air and a squealing sound came from a small twitching heap on the ground. Kenji hesitated, put his hand over his nose, and kept walking, thinking he might draw more attention to himself if he suddenly turned back and went the other direction. If he could just make it past them, the mask shop wasn't far.

"What are you looking at?" one of the men turned and snapped at him.

Kenji bowed quickly and kept his gaze downward, heart beating as he walked faster. He heard the men laughing but didn't dare look up. When he was far enough away, he turned back, saw them kicking the small bundle on the ground, a rat, he guessed from the long tail that twitched as smoke rose from the dark, convulsing creature. Kenji turned around and felt sick to his stomach as he hurried away. He never said a word about it to anyone.

Kenji shook his head in the darkness of their room but couldn't tell his brother what was really on his mind. He was proud of Hiroshi, but even more so, he was afraid for him.

"What did *obachan* say?" he asked.

"Nothing. I haven't given the *mochi* to her yet. I told her I would stop stealing."

Kenji swallowed. Like his *obachan,* he didn't want his brother stealing anymore, taking chances that might get him hurt or in trouble with the military police and taken away to prison. Even his brother's skill and speed as a wrestler wouldn't help him then. For as long as Kenji could remember, Hiroshi had never backed down from what he believed. It was what he admired about him, and also what he feared. If his brother's life were a Noh play, Hiroshi would be an *Ayakashi,* the warrior who returns to earth to avenge his family and good name. Yes, Hiroshi would always be the avenger. Kenji could see the mask now, the sharp piercing gaze and dark flowing beard. He'd also come back and seek the love he'd left behind. Kenji's mind wandered and he wasn't sure how long they had remained silent until he recaptured his train of thought, breathed in deeply, squared his shoulders, and whispered from his futon, "I think you should stop stealing, before something really goes wrong."

There, he had said it. When Hiroshi didn't answer, Kenji waited in the darkness of the room as the winter winds blew, rattling the shoji windows behind the rough blackout curtains. In the dimness, he reached out, let his fingers lightly brush against his brother's blanket, his shoulder or arm just underneath. Kenji listened, until beyond the rattling, the soft sounds of Hiroshi's even breathing let him know that his brother was already asleep.

The Shogatsu or New Year of 1943 had passed quietly. His *obachan* cleaned house but there were no decorations, no going to visit the shrines or friends, and no traditional three-day holiday filled with *toshikoshi* soba, the buckwheat noodles Kenji loved. *Ozoni,* the soup with *mochi,* was only a memory that left his stomach aching. Hiroshi gave his *obachan* the box of Okata's *mochi,* but only after he solemnly promised never to steal again would she allow them to be eaten.

Instead of forgetting the troubles of the old year, they worried about the ongoing war. On New Year's Eve, they listened for the *Joya-no-Kane,* the traditional gongs, struck one hundred and eight times with a wooden log in the Buddhist temples and shrines. Ever since they were little, his *obachan* had told them it was to drive away the 108 hindrances that each person carried. What's a hindrance? he had asked. His grandmother called them evil thoughts. The gong was struck until the morning light of the New Year appeared.

"What are these evil thoughts?" Kenji asked his *ojichan* every year. To think badly of others? To lie to your grandparents? To cheat on an exam? To steal? To touch yourself until you're excited? Was Hiroshi evil because of his stealing, even if it was to help his family? Kenji didn't want to admit that he was already guilty of some evil thoughts. Still, he believed there was no greater evil than the *kempeitai*. What could be more evil than hitting women, stealing food from those who had so little, and burning defenseless animals alive? Kenji shook away the thought, and the acrid stench that he still smelled.

"All that it means to be human," his *ojichan* always answered.

"But that doesn't answer my question," Kenji persisted this time. He wanted real answers. "And aren't some evil thoughts much worse than others?"

His grandfather laughed and nodded. "Yes, Kenji-chan, but we're talking of the small evils that we hold in our hearts. You know the answers, deep inside, when you've had a bad thought, or said something wrong to hurt another person."

Kenji breathed a sigh of relief. Well, it wasn't so bad then — evil thoughts came in all shapes and sizes. Surely he and Hiroshi must fall into the "small evil" category.

Every New Year, when Kenji heard the resonant brass gong being struck, he felt each evil hindrance rise from his mind and body, leaving him with a feeling of weightlessness. This year, there was only a suffocating silence. The *kempeitai* wouldn't allow the traditional striking of the gong to interfere with their blackout rules and disrupt communications. And though no one said a word, Kenji now knew that the old evils of the previous year would remain in Yanaka. He saw the same sad recognition in his *obachan*'s face as she stood and walked slowly up the stairs to bed.

INVISIBILITY

Six-year-old Aki awaited the *Joya-no-Kane*, the thing she loved most about New Year's Eve. Like last year, she would lie in bed next to Haru and count each strike of the gong until she fell into a deep sleep. The rhythmic lullaby rang on into early morning. But this year there were no gongs and Aki couldn't sleep. She whispered Haru's name but her steady breathing told her she was already asleep. Thoughts didn't run wild in her sister's head and keep her awake as they did Aki. Never mind, Haru would only tell her to close her eyes and count to fifty . . . *ichi, ni, san, shi* . . . and she would soon be asleep. Just what Aki didn't want to hear. She lay perfectly still, tried to conjure up the gong's reverberation in her head as in previous years, but it was no use, there was only silence.

Aki pulled away from the warmth of her sleeping sister and rose slowly from the futon, quietly slipping on her sandals. Things were different now than they were last New Year's, and not just because all the big boys had left the stable. Even her parents were act-

126

ing strange lately. Her mother jumped at every sound and never had energy to play with her. And her father never stayed at home for long. When he did, he sat alone in his office at the stable, or stood and stared at the empty *dohyo* in the *keikoba*.

No one would tell Aki what was wrong. Even Haru avoided her questions. Just that morning, as they finished their watery congee, Aki had asked, "What's wrong with Mother and Father? What's happening?"

"We're at war," Haru calmly answered like an adult. "We're trying to find our place in the world," she added.

"Isn't our place right here at the stable?"

Haru shook her head, "You're too young to understand these things," she answered. Aki looked at her pleadingly. She *could* understand if Haru explained. But the grave, serious look on her sister's face told Aki to stay quiet.

Aki tiptoed out of their room and into the hallway. She paused a moment at a strange sound coming from the courtyard, a distant moan. Could it be a cat? Her parents had told her over and over she was never to leave the house after dark, but Aki thought if she counted to fifty, she could be outside and back again before anyone knew. *Ichi, ni, san, shi* . . . She passed her parents' dark and quiet room and was down the hall. *Go, roku, nana, hachi . . .* She was almost at the front door. It wouldn't hurt to just take a peek outside. What if the kitten needed help? Father would be proud that she checked. *Kyu, ju, juichi, juni . . .* Aki reached down and unlatched the lock, slid the door open slowly, slowly, so she wouldn't wake anyone up, just enough to take a look and listen to where the whimpering sounds were coming from. She poked her head outside. The night air was icy and felt like glass. There was the moan again, not like a cat sound exactly. Perhaps it was another animal that needed help. *Jusan, juyon, jugo . . .* One step after another and Aki was in the courtyard, the scratching of her sandals making too much noise, so she lifted her feet higher and moved quietly. The sound again. It was coming from the other side of the courtyard, near the stable where Hoku, the stable caretaker, stayed. *Juroku, junana, juhachi . . .*

Aki stopped when she saw the shadow, something pressed against the wall — big and dark. It was moving back and forth and the whimpering moan was coming from it. Aki became invisible. Ever since she could remember, she turned invisible when something frightened her. Now, no one saw her, not the dark *obake,* not the big monster that leaned back and moaned.

Then all at once, there were two shadows.

128

Aki turned around and ran back to the house, her sandals clacking against the stone walkway. "Who's there?" a voice shot through the cold air. It sounded like Hoku but Aki didn't stop to find out. She slipped into the house and latched the shoji door behind her. Quickly, she retraced her steps down the hallway to her and Haru's room and fell onto the futon. Breathing hard, she moved toward her sister's warmth. Only then did Aki make herself visible again. She closed her eyes and began counting to fifty from the beginning: *ichi, ni, san, shi* . . .

6
THE PAST AND THE PRESENT
1943

Yoshio leaned against the wooden post of the tower, sucked on his pipe, and let the smoke drift, floating upward into the wet April evening. Since the "Sacred War" showed no signs of coming to an end, he only smoked once in a while now, usually after dinner. Tobacco, along with everything else, was almost impossible to obtain, even with ration coupons, or when possible through the black market. It was a luxury, usually hoarded and kept in a tin can with a box of matches beneath one of the kitchen floorboards, along with Fumiko's wedding ring, her silver pin, and pearl earrings wrapped in a silk scarf. He inhaled again, tasting hints of vanilla and cinnamon on his tongue, savoring it.

For the past week, Yoshio had been living his life completely in the dark, though he kept it to himself, not wanting Fumiko to worry further or to disrupt the boys' lives any more than the war and rationing already had. He took another puff from his pipe, remembered the scatter of glowing lights from neighboring houses, the night air filled with floating voices. Blindness mattered little, since the blacked-out windows and air-raid curtains scarcely let a sliver of light seep out. His face turned upward to the wide canvas of dark sky. He mourned the absence of moonlight. Since February, he'd strained to see any faint glow that might be a star, any remnant of moonlight. Now he could no longer see if there were stars in the sky, something he'd once loved to do with Fumiko when the boys were little and asleep. She loved stargazing. "They never leave," she had whispered to him. "They may hide behind the clouds but I know they're always there." For Yoshio, those stars would forever hide behind the clouds and he would have to learn to believe with the same faith that Fumiko had. They were there.

Now that Yoshio was completely blind, it made less difference than he expected. In many ways it was easier; he no longer struggled to make out the faint shadows around him, but simply gave in to the darkness. And by doing so, his other senses became more acute. Or perhaps he just concentrated on them more. It helped that he was blessed with a vivid memory — the fifteen steps leading up to the watchtower from the kitchen, the one hundred and eighty-three steps from the front gate to the bar down the street, the two-inch scar on Fumiko's lower right side from when she had had her appendix removed as a girl. In fact, there were times when Yoshio preferred to follow his memories rather than the calculated steps through this world gone mad. Not that he could ever voice such unpatriotic thoughts aloud; what with the neighborhood associations keeping watch on their every move and the National Defense Women's Association on each corner, the smallest indiscretion might bring the *kempeitai* to their doorstep.

It had been a difficult day and his thoughts simmered. Since the rumors of heavy Japanese losses at Midway and Guadalcanal, followed by the destruction of the entire Japanese convoy at the Battle of Bismarck Sea, which he learned about through a letter his friend Taiko had received from his son, Yoshio felt that the tide had turned for his country, even as radio broadcasts proclaimed otherwise. It was just a matter of time, he thought.

Okata from the neighborhood association now came by once a week, expecting each household to donate anything that would help with the war effort. Rumors circulated around the neighborhood that the Okata household lacked for nothing — there was always ample rice on his table; payment for his scavenging for the military. And each week he seemed to be more aggressive. Yoshio had never liked Okata; he was the kind of man who always needed to be noticed.

So when Okata came from down the street at noontime today, Yoshio was already agitated. He was glad the boys were at school. His neighbor's insistence upon coming in somehow frightened him. Okata immediately bragged about the Buddhist temple bells and altar brass that were donated to him just that morning for the metal drive, and how the authorities would be pleased.

"Yes," Yoshio had said. "And we know how important it is to please the military."

Okata had let the remark pass; without a pause, he'd added that Oda-san down the street had donated his entire tool set.

In that same moment, Yoshio remembered Fumiko had forgotten to take off her gold wedding ring. He had felt it when he brushed across her hand at breakfast. Usually, she removed it every morning in case there was a surprise visit from Okata, but she liked to put it back on when they went to bed. "It's hard to sleep without it," she'd said, just last night.

Okata had caught sight of it, too. "Ah, your gold ring, Fumiko-san! You must be so proud to be able to serve our nation by donating it." Yoshio could hear the greedy smile in Okata's voice. "Every little thing will lead to our nation's victory."

Yoshio heard a whisper of reply from Fumiko, the sharp intake of breath as she

133

twisted the ring off her finger, followed by the slow release of air, as if she were deflating.

"Okata-san," he said quickly, without thought. "I'm sure one small ring won't do much to help the nation."

In the silence, he felt Okata staring at him, judging him, deciding what this meant for him to oppose the neighborhood authorities.

"Yoshio-san is just being a sentimental old man," Fumiko interjected. "What does a ring matter, a small piece of metal that can be easily replaced when our nation is victorious."

Then Okata laughed loudly, "Yes, Yoshio, this is not the time to be sentimental. Our nation needs all our help until victory is achieved."

Yoshio remained silent, barely able to swallow. It was Fumiko who bravely carried on, giving Okata another iron pot and a silver hair ornament, her voice light and animated, never once revealing her grief.

Standing high in his tower, sucking on his pipe, Yoshio let go of the day's difficulties until he felt as if he were far away from all that troubled him. A mild wind stroked his face; he closed his eyes to his memories. Their story, Fumiko's and his, had begun with a dance. He smiled at the thought of his body once being so limber, so full of power and vanity. He had grown up on the sea coast of Hokkaido — in the port town of Hakodate — and Fumiko, in the larger city of Sapporo. Yoshio always believed people who lived by the sea carried within them a lighter, more fluid water spirit. His father had been a fisherman and Fumiko's a shopkeeper, humble people who never wanted more from life than to provide for their families. Still, Fumi-chan had always been a big-city girl in his eyes.

Fumiko had an aunt, uncle, and cousin who lived in Hakodate and she spent several summers there with them. Yoshio first saw her at the Bon Odori during Obon, when everyone in town gathered together to dance in honor of the spirits of the dead. The raised platform of the *yagura* was set up in the middle of the dance grounds, a *taiko* drum on it. Men, women, and children danced around the *yagura* to the rhythmic beat of the drum, the clicking of bamboo sticks, the raised fans, the simple, repetitive steps, each executed in the pure expression of joy, free of their usual shame or inhibitions. Yoshio had begun dancing at the Bon Odori as a little boy, adapting to the steps with ease and grace. Every year he joined the circle and felt the lightness of the spirits inhabit his body.

And the colors. Once again they soared through his darkness — the red, green, and yellow lanterns strung from the *yagura* high above their heads, matched by the patchwork kimonos and the round bamboo and parchment fans that floated in the air like white masks. The first time he saw Fumiko was the summer she was fifteen — a white blossom in her black hair, wearing a yellow *yukata* kimono, walking carefully on her cloglike wooden *geta*. Seeing Fumiko struck him like a bright flash of lightning, a surge of energy. The lanterns cast a bright glow over everything as he watched her across the circle. The rhythmic beating of the *taiko* drum began, each *step-beat, step-beat* became his heart pounding. At seventeen, he was frightened and astounded. So, this was love. Yoshio followed Fumiko in the dance around the circle, trailing the yellow of her kimono, the white flower that peeked in and out from the crowd, the beckoning of her fan — the *step-beat* that he still felt now. She moved as if she were floating, as if the lightness in her step reached up and met his. Four years later, he had saved enough for the gold ring, even before their families sat down for the marriage negotiations.

Now he heard Fumiko down in the kitchen cleaning up after their meager dinner, the flow of water echoing against the hollow kettle, the clinking of rice bowls in the hot water, her low, soothing hum that still gave him comfort after forty years of marriage. Yoshio turned toward the sounds and smiled

136

in his new sightlessness. Then carefully, with a calm assurance, he took the first step back down to her.

THE RING

Fumiko poured the rest of the boiling water into the sink to rinse the last of the bowls. Her thoughts rose with the steam, which clouded her vision, and her soft humming became a choking sob. Did Yoshio think she was a fool? That she wouldn't know he'd completely lost his sight? They had been married so long that she knew what he'd do even before he did it. It was as subtle as the arrangement of stones in a garden — the increased time he spent alone up in the watchtower, the way he no longer looked but tilted his head to listen, even the way that he touched her felt different, as if he were seeing with his hands. She knew. It was a marriage that hadn't faltered in forty years, despite the heartache of losing Misako and the raising of their grandsons. They had lived two separate lifetimes together, nurtured two families, and even with the hardships of war and rationing, she never felt their family strength waver. But the moment she slipped the ring off her finger and handed it to Okata, Fumiko experienced a shiver along the back of her neck, the breath of a bad omen. In that instant, she knew Japan would never win the war and that even greater sacrifices would follow. If even a small sliver of gold from a ring was needed, what hope was left?

Since midday, a silent rage had smoldered inside of her. She tried to calm herself by sewing the padded head coverings they were instructed to wear during air raids, and writing or embroidering their names on the inside of their clothes in case of an emergency. She was thankful her husband couldn't see the look of pleasure on the bastard Okata's face as his sweaty palm closed around her ring. Yoshio would have struck him, just as she had imagined herself doing a hundred times since Okata left this morning. What stopped her was his connection to the *kempeitai,* and the fear that he might suspect Hiroshi of stealing from him. Quite unexpectedly, Okata had spoken of Hiroshi the last two times he'd come to the house. "Fumiko-san, your older grandson is becoming quite a young man, so tall and strong." And just this morning, "Perhaps Hiroshi has thoughts of joining our emperor's Imperial Army?" Coincidence? Fumiko shook her head and knew it wasn't. Okata never said anything that didn't mean something else. In the end, the ring wasn't important, but the well-being of her grandsons was another matter. For the first time, Fumiko realized she would kill for them.

She looked up when she heard Yoshio coming down the stairs, rubbed her eyes so he wouldn't know she'd been crying, then remembered that it was the quality of her voice she had to control now. Could she find the right balance between fear and hate? She watched him pause at the bottom of the stairs, and then take the five steps to his chair by the table.

"Tea?" she asked, her voice steady and controlled.

He nodded, looking pale in the dim light. "It's a calm night."

"Best to enjoy them while we can," she said, regretting the ominous undercurrent.

Yoshio looked at her, squarely in the face, as if he could still see her. "They are numbered," he agreed.

After a moment of silence, Fumiko said, "Perhaps we should discuss Reiko-san's offer?"

"Hai," he answered quietly.

Fumiko knew that a number of families from the neighborhood had begun to evacuate to the safety of the countryside to wait out the war. But until that moment, they hadn't spoken seriously about sending the boys to his niece and her family outside of Nagano.

"It's something to think about," he added.

"Hai." Fumiko heard the unexpected rise in her voice as she agreed.

She poured tea into a clay cup and placed it in front of Yoshio. But before she could turn away, he reached for her hand, his familiar warm grip holding tight.

THE TRENCH

Hiroshi pushed his shovel with ease into the muddy ground, which was still saturated from the April rains. Murky puddles stood at the side of the road as he and his classmates Mako and Takeo began to dig. Digging trenches was far from the work in munitions plants or airplane-parts production they had hoped to be doing to help their nation's war effort. Soon, their clothes would be covered in mud. He knew his *obachan* would shake her head when he returned home, take the small amount of fuel they had and hurry him to bathe, while she soaked his clothes in a tub of water.

At fifteen, Hiroshi was too young to fight for his country, but too old to be considered a child. He and his friends were all members of the Great Japan Youth Association, mobilized through schools to help in any way. Two days a week, upper-grade classes were suspended so that students could help dig slit trenches along the roadway. When the air-raid sirens sounded, students jumped into the nearest trench to squat or lie facedown with their hands or schoolbags over their heads. Hiroshi knew the trenches were important protection, but they still looked like open graves to him, waist-deep furrows long enough to hold a dozen or more people.

Several of his classmates had already left to work in factories, but he would have to wait until the schools were completely closed. The most important thing to his grandparents was his and Kenji's education, even if it meant days of digging trenches, practicing air-raid drills, and writing slogans. As long as the schools were still open, his grandparents expected him to attend.

As Hiroshi dug, he carved out the sides and packed the mud together with the back of his shovel. The sharp smell of wet earth brought back childhood memories of going down to the Sumida River with his *ojichan* when he and Kenji were little. As they stood on the wooden bridge, looking down at the flowing water, his *ojichan* told him of growing up in Hakodate. "As a boy, I swam every day during the summer months. I couldn't get enough of the water. I'll never forget your . . ." And then his voice trailed off and Hiroshi wondered if he was thinking of his daughter. He noted his grandfather always paused between words and his voice softened when he spoke of her. But his *ojichan* never avoided speaking of his mother, and he continued, "I was too busy working when your *okasan* was young, I never taught her to be comfortable in the water, not like with you boys."

"Do you think she suffered?" Hiroshi had once asked. He was ten years old and couldn't help wondering what it must have felt like surrendering to the dark, cold water, giving in after the struggle.

His *ojichan* watched the serene waters below. "I believe that what she must have suffered most was the thought of leaving you and Kenji."

A puddle of muddy water formed at the bottom of the trench as Hiroshi dug, and deepened as water streamed down the sides of the embankment. Watching the shallow pool grow, he realized that someone lying facedown in it could drown, and what an irony that would be.

"Keep digging!" a voice shouted down at him.

Hiroshi looked up to see a thin, narrow-eyed *kempeitai* officer who didn't look much older than he was.

"Hai," he shouted back, catching quick glances from Mako and Takeo as they worked.

Hiroshi gripped his shovel and dug faster and deeper. Then just as the officer turned away, he tossed a shovelful of mud up on the ground, close enough to splatter across the officer's boots and pant legs.

"You stupid bastard," the officer shouted. "Look what you've done!"

"Sumimasen." Hiroshi stood straight and

apologized. He bowed slightly, suppressing a smile.

"I'll teach you . . . ," the officer began.

From the corner of his eye, Hiroshi saw the policeman's muddy boot rising toward his head. As he dodged sideways, a spray of mud slapped against his cheek. Kicking air, the officer lost his footing and slipped backward onto the muddy ground, amid laughter from the boys. By the time he regained his footing, Hiroshi had scrambled up from the trench, slick with mud, and stood above him, tall and broad. They stared at each other, neither moving, until the officer leaned forward and muttered, "This isn't over." Mud covered the length of his back as he walked away.

"What did he say to you?" Takeo asked.

Hiroshi shrugged and jumped back down into the trench with a splash, only to realize that the water had risen a good three inches above his ankles.

RESISTANCE

All through May as the skies cleared, dry, warm days settled in. Hiroshi and his family each had their own diversions — his *obachan* still managed to put food on the table each night, while he and Kenji went to school, did volunteer work, and looked to a future of sumo and Noh masks. In their hurry to cover the void created by the war, his *ojichan* had been left behind. Hiroshi couldn't say what it was, but he noticed a change in his grandfather, how his restlessness and despair had suddenly given way to calm. He began to watch his *ojichan*'s movements, his seeing without seeing, and he knew that his grandfather had gone completely blind.

One balmy May evening as they climbed the narrow stairway to the tower, Hiroshi's suspicions were confirmed by the careful way his *ojichan* made his way up the stairs, and his complete tranquility in doing so. Usually, his *ojichan* strained to catch any flicker of light, his face tense with concentration. Now, he looked straight ahead, as if he had accepted the fight was over.

"Are you all right?" Hiroshi asked as they stood gazing out at the darkening sky.

"Never better."

Hiroshi watched his *ojichan* closely. "Does all the darkness frighten you?"

His grandfather shook his head. "What is there to be frightened of? If all the glorious victories we hear about continue, we should have lights blazing and food on our table again by spring of next year."

Hiroshi swallowed. "Not the war. Your darkness."

His *ojichan* turned toward him and smiled. "Since I've stopped resisting the inevitable, all is well." He pulled out his pipe, used his thumb to pat down the pinch of tobacco he allowed himself, and never once fumbled. "You know, Hiro-chan, things can be just as frightening in the daylight."

Hiroshi watched in silence, as the small spark of his match flared and settled.

"At least I'll never have to worry about the blackouts," his *ojichan* joked.

Hiroshi's laugh strangled in his throat. It was like a candle flickering to its end, his *ojichan* had once explained to him, the room darkening slowly. The night voices hummed below them like persistent mosquitoes. He wanted to swat them all away.

"It's going to be all right, Hiro-chan," his grandfather said softly, laying his arm across his shoulder. "Now tell me, what do you see?"

Hiroshi opened his eyes wide and stared hard until they watered. "Shadows," he answered.

"Behind the shadows, do you see that wooden stool in Yoshida-san's courtyard to your right?" his *ojichan* asked, pointing in the exact direction.

Hiroshi gazed down to their neighbor's courtyard and realized his grandfather had memorized it all — each beauty and blemish etched into his mind.

"Yes," he answered.

"Even when it's gone, thrown out, or used for firewood, I'll still see it there. I'll always see Mariko-san sitting on that stool practicing her cello. Do you remember when her music filled the air every night? We didn't realize how lucky we were then," his *ojichan* said wistfully.

Yes, Mariko-san's music, Hiroshi thought. He heard again those clear, vibrant notes, a low, steady lament, or quick hops of happiness over the strings of her cello that used to fill their neighborhood with life. Hiroshi wished for them again.

The Yoshidas had been his grandparents' neighbors since before he and Kenji had come to live with them. Mariko was five years older than Hiroshi, not beautiful, but always pleasant and sweet. When he and Kenji were little boys, she babysat them on the afternoons his *obachan* went to help Ayako-san at the bakery when her daughter was expecting a child. Almost three years ago, just after his thirteenth birthday, Hiroshi developed a crush on Mariko. He peered every day through an opening in the bamboo thicket as she returned home from the conservatory, her arms wrapped around her cello the way he wished they were wrapped around him.

She caught him once. "Hiroshi, is that you?" she asked, stopping and peering into the thick bamboo that separated their houses.

He hesitated a moment, just a moment, watching the question remain on her thin lips. "*Hai,* yes, it's me," he answered, parting the bamboo curtain.

146

"What are you doing there?"

Again, he hesitated, his gaze on her smooth white hands that cradled the cello.

"Are you playing?" she asked. "Is this a game you're playing?"

He remembered feeling hurt that she thought him a child playing. He had answered, *"Hai,"* though he wanted to say, "I was waiting for you. For a glimpse of you."

For as long as Hiroshi could remember, Mariko had played the cello. Accepted into the conservatory at fifteen, she often practiced in her family's courtyard. He watched her with unabashed joy. It didn't matter that she was older and had grown-up plans. One day she would see that he had grown up, too, and she would love him as much as she loved her music.

Now, Hiroshi brushed aside the thought. His youthful passion for her had lasted one summer. Still, he could never look her straight in the eyes afterward. Just last week Hiroshi saw Mariko on the road, where she stood waiting for another stitch on her fiancé's *sen'ninbari* belt. "So that he will remain safe from the enemy's bullets," he heard her tell a passing woman. And for the hundredth time, Hiroshi realized that the war had ended more than just his dream of becoming a *rikishi.*

Two evenings later, as Hiroshi stood with his *ojichan* up in the tower again, they were taken by surprise when the strains of cello music wafted up through the night's darkness and enveloped them, at first tentative, then gradually growing stronger, louder.

"Mariko," his *ojichan* whispered joyfully, closing his eyes to listen. "Bach's First Cello Suite."

Hiroshi looked down to Yoshida-san's yard but could only make out the shadow of Mariko sitting on the stool, the ghostly white of her kimono sleeve moving back and forth. Did she hear them speaking of her? Why was she playing now, just before blackout, and outside, in full view of the neighbors? Okata would surely notify the *kempeitai*.

"Why now?" Hiroshi asked.

"Music is in her blood," his *ojichan* answered. "Perhaps she couldn't resist any longer."

They stood perfectly still, letting the low moan of notes move through their bodies with an almost cleansing sweep. To Hiroshi, the music felt like a moment of normalcy, a sudden light in his *ojichan*'s darkness, another chance for his grandfather to feel the life that surrounded him.

The next night after sunset, Mariko came out to the courtyard and began playing again, her notes soaring furiously into the night just after blackout. Hiroshi's *obachan* hurried next door and pleaded with the Yoshidas to stop her before the *kempeitai* came to their door and ordered her to stop. But after a moment's quiet, Mariko began playing again. Hiroshi's grandmother returned, shaking her head sorrowfully. Mariko's fiancé had been killed in the Philippine Islands and she was inconsolable. Her tears stopped only when she played.

Hiroshi remembered the dog down the street that the military police had ordered killed because of his frenzied barking just before each air raid. They called it a disruption of army communications, anything that might interfere with information concerning the enemy's approach. Mariko's cello music directly disobeyed blackout rules, though Hiroshi couldn't understand how her music was anything but soothing in these difficult times. He knew her cello would be confiscated, and, worse, she might be taken in and questioned. Still, Hiroshi understood her grief and admired her courage as he watched her play, falling a little in love with her all over again.

On the third night of her playing, Hiroshi took a piece of white origami paper and folded it into a crane, just as she had shown him as a little boy. "It's the symbol of luck and happiness," she'd told him. This time he inserted a stone inside to give it weight. When Mariko sat down and began to play, he threw the crane over the bamboo thicket and into her courtyard, where the small white shape landed beside her right foot. She never paused to look up, but played on, lost in the music. But Hiroshi knew the crane was there, right next to her, a small reminder of happiness.

Minutes later, Mariko's mother's screams brought them rushing from their houses to the Yoshidas' front gate. Hiroshi pushed his way to the front of the small crowd, only to be stopped by a military policeman who held out his rifle, its bayonet pointed at his chest.

"No further," he directed.

Hiroshi stopped, and looked over the shoulder of the policeman and into the courtyard.

"Stop!" he heard an angry voice yell. "Stop now or you'll suffer the consequences!"

Mariko sat on the wooden stool, dressed in a white mourning kimono, her wide sleeves moving back and forth like wings, the origami crane still lying on the ground by her stool. Hiroshi recognized the sad Bach cello suite she played. As the music filled the air, she closed her eyes again; a thin smile crossed her lips. She was oblivious to the policeman ordering her to stop.

"I said, stop right now!" the policeman ordered again. He glanced toward the small crowd, and grew more furious at Mariko, who dared to disobey his orders in front of others. Then, with a motion so swift Hiroshi didn't see it coming, he pulled out his pistol and fired a shot into the air. The pungent smell of gunpowder rose into the night.

The crowd scattered. Hiroshi saw his *obachan* lead his *ojichan* away but Hiroshi remained. If only he could get to Mariko, he would convince her to stop. He heard the frantic pleading of her parents, "*Dozo,* Mari-chan, please stop," mixed with the angry police commands.

Hiroshi rushed forward, pushing past the guard, who pushed back, a look of surprise on his face. In the next moment, Hiroshi felt a quick sting as the sharp tip of the guard's bayonet slashed his forehead. He stepped back and swung a fist at the guard but the rifle butt slammed into his ribs. Doubled over in pain, Hiroshi forced himself to look up. A gush of warm blood blurred his vision and covered his right cheek. Just then, the other policeman lowered his pistol and fired again, this time not into the air, but straight at Mariko's cello.

Days later, despite his throbbing wound, now closed with thirteen stitches, despite his ribs bruised purplish-green, Hiroshi remembered this: a split second after the gun was fired Mariko opened her eyes in surprise, tipped her head, and glanced downward. Did she see the white crane beside her foot? Hiroshi liked to think so. No, he knew so. But there followed a moment in which everything seemed to freeze, all except the final exquisite note from her cello that hung in the air as she fell to the ground.

OMIYAGE

The week after Mariko's death, the days turned hotter, and the humidity suffocating. For Fumiko Wada, the war had taken a horrific turn — the murder of Mariko and the wounds Hiroshi suffered made it personal. Survival had taken on a new face — it was no longer about foraging for food or losing her wedding ring or honoring her emperor and country. It was about her family, and had nothing to do with the war fought in distant places. This war took place right in Yanaka. The anger and despair she felt was oppressive like the heat, pressing down on her like a great weight.

She ran up and down to Hiroshi's room, making sure he was comfortable, snapping at Kenji, who sat by his side from the moment he returned from school until he left again the next morning. "Let your *oniisan* sleep," she told him. But he shook his head and remained as silent as his brother. It was all Fumiko could do not to scream.

So when friends and neighbors came to visit, bringing *omiyage,* small gifts, it was unexpected. So many traditions had been abandoned since the Pacific War. They came to see Hiroshi, to mourn Mariko's death and honor her grandson's courage. Each *omiyage* meant so much more because there was so little to give. Before the war their gifts would have been a box of *mochi* filled with red bean, a tin of dried seaweed, green tea, a box of chocolates, or her favorite butter cookies, each beautifully wrapped in *noshi* paper and *mizuhiki* string. Now, as Fumiko bowed low and received each gift, it was accompanied by an embarrassed glance or an apologetic word for its modest presentation. Fumiko accepted each *omiyage,* touched beyond words.

Later, she carefully untied each *furoshiki* to see the cloth wrappings made from material scraps cut out of kimonos, tablecloths, even a cotton *yukata* robe she remembered seeing Mori-san wearing. And in each, Fumiko found small tokens of her neighbors' lives, three polished stones, a conch shell, a pair of lacquer chopsticks, and a paperweight with the word "Sweden" carved in its wood base. But it was Ayako's gift, the packet of ginseng tea, that moved her to tears.

"To give Hiroshi strength," Ayako said, stepping into the *genkan,* and handing her the folded paper packet. Only her old friend had dispensed with the formalities of gift giving and pulled the packet from the folds of her kimono sleeve.

Fumiko bowed to her old friend. "It's as if

the world has gone mad," she said, upon rising. "I just thank the gods Hiro-chan's wounds will heal."

Ayako agreed. "Hiroshi is a strong boy." Then she raised her voice angrily. "You would think they'd use their strength to fight this war rather than kill the innocent!"

Fumiko quickly ushered Ayako inside and slid the door closed. With Okata prowling around the neighborhood, she remained extra careful.

"Mikiko and I must close the bakery," Ayako said, lowering her voice. "The *kempeitai* have confiscated the rest of our equipment."

"*Iie,* no!" Fumiko shook her head and reached out for her friend's arm. "What will you do?"

"We'll go to Hiroshima and wait out the war. Mikiko's husband has family there and they would love to see Juzo. And when this is all over, we'll return to Yanaka and reopen the bakery."

Fumiko could hardly speak. Along with everything else, Ayako's leaving had knocked the wind out of her. "When?" she whispered.

"The end of next week." She smiled at Fumiko. "Don't look so sad. It will only be for a short time."

Ayako, Ayako is leaving! It can't be true! Fumiko thought, her dearest friend moving so far away. She knew there were words that needed to be said, as she watched Ayako talk of the move and what they would leave behind, but she could only nod in agreement.

SCARS

While Hiroshi's wounds healed, Kenji stayed by his brother's side. He wanted to protect him though he didn't know how. Even when Hiroshi was asleep or lay staring at the ceiling, ignoring him, Kenji stayed. He was afraid that his brother would die, leaving him an orphan a second time. He tried not to think of the parents he'd never known, because losing Hiroshi wouldn't be the same. His mother and father were ghosts to him, while Hiroshi was flesh and blood.

When he had told Yoshiwara-sensei that he wouldn't be returning to the mask shop until his brother was well again, Yoshiwara handed him a tin of biscuits for Hiroshi. "With hopes that your *oniisan* gets better soon," he said. Speechless, Kenji bowed low to his sensei.

Hiroshi hadn't spoken since that terrible night. He lay on his futon, pale and thin, his head bandaged, and his thoughts far away from Kenji's small talk. "Mako and Takeo would like to visit," Kenji droned on. "And Futabayama won another match last night." Hiroshi turned away from him. Kenji couldn't help but think that they'd somehow changed places; he had always been the serious, introverted one.

And while his grandparents worried, they decided to leave Hiroshi alone. "Give him time," his *ojichan* advised. "He'll talk again when he's ready."

But Kenji wanted his strong, gregarious brother back. He heard the doctor tell his *obachan* that Hiroshi would always have a scar on his forehead. At first, the stitches looked like small angry knots, the wound red and raw when his *obachan* changed the bandage. But Kenji secretly admired the scar, the curve that abruptly ended at his brother's temple. He couldn't stop staring at it. It was a mark of Hiroshi's courage, a scar that Kenji could only hope for.

Initially, his brother's silence bothered Kenji, until he became used to the new sound of his own voice. The change had taken place the year before, when his voice suddenly fell an octave. Each day after school, Kenji sat with Hiroshi, reading to him from Japanese folktales, sumo magazines, even occasional descriptions from The Book of Masks, whether he listened or not. Kenji hoped that if nothing else, he might slowly draw his brother's attention back as his *obachan* always did with her stories. By the end of the week, as he read, Hiroshi turned and winced, gave a low moan. Kenji dropped the book and looked anxiously at his brother to see if there was anything he could do. But Hiroshi had already turned away and lay quiet again.

"Let me tell you another story." Kenji cleared his throat. And before Hiroshi could make a move or protest, he was repeating the story of *Hagoromo*, or *The Robe of Feathers*, the Noh play he had seen last year with Yoshiwara-sensei.

"There once was a fisherman called Hakuryo who found a brilliant, feathered robe hanging from a tree and wanted to take it home. Only, as he was about to leave with it, a beautiful woman angel appeared out of nowhere and asked for the robe back, or else she wouldn't be able to return to heaven. At first, the fisherman stubbornly refused, only to relent, making a deal with the woman; if she would dance for him, he would return the robe to her. She in turn told him that she couldn't dance for him until he returned the robe to her . . ." Kenji paused. He had heard enough of his grandparents' stories to know when to capture a moment.

Hiroshi stared up at the ceiling. "What did the fisherman do?" he asked at last, his voice a thin, dry whisper.

Nervously, Kenji continued. *"When the fisherman finally agreed to return the robe to the woman, she gratefully put it on and became an angel once again. Then she sang and danced for him happily, before she flew away to heaven."*

Kenji stopped and the quiet felt abrupt,

leaving a long silence between them. Too soon, he thought. I've ended the story too soon. But before he could think of anything else to say, Hiroshi spoke again.

"And they lived happily ever after, just like in all the stories."

He wasn't sure whether Hiroshi was being sarcastic, but he didn't care. His brother had found his voice.

Hiroshi turned to look at Kenji for the first time. "Do you think Mariko's become an angel in heaven?" His face was drained of color and his eyes had dark shadows below them.

"Yes," Kenji answered. "She might have even found her fiancé again." His answer was surprisingly calm and definite.

"Hai," Hiroshi answered, "I hope so."

"Are you all right?" Kenji asked.

Hiroshi nodded. He shifted his body toward Kenji and winced once more, but this time he didn't turn away.

The sticky, malodorous heat of August stifled Yanaka during the day, without cooling off in the evenings. It was the breathless heat of decay, trapped and smoldering behind blacked-out windows at night, leaving tempers on edge. The smallest irritation led to sharp words, the low murmur of arguing voices — the suffocating remnants of the day.

Three months after Mariko's death, while

walking home in the thick heat from the mask shop, Kenji saw a crowd gathered at the small park a few blocks from their house. Usually, Kenji would have kept going, but something about the animated faces made him slow down, push his way through the sweaty crowd to see what was happening. Their voices attracted him, voices he recognized from before the war, open and enthusiastic.

Within a circle of rocks, on a makeshift *dohyo*, were two young men stripped of their shirts and shoes, wrestling. It took only a moment for Kenji to realize that Hiroshi was the smaller of the two wrestlers. Kenji pushed closer and watched his brother move slowly around the circle, light and fast, a serious, concentrated look on his face. Kenji saw his wounds as well — the puckered scar on his forehead an angry half-moon, the yellowish bruise of his ribs still visible.

What was Hiroshi doing wrestling at the park? Kenji hadn't seen Hiroshi fight in almost two years; he'd hardly attended any of his practices before then, or understood the enjoyment his *ojichan* and brother found in sumo. His grandfather had lamented that word had come from the sumo association that all matches would be halted after the New Year. But watching Hiroshi now, he saw something akin to a dance as well as a sport. He had never liked the violence of wrestling, but the way his brother moved was another thing, like a Noh actor onstage, each movement meaning more than met the eye.

Kenji's heart raced as he watched his brother slip out of the other boy's grasp. The bigger boy had let go of any pretense of a dignified sumo match, and was now street fighting, arms flailing as he tried to punch his opponent. Hiroshi moved quickly out of the way when the boy charged him. Instead of knocking him down, Hiroshi used the other boy's own momentum to send him toward the edge of the circle.

"Stupid fool!" an older man yelled from the crowd. The boy steadied himself. The crowd surged around Kenji. "If you expect to eat, you had better win," the man yelled again. The boy glanced his way and Hiroshi made his move, charging at him with all his force and knocking him out of the circle. Cheers from the crowd filled the air, and Kenji felt a sudden joy racing up his body, his cheer joining theirs.

"Enough!" The man's voice rose above the crowd.

Kenji thought the *kempeitai* had arrived and Hiroshi would be taken away to jail. Instead, it was the same man who had taunted the boy to win. Short and solid, he stepped forward and handed Hiroshi a burlap sack, bowing just enough to pass for respect.

The man pushed the other boy, who stumbled forward. "Come along," he said.

160

"Look at you. You're a disgrace to our family name!"

The boy grabbed his shirt and sandals, bowing quickly to Hiroshi before chasing after the older man. Kenji turned to see his brother's friends Takeo and Mako across the crowd, laughing, grabbing Hiroshi by the neck, and slapping his back in congratulations.

And then Hiroshi saw Kenji in the crowd, gestured for him to come over, and happily told him the story: Tonuki was the name of the boy he was wrestling with. Hiroshi had heard his uncle was the farmer assigned to raise livestock for the *kempeitai*. According to Takeo, Tonuki also liked to gamble, mostly cards and small yard bets. After a fair amount of needling over the past weeks, Tonuki had agreed to fight. It was arranged that they would meet at the park for the match, between the late afternoon and early evening, when the *kempeitai* changed shifts. The prize would be a chicken. If Hiroshi lost, he would be cleaning their henhouse for a week. Even *obachan* would be happy. A chicken won fair and square. His words came out in a breathless rush.

Kenji peered into the sack, a spray of brown feathers floating through the air as the chicken fought to get out. A film of dirt like two handprints streaked Hiroshi's chest where Tonuki had pushed him. He had never

161

been prouder of his brother as they walked home; Hiroshi's forehead glistened with sweat, his scar still red and intimidating. Kenji knew the scar would fade in time, become invisible to many, but to him it would always be there, never losing its significance.

7
THE FALLEN SUN
1944

A cold wind, though not as icy as the week before, blew through the tower. Yoshio's tobacco was long gone but he still felt solace in holding the pipe, placing the stem between his lips and biting down. He must be regressing in his old age, he thought, needing to suck on an object for security like a child. In the next moment, Yoshio cupped the pipe in his palm and with one violent swing threw it as hard as he could. He didn't need an empty pipe for security. He imagined it sailing high and far, most certainly landing like an uninvited guest in someone's courtyard. He leaned forward and listened for the dull thud of its landing but never heard it. What Yoshio heard instead were voices at the front gate. He recognized Okata's voice from the neighborhood association, followed by two unfamiliar voices, and hurried downstairs to the kitchen.

Yoshio listened as the front door slid open, then Fumiko's voice, then a rough, disrespectful grunt demanding, "*Go-shujin,* your husband!" No formalities. The two with Okata must be *kempeitai.* He heard Fumiko's pause, that minute intake of breath before she began to say something, only to be abruptly cut off. Then Yoshio heard Okata's scheming voice give directions down the hallway, heard the heavy thump of boots as they came directly to the kitchen, where he sat, waiting for them.

The command was hard and terse. "The watchtower in your backyard must come down immediately," ordered one of the policemen, his voice coarse, his words laced with a strong country dialect. Yoshio gazed out the window in the direction of the tower and back toward the policeman. Okata didn't say a word.

Then, as if the policeman thought Yoshio's silence meant he hadn't heard or didn't understand, he repeated, "The tower must come down. There will be no allowances. Some men will be here tomorrow to take it down for you. I'm sure you will donate the wood afterward."

The only surprise was that Okata hadn't reported him long before this. Yoshio sat back, looked again out the window and in the direction of the tower. He had built the watchtower with his own hands, and he would be the one to take it down. He refused to waste words on the fools. Yoshio simply turned back to them and nodded.

Then he heard the same heavy thumps down the hall and they were gone. He could still smell remnants of their presence, sweat and cologne and, even worse, the flowery scent of Okata's hair oil, which made Yoshio sick to his stomach.

After Okata and the *kempeitai* left, Fumiko came into the kitchen and put hot water on to make tea as she did every afternoon, even when there was no tea, only the hot water. Yoshio listened to all the sounds that filled their silence, the hollow kettle being filled, the soft scrape of her slippers against the floor, her quiet sigh.

After a long while, Fumiko asked, "Do you remember the ginkgo tree in my uncle's yard?"

Yoshio thought back. Hakodate was such a long time ago.

"The one you were sitting under the afternoon I dared to speak to you?" he asked.

"Hai," she said, softly.

He heard her fingers scrape the bottom of the tin for a pinch of green tea to put into the hot water.

"So long ago. Do you think it's still there?" he asked.

She placed a cup in front of him, the steam rising. "It doesn't really matter, does it? You have always told me that once we have a memory, it never leaves."

165

"Hai," he answered. Until illness or death, he thought.

She sat down beside him and he leaned toward her warmth. "And so it will be the same with the tower, *neh?*"

How could he not love her? In his darkness, he saw the beautiful girl sitting under the ginkgo tree, the young girl dancing with the white flower in her hair, the *step-beat* of his heart once again.

"Hai," he whispered.

After tossing and turning most of the night, he had no more dreams. Yoshio lay still in bed, listening to Fumiko's steady breathing. On their futons, they hadn't said a word to each other in the dark. And in the stillness, Yoshio's decisions were made; the sudden dismantling of their lives would begin with the tower, followed by the departure of Fumiko and his grandsons to the safety of the countryside. They would evacuate to Nagano, to stay with his niece Reiko's family until it was safe for them to return. Yoshio swallowed his fear, filled his darkness with the light of his grandsons, his many years with Fumiko. He knew the house, knew the alleyways, the small corners and crevices of this world he loved. It was too late for him to adapt to a new place again. He would stay in Yanaka, alone.

■ ■ ■ ■

When the first whispers of morning arrived, Yoshio rose quietly from the futon into the cold darkness of late winter. He took each step up to the tower with steady purpose, and stood silently gazing up toward the sky. He imagined the light slowly revealing each detail of the world around him. He had built the tower to honor his daughter, Misako, and for the boys, only to realize that in the ensuing years, it had become his place of refuge. The watchtower stood just above the real world, where he mourned the past and welcomed the future. Now, it, too, would be gone and the future felt bleak.

Yoshio made his way down the steps and back into the kitchen. He knew every piece of the tower, had quickly determined which of the support beams to weaken first in order to bring it down. He took eleven steps, turned to the right, and knelt down. By the window was the second wood plank he had loosened, hollowing out the earth underneath. Now his fingers dug still deeper into the dirt, until he touched the cloth he'd wrapped the sledge-hammer in, lifting its solid weight with both hands.

Yoshio slipped back out the kitchen door. He stroked the wooden beams for one last time, felt for the joints, and carefully removed the wooden pegs that held them together. If he weakened the crossbeams in the right place, he judged, the tower would collapse within itself, out of harm's way. Yoshio took a deep breath, stood to the right of the first beam, and swung hesitantly as the sledgehammer connected with a dull thud against the wood. He pulled back and swung again. With each swing, Yoshio felt lighter, just like when he heard the *Joya-no-Kane*, the traditional New Year's gong being struck, each toll dispelling an evil hindrance, a malicious thought from his heart and mind, each swing carrying with it a private wish that he could never explain to Kenji. *Death to Okata!* He swung hard, hearing the wood crack. *Death to the kempeitai!* Yoshio swung again harder, crashing into the beam, revitalized with a strength long diminished by age and hunger. *Death to this imperial war!* His blood raced. Sweat clung to his back. He swung once more, heard the groan of the wood splintering. He paused a moment, swaying from side to side, then stepped over to the second beam, anxious to finish before his strength failed. With each blow, the watchtower creaked and shifted. Yoshio felt a long, sharp moan throughout his body as each evil hindrance left him, floated up and away into the early morning light.

Hiroshi woke with a start — a rhythmic pounding echoed through his dream and into his waking. At first he thought it was his own heart pounding, but the thumping reverberated through the entire house. Kenji had thrown his comforter over his head and didn't stir. The windows were blacked out and Hiroshi couldn't tell whether it was light or dark outside. He flickered through the possibilities of an air raid or earthquake as he rushed downstairs to the kitchen. The pounding grew louder. His *obachan* stood motionless at the window, pushing aside the blackout curtain as the early morning light filtered in.

"What is it?" Hiroshi asked. His voice was hoarse, still dazed with sleep.

"The tower," she whispered.

Hirsoshi hurried to the window and saw his grandfather swinging a sledgehammer, striking the support beams that held up the watchtower.

"He'll hurt himself."

His grandmother reached out and grabbed his arm. "Hiro-chan, listen to me," she said firmly. "Your *ojichan* needs to do this himself."

Hiroshi looked to his grandmother but she remained quiet. "*Obachan,* you must stop him. He can't even see what he's doing," he pleaded.

His grandmother turned slowly, as if she had suddenly lost all strength, and braced herself against the wooden table. "What you don't understand, Hiro-chan, is that there are many ways to see," she said.

Kenji padded into the kitchen a moment later. They stood and watched as his *ojichan* swung once, twice, each time connecting with wood, a grunt coming from deep inside him. His *ojichan* was tired, straining to lift the hammer, blow after blow, cracking the last of the main beams with a final booming strike. Hiroshi heard a faraway dog barking and knew the entire neighborhood must be awake.

"Shi oeru," his *obachan* said to them. "Now it is finished."

His *ojichan*'s hands trembled as he dropped the sledgehammer to the ground, stepped back, and bowed very low toward the watchtower. Hiroshi didn't move. He was reminded of being a little boy and knocking down all his blocks with one clean sweep of his arm. The watchtower had stood for all these years, a symbol of his childhood and his grandfather's strength. Silently, they waited for the fall.

What Hiroshi would always remember was how the watchtower refused to fall. There would never be any explanation. It only happened when the *kempeitai* arrived to tear it down, and their voices rose to a frantic pitch as they scrambled away from the area of the weakened tower. Only then did the support beams suddenly creak and splinter, give in to the weight as the watchtower bowed to the ground. And not in pieces like his childhood blocks, but as a whole — like a body slowly falling.

FORTITUDE

By late spring, Hiroshi and Kenji began digging an air-raid shelter where their *ojichan*'s watchtower once stood. Unlike all the slit trenches Hiroshi and his classmates dug along the roads, this was his most ambitious undertaking yet, a hole in the ground large enough to accommodate all four of them. An underground room with walls carved out and held up by pieces of wood scrap, and a roof made from a piece of corrugated metal he found behind Fukushima-san's boarded-up *sembei* rice cracker store. For days, he and Kenji dug, deeper and deeper, excavating dirt and rock, and building up a three-foot dirt wall on all four sides. Every morning his muscles were so sore he could hardly lift his arms, and Kenji moaned at the thought of digging again. But by the end of the week, the air-raid shelter, a three-by-six rectangular pit, was complete.

The air-raid sirens screamed with more frequency now; at least once a week in the early hours of the morning, the Americans targeted strategic spots — airports, factories, and munitions warehouses — mostly located outside of Tokyo's residential areas. Still, every time the sirens blasted, the family dragged themselves from their futons and into the shelter, listening for the dull thuds of bombs falling in the distance, feeling the rumble of the earth beneath their feet, waiting until the all-clear signal sounded, and wondering how much longer it would be until the bombs reached Yanaka.

Akira Yoshiwara

Akira Yoshiwara packed only what he needed. He reached up for the tin behind the paints and pulled out the envelope of yen notes and slipped it into his pocket. It was an already hot August morning when Nishihara, one of the young artists, came stumbling into the shop just after dawn, breathless and fearing for his life. Most of the artists had been rounded up by the *kempeitai,* and he had escaped, just barely, only to come and warn Akira that they were on their way to take him in for questioning. There was no time to spare.

"How did they find out?" Akira asked.

Nishihara shrugged and poured water into a clay cup, drinking it down too quickly. "They've been watching us from the beginning," he said, coughing.

The stupidity of it all, Akira thought, though he kept silent. He'd gotten caught up in their youthful exuberance, and his own belief that the war was senseless. Now, it had caught up with him, and after Otomo Matsui had used his influence to keep him from being drafted, he packed the ivory cat given to him by Matsui, his set of chisels, and an unfinished *Okina* mask in the middle of his bag of clothes, a reminder that he needed to return to finish it. He looked around the small shop, bright in the sunlight, where he had lived and worked for the past fifteen years. At first glance, it might have appeared just as bare and empty as when he first entered it, but Akira knew otherwise; the past three years had brought Kenji — and new life — to it.

He thought of how the boy would come and find the door locked and him gone. Kenji was the perfect protégé, but now Akira might never know the outcome of his talent. He had also been the closest person Akira had to a family.

He wrote a quick note for Kenji to find. "I must leave. No time to explain. Perhaps another day." He didn't write his name or anything else the *kempeitai* might use to find him. That done, nothing else mattered, except . . . "Nazo," he called. He heard something from the other room and hurried back there. Nazo sat on the counter, waiting.

"We have to go now," he said, as if talking to another person.

Nazo watched him, not moving. It was his right of refusal, though he had no say in the matter. Akira Yoshiwara scooped the cat up with one hand, grabbed his bag, and followed Nishihara out the door, locking it behind him. He left the note for Kenji wedged in the corner seam of the front window. Early on, the boy had spent so many hours standing there, gazing at the masks, it now seemed the right place, and one the *kempeitai* might miss in their abrupt way of seeing and not seeing. Akira knew there was only a slight chance Kenji would find the note before the military police arrived. Even so, he believed that life was made up of chances.

VANISHED

The decision for Kenji and Hiroshi to leave for the countryside was settled. They would leave at the week's end in the midst of the lingering heat. The week before, Kenji had heard his *obachan*'s raised voice coming from the kitchen, bringing him and Hiroshi downstairs to witness a rare argument between his grandparents. Usually their disagreements were settled with a quick, sharp word that reverberated through the room and landed with finality. This time, the words streamed

174

from his grandmother's lips as if she'd been waiting all these years to release them. "Don't be foolish, old man; do you think I would leave you here alone?" Her eyes blazed, her mouth snapped open and closed like a turtle's at his suggestion of her leaving Yanaka without him.

"I'm not a child," his *ojichan* answered.

"A child would have more sense," she added.

His *ojichan* cleared his throat and remained silent.

Kenji's *obachan* would stay in Yanaka with his *ojichan* and that was that. He could see the sweat glisten on her forehead. *"Iie,"* she said again, calmer and more definite. "No, not without you." Her gaze moved past his *ojichan* and out the window to the empty space where the tower had stood. "This is my home, too. The boys will be fine with Reiko-san." It was final then, like a door slammed shut. His *ojichan* sat back looking thoughtful, the shadow of a smile on his lips.

The following morning Kenji hurried down the back alleyways to the mask shop. The air was already hot and still. He wanted to tell Yoshiwara-sensei he was leaving for the countryside in six days. In his schoolbag, he carried *The Book of Masks* to return to his teacher. Even as the war spun around him, Yoshiwara worked on creating his masks. He

175

paid little attention to the hardships or to the orders given by the *kempeitai,* other than putting up blackout curtains. When the sirens blared, Yoshiwara simply closed the curtains and went back to work. So far, he'd been lucky the bombing never reached Yanaka.

Besides the thought of leaving his grandparents, Kenji dreaded not working at the mask shop every afternoon, with its intoxicating smells of cypress wood and paints, the rhythmic lull of the sanding. The intricate painting of the masks had become his passion. Day by day, he learned a little more from his sensei, what Yoshiwara called the "hidden secrets" that would make him a mask artisan of distinction — the slight arch of an eyebrow, the thickness of the lips, or just how deep a furrow should cross the forehead. "Remember this, Kenji, there are many people out there who can make a mask," Yoshiwara told him, "but not many who can make a mask come alive."

Kenji pushed at the door and was surprised to find the mask shop locked. The sun beat down hot and unrelenting on the quiet alleyway. He rapped lightly on the door and waited. In the three years he'd been apprenticing with Yoshiwara, his sensei had never been away from the shop for more than an hour or two, and only to buy paints or do a quick errand. Kenji knocked again, hard and loud this time, but all that greeted him was silence. He walked to the front of the shop and peered through a crack in the closed curtain, past the empty display window that once held the masks that still mesmerized him, and into the shadowy shop. He suddenly felt again like that boy who longed to hold those brilliant masks in his hands. After three years, he saw in his reflection that nothing had changed. Beyond the curtain was the same spare, dusty room, the same desire to be on the inside looking out.

Kenji was about to turn away when a slip of white paper wedged into the corner seam of the glass caught his eye. He reached for it, unfolded the note, and recognized his sensei's writing, the quick, elegant strokes in black ink that told Kenji he was gone. He stepped back slowly in disbelief. How could his sensei leave without telling him? Then, not knowing what possessed him, he picked up a rock and threw it at the window, shattering glass as he turned around and ran.

The next afternoon when Kenji stopped by the mask shop again, he found the shop had been broken into and the door left ajar. The remnants of the *kempeitai* were everywhere, boot prints in the wood dust, the shop stripped of everything, his sensei's equipment, the wood shelves, and even the clay teacups they drank from. The little left behind was in ruins, as if Akira Yoshiwara and his mask shop had never existed.

Kenji's hope of seeing his sensei again grew just as empty. As each day turned to dusk, Kenji felt increasingly sure that his teacher was gone for good; that the war had finally caught up with him. He wrapped Yoshiwara-sensei's *Book of Masks* in an old sweater and packed it in the bag he was taking to the countryside. Each night before he dropped off to sleep, he invented explanations that placed his sensei out of harm's way: Yoshiwara had left for the safety of the countryside. He had gone to visit his family, though Kenji never heard him speak of any. Or maybe he had been commissioned to carve a brilliant new mask in another district, and there was no time to leave him details. These thoughts were followed by a darker possibility. The *kempeitai* had heard that Yoshiwara was an agitator and had come to arrest him, but he had managed to get away before they came, or why else the note?

Kenji grieved for his sensei and all the masks that might never be made. He saw them when he closed his eyes, felt the smoothness of the wood in his hands as his head spun with uncertainty. The last time he'd seen Yoshiwara, Kenji was hurrying out of the shop, late to go home again, knowing his *obachan* would be worried. His sensei barely looked up from his work, and said as

178

he always did, "*Ashita*. Tomorrow, then." But then he glanced up and added, "Or the tomorrow after that." Kenji wondered now how many tomorrows it would be. Or, did it have something to do with *him?* Kenji had never voiced these thoughts aloud, though they swam in the back of his mind. What was it about him that made the people he loved vanish into thin air?

THE MOUNTAINS

Akira Yoshiwara parted ways with the young artist Nishihara at the train station. Separately, they could better blend into the crowd. The air was thick with humidity, making him wish he could peel away his skin. The noise of the station was unbearable — the chaos of frantic voices, metal grinding against metal, the nervous heat of desperation as he merged with the crowds and kept away from the *kempeitai* patrolling the platform. Nazo pushed against the cloth bag he carried and Akira loosened the tie just enough for the cat to stick his head through. "Not yet," he said, as Nazo struggled to climb out. "As soon as we're on the train," he reassured, and the cat relaxed, narrowing his eyes at all the movement around him. Akira touched his pocket to make sure he had his money and travel voucher, bought at ten times the normal price. Still, he was lucky to get one on such short notice. It would have taken days if he hadn't had the money to expedite things. When the man at the ticket counter had asked, "Where to?" he'd answered, "The mountains," not caring where the train would eventually take him as long as it was far away from Tokyo.

It wasn't until Akira finally stepped off the train with Nazo in Oyama, hundreds of miles northwest of Tokyo in the Japanese Alps, that he relaxed. From the one-room train station, he emerged into the cool, thin air, which he breathed in hungrily. He walked through the small town of low wooden houses and narrow streets, framed by the tall mountains. Despite the quiet simplicity of the place, Akira felt unsettled. He paid an old man named Tomita with an ox and cart to take him farther up into the mountains, to the village of Aio, where the old man was returning. The madness of the war made him want to completely disappear.

As the cart moved slowly up the mountain road, the air grew cooler, and the outskirts of the town gave way to a rutted road bordered by pine trees that blocked the sun and left the slow-moving cart in dark shadows. It felt as if he were stepping into another world, that Tokyo, the mask shop, and the war itself had all been a dream. Akira lifted Nazo out of the bag, set him unsteadily on the bed of the rough wood cart, where the cat hesitated, then lay down and stayed there for the rest of the journey, his claws gripping tightly to the wood. As the cart rounded the bend, Tomita pointed up the mountain. "See there?" he asked. "In the trees?" Akira stared hard among the large pines, until the dark outlines of houses with tall, pitched roofs appeared, nestled among them. The old man turned back and grew talkative, telling Akira they were called "praying hands" houses because of the appearance of the thatched gable roofs. "They're said to resemble two hands pressed together in Buddhist prayer," he added, with a toothless grin. He made a sucking sound and shook his head. "If you ask me, it's for a more practical reason. It's to keep the snow from piling up during the winter." He waved his hand downward. "Slides right off the roof." The old man laughed to himself. His family had lived in Aio for hundreds of years and very little had changed. "What brings a young man alone to a place like Aio?" Tomita eyed him and waited for an answer.

"Illness," Akira answered. It was the first thing that came to his mind. "I've come to the mountains to recuperate."

Tomita nodded.

Akira had no idea if he believed him or not, but he was too far away from anyone or anything to care. The old man finally stopped the cart at the edge of the village, directed

181

Akira to find a room at the second-to-last wooden building among a small cluster of others. "Behind the sake shop, they usually have a place to rent," he said. He clicked his tongue and continued up the hill.

As he stepped down from the back of the wooden cart, Nazo safely back in the cloth bag, Akira Yoshiwara saw a woman sitting by the side of the dirt road in front of the small dry-goods store. Her worn kimono, once the color of persimmons, was faded to a pale pinkish hue. She wore a dark scarf on her head and leaned forward over a wooden box. He mistook her for an old woman, until she looked up and the brightness of her eyes told him otherwise.

"Turnips?" she asked, in a voice so filled with youth and hope, he thought it came from someone else.

He followed her gaze to the wooden box, where there were two lone turnips. The pungent scent of decay drifted upward. Upon a closer look, he saw the brown spots of rot already staining the bottom of the box.

"I'll take both of them," Akira finally said. He reached down and dropped several yen coins into the box. Then he picked up the turnips and walked toward the buildings, leaving the woman behind.

The night before they were to leave for the countryside, Hiroshi shook Kenji awake as they lay on their futons. Kenji was just drifting off to sleep and he pulled away from his brother, irritated.

"I won't be going to Nagano with you," Hiroshi whispered. "I'm staying to work in a munitions factory with Mako and Takeo, right outside of Tokyo in Chiba. That way, I can still watch over *ojichan* and *obachan.*"

Kenji turned to face Hiroshi, suddenly wide awake. In the darkness of their room, he could barely make out his brother's shadow facing him.

"Then I'm staying, too." Kenji insisted.

Hiroshi paused. "No," he said. "They need to know that you'll be safe in Nagano."

"What about you?"

He felt Hiroshi's hand rest on his shoulder. "One of us has to stay," he answered. "They'll need help here, just in case of an air-raid attack or evacuation. *Obachan* can't handle everything alone."

"Then why can't we both stay?" Kenji asked. He hated the way his voice sounded, childish and demanding. Couldn't Hiroshi see? It was hard enough being separated from his grandparents after Yoshiwara-sensei's disappearance, and now even Hiroshi was abandoning him.

His brother took his time answering, and when he did, Kenji thought he sounded older, more like a father than a brother. "*Ojichan* sees the future in us. You and I. If anything were to happen to us, there would be no future."

Kenji was glad it was too dark for Hiroshi to see he was straining against tears. "Isn't that why we're being sent to the countryside? To be safe."

"*Hai,* but I need to know that they will be safe here, too," Hiroshi said. "Kenji, try to understand that this is for the best."

Kenji was embarrassed by his selfishness. How could he not understand that Hiroshi would always be the *Ayakashi,* the warrior protecting his family?

"*Hai,*" he answered, his voice strong and clear.

Train schedules were erratic. On the warm, August morning he was to leave, Kenji watched his *obachan* light the thin, fragrant stick of incense in front of his parents' photo, praying softly for him to have a safe journey. At fifteen, he'd never been farther from Yanaka than central Tokyo, and even then, never alone. He anticipated leaving with fear and excitement, a bittersweet edge that coated his stomach. He had assumed, like his grandparents, that Hiroshi would be going to Nagano with him. Instead, he would be going alone.

The train was stifling and crowded with families, every empty space filled with suitcases, wooden boxes, straw baskets, cloth *furoshiki* hiding small bits of food — entire households reduced to what they could carry. Since the start of the Pacific War, people moved in waves of crowds. They gathered at train stations, on the streets, in front of Takahara's Dry Goods Store, filling the space with the low murmur of voices and the uneasy laughter that Kenji knew was fear.

Kenji pushed toward the window seat to get another glimpse of his grandparents. They appeared so old and frail, standing on the platform. Hiroshi stood tall beside them. All around, crowds of people clutched their travel vouchers and scrambled to get on the train, to get away from the military police, to leave the beggars and black marketeers behind.

Kenji could hardly breathe and struggled to open the window, giving up in a sweat. He sat back in his seat and heard his *ojichan*'s voice again.

"Take care of yourself," his grandfather whispered to him on the train platform.

He felt a flicker of fear. Of course he would. "You and *obachan* don't have to worry about me," he answered.

"I'm not." He smiled. "But you know how it is when you get older. We're never satisfied

185

unless we repeat ourselves." He pushed several yen notes into Kenji's hand and smiled. "One day, you'll know."

Kenji hugged his grandfather tighter, then pulled away and bowed to him, forgetting for a moment that he could no longer see. But his *ojichan*'s hands reached out and caught his shoulders. "You and Hiroshi are the future. No matter what happens, you must remember to look forward, to bring honor to our family and to yourself."

Kenji nodded, his throat closing. He tasted bitterness on his tongue and his throat hurt at the thought of leaving. And where were Yoshiwara-sensei and Nazo at that moment? He bowed low again with the weight of his grandfather's hands still on his shoulders. He stood straight to see that his *obachan* was crying, something he'd rarely seen growing up.

The train slowly pulled away, jerking forward, then hesitating before finding its rhythm. Kenji swallowed and didn't turn away from the window until the last glimpse of his grandparents and brother had vanished from his sight. The train picked up speed as it rumbled through the outskirts of Tokyo. It looked like a battlefield. Slit trenches lined the roads like open wounds, buildings were boarded and abandoned, long snaking lines of women and children waited for rations under the lifeless gray sky.

But as the train continued northwest toward Nagano, he saw the scenery change. The stark rubble of buildings became flatlands, giving way to the slow rise of mountains and valleys as the train hugged along the sides. A rush of wind rattled through the car as drops of rain whipped the window, cooling the stagnant heat. As the rain grew in strength, Kenji gazed at the mountains, half-hidden by fog that hovered like smoke over the trees. The peaks rose in varying shades of brown and green that lightened as they reached up toward the gray sky. They made him think of Hiroshi and reminded him of sumo, powerful and majestic. Below, there was a scattering of wood houses on the valley floor, crisscrossed by rice paddies and fields of brown earth and patches of green. Kenji took a deep breath. Even in the crowded, stifling train, he imagined the air down in the village of Imoto to be sharp and sweet, like a mouthful of cool water.

8
FOXFLARE
1945

By February, the bombing had grown more intense. The air-raid sirens blared at least twice, sometimes three or four times a week. Yoshio sighed, relieved that Kenji was safely in the countryside with his niece Reiko, and though he wished Hiroshi were, too, he was secretly glad that his older grandson had stayed with them. At almost eighteen, Hiroshi was a tall and strong young man. Yoshio couldn't imagine how he and Fumiko could cope without him. Even with so little food, he grew taller, like a weed that pushed through a small crack. Fumiko had told him as much each night, describing even the smallest changes she saw in the world around them. Yoshio knew his daughter, Misako, would have been proud of both of her sons.

His sight was taken over by sounds and smells. Yoshio stood in the kitchen and heard a distant buzz. He knew the planes were coming again. The sirens would follow. During the past year, it seemed that the Americans bombed specific targets, and now, with each Japanese defeat, the explosions grew more frequent and inched closer to residential areas. It became routine to rush to the bomb shelter in the backyard where the watchtower once stood. For once, Yoshio was glad for his blindness, for the darkness that shielded the anger and shame, the weight of sadness that sent them down into the ground instead of up toward the sky.

The sirens usually blew just after sunrise and they scrambled to the underground shelter in a practiced order — first Fumiko, donning the padded cloth headgear she had sewn for each of them, followed by Yoshio, who was carefully guided down into the dirt cavern by her, and lastly Hiroshi, who carried the water and first-aid bag, and secured the opening with a door he'd fashioned out of wood scraps salvaged from the tower. It wasn't more than a hole in the ground, shored up by random pieces of wood, but they squeezed in and sat down on the damp earth. Yoshio leaned back and pressed against the cool soil. A sudden, sharp explosion shook the earth and sent loose dirt raining down on them. Yoshio tasted the sharp, salty dirt that whipped against his cheek. He shivered at the closed dampness of being buried alive and squeezed Fumiko's hand as he felt her lean toward him.

In the cramped space of the shelter, Yoshio

thought of his parents for the first time in a very long while. Although they'd died more than twenty years ago, he still heard his mother's voice as if she were right there with him. *"It is the Kitsune,"* she told him, *"the devious fox that has led the Japanese people into yet another terrible situation. It is the kitsune bi, the foxflare that illuminates the path that will lead Japan to disaster."* He shook his head to dispel the long-forgotten folktale his mother had told him as a child.

"Kitsune," he mumbled aloud.

"What are you saying?" Fumiko asked, releasing his hand to the winter air.

Yoshio shook his head. Another distant explosion shook the earth and he wondered how fast they might die if the shelter should cave in on them. How had they come to this point, hiding in a hole in the ground, tormented by a hunger that would kill them if the bombs didn't? He breathed the dank air and cleared his mind of such ideas. Instead, he thought of his mother again, recalled how she had said that a black fox was a sign of good luck, while a white fox meant calamity. And what was the last myth? He concentrated and saw only darkness. Another bomb fell, closer still, so loud he could feel it in his teeth. The impact shook more dirt loose; it rained against his back and down his neck. He heard Hiroshi whisper, "It will be over soon," while Fumiko chanted softly in a rhythmic murmur that once again put him at ease. He closed his eyes and waited. Ah yes, now Yoshio remembered the last myth; three foxes together foretold disaster. And here they were, like three foxes trapped in a hole with disaster just above them.

THUNDER

The distant roar of the planes sounded like thunder to eight-year-old Aki, a low, faraway rumbling that followed the lightning streaking the black sky, as it did before a bad storm. After each flash of light, she counted the seconds before the next loud rumble, just as her father had taught her when she was little. *Ichi, ni, san, shi, go* . . . the five seconds between meant that the thunder was a mile away. Rain would then follow and there was nothing to be afraid of. It's just nature's way of having a fit of temper, her father had assured her, and he never told her anything that wasn't true. Still, the noise of the planes was something else, a thunder she couldn't keep count of when it came with no lightning before and no rain afterward.

More than anything, Aki wanted to go home. She didn't like being in the countryside, almost four hours from Tokyo in the village of Ikaruga, away from her parents and living in a boardinghouse, southwest of Nara, with the rest of her classmates. Under the Group Evacuation Law, students were rotated out to the countryside every six months. They'd been there for five months since October, the winter months dark and desolate. Even though Haru was with her, her sister slept in another room with the older girls and she hardly saw her except at their evening meals. During the day, there were classes and work in the fields or factories to provide more food and supplies for the military.

Occasionally, she heard the roar of the planes overhead in the afternoon and looked up to see the scattering of big metal bugs swarm the sky, dark and menacing. And then they were gone. Recently, the roar of the planes came just after sunrise, waking the girls from a deep sleep, as they were hustled, cold and groggy in their *monpe* pants and cotton padded headgear, toward the air-raid shelters. When the siren went off again, signaling the all clear, they trudged back to their beds, sometimes forgetting to take off their padded headgear as they fell back into an anxious sleep before the morning bell rang.

During the afternoon, Aki and her classmates worked in their assigned groups to clear the fields, while Haru worked in a mosquito-net plant near the school they attended in the mornings. Aki didn't like her group, which was made up not only of her classmates but also village students. They were rough and without manners, and often got her entire group into trouble. If one student from their group had to be disciplined, they all were. Aki hated it when they were made to line up in two rows facing each other. Upon the teacher's command of "Now!" they took turns slapping each other across the face, once or twice, sometimes more, depending on the teacher. The first time Aki felt the sting of a slap across her cheek, she pulled back and slapped the boy across from her just as hard, and saw the pink welt of her handprint spreading across his cheek.

"I want to go home," Aki whispered to Haru at dinner.

"We can't go home yet."

"Why?"

Haru pushed her hair away from her eyes. "We have to stay for six months until the next group of students comes."

Aki had lost track of how long they had been in Ikaruga but it seemed too long already. "How much longer?"

She didn't tell her older sister that sometimes she cried at night because she was so unhappy. Some of the teachers in Ikaruga were abrupt and mean, always looking over their shoulders as if someone were sneaking up behind them. Aki thought they had moved to the countryside to be safe, but instead, she was frightened by the strict, unfair discipline, all the open space around her, and by the thundering planes that flew overhead toward the big cities where people like her parents and the sumo stable were.

"It won't be much longer," Haru said.

"How much?"

"One more month," Haru answered. She pointed to Aki's bowl and made her eat all of her sweet potato. "Then we'll go home, I promise."

Aki smiled, poked at the sweet potato with her chopstick. She was tired of eating the same thing night after night and never feeling full. Slowly, she finished eating as Haru watched her. She couldn't remember the last time she'd had rice or soba noodles. It made her happy to think that soon she wouldn't have to work in the fields any longer, or sleep in the room with all the other students, or be watched day and night by the teachers. Aki wanted it to be like before the war, back at the sumo stable, where she was free to run about and watch her father train the big boys to be *sumotori.* That night, lying on her cot, she began counting the days until they returned home, just as she counted the seconds before she heard the next roar of thunder and knew how far away it was.

Six months ago, in August, when Kenji had arrived in the village of Imoto in the Nagano prefecture he had been disappointed that the mountains he saw from the train were mere shadows looming in the distance. The village itself was spread out on the flatlands, small farms dotting the landscape, their fields a muddy mess against the endless gray sky. Most of what they grew, the barley and sweet potatoes, was given to the military. Still, Kenji relished the calmer, slower pace in the countryside.

Aunt Reiko was waiting on the platform, thin and dark-haired, with streaks of gray that made her appear older than Kenji had imagined. She waved when he stepped from the train. He put down his suitcase, and bowed low upon meeting her. He hoped to see traces of his *okasan* in his aunt, since they were blood cousins and not far apart in age. He searched for some resemblance, but the woman who stood before him looked nothing like the photo of his mother. Her thin shoulders were stooped as if she carried a great weight, and her hands were rough and red from farmwork. But once he looked into her eyes, he saw a glint of youth and beauty, eyes that could bring life to the most inanimate mask. And when she spoke, her voice was open and straightforward, drawing him in.

"You must be Kenji-chan." She bowed to him. "And this is your uncle Toki," she said, smiling.

A short and stocky man with close-cropped hair stood next to her. When he turned, Kenji saw that his right arm was missing.

Uncle Toki looked Kenji up and down and grunted. He pointed at his suitcase. "Any more?" he asked.

"No," Kenji answered.

"Then come," he said, turning around abruptly. "There's work to do."

Aunt Reiko smiled shyly and touched Kenji's arm lightly in reassurance. "We are terribly happy that you're here," she said softly.

Kenji was wrong; he was sure there was a resemblance to his mother, after all. He picked up his suitcase and followed her outside. The station was no more than a one-room wooden building, and beyond it, a small village surrounded by flat brown fields.

At the edge of the village was a burned-out building. Kenji caught up with his aunt. "Was that building bombed?" he asked, pointing to the charred frame. He knew the Americans had increased their bombing raids now that they had captured the Mariana Islands.

Aunt Reiko shook her head. "Imoto has been untouched by the war so far. Except . . . ," she began, then stopped with a glance at her husband, Toki.

Kenji remembered his grandparents saying that his uncle had lost his arm during the fight for the Philippine Islands. What must it have felt like to wake up and have your arm missing? He wondered if the arm were still somewhere in the Philippines, withered down to the bone, once white, now darkened by time and dirt and neglect. Or if the wound, now healed to a shiny-scarred nub, still hurt with a phantom pain that throbbed and ached constantly.

"This fire began from lightning," Aunt Reiko said.

"Lightning?" he repeated, catching the last of his aunt's words.

"A dry storm. We never did have rain that night, just the lightning and thunder."

Kenji glanced back at the building, imagined the thin veins of light coming closer, touching down on the building, which exploded into flames. Uncle Taiko, his *ojichan*'s friend from the bar, had once told him that lightning without rain signified impending disaster. Kenji felt a stab of uneasiness but nodded to his aunt and kept the rest of his thoughts to himself as he followed along. It was lightning that had destroyed the building. If only Japan could harness lightning as its secret weapon, he thought, perhaps then they really could win the war.

The farmhouse is brighter than I expected. I'm

sure it's Aunt Reiko's touch that fills each room. I was greeted with a piece of art just as I walked into the entrance hall — a raku vase with muted colors and fine lines. It surprised me, leaving the vase out on display with no fears of it being confiscated by the kempeitai. *And what a breath of fresh air! Not one officer in sight since arriving in Imoto.* Kenji wrote down his first impressions of Imoto in his notebook, hoping to share them later with his grandparents and Hiroshi. But on his first evening at the farmhouse, he knew as soon as his pen touched the paper that it was Yoshiwara-sensei he was writing to.

Aunt Reiko and Uncle Toki had two children, Kenji's second cousins, an older daughter who was married and living in a village nearby, and a younger son, Hideo, who at sixteen was a year older than Kenji. After a few strained days of getting to know each other, they fell into a quiet rhythm working together in the fields and going out to harvest fodder for the military horses that were starving like everyone else.

Hideo doesn't talk much, Kenji wrote, *but neither do I. Yet in some strange way, we seem to understand each other. It's no wonder, with his father, Uncle Toki, so abrupt and angry; I'd be afraid to say anything, too.* He noted that his cousin was shorter and more compact, resembling his father's side, while he had grown taller and thinner in the past months.

Kenji was fortunate to have his own small room, which used to belong to Hideo's now married sister. He put down the pen, stood up from the desk, and rubbed his hands. In less than a month, his were as rough and red as his aunt's. And his fingers were always cold and stiff, as if the blood no longer traveled to the tips. It brought to mind Yoshiwara-sensei opening and closing his fists after a long day of working on a mask. Kenji did the same now, remembering the warmth of the wood as he sanded each mask with light, even strokes. He carefully took out *The Book of Masks,* still wrapped in his sweater, his fingers growing warmer as they traced the dark lines of each mask.

Throughout the fall and winter, Uncle Toki sent them out to the far field to collect anything they could find to feed the military horses, any shrub or weed that had withstood the winter. Now, as spring approached, grass was scarce even though the skies had cleared in the past week and brought the sun's warmth.

"Be careful," his uncle warned.

Of what? Kenji thought. He was safely in the countryside.

"More and more people are coming from the cities," he added, answering Kenji's silent question. "They'll do anything for food. You can never be too careful."

They walked farther out into the fields, away from the row of trees where the grass hadn't sprouted to an area that received more sun. Hideo threw his cloth sack over his shoulder and reasoned the grass would be longer there, and, if not, the weeds certainly would be. They walked farther out, the open space always loosening their tongues and putting them at ease.

"It must be much different living in Tokyo," Hideo said. "With so many more people."

Too many, Kenji thought, but answered, "Yes, it's very crowded. But the city's exciting."

"And the schools must have many more students?"

Kenji nodded.

"I hope to go to the city to study later," Hideo added.

"What do you want to study?"

"Engineering." Hideo smiled.

Kenji smiled back. "I'll show you around Tokyo. And you can meet my brother, Hiroshi. He's a formidable wrestler."

"Sumotori?"

"Hai."

"Then I'll be welcomed everywhere in Tokyo with a famous *sumotori* as my cousin. And you? What do you want to do, Kenji-chan?"

Kenji hesitated. He hadn't said the words aloud or told anyone that he wanted to be an artisan; only Hiroshi and his grandparents understood his desire.

"I like art," Kenji answered, "and the theater."

Hideo readjusted the bag on his shoulder. "My father always says that it's hard to create something out of nothing. That's why art is truly a gift."

Kenji was surprised to hear Hideo quote his father, a sullen man who hadn't said ten words to him since he had arrived.

Hideo seemed to pick up on his thoughts. "If you'd met my father before the war, you would have met another man. Do you know that all the pottery in our house was made by him?"

Kenji was amazed. Even his cousin's respect and admiration was unexpected. Then he remembered the lovely raku vase in the hall. He never guessed that Uncle Toki had made it. He couldn't imagine what it must have felt like to lose not only his arm but also his art. In that instant, Kenji realized that the war had taken away much more from his uncle than just flesh and bone.

Out in the fields, it was difficult to fill both sacks with anything but weeds, so Kenji strayed farther. He stopped pulling when he heard a distant, low buzzing. For a moment he felt immobilized by the faraway hum, a sound he knew all too well from Tokyo, where he always made a mad dash for the air-raid shelter. He wanted to believe that warplanes would never be flying so far out into the countryside, that they would leave Imoto untouched, as his aunt had said. But the drone grew louder. He dropped his cloth bag and looked up to the sky, shading his eyes against the sun. At first, in the glare, he didn't see anything, but then, just beyond the horizon he spotted the dark shadows approaching. Two planes. This far away from any city, they were most likely on reconnaissance missions. Uncle Toki had warned them to be careful, but he never expected planes. Kenji waved and yelled for Hideo to take cover but he was too far away to hear. He turned and ran toward his cousin as the roar of the planes grew closer, and he felt their enormous dark shadows swallow him as they flew overhead. He looked up and caught a glimpse of the American flag on the tail of one of the planes.

He prayed it wasn't worth the pilot's time to return and chase down two teenagers. In the distance, he saw Hideo running toward the trees that bordered the field. Kenji's heart pounded as he struggled for breath and paused long enough to see one of the planes circle in the distance and return in his direction.

"Run," Kenji shouted, "run, run, run!" He wasn't sure if he was saying it aloud or in his head, but he knew Hideo had a good chance of making it to the trees even if he couldn't. He suddenly felt as if he were Kenji the ghost again, with all the kids in the yard chasing after him. He heard the thunderous roar of the plane come closer, its engine sputtering behind him just as he heard the footsteps of his classmates within reach of grabbing his shirt. Kenji ran faster, turning back to see the plane banking and coming in low, but his foot struck a depression in the ground and buckled under him. The pain in his ankle was sharp and excruciating as he fell to the ground. On his back, he faced the oncoming plane, the way he should have faced his classmates all those times before.

The plane angled in so low Kenji saw a goggled face behind the windshield. He saw the sparks fly first — quick flashes of light from the guns, followed by the rapid popping noise as bullets thudded across the ground and kicked up a dry storm of dirt in two straight lines rippling toward him. Lightning first, always followed by thunder. In that split second, Kenji knew he'd have to get his body between the stream of bullets or roll to the side before they reached him. He rolled just as the bullets careened past him. Kenji covered his head with his arms against the spray of dirt and rocks as the shadow of the plane roared over him. He looked up as the bullets chased Hideo into the trees before the plane pulled upward. As soon as it vanished into the clouds, Kenji pushed himself up. He could barely stand. His ankle throbbed but he didn't think it was broken. He hobbled as fast as he could; he dragged his foot toward the direction he'd last seen Hideo, praying that his cousin had made it to the safety of the trees. The plane hesitated, then flew off rather than circle and drop down for another round of strafe. Kenji stopped and sank to the ground. From the corner of his eye, he saw Hideo running toward him.

Later, aside from a badly twisted ankle and minor cuts and bruises, Kenji and Hideo were otherwise unhurt. Kenji wondered if that American pilot had had any real intention of killing them, or whether it had been just sport? Sport, he decided. The thought made him sick to his stomach. Now he knew that even the countryside of Imoto wasn't safe from the storm. *The swelling in my ankle has gone down and I can stand on it again. I'm going home, where I can be of some help to my family,* he wrote a week later, the night before he boarded a train and returned to Yanaka, not five days into March.

Haru had kept her word to Aki. By the first days of March they were sent home to Tokyo, replaced by another group of students evacuated to Ikaruga. For the six months they'd been in the countryside, Haru never told Aki how much she missed home and wanted to return. She hated the strict teachers and long hours working at the factory making mosquito nets. But she had to be strong, to help her younger sister endure what she herself could barely stand.

The moment they arrived home, Haru breathed a sigh of relief. Aki ran from room to room and out to the sumo stable, hugging her parents and wanting to be picked up as if she were a little girl again. Haru wanted to do the same, but something stopped her. In the months since she'd seen them, her parents had aged years, especially her mother, who appeared pale and gaunt, her once black hair now sprinkled with gray. Darkness had fallen over her father's beloved sumo stable; the constant search for food, the weekly visits from the neighborhood associations, and the death of one of her father's young *sumotori,* Makahashi, who had been killed in the Philippines, where another wrestler had had his leg amputated, had taken their toll.

When Aki followed her father out to the *keikoba,* Haru took the chance to speak to her mother.

"*Okasan,* is everything all right?"

Her mother touched the back of her hair and laughed nervously. "Of course, why do you ask?"

"You seem so thin," Haru dared to say.

"We are all too thin," her mother answered. "It would be strange if I weren't thin during this awful time."

"*Hai,* but —"

"But what, Haru-chan?" her mother interrupted. "What are you saying?"

For the first time, Haru heard fear in her mother's voice, and saw it in her beautiful, dark eyes. She glanced away from Haru and waited for an answer.

"Nothing," Haru replied. She wanted to ask her mother when this awful war would be over, but Haru felt some fragile thread might break in her mother if she asked too many questions. Like Aki, she wanted life to return to the way it was, when their days were filled with noise and laughter, when her father's teaching voice and the rough grunting noises of the *rikishi* at practice meant her father was doing what he loved best. Back when the reception room was filled with gifts her father used to receive — tins of fish eggs and dried beef, expensive foreign chocolates, bottles of sake and whiskey — and her mother's days were filled with her dance class and afternoon teas with friends and there were no fears.

"Shall we make some tea?" her mother asked, suddenly smiling again.

"*Hai,*" Haru answered, happy to see the mother she knew and loved back again.

Still, something in the air made Haru feel heavy, as if some great weight were slowly descending on all of them.

Three days later, a cold north wind blew all day. Before the war, a strong March wind meant the excitement of kites rippling high in the sky, an assortment of red, yellow, and green colors in all shapes and sizes. Haru remembered her father taking her and Aki to the park, along with two of his youngest sumo students, teenage boys who appeared just as excited as they were. The winds were so strong, her father had carried Aki most of the afternoon — afraid that she might be blown away, he had teased. The two students controlled the kites, their weight a solid anchor against the blowing wind.

Now the wind only made Haru feel restless and uneasy, as if something bad might ride in on the tail end of it, and there were no more *sumotori* left to anchor them down. She was only too happy to fall onto her futon that night and end the day.

The scream of the siren woke Haru in the night. It was still dark outside when her father stormed into their room to get them out of bed. Aki sat straight up as if awakened from a bad dream.

"Hurry," her father urged, "we have to get to the school as quickly as possible."

Haru rubbed the sleep from her eyes. Everyone in their neighborhood was supposed to assemble at the nearest school in an emergency. Was this a real emergency? Weren't most of the air-raid sirens in the early morning hours? Her answer came with the scream of more sirens, followed by a volley of explosions that sounded like distant fireworks.

Haru and Aki jumped up already dressed in their *monpe,* which they'd worn to sleep ever since returning from the countryside. They stumbled down the hall after their father to where their mother waited, with their cloth headgear and first-aid supplies. A series of loud explosions went off in the distance. Their house trembled and the floor shook with each impact.

"Hurry," her father repeated.

Her mother hugged Aki close and stayed silent, as if she were holding back a scream.

Outside, Haru saw the entire sky to the west alight with a strange orange and red glow. Long strips of flames fell from the dark sky. The heavy smell of smoke filled the air; it stung her eyes and made them water. She could hear the drone of planes overhead, a roar that shook the ground. "Incendiary bombs," she heard her father shout to her

208

mother. Wherever the planes flew over, fires erupted. Squeezing Aki's hand tighter, Haru followed her parents through the smoke-filled air the four blocks to the school.

"Where's Hoku?" she heard her mother ask. She thought her father answered, "Nowhere . . ." The rest of his words were lost in all the noise. Where was Hoku? His caretaker's house sat dark against the smoky sky.

Neighbors were running toward the school, where they squatted in open trenches for shelter. There were so many people, babies crying and children calling for their mothers, Haru closed her eyes in all the confusion.

"You'll be safe here," her father said, climbing out of the trench wearing his iron helmet. "I have to report to my duty station," he said. "I'll return as soon as I can."

"Please, please, be careful," her mother pleaded.

Haru had never seen her mother so distressed. Her father leaned over and hugged both her and Aki together, then kissed her mother on the lips, something she'd never seen before. Aki held on to her father's arm until he jerked roughly away, leaving her in tears. The winds picked up, bringing a thick black smoke toward them. After her father disappeared into the night, Haru saw her mother still touching her lips.

The whizzing sounds of the incendiary

bombs, the deafening roar of the planes and wind overhead continued as they crouched in the trench. Haru counted the continuous explosions, as they grew louder and the line of fire inched closer and closer to the school. The American planes had never attacked their neighborhood before. Someone screamed. The oncoming fire and smoke chased people out of the open trenches, sending them running for their lives. Aki was wearing her cloth headgear, with her eyes squeezed shut, her hands covering her ears as the teachers had told them to do in school. What use was it all now? Haru thought. She could see her mother panicking, not knowing if she should listen to the shouting voices that screamed, "Run, run!" and "If you stay here, you're sure to die!" Or if they should wait, as her father had directed? Haru's impulse was to run. She sat up, lifted her hand, and felt the hot wind against her palm. She pulled at her mother's arm and, without waiting, climbed out of the trench. She wouldn't stay a moment longer in that open pit only to be burned alive. No sooner had she climbed out than her mother and Aki did the same.

"Go south!" a voice shouted. Haru felt someone pushing her from behind. The fire was fueled by the strong north wind, the wind that left her feeling so uneasy. South was downwind. If they ran upwind, they would most certainly meet a wall of fire. They stood paralyzed; there was no safe passage. On the horizon, it appeared the entire world was ablaze as the fire quickly pushed its way toward them.

Her mother pulled them in the direction of Sunamachi, in the south, where there were many bridges and rivers. "Don't worry," she reassured them, "we'll be all right." It made sense to head toward water and Haru was relieved to see her mother taking charge again, as if she'd awakened from a trance. They gripped each other's hands and ran.

The bridge on the Onagigawa River was crowded with people trying to cross. Houses exploded all around them, debris whipped through the air as electrical wires sparked and fell across the road, sweeping a woman with a baby on her back off her feet. Just as quickly she was lost in the thick, black smoke. The wind and flames merged with a terrific force. The air was on fire. Haru saw bodies ablaze hurl themselves into the river, smelled the burning flesh. When the vomit reached her throat, she stopped, then felt her mother's hand slip away from hers.

"Okasan!" she screamed, her voice lost in the howling firestorm, unable to see her mother and sister. *"Okasan!* Aki!"

Haru's voice was raw, and the smoke scorched her throat. She felt someone grab her arm and for a moment thought that her mother had found her, only to realize that she was being pulled by an old man into a small ditch under the bridge by the river. All around them, she heard screams swallowed up by the roar of the firestorm. Was it her mother or Aki? What had they all done to deserve such a fate?

She pulled away but the old man held her down, leaned close to her ear, and said, "Do you want to get swept away? You have to live in order to find your family."

Haru stopped fighting and felt the old man's grip loosen. She allowed herself a moment of reprieve from the hell just above her, leaning back against the dirt and rocks as her eyes filled with tears.

Haru didn't know how long she stayed in the ditch under the bridge before she climbed back up to the road again. Had she even said thank you to the old man? The howling wind swept another wave of fire toward her. Surrounded by fire on all sides, she had nowhere to go. She could barely see what looked like a slit trench on the other side of the road, dug all over Tokyo by volunteers and students during emergency air raids. Without thinking she ran and leaped through the fire, tumbling hard into the trench. Haru was still stunned she had survived the jump without getting hurt when she saw Aki crawling toward her.

"Haru-chan!"

"Aki!" She hugged her sister tightly. On the other side of the trench, another woman who wasn't her mother hovered low.

"Where's *okasan?*" She raised her voice against the howling wind. "Is she all right?"

Aki didn't answer, couldn't answer. She shook her head and buried her face in Haru's shoulder as they pressed their bodies against the dirt. She heard the other woman scream as the fire began showering down on them. The back of the woman's blouse had caught fire, spreading down the length of her body. Before Haru could do anything, the woman had bounded out of the trench and was blown away by the roar of the wind and fire. It was as if she never existed. Haru turned when Aki suddenly screamed, her padded headgear ablaze. She pushed her down quickly and used dirt and her own hands to smother the flames, then ripped off the foolish headgear. Miraculously, Aki's hair and a bit of her head were singed but she was otherwise unhurt. It was only then that she felt the stinging pain and throbbing of her own burned hands, her palms red and raw, already blistering. She shifted her body on top of Aki, to protect her from the fire, and placed her palms against the cool dirt, waiting for the pain to subside. It was the only thing she could do. She held Aki close, heard her sister whispering, "*Ichi, ni, san, shi, go . . .* I'm invisible. No one can see me."

They lay flat in the trench as the fire and wind roared just above them.

When Haru dared to raise her head at dawn, there was nothing but silence. She saw a heavy, smoke-filled sky. The firestorm had blown itself out. They slowly climbed out of the trench to see a steaming world she no longer recognized. Most of the houses were burned to the ground, only concrete structures had survived. Trees were nonexistent and dead bodies floated in the river or lay by the side of the road, their charred remains smoldering, while other bodies were still in sitting and kneeling positions. She imagined them too hot to touch and her palms burned at the thought. She forced herself not to be afraid, to keep walking through the gray, gritty air, shielding Aki until they were away from the river.

"Wait here for me," she told Aki. "I promise I won't be long."

"Where are you going?" Aki held on to her arm and only reluctantly let go.

"I'll be right back."

Haru hurried back to the river and climbed down the embankment to the ditch under the bridge, her hands throbbing with pain. She had to see if the old man was all right, and to thank him for saving her. She bent low and peeked. Tucked in the corner, Haru could see he was still sitting there.

She called out hello.

When the old man didn't answer, she inched closer to see if he was all right. Only then could she see his eyes were wide open as he stared blankly out at the river. The fire had just touched his body, but she imagined the heat or smoke might have overcome him first. Her body could have easily been lying there beside his had she not had the impulse to leave, to find her mother and Aki. Haru bowed quickly in respect and turned to run back up the embankment as fast as she could.

"What do we do now?" Aki asked, still clutching the charred headgear, strangely calm, standing amid the devastation.

"We go home," she answered. Haru didn't know where else they could go. There was a chance her mother had found her way back home, and, if not, surely her father would come back for them.

They began to walk and then they ran.

THE VALLEY OF DARKNESS

Hiroshi had just fallen asleep when the first siren went off, startling him awake. His heart raced, and he instinctively knew this time it was something more than a usual air raid. It was the middle of the night; usually the sirens went off just after dawn. Kenji must have felt it, too, for he was up from his futon by the end of the siren's first wail. Kenji's ankle was still tender, his limp still pronounced since returning from Imoto just four days earlier. Hiroshi watched him grimace as his weight landed on the foot. His grandmother had cried the day Kenji returned. The grandson they had sent to the countryside to be safe had been in more danger than they were in Yanaka.

Ever since his brother's return, Hiroshi felt a change in him, and saw it in each quick, assured gesture. Unlike the shy young boy who left, Kenji exuded a newfound confidence.

"Ojichan?" Hiroshi asked.

"I'll help them down to the shelter," Kenji answered, hobbling quickly out of their room.

"I'll get everything else," he said, grateful that his brother was back to help. He gathered the *furoshiki* of meager supplies, the water and the first-aid kit, the cloth headgear his *obachan* sewed for them, and one more thing this time, a fan for his grandmother to move the air when it became too thick and still. During the last air raid, he had watched her close her eyes, chanting something between her lips as she swayed from side to side.

They spent most of the night and morning huddled in the backyard air-raid shelter, cramped and stiff but otherwise unharmed. The air became so thick and solid Hiroshi thought they would suffocate. Relentless explosions shook the ground. Dirt sifted from the earthen walls around them as the planes droned overhead. All Hiroshi could think was that they had saved someone the trouble of burying them. And when they were able to emerge at last from their shelter hours later, it was into a fragile silence. Later, they would learn the greater shame of having survived a night in which so many had died.

Yanaka had been spared once again. Just as the area had been left virtually untouched during the Kanto earthquake of 1923, the winds had blown the firestorm in other directions. Hiroshi remembered the story his *ojichan* told them when they were boys, how the temples surrounding the Edo castle were moved to Yanaka for safety after the earthquake. And when the roar of the planes finally vanished and the ground stopped shaking, the thick, acrid, smoke-filled air hovered, clearing just enough to see in shadows that the temples still stood. Hiroshi wanted to know what god had protected Yanaka from the firestorm. What gave them the right to live when so many had perished?

The day after the firestorm was eerily quiet. It was as if the entire world surrounding them had turned to ash. Hiroshi went against the wishes of his grandparents and volunteered for the committee to help clear away the dead, with hopes of notifying their families and giving them a proper burial. How could he not help? he asked his grandparents.

Before March 10, 1945, Hiroshi had never seen a dead body, now they lay all around him — some like blackened statues still in sitting positions, others with their skin melted away from a heat that burned like a furnace, leaving only fragments of bone in dust. The flames that had been swept forward by the winds left no escape for anyone caught in the storm. Amid the rubble, Hiroshi also found small miracles — some bodies untouched where they fell, or a wayward cloth helmet and baby's sock that hadn't burned.

The air was still thick and smoky as the neighborhood committees scattered in groups of four or five, his led by a man named Iwada-san. Hiroshi began coughing, his eyes burning from the smoke. One man, whom he recognized as the father of one of his classmates, passed out white handkerchiefs for them to tie around their mouths. They walked silently down the road toward the Onagigawa River looking like bandits. Once green and tree lined, there was nothing left on either side of the road. As they approached the river, it was as if the once lush landscape had been wiped clean, the blank surface covered in gray ash like snow. All that was left was the charred stone bridge. Hiroshi heard the water flowing below the embankment then saw the burned bodies that lay along the slope, while other bodies floated in the river. He heard one committee member, an older man, say that those who ran toward the river were trapped by a wave of fire, which suddenly had surrounded them from all directions. Many who jumped into the river to escape the fire were asphyxiated by the smoke and burning air. The man nudged one of the bodies with his foot and stepped quickly back when a large piece of the charred leg broke away. Hiroshi knew that so many bodies would never be identified.

It made Hiroshi sick to his stomach as he worked furiously to retrieve the swollen and bloated bodies from the river. He climbed back up, half-soaked, and retched on the bank, but knew that if he stopped, he would never be able to continue. He held down his next bout of nausea and faced his fear, or it would always return to haunt him. A sudden movement down by the side of the river caught his eye, a woman's body floating against the bank, her clothes caught on some branches. Carefully, Hiroshi made his way back down the embankment until he reached the body, her back burned to the bone. When he turned her body over, her face was distorted, blackened and bloated but not burned. He checked to see if her name and address was sewn into her clothes as they'd all been instructed to do. And there, on the inside flap of her jacket, were the characters that told him her name was Noriko Tanaka.

DESTINY

Hiroshi's *unmei,* the destiny his *obachan* had told him about as a boy, came to light on that day when all else was steeped in darkness. It was Iwada-san, the head of his search committee, who recognized the name Noriko Tanaka as they gathered to identify the multitude of dead found by the Onagigawa River. Hiroshi hadn't known his heart could hold so much sadness, and wondered how to keep it from bursting. That morning, he had found the body of Tanaka-oyakata's wife, though he didn't know it was the great sumo coach's wife at first. There were so many dead and dying, so many nameless bodies. But it was her face that struck him as he turned her body over, bloated in death, yet strangely calm. He tried to wipe her face of ash and dirt, picked the debris out of her hair. Even when he discovered the name sewn in her jacket, he didn't make the connection to Tanaka-oyakata, thinking only what a terrible loss it was to the family waiting for her to return to them. Her body was wrapped in a sheet and lined up among the dozens of others until her family could be reached.

It wasn't until Hiroshi and Iwada-san entered the still smoldering Katsuyama-beya later that afternoon that it was confirmed that Noriko Tanaka really was Tanaka-sama's wife. The *oyakata* stood before him, a big, defeated man. With him was a pretty girl Hiroshi assumed was his daughter, with her hands wrapped in white bandages like two thick gloves. Her dark, piercing eyes peered out at him from behind Tanaka. He looked away, his throat sore when he swallowed.

"Tanaka-san, if you could come with us to identify the body. We've set up a medical tent down by the river," Iwada-san said softly.

"*Hai,*" Tanaka answered. Without saying another word, he bowed low to Iwada-san.

"It was Hiroshi-san who found your wife's body," Iwada said, bowing back.

Hiroshi watched Oyakata-san's lower lip tremble. His daughter stood there, her bandaged hands seeming to weigh her down, while tears streamed soundlessly down her cheeks.

Tanaka-sama touched Hiroshi's arm and bowed low to him. "*Domo . . . ,*" he began, his voice breaking. "*Domo arigato goziamasu,* Hiroshi-san, for finding my Noriko."

"I'm very sorry," Hiroshi said, bowing back. He wasn't sure Tanaka-sama heard a word he said, or remembered him to be the young recruit whose sumo career had been cut short by the war. The wind had picked up again, a sudden rush of smoke swept by, and he heard the little girl whimper, step forward and raise her bandaged hands as if to protect her father. Tanaka put his arm around the little girl's shoulders.

Once outside the gate, Hiroshi turned around to see that the main house still stood, but all he saw left of the Katsuyama-beya was one building, darkened by fire.

Everything else was gone.

9
VOICES
AUGUST 1945

The voices told what had happened after the atomic bombs fell, like the whispered words of ghosts. *Can you imagine a wind so strong that it ripped a man's face away where he stood? Can you imagine how internal organs exploded, clothes and bodies burst into flames, disintegrated on the spot? Can you envision a mushroom cloud formed by smoke and debris that could be seen for miles by the naked eye, followed by a black rain falling, black tears they called it, radiation spreading in its wake? Those who died were the lucky ones,* the voices continued. *Those who lived through it would never be the same.*

Nine days after the atomic bombs fell, on August 15, Hiroshi and his family knelt in front of the radio and heard the static, high-pitched voice of the "divine god," their imperial emperor, for the first time. Hiroshi was stunned; it was the calm voice of a mild-mannered man who sounded more like a scholar than a leader. The voice said the war "had not turned in Japan's favor," and they must now "endure the unendurable, and bear the unbearable." Hadn't they already lived through the unbearable? Died for it? It was the voice of a man who spoke in formal, stilted classical phrases, a voice that sounded very far away from the Japanese people.

■ ■ ■ ■

PART TWO

■ ■ ■ ■

Ah, summer grasses!
All that remains
of the warrior's dreams.

— Basho

10
SHADOW FIGURES
1945

Fumiko Wada hurried down the crowded alleyways to wait with other women in food lines that grew longer with each day of the occupation. At sixty-three years of age, she fought to keep her anger and sorrow at bay. The number of lives lost abroad and at home was staggering. And in the end, what was it all for?

The first three months after Japan's surrender in August were heavy with despair, the sky a thick, smoky blanket that wouldn't lift. But by early November, the air had become an icy chill. Fumiko feared a long, cold winter and stayed close to home, urging Hiroshi and Kenji to do the same. But it wasn't just the despair and destruction that disturbed her about this new postwar Tokyo. She edged past another pair of cigarette-smoking, gum-chewing, chocolate-giving *gaijin* soldiers who patrolled the streets. Fumiko loathed these towering men with their strong smells and loud voices, the *pan-*

pan women who entertained them, and the gang-run black market, which charged exorbitant prices for food and goods. Even with the blackout curtains taken down, the slit trenches filled in, and the nightly scream of air-raid sirens silenced, the Japanese people still went hungry. They moved through the streets like shadow figures, and it felt to Fumiko as if another kind of war had just begun.

Despite the Allied forces' steady presence, Fumiko was lucky if she could bring home a bit of rice mixed with soybeans, or powdered milk, or eggs for Yoshio and her grandsons. Food remained scarce, government distribution chaotic, and the high prices on the black market forced most people to survive on watery soups, sweet potatoes, the roots of plants, acorns, insects and rodents, and a type of steamed wheat bran bread that was formerly fed only to cattle and horses. People were still dying daily from starvation. Each time Fumiko bit into the coarse, bland bread, she imagined what Ayako would say. *"It isn't even good enough for cattle and horses!"* Then Ayako's laughter would fill Fumiko's mind as it used to fill the small room behind her friend's bakery.

One day, Yoshio simply refused to eat the bran bread anymore. "It upsets my stomach," he said, preferring to pick at the boiled sweet potato in his bowl. Hiroshi and Kenji were cleverer; she knew they pocketed the bread, most likely to feed the stray dogs. She didn't think it was possible for them to lose more weight after the war, but they became shadow figures like all the rest. When Fumiko felt the bread lodge drily in her own throat, she had only to remember her friend's sweet, light *kasutera,* the thin, loaf-sized sponge cake, and her mouth would water.

She often thought of Ayako while she waited in the food lines, and her sorrow ran even deeper than her anger. She felt as if her breath were squeezed out of her. Three months past the surrender, Ayako was still missing. Ayako-san, along with her daughter and grandson, had moved to Hiroshima to stay with relatives until the war's end. After the bombs were dropped, Fumiko could only wait, praying that they'd been spared. Each morning she braced herself, fearing the news she waited for day after day. Had Ayako gone into the other world where her two husbands and lost child waited for her?

Sometimes, Fumiko felt Ayako's loss was unbearable, a current that flashed through her body, growing more severe as the days passed. Some nights she lay still on the futon, so as not to wake Yoshio, and she wondered if he could feel that current surging through her or hear the slight hum that grew louder each passing week. When she closed her eyes, images of Ayako, Mikiko, and little

Juzo flickered through her mind, keeping her awake. The following day she moved through the world in a daze, dozing wherever she sat down.

Fumiko glanced at the long, hopeless food lines and kept walking, no longer cringing at the loud American soldiers who took up most of the walkway. She ignored them like a dip in the road and slipped past, her sandals click-clacking as she went about her own business. "Slow down, Mama-san, what's the hurry?" a soldier called out, but she just pulled her kimono tighter and walked faster, shaking his voice away.

She kept walking until she neared the train station. She thought of returning home and making Yoshio walk with her; it would do him good to get out into the fresh air, but she could already hear him say to her, *I see all I need to see from here.* But the sky had cleared to a pale blue, like an open door that suddenly made her feel courageous. She held her head high and looked clearly around for the first time in a long time. With so many buildings destroyed in the bombings, it was a miracle that so many train lines were still running. Fumiko marveled at the crowds of people hurrying in and out.

The faces she saw changed as she entered the train station, no longer just anxious women waiting in food lines, but beggars and soldiers, vendors and the homeless who had nowhere else to go. On the platform, Fumiko found herself pushed by the hordes as a train rattled slowly into the station. People crowded off and then on, pulling her along as they boarded.

Downtown Tokyo near the Sumida River looked like a wasteland. Where tall buildings once stood, Fumiko saw only rubble for miles around. Occasionally, a lone building stood, like the last can on a shelf. No space had been wasted, however. Flattened and bombed-out areas had already been turned into vegetable gardens. On every block were notice boards with handwritten sheets of paper that described missing persons. When the wind blew, they looked like hundreds of white flags flapping up and down in surrender. The homeless families increased in number as she walked along the downtown streets, their scant belongings tied in bundles beside them. Stories of the displaced spread through every household as war widows and orphans wandered the streets begging for food. "Anything, anything," they whispered, forcing her to look away. And yet, the most heartbreaking faces Fumiko saw were those of Japanese soldiers who had returned from war, having cheated starvation and death, only to find their homes incinerated and their families missing or dead. With nowhere to go, they roamed the streets aimlessly, dazed and despondent like phantoms, still dressed in their ragged uniforms. She was furious at a government that would abandon its soldiers. Fumiko longed for the suffering to end as she walked slowly down the ravaged streets going nowhere in particular. She looked upon the bleak city in ruins, hoping against hope that it might someday be rebuilt.

Shelter

After the surrender, Hiroshi stayed close to home as his *obachan* wanted him to do. But a few weeks later, when the call came for volunteers to help fill in the slit trenches that had been dug for defense purposes, he was more than happy to sign up. The occupying forces hoped to quickly erase any outward signs of the war. Hiroshi was just thankful for the pure, physical work of digging; it made him wake up each morning and shake off his stupor, the listlessness that slowed his movements. He wanted nothing more than to work his muscles again until they ached, until his clothes became stiff with dirt and sweat. He wanted to draw long, slow breaths in hopes that the air around him might lighten his heart and mind. At eighteen, he could do little else for his devastated country but fill in the slit trenches he had once helped to dig. Every day there were new rumors of food shipments coming in, of buildings that would be resurrected, and of schools reopening, but week after week, everything remained in flux. By the end of November, Hiroshi was sure of only one change: the long, narrow scars by the side of the roads had all but disappeared.

A few days into December, Hiroshi awoke early and realized he'd forgotten to do one important thing. He dressed quickly without waking Kenji. Downstairs, his grandparents were surprised to see him up so early. *"Ohayo gozaimasu,"* he said, as he walked through the kitchen and out the back door so quickly, he scarcely heard his name and the sound of his *obachan*'s questioning voice trailing behind him.

In the backyard, the sky was just awakening, a pale gray light that gradually revealed the outlines of a world he'd known all his life. It was like a photo being slowly developed. The air was thin ice as the yard came into focus. He stretched his tall frame, shook loose his arms and hands, and did a few leg squats until he felt the pull of his calf muscles. Why hadn't he thought to fill the gaping wound in his own backyard before this morning? Wasn't it the most personal scar of all, mocking them every day?

Hiroshi pulled away the plank that covered the entrance to the air-raid shelter, and stepped down into the dark, closed tomb. He lit a lantern and shook his head. To think the flimsy structure could have provided any kind of real protection! He shivered from the cold and the damp, earthy smell, then quickly set to work removing each board that had been wedged in to support the dirt walls. One by one, he dragged the pieces out before he emerged a final time to pick up the shovel. The ground wasn't frozen yet, as in some winters. He and Kenji had built up the dirt walls and laid a piece of corrugated metal on top as a roof before covering it with more dirt. He began digging until his shovel tapped metal, then he cleared away the dirt and pulled the roof off, leaving a gaping hole. Hiroshi swung the shovel against the raised dirt walls of the shelter with a *thwack,* followed by several more hard blows — *thwack, thwack* — against the walls. He went another round of hits before he heard the earth breaking apart, gradually giving way. He stepped back and watched the dirt sink into the hole as big as the oversized graves he'd helped dig to bury the countless unidentified dead after the firestorm. He wanted to bury this air-raid shelter, too, and with it, the past. He shoveled the rest of the earth into the hole and thought of his *ojichan* taking down the watchtower, which had stood on the same spot but had risen above the ground. It was time, Hiroshi thought, to move forward. Warm from the work and his desire for a stronger, better future, he knocked down another side of the wall and watched it collapse into the gaping hole.

SURVIVORS

Sho Tanaka picked up a piece of charred wood that fell apart in his hands. The two-story wooden building where his sumo students slept and ate had burned to the ground, along with Hoku's caretaker house. "Hoku," he murmured to himself. He hadn't been seen since the morning of the firestorm, nine months ago. It was Hoku who had pounded on their door that fateful night. "The planes are coming this way," he warned, quick and urgent. By the time Tanaka had gathered Noriko and the girls, Hoku was gone.

On the other side of a stone walkway, the building housing his office and the practice area had miraculously survived. Had the winds suddenly shifted, the fire gone elsewhere? Tanaka shook his head and continued to clear the debris into a growing pile. The Japan Sumo Association financed most sumo stables, including the Katsuyama-beya. Tanaka could only guess when they'd be able to help restore the stable amid all the other destruction. Until then, he would have to get the stable back up and running on his own.

With the girls back in school, Sho Tanaka spent most afternoons sitting in his small upstairs office, which was drafty in winter. Occasionally, a quick shot of black-market whiskey, or sake, warmed him against the cold and the loneliness. The persistent smell of smoke filled the room and seeped into every crevice. He ran his hand over the top of his smooth pate. When the war ended in August and he began to lose his hair, Tanaka feared the cloud of radiation from the atomic bombs dropped on Hiroshima and Nagasaki had somehow poisoned him. He'd read accounts of survivors' symptoms, and couldn't bear to think of leaving his young daughters without both their parents. The doctor had found no medical explanation for his hair loss, and Tanaka had scoffed when he suggested an emotional cause. After all, the entire country was emotionally devastated. He didn't tell the doctor that deep down, his terror grew when he lay alone at night, his thoughts bouncing between raising two daughters alone and trying to rebuild the Katsuyama-beya from its burned ruins.

The morning after seeing the doctor, not two months after the bombing, Sho Tanaka had risen and shaved his head, ignoring the dull rasp of the razor scraping across his pale skin. When he finished, the water was murky with tufts of black and gray hair floating at the top of the wooden bucket. He felt a sense of calm for the first time since the war ended. No longer would he worry if he found strands of his hair on his clothes, or at the bottom of the bath. He'd taken matters into his own hands.

His daughters, Haru and Aki, covered their mouths in laughter when they saw him for the first time, his head pale as a baby's bottom. From then on, they often reached up and stroked it, "for luck," Haru said. And he did believe it would bring him luck, or perhaps just more attention as the *oyakata* of the Katsuyama-beya. He smiled to think that at each major tournament to come, he would be more visible; his shaved head would be a stark contrast to the prized *chonmage,* the oiled topknot that each *sumotori* wore with pride.

A December chill had settled onto the small office. Sho Tanaka rubbed his eyes and gazed at the photo of his wife and daughters on his desk. It had been taken during a time of great happiness, the moment frozen on their beautiful faces. Now, Noriko was dead, Haru's hands still hadn't healed, and Aki's voice had gone silent. He swallowed the sourness that rose to his mouth.

He still believed Noriko might enter his office at any moment to tell him she was on her way to the market, a barely visible smile rising at the corners of her lips. The same slight smile he'd seen twenty years ago at the teahouse where they'd met. But he was no longer the young, strapping *sekitori* of so many years ago, who sat in the Sakura teahouse — one of the finest geisha teahouses in the Akasaka district in Tokyo — celebrating his advance to the rank of a professional wrestler. He'd heard that many of the geisha at the teahouse had trained in the famous Gion district of Kyoto. Only through a formal introduction, or as a guest of a long-standing client, such as his *oyakata,* could he be welcomed at the Sakura.

Sho Tanaka was twenty-five, his head spinning from the beer he had already consumed at the stable with the other *sekitori* wrestlers. He should have lain down to rest instead of going to a geisha house with his *oyakata* and other high-ranked wrestlers, but they wanted to celebrate his promotion from the ranks of apprenticeship. He sat and drank more beer with them, waiting to be entertained.

Tanaka looked up when the shoji door slid open and two geisha knelt just outside; then they entered to pour each guest more beer and sake. He watched their smooth, white faces, each a perfect mask, and their swift, delicate movements around the low table, the sweet scent of their perfume lingering as they bowed and retreated from the room.

His good friend, the wrestler Fujimoto-san, leaned over toward him. "It's a good time for you to meet some women," he teased. "You're a professional wrestler now, you're free to marry."

"I'm too busy winning matches," Tanaka had answered, raising his glass. The truth was, he didn't allow himself to think much about women. Throughout a wrestler's early training, marriage was discouraged until he reached the *sekitori* division. Before then, there was little time or money as an apprentice *sumotori*. His life was that of a *rikishi,* and once he stepped into the stable, the door was closed to the outside world. Even with this promotion, it would be a struggle to support himself with what he was making as a lower-ranked *sumotori*. He could rarely spend an evening with a geisha, much less support a wife.

Sho had been lost in the hazy spinning of the room, the loud conversation and laughter, when the door slid open again and two young *maiko,* geisha apprentices, entered. Three older geisha who carried instruments — a drum, a flute, and a three-stringed *shamisen* — followed them in. The room fell silent as the music began and the young geisha apprentices began the *Tachikata,* moving in precise, fluid movements through the traditional Japanese dance.

"Each dance tells a story," his *oyakata* whispered to him.

But Sho wasn't interested in how each movement added to the progression of the story. He couldn't take his eyes off one of the geisha apprentices, the taller, thinner of the two, her red collar against her pale skin, her eyes the color of black pearls. The dancer captivated him, and he saw in her a fragility that he wanted to protect. Later that evening, he discovered her name was Noriko-san.

Even when they secretly began to court the following year, he never believed she would leave the *o-chayo* at twenty to marry him. But she had. Four years later, when he began to lose tournaments at the age of thirty, and had decided to retire from tournament wrestling after twelve years, rather than lose his rank, Noriko stood by his side. At twenty-four, she embraced the position of *okamisan,* the stable master's wife, as if it were always meant to be her life's work.

In the past few years, he'd seen more than traces of Noriko in his daughters, in Haru's slender, graceful limbs, and more predominantly, in Aki's black-pearl eyes and fair complexion. As the girls grew older, he couldn't look Aki directly in the eyes without seeing Noriko. Through them, Noriko's absence still struck him at the most unexpected times, moments of sorrow that caught in his throat and brought tears to his eyes. They would always be an enduring reminder that in the end, he hadn't been able to protect her.

Aki's voice sang out *"Otosan"* when her father returned to the stable after the firestorm. Walking toward her covered in black soot, he looked like a monster in a movie she'd once seen. She shouted out his name and ran to him. He picked her up and held her tight. Her arms went around his neck and she looked hard into the distance, hoping her mother would be coming through the smoky shadows, too.

Afterward, Aki went to stay a few days with relatives, while her father took care of Haru and the burns on her hands. When she returned to the stable, Aki saw Haru's bandaged hands like two bound stumps and began to cry. It was her fault that her sister had to suffer, while she had escaped relatively unharmed. She touched the small, raw spot on the back of her own head. She could barely swallow her throat was so sore.

The day Aki finally lost her voice was when she entered the temple to say goodbye to her mother, though it was only an empty body; the mother who had laughed and danced for her was already gone. The words of farewell began to roll and tumble over themselves in her head but wouldn't come out of her mouth. It was as if her voice had slowly burned away in the intense heat of the fire. If her mother had to die and Haru had to suffer from her burns, then so must Aki.

At first, her father and Haru thought Aki's silence was from the shock of losing her mother, of having to witness and survive the devastating firestorm. The doctors who had cleaned the singed skin on the back of her head couldn't find anything else physically wrong. Aki knew better. She still had conversations in her head, but the words refused to emerge. How could she tell her father that she didn't remember what had happened to her mother? She knew he needed to hear something, anything, to lighten his grief. But she remained silent, as if her words were held captive in a dark, airless room. It had happened so quickly — engulfed by the smoke, the wind, and the heat of the flames — her mother there and then not there. Forever and ever, Aki would be the last one to have seen her mother alive.

Her father shook his head sorrowfully and told Haru, "Aki-chan will be better in a few days. Give her time." Aki watched her father in silence. Already he was talking around her. Why did he think that just because she didn't speak, she had disappeared? She quickly looked down to see if she was becoming invisible again, as she used to be when she was afraid. *Ichi, ni, san, shi* . . . But no, she held up her hands, looked down at her legs, her flower-patterned kimono, Haru leaning over to touch her hand with her own bandaged one.

The moment Aki stopped talking, everything around her changed. Life felt charged with both distance and clarity. While her lack of speech made her invisible to some, she saw and heard much more than before. There was something comforting in the silence of her own voice. She remembered things long forgotten, like being small and taking a nap, wrapped up tightly in a silk comforter, while her mother told her to close her eyes. And slowly, slowly, she would drift off to sleep. But strangely enough, when she lay quietly in the dark room those first nights staying with relatives, listening to all the strange sounds of a different house, it wasn't her mother she missed but Haru. She wondered if this somehow made her a bad person.

For months, Aki answered questions with a nod or a shake of her head. Her father lost himself in plans to reopen the stable and rarely spoke to her directly. In her mind, she knew he was angry with her for losing her voice, for not telling him what happened to her mother. "I'm sorry," she wanted to tell him, but the words lodged in her throat. Only Haru spoke to her as always. Even though she didn't answer, her sister's eyes focused on hers with infinite patience.

■ ■ ■ ■

In late December, just after her tenth birthday, Aki was in the kitchen helping her sister stir the rice gruel, dropping in the green leaves and the stem that came from the pumpkin Haru was cutting into pieces.

"Fukata-san tried to cheat me," Haru said, her voice filling the kitchen. She seemed to speak twice as much to compensate for Aki's silence. "He wanted to cut off the stem and leaves, only to resell them to someone else. I refused to buy the pumpkin until he agreed to leave them on."

Aki smiled. Her sister had become as capable as her mother in going to the market, waiting in food lines, and bargaining every day to make the most of the little she brought home. She often wished she had Haru's talents. Her thoughts were interrupted by a soft rustling noise like that of her mother's slippers against the tatami. She assumed it was her father coming in, but when she looked up, it was her mother standing in the doorway watching them with a contented smile on her lips. She looked beautiful and young again, dressed in her favorite maroon kimono with the white chrysanthemums on it. Aki dropped the wooden spoon on the floor and cried out, *Okasan!* Her heart skipped with a quick joy.

244

Her voice resonated through the room. It took Haru a moment to realize that she'd spoken. Her hand rose to her mouth as if containing a scream of joy or surprise. "Aki-chan?" she asked, as if unsure any other words would follow.

Aki's gaze fell on her sister's hand, discolored from the orange veins of pumpkin, the same hand that had been burned red and raw. "Over there," she said, pointing to the doorway. Her voice sounded strange to her, low and throaty. But before she could say another word, Haru rushed over to embrace her.

Aki pulled away from her sister to tell her it was their mother who had brought her voice back to her. "Over there," she said once more. "At the doorway." But when she looked again, her mother was gone.

THE PRAYING-HANDS HOUSE

More than a year had passed since Akira arrived at the village of Aio with no idea how long he would stay. He'd rented the room behind the small sake shop that was now closed, and emerged only for food and to take long walks into the mountains through the late summer and fall, when the leaves blazed an angry orange-red. The village survived on its trees, the residents making wood charcoal and taking it down to the larger town of Oyama. Akira liked the idea of coming to a place were wood was of such importance, just as it always was for him and the masks. He began to read and draw again in both pencil and charcoal — the mountains, the tall pines with the sloped roofs peeking through. He felt like an art student, with the freedom to do as he pleased, discover what he would. The masks faded in and out of his thoughts; the one unfinished *Okina* mask he'd taken with him was safely tucked away under his bed with his chisels. He couldn't bring himself to finish it, because then what would be left for him to do?

It was on one of these walks his first winter there, late in 1944, that he had met Kiyo. Snow was falling. He looked up at the pale gray sky and the white blanket that covered the mountains, and pulled his coat closer. Was this mountain village, nestled high above the world with its steep-roofed houses that resembled praying hands, enough to keep him sane until the war ended? Could he live out a year or more hiding in such a solitary place?

When he heard the dull crunch of snow, he turned and saw her standing there, a thin girl of nine or ten, with long hair. In the freezing wind, she wore only a dark cotton kimono and *tabi* socks with her sandals. She stood at a distance and watched him with curiosity.

"Why are you always by yourself?" she asked.

The question rang through the cold, clear air and startled him.

"How long have you been watching me?" he asked. His breath drifted out like smoke.

"Long enough to know you're always by yourself," she answered, without any shyness or restraint. The girl's focused gaze didn't turn away from him.

Akira was amused. "Some people enjoy being by themselves."

She eyed him closely. "There aren't many visitors to Aio who stay. Why have you stayed?"

He laughed out loud at her directness, so unlike other children he'd known. He thought of Kenji and how shy he'd been the first time he took him back to the shop.

"I enjoy it here in Aio," he answered her. "And I'm not totally alone, I have a cat."

The girl took a step forward and bowed slightly. "Then, if you're staying for a while, my name is Kiyo."

He bowed low and with great ceremony. "And I'm Akira Yoshiwara. And now that we're no longer strangers, I think you should go home. Do your parents know you're out in the cold without a coat? You must be frozen." He glanced down at her feet.

Kiyo looked away. "I'm used to the cold."

They both turned their heads at the scraping sound of a door sliding open in the distance. Before Akira could say anything else, Kiyo whispered, *"Sayonara,"* and turned to run back toward one of the old pitched-roof houses, disappearing inside so quickly he wondered if she had really been there. From the stone chimney, a great billow of smoke rose up into the sky.

Afterward, Akira saw Kiyo on his walks several times a week. She sometimes waited for him, but all they did was exchange a few words and she disappeared again, or she walked with him a short distance before turning around and heading home. He began to look forward to seeing her. He loved her quick questions that enlivened his long silences. Then one day in March when he came up the dirt road, he saw her standing beside the house with a slender woman, dressed in a plain brown kimono, her long, dark hair pulled back.

Akira bowed upon reaching them.

"Akira-san, this is my mother, Emiko," Kiyo said.

He bowed again.

"I have heard a great deal about you. I hope Kiyo-chan hasn't been bothering you," Emiko said and bowed.

"Not at all." Akira recognized the eyes as soon as he looked into them. No longer bent over a wooden box, a scarf around her head, she appeared younger and quite attractive.

"The turnips," he said.

She looked down shyly. "I wondered if you'd remember."

Akira smiled.

"I wanted to thank you for being so kind to Kiyo. She can be quite talkative."

"It's a pleasure to have her as company," Akira said.

"I told you," Kiyo piped up. "I told you he doesn't mind."

Emiko shook her head at her daughter and invited Akira in for tea. Inside the steep-roofed house, he was reminded of pictures in a book of fables from his childhood. As his eyes adjusted to the darkness, a large, open room with high rafters came into focus. Emiko followed his gaze and said, "They used to house silkworms in wooden boxes up on the rafters a long time ago. The heat from the fire rose and kept them warm, before wood charcoal became more lucrative." She hurried to the *irori,* the large hearth in the middle of the room, and set more wood on the small fire. In its tentative light, Akira glimpsed the sloping thatched roof above the rafters, the smoke-darkened wooden walls, and the spare furnishings.

"Have you lived here long?" he asked Emiko. Kiyo had disappeared to a back room.

"The house has been in my husband's family for more than a century."

Akira turned away from the blackened

kettle hanging on its rusty hinge above the sparse fire. Flickering flames made the lines of Emiko's face waver between young and old.

"My husband has been dead for several years now," Emiko went on, "and it's difficult to keep up . . ." Her voice faded.

"I'm sorry."

Emiko bowed her head. "Forgive me, I'm feeling sorry for myself. The war has been difficult for everyone."

Akira nodded. *"Hai,"* he said softly.

As they sat in silence, the smoke made his eyes water, his throat close. He looked up, glad for the ringing voice of Kiyo as she thumped back into the room.

From that day on, Akira was often a guest in that house, and in the spring of 1945, he helped the widow Emiko and Kiyo run their small farm, chopping wood, planting turnips and carrots, and harvesting whatever they could. Although they were safe from bullets and bombs, they suffered from the winter cold and gnawing hunger that left the entire village listless. The land, either parched or frozen, grew miserable turnips and carrots, weak and small but edible. Once in a while, Emiko went down the mountain to trade turnips at the dry-goods store for miso or a half-cup of rice. One afternoon in mid-March, she returned with the news that firebombs had destroyed much of Tokyo and killed more than one hundred thousand people. Akira was stunned. So many lives lost, while there he was, tucked safely away in the mountains. He hoped that Kenji and his family had somehow survived.

Throughout the spring and summer, bombs continued to drop. More deaths than Akira dared to think about. In August, Japan surrendered and was soon occupied by American soldiers. But by the time autumn came again, Akira wanted no part of the occupation, just as he hadn't wanted any part of the war. Even if he could return to Tokyo without repercussions, what of his old life was left for him there? Aio was a forgotten place, which suited Akira just fine. At least in Aio he had Emiko and Kiyo, the widow and her daughter, and he was content to know that he helped them in small ways. It wasn't exactly happiness, but something close enough to it.

11
ASHES
1946

By the end of April, the courtyard was alive again with colors Haru had never paid attention to when she was young. Now, it was her favorite time of year; blooming shades of green, purple-blue lilies, pink azaleas, the yellowish green unfurling of buds. If Haru were to look back and search for the defining moment when she came to love the mysteries of plant life, it would be just after the firestorm, with the world around her desolate, mirroring just what she felt inside. All she saw for months and months were shadowy tones with a black edge, as if she'd gone color-blind. The air was filled with gray ash that found its way onto every clean surface and into every crevice. Like an endless winter, the lifeless sky reflected a blanket of dingy snow that covered the ground. There was so little Haru could do, and so little hope left. She knew it was exactly what grief looked like.

Still, every day after the firestorm Haru went outside, a scarf covering her face and mouth, her hands bandaged, hoping the world might have returned to the way it was. In her mind, she played I See, a game she and Aki had played as small children. *I see a cat . . .* , she began, which was followed by Aki's *I see a cat with black, black eyes . . . I see a cat with black, black eyes and a long, bushy broom tail . . . I see a cat with black, black eyes and a long, bushy broom tail that sweeps the floor . . .* It went on and on until Aki couldn't remember any more and became silly, or gave up, her attention already focused on something else.

Haru looked at the devastation around her. *I see a world covered in gray ash. I see a world covered in gray ash with flecks of white bone. I see a world covered in gray ash with flecks of white bone of all those who will never rise again . . .* She walked around the sumo stable seeking signs of life, thinking in her twelve-year-old mind that not until she found it would she believe things could return to normal.

Several weeks after the firestorm, in April, she spied a thin green stem between two cracks in the courtyard pushing its way up toward the light, a tiny speck of color in an otherwise sullen world. Stabbed by the surprise at her discovery, she felt a fragile connection to the green speck — if a living plant could rise from the ashes, then her hands would heal, Aki would be okay again, and their father would rebuild his sumo stable. It wouldn't ease the grief of losing her mother, but it seemed like a promise that life would continue. It was all Haru needed; a thin thread of hope that filled her with joy.

THE INVITATION

Since the occupation, all sumo tournaments had been canceled, but when the weather warmed and the May days grew brighter, Hiroshi received a note from Tanaka-oyakata inviting him to the Katsuyama-beya. Hiroshi and his *ojichan* tried to keep track of the sumo news that trickled out to the public through the radio or neighborhood gossip. Grand Champion, Yokozuna Futabayama had officially retired in 1945. Hiroshi's grandfather shook his head angrily when the Kokugikan, the national sumo stadium, was taken over by foreign troops and renamed "Memorial Hall." Its offices were now used for administrative personnel and the arena turned into an ice-skating rink.

Hiroshi reasoned the invitation was the *oyakata*'s way of thanking him for finding his wife's body after the firestorm. Still, he was excited to see the stable. He tossed and turned all night and awoke late to a faint hum of voices rising from the kitchen. He unfolded the dark blue raw silk kimono that had once belonged to his father and fingered the three white wood sorrel crests. His *obachan* had given it to him to wear on special occasions. At nineteen, Hiroshi had finally grown into the kimono. It was still loose around the stomach, but it now fit his shoulders and its length was right.

"Are you going to try out for sumo wearing that?" Kenji joked when he stepped into the kitchen.

Hiroshi ignored him.

"You've grown so tall, Hiro-chan," his grandmother fussed, pulling at the kimono and tightening the sash.

"I knew he would be," his *ojichan* added.

His *obachan* laughed. "Even when you could see, you never paid attention."

"Only to you," his grandfather said, smiling.

Hiroshi laughed, too, said his goodbyes, and slid open the front door. Outside, he could still hear his grandparents' teasing voices.

It had been more than a year since the dark day that Hiroshi first visited the Katsuyama-beya. Now, as he approached the sumo stable, he felt a knot tighten in the middle of his stomach, a reminder of the sadness he had carried with him through the gate the last time. When the smoke from the firestorm had finally cleared, people seemed to hold their breath in stunned silence as Japan surrendered. Then little by little, life found a way back. The first signs came when the birds returned, circling tentatively before landing on the charred remains of buildings or tree stumps. Every morning Hiroshi listened for their singing and squawking before he allowed himself to believe that things might one day be all right.

As he passed through the gate of the sumo stable, Hiroshi was astonished at the transformation. Signs of life were everywhere. Leaves had sprouted from branches, birds whistled through the air, and the skeletal frame of a new building was up, reminding him that this was once the sumo stable where Yokozuna Kitoyama trained to become grand champion. Hiroshi paused to catch his breath and tightened his sash, wishing his *ojichan* were there with him.

"Are you here to see my father?"

Hiroshi turned around. He knew this young girl. She was with Tanaka-oyakata the last time he was there. Only now she was taller and her hands were free of bandages. At twelve or thirteen she also seemed more self-assured. Next to her a younger girl stood quietly by, with strikingly beautiful iridescent black eyes. Both girls were dressed in light blue cotton *yukata* kimonos.

Hiroshi bowed. "*Hai,* I've come to see Tanaka-oyakata."

The older girl shifted from foot to foot, eyeing him closely as if just recognizing him, her hands tucked in the folds of her kimono. "You were here before," she began, but then looked at the younger girl and stopped.

"Hai," he said. "A long time ago."

The girl appeared thankful he didn't say more. She paused and then pointed toward the wooden building across the courtyard. "You'll find my father upstairs in his office."

"Domo arigato gozaimazu." He bowed low, then straightened and added, "My name is Hiroshi Matsumoto."

A faint smiled crossed the girl's lips. She looked up at him. "I'm Haru Tanaka and this is my sister, Aki."

Aki bowed but remained silent, her eyes darting up at him again.

"You'd better go," Haru added before he could say anything else. "My father doesn't like it when his *rikishi* are late."

Hiroshi smiled to himself. She thought he was a sumo wrestler. He bowed once more. When he reached the building, he glanced back to where they stood, still watching him. Haru already poised and graceful, older than her years, while Aki was the most beautiful little girl he'd ever seen; he could already see her resemblance to her mother.

Hiroshi pulled open the wide wooden door and stepped into the cool darkness of the building, inhaling the smell of smoke and earth. He felt a soft dirt floor underfoot, looked up at the row of narrow shoji windows above the wood-paneled walls. Pale streams of light fell on the white outlines of the *dohyo* in the center of the large, open room. This was the *keikoba*, he thought. To one side of the practice area was a tatami platform where viewers came to watch practice. He walked carefully around the *dohyo*, behind which wooden stairs led to the second floor.

Tanaka-oyakata sat at his desk in the small, warm office. The door was open and Hiroshi was surprised to see he had shaved his head, which made him look just a bit more intimidating. His whole presence seemed to fill the room.

Tanaka-oyakata looked up and stood, greeting him with warmth. "Matsumoto-san, I'm happy you could make it."

Hiroshi bowed. "Thank you for your invitation."

"Please sit." Tanaka sat back down in his chair and cleared his throat. "I hope all is well with you and your grandparents?"

"Very well." Hiroshi was surprised the *oyakata* remembered he lived with his grandparents.

"Ah good." Tanaka lined up a stack of papers on his desk. "Let me tell you why I asked you here. During the past year, my greatest hope has been to rebuild Katsuyama-beya again. As you can see, we're proceeding slowly. About half a dozen of my old *rikishi* have returned since the occupation. They're helping me to rebuild with what little we have. We've also begun training again on a regular basis."

Hiroshi sat up straight, his fingers numb from gripping the arms of the chair, his heart racing at what this might mean. He heard footsteps on the stairs and saw Haru carrying a tray with tea. She poured a cup for her father and one for Hiroshi, glanced in his direction, and left without a word.

"How can I help you?" Hiroshi asked.

"I have seen the way you move, Matsumoto-san," Tanaka said, his voice low and calm. He sipped his tea. "It was disappointing that you weren't able to join the stable before the war when you were a boy. So, I'm asking you now, as a young man, if you still feel you have what it takes to be a *sumotori?*"

At nineteen, Hiroshi hadn't yet thought of himself as a man. Men were Tanaka-sama, or his *ojichan,* or his father standing tall and determined in the black-and-white photo in the receiving room. But there was never a moment when he hadn't dreamt of being a *sumotori.* He stood and bowed to Tanaka-oyakata. Without hesitation, he answered, *"Hai."*

THE SCHOLAR

Kenji dreamed of the masks once more. The war had nearly deadened his need for them, but when the surrender came, his imagination returned full-blown. He walked down the alleyway on his way back from school, the June sun pressing warmly against his back. Everything around him was a reminder of the masks — the curve along the table became the jaw of a *Kinuta* mask; the shape of the moon, a *Ko-omote* mask; a caterpillar, the brows of the *Warai-jo* mask. Nothing escaped his wonder and longing for their faces. And with the masks, his thoughts returned to his sensei. Kenji wondered where Akira Yoshiwara was, or if he was still alive. He turned down another alleyway, tracing the steps he had taken almost every afternoon for three years to the mask shop. The war *had* changed him. Before, he would have assumed his sensei was alive, but now he presumed him dead. At seventeen, Kenji sometimes found it easier just to accept the inevitable.

Kenji stopped in front of the vacant mask shop and looked into the window, but through layers of grime, he saw no sign of the colorful masks that had drawn him here so many years ago. During the bombings, as he sat in the dark, dank air-raid shelter fighting his fear of being buried alive, all that kept him calm was his vision of the masks.

Even now, the memory of that dirt hole made him shudder. The humid air was thick and stale with their labored breath as planes rumbled overhead. He tried not to breathe in too much air so his grandparents and Hiroshi would have enough. He had so much to say to them but didn't speak — no one did — for the lungful of air it would cost them. Instead, Kenji closed his eyes and focused on the Egyptian death masks worn by pharaohs he'd read about, made of gold and embedded with priceless jewels, the high, straight nose, the closed lids so serene and beautiful in death. Would there be anyone left to make such a mask for him?

Kenji wiped the window with the palm of his hand. The pane he had shattered with the rock had been boarded over. He peered into the deserted room and saw the rock still lying on the floor. He used to imagine he'd go back one day and Yoshiwara-sensei would be at work on a mask as if nothing had happened. Yet, every month since the war ended, he returned to find it was all a foolish dream.

Kenji was finishing his last year in high school. When classes began again in early 1946, he was happy to return to his old life as a student. He studied hard, and to his surprise, he scored the best in his class at the end of the year and won an academic citation that brought his grandparents great happiness. His *ojichan* took to calling him *gakusha,* the scholar, which made Kenji uneasy. He knew his grandparents always wanted him and Hiroshi to have good educations, but now that his brother was training to be a *sumotori,* it was up to Kenji to finish school. He swallowed his dreams of carving masks and tried to live up to the title of *gakusha.*

Yet while Kenji focused his energies on his studies, the masks still haunted his dreams. Even if he should venture to open his own mask shop after graduating from school, could he possibly make a living? No matter how he tried to justify giving up college for becoming an artisan, he couldn't.

Kenji turned away from the mask shop and hurried back down the crowded alleyway. He knew his *obachan* worried if he wasn't home by dinner. Now, as Japan stumbled, then crawled and learned to walk again under the Allied occupation, Kenji also had to find his way. Ever since Hiroshi had moved to the Katsuyama-beya, Kenji missed his brother more than he could say, but he knew his grandparents were delighted. Proud. Everyone was proud of Hiroshi, and so was he. That was the way it had always been, but every once in a while, Kenji felt something in the back of his throat, the bitter taste of jealousy. He hated himself for it, knowing he would never love anyone as much as he did

Hiroshi. Yet he couldn't help but wonder why life always fell into place for his brother, while everything was such a struggle for him. Since they were boys, Hiroshi was always the hero, Kenji the ghost.

But every night since April, when Hiroshi had packed and moved to the Katsuyama-beya, Kenji would close his shoji window and turn back to stare at the six-tatami-mat room he had shared with his brother all his life. While it had always felt too small for both of them, it now seemed cavernous without Hiroshi. Kenji looked at the empty space next to his futon and wished his brother, his strongest connection to the parents he would never know, were still sleeping beside him.

Kenji hurried past old Sakahara-san's tobacco store, another tragedy of the war. When tobacco became scarce, Sakahara closed the store, boarded it up, and told his friends he was going to live with his daughter. Weeks later, when a foul odor began to seep from the building, authorities broke in, only to find Sakahara's decaying body. He'd chosen to stay and die of starvation rather than leave his store and impose a burden on his child.

Kenji turned the corner and stopped walking at the sudden sound of a familiar voice. Like a bad memory it returned, brash and boisterous and cruel, the same voice that had coerced their neighborhood out of prized personal possessions for the good of the nation. For Okata's own good, Kenji knew. He paused outside Fujiwa's store and listened. Just inside, he saw Okata, the bastard puppet for the *kempeitai,* trying to trade something for a bottle of sake. Kenji waited for Okata to emerge, and saw that he looked old and disheveled as he moved unsteadily down the alleyway carrying a bottle of sake. Kenji followed him, uncertain of what he was doing. Okata shuffled down a quiet street and then another that came to a dead end as he turned abruptly to face him.

"You, boy! Why are you following me?"

Kenji was taken by such surprise he could hardly get words out. He mumbled something about his *obachan*'s wedding ring, about wanting it back. Okata laughed, said it was freely donated for the good of the nation. It was long gone. He spat a glob of phlegm near Kenji's foot.

"There, you can have that!"

For the first time in his life, Kenji lunged without thinking. His fist connected with Okata's cheekbone, snapping his head sideways, and his ragged body followed as he hit the ground hard. The bottle shattered. Kenji turned and walked away, his hand throbbing. He didn't look back.

All year, Fumiko had written letters to the address Ayako left with her, hoping for news. She appealed to both the Japanese and American authorities for information every month, but to no avail.

On the first anniversary of the Hiroshima bombing, she woke up with heaviness in her chest and remained quiet and sullen all morning. Everything irritated her, from Yoshio's humming to Kenji's reading aloud to his grandfather. "Take your voices outside," she snapped, throwing her dish towel on the table.

When she had returned home angry and frustrated, after standing in the long food lines, Yoshio quietly said to her, "Fumi-chan, you have to let Ayako-san go now."

Fumiko began to cry. They sat at the kitchen table and suddenly she couldn't stop. The last time Fumiko had cried so hard was at the deaths of her daughter and son-in-law, Misako and Kazuo. She looked up. Yoshio was looking directly at her, even if he couldn't see her.

"What if she isn't dead?" she mumbled through tears.

"Then she will find you," he answered.

"What if she can't?" Fumiko asked. She was being childish, but she couldn't let Ayako go without a fight.

Yoshio remained silent for a moment. The warm August afternoon was thick and still. Then in a voice gentle and measured, he answered, "If Ayako is gone, perhaps it's part of your *unmei,* the fate you've always trusted in, and now you must obey it. I have no doubts you'll see each other again in the other world."

Fumiko paused. She was the one who believed in the randomness of destiny, who believed it was something no one could control or change. She'd stood by this belief for a good part of her adult life and imparted it to her grandsons. When Yoshio teased her about it, saying Fumiko could control her own fate if she wanted, she shook her head and pretended not to hear him. How could she tell him that she feared the unpredictability of life; that after Misako's death, there was no such thing as control? From that moment on, Fumiko couldn't help but wonder what lurked around the corner. And now Yoshio, who always sought to balance her vision, was acquiescing to her.

Yoshio remained silent as she cried. When she finally stopped and took a deep breath, her entire body shuddered. She sat very still for a moment until she realized that the current that had pulsated through her body for the past year had ceased. Though tired, she felt strangely at peace. She wiped away her tears and blew her nose. How frightful she must look. For once, Fumiko was grateful Yoshio couldn't see her. She leaned closer to where he sat by the window. He liked to feel the wind against his face, as if it somehow freed him from the darkness. His was the face she had loved for forty years, now so thin and tired. She reached for his warm, wrinkled hand and kissed it, and then held it against her beating heart.

During the week of Obon, Fumiko wrote her friend one last letter. *"Dear Ayako,"* she began, *"if you were here . . ."* But she didn't mail it.

HIDE-AND-SEEK

In the waning light of October, with the war over for more than a year, Akira Yoshiwara chopped the last of the wood and stacked it by the barn, then slipped a slim package of pencils into a space between two of the lower logs. He picked up a log and weighed it in his hands. Too heavy and coarse for a mask. The Japanese cypress he needed was light and smooth; the masks he made from it fitted each actor like another layer of skin. It seemed a lifetime since he'd shaped one, and he missed the masks as he might miss a lover, his fingers defining the slowly emerging features.

Akira dropped the log on the pile, rubbed his calloused hands together, and walked back up toward the house. He knocked lightly on the door and stepped out of his sandals. It had become a ritual each evening, after he finished chopping wood or patching the roof, to savor a cup of green tea by Emiko's fire before returning to his room in the village. Grateful for her welcome, Akira would sip from his cup and feel the ache of the day's work in his shoulders. Each night Kiyo would rattle on happily as he and Emiko sat by the fire, listening to a trapped cricket as darkness fell, the anxious scraping of its thread-thin legs somewhere in the house. He watched the dancing shadows of the fire against the walls and when he looked up at the soaring roof, he no longer saw praying hands but empty ones. Still, for the first time in his life, he felt something close to peace.

Now, he heard Kiyo sliding the door open and bounding out of the back room.

"Can I look now?" she asked. Her face glowed pale white in the deepening dusk.

Akira smiled and nodded. "Somewhere over there." He pointed toward the woodpile he'd just stacked.

She bolted past him down toward the barn. Akira stepped into the house and Emiko greeted him with a bow.

"You'll spoil her," she said, not with anger but gratitude.

"Pencils for her schoolwork," he said.

They'd begun this game of hide-and-seek

with small gifts during the summer. He hid a box of rice candy in the hollow of a tree and it took her all morning to find it. The following weeks, she found a small lacquer box, a hair clip, a pair of chopsticks, and a cat charm he'd bought down in Oyama. Kiyo lit up at each small present, and he wondered just how many gifts she'd received during her childhood.

"The tea is ready," Emiko said.

He followed her into the open room and they sat by the hearth sipping their tea in silent comfort until they heard Kiyo's high squeal of delight, which brought a smile to both their lips.

THE KATSUYAMA-BEYA

Since moving to the Katsuyama-beya, nineteen-year-old Hiroshi had learned how to live his life all over again. Every morning before the sun rose, Hiroshi was shaken awake by the young wrestler Fukuda. He pushed his friend's hand away. "Don't bother me," he growled, and turned over on his futon.

"It's time to get up, Matsumoto-san. If you want to reach the rank of *yokozuna,* you must sacrifice all, including sleep!" Fukuda whispered, repeating the words Tanaka-oyakata drilled into them every morning during practice.

As a lower-ranked wrestler in the Jonokuchi Division, Hiroshi rose at four-thirty every morning in the makeshift dormitory-style room, careful not to wake the others. The outside world seemed very far away as he heeded the rules and training schedule of Tanaka-oyakata. Due to their low rankings, he and Fukuda were assigned the most menial jobs. It was up to them to turn on the lights, get the towels, put the salt and the power water in place, and check the *dohyo* before the other *sumotori* entered the practice area each morning.

Hiroshi groaned and turned back to face his friend. "A moment longer." He closed his eyes again and felt more tired than ever in his life. If he were at home, he'd still be asleep next to his brother, awakening hours later to the soft murmurs of his *ojichan*'s and *obachan*'s voices floating up from the kitchen. They were more reliable than any clock. Sharing a room with Kenji alone seemed a luxury now, and moments of quiet to think about his family were few and fleeting.

"Now!" Fukuda pulled at him. Fukuda was only sixteen, but already big for his age, weighing close to two hundred pounds. He was the only *rikishi* at the stable who was lower ranked than Hiroshi.

As they hurriedly dressed in the chilly morning air, Hiroshi helped Fukuda tighten his heavy black *mawashi* belt. Weighing ten pounds and measuring thirty feet long, it required a complicated process of winding and tightening the two-foot-wide canvas strip around his waist and between his legs. Hiroshi directed him step by step, and, as usual, Fukuda expressed gratitude for his guidance. At the stable, there seemed no place for sentiment or any other comfort.

It had taken Hiroshi several weeks not to feel self-conscious training among the other *rikishi,* huge men in their *mawashi* belts who pushed their bodies to the limit. Now, he moved through the daily routine without thinking. By five every morning the practice area was crowded with movement. "Faster, faster!" He heard the bamboo switch smack against the palm of the upper-ranked wrestler in charge. Hiroshi's heart pounded as he began the day with routine exercises, performing hundreds of *shiko,* alternately lifting his legs as high as possible and stomping on the ground. The leg lifts were followed by the *suriashi,* starting from a crouched position and jumping with both feet together, pushing out his arms while staying low to the ground. Next were the *matawari,* or thigh splits, and the *teppo,* a striking exercise for the arms and shoulders against a tall wooden pole, in which he slapped it with the open palms of his hands. Grunts and dull thuds filled the breathless, humid air. He watched Fukuda struggle through each set.

The first few weeks Hiroshi's feet were blistered and every muscle in his body ached as he silently endured the daily regimen. Some evenings he could barely lift his arms, yet he pushed through the pain the next morning. After their morning exercises came hours of wrestling without a break. It was followed by more leg-strengthening exercises. As the months passed, Hiroshi's sore muscles hardened and became accustomed to the strenuous regimen, while each move felt increasingly natural and vital.

After hours of morning exercises and practice, there were challenge matches among all the *sumotori* — the only time a lower-ranked wrestler like Hiroshi or Fukuda could fight a higher-ranked one. There was only one *sekitori,* an upper-ranked wrestler who had reached the *sekiwake* level, the third-highest rank in the top Professional Division. Daishima had trained with Tanaka before the war. He was the *heyagashira,* the highest-ranked wrestler in the stable. He was a big man, heavy in the stomach, with thighs larger than Hiroshi had ever seen. He obviously enjoyed his authority, speaking only to those he liked and ignoring all the rest.

Still, Hiroshi felt unprepared when Tanaka-oyakata called out his name to step onto the *dohyo* in a practice round against Sekiwake Daishima. He didn't think he was ready.

Fukuda pushed him forward. Hiroshi felt his empty stomach burning as the entire stable gathered around the *dohyo,* along with Tanaka, who watched intently as Hiroshi was knocked flat during the first charge. It happened so quickly, he felt as if he'd been run over by a steam engine; a half-gasp of air caught in his throat as he hit the *dohyo* hard. By the time he picked himself up off the ground, streaks of dirt across his back where he'd fallen, Tanaka had already turned away. Hiroshi bowed and stumbled out of the ring. Brushing himself off, he noted the bored look on Daishima's face as yet another young wrestler took his place.

After morning practice, Hiroshi and Fukuda's real work of the day began. They were also *tsukebito,* apprentices assigned to assist Sekiwake Daishima. In hierarchical order, each lower-ranked wrestler was also responsible for cooking, cleaning the practice room, doing all the laundry, scrubbing the backs and washing the hair of all the higher-ranked wrestlers. By noon, while the other wrestlers ate and bathed, Hiroshi and Fukuda stayed to clean up the training area. The towels were covered with dirt from the *dohyo,* the air thick with the musty stink of earth and sweat. Hiroshi was starving, having eaten nothing since the night before. He felt a gnawing in the pit of his stomach, though it was a different kind of hunger than he'd experienced during the war. Whereas bitterness lined his stomach then, now it was a raw need that burned within him, a need to do his best, to be the best. While food gave Hiroshi the sustenance to train, Fukuda never had enough to eat. Good-natured and with a sweet disposition, he came from a school in the countryside, where Tanaka had recruited him earlier in the year. Hiroshi wondered if Fukuda had the right temperament to be a *sumotori.* Most of the wrestlers grew stronger and harder with each fight, planning and calculating what might bring down their opponent the next time in the ring. Not Fukuda. While he had the size and bulk, there was something inherently gentle about him.

There was little time to waste. After cleaning up the practice room, Hiroshi had to give the demanding, difficult Sekiwake Daishima a massage and wash his hair. Then the highest-ranked *sumotori* would enjoy a long, hot soak, while all the other wrestlers waited their turns. Hiroshi swept quickly and watered down the *dohyo,* threw salt into the ring to purify it, and placed a Shinto *gohei,* a wooden stick with white paper folded around it, upright in the ring to mark the area as sacred.

Daishima was waiting for Hiroshi in the soaking room. The warm, damp air let him know the coals had been lit and the water was hot and ready for soaking. The *sekiwake* sat on a low wooden stool and poured cold water from a bucket over his head. He turned and grunted when he heard Hiroshi approach, which always signaled he wasn't in a talkative mood.

"Sekiwake Daishima, I'm sorry to be late." Hiroshi bowed, then opened and closed his hands, stretching his fingers so they wouldn't be tired after kneading Daishima's thick shoulders and his bear of a back.

Daishima grunted again, lowered his head and leaned forward for his massage. Hiroshi began kneading his thick neck, working his fingers to loosen the tight muscles. Fukuda had been chastised repeatedly for not giving Daishima an adequate massage. The entire stable heard him dismissing Fukuda for a fool. From then on, Hiroshi had taken on the task, while Fukuda transported the *chanko* from the main house to the stable for their first meal of the day. He felt the *sekiwake*'s neck muscles relax as his fingers squeezed harder, dug deeper.

"It's understandable that you're late," Daishima retorted, his booming voice filling the humid room. "Of course it would take you longer to get up off the *dohyo* this morning after our match."

"*Hai,*" Hiroshi answered. He'd learned quickly to always agree with whatever

275

Daishima said.

The *sekiwake* laughed and swung a wet towel over his head. "To the left," he directed.

Hiroshi shifted his attention to the left side of his neck. The stable was too small to butt heads with the highest-ranked *sumotori.* He would bide his time, doing what was expected of him as he climbed the ranks. It was the sumo way, one of honor and hard work. Most important, he wanted to restore hope to his country and countrymen, much as Yokozuna Futabayama had done during the war. Not until Futabayama retired was his secret revealed to the public: he was blind in one eye. It didn't matter if it would be hours before Hiroshi could eat and lower his own tired body into the lukewarm water of the soaking tub, too exhausted to bother with heating the coals, even if there were any left.

Superstition

Akira Yoshiwara spent the coldest weeks of his second winter in the village of Aio snowed in, cocooned in blankets and huddled in his room writing and drawing, while Nazo paced back and forth, jumping up on the wood table, his cat eyes narrowing at the falling snow, which meant another afternoon in captivity. He glanced about the room before he settled down to licking his paws.

Through the window Akira saw nothing but

a blinding whiteness that hurt his eyes. All thoughts of walking the mile up the mountain road amid the storm that morning were quickly surrendered. The mountains could be harsh and temperamental. He thought of Emiko and Kiyo, the mother's measured words balancing the daughter's endless chatter, and admitted to himself that he missed their company, their voices, both soft and boisterous, and the warmth of other bodies near his.

Akira threw off his blankets and reached under his cot for his set of chisels, turning each one over in his hands, sharp and clean to the touch. Once a week he used a rag and oil to make sure they remained in perfect condition. He had avoided finishing his last mask, afraid that, if and when he did finish it, it would be the end of his mask-making life. He smiled and shook his head at his own superstition. He would carve hundreds of masks in his lifetime, and, should he decide to grow old in Aio, he'd have blocks of Japanese cypress sent to him. He looked through his bag, finding the unfinished *Okina* mask, unwrapped it, and slowly, carefully, began guiding the fine blade against the soft, smooth wood. When he next looked up, it was dark outside, glints of white snow still falling against the window.

As the winter cold seeped into the drafty *heya,* the *rikishi* shivered through morning practice, stretching and working through colds and fevers, their bodies moving in quick, jerking movements to keep warm. Hiroshi was grateful his hair had grown long enough to cover his ears, and when it grew to touch his chin both in front and back, Tanaka-oyakata asked a *tokoyama,* the stable's hairdresser, to come in and style his hair into a *chonmage,* a *sumotori*'s identifying topknot.

The *tokoyama,* a short, stocky man named Tokohashi, gave a quick, loud laugh. He was a friend of Tanaka-oyakata's and the longtime hairdresser for the stable. Like other *sumotori* hairdressers, he told Hiroshi, the first part of his name came from his adopted profession, but "hashi" came from his own family name. As he talked, Tokohashi laid out his assorted picks and combs and a tin of *bintsuke* wax on a dark piece of cloth with a peony pattern on the edge. He combed through the knots in Hiroshi's hair without restraint, ripping through it in quick jerking movements, bringing tears to his eyes, until the wooden comb sailed through his hair with ease. Then Tokohashi pulled it tautly upward before applying the *bintsuke,* a special wax derived from soybean, to stiffen and keep his hair in place. Hiroshi felt the sharp pull along his hairline and at the base of his neck. For a moment, he wondered if the hairdresser's sole job was to inflict pain. Tokohashi tied his long hair securely at two different sections with white strings. The sweet, flowery smell of the *bintsuke* was intoxicating.

"I'm warning you, Hiroshi-san, many think the scent of *bintsuke* is an aphrodisiac. The young women will never leave you alone again!" Tokohashi teased. He leaned back to make sure there were no stray hairs sticking out.

Tanaka-oyakata laughed. "I'm afraid, Hiroshi, it's the fate of all *sumotori*."

"You should have seen all the women Tanaka-sama had to fight off," Tokohashi added.

"Yes, but it was Noriko-san who saved me," Tanaka said. Her name hovered in the air for a moment.

"*Hai,* Noriko-san." Tokohashi lowered his head. "The Sakura was —"

"One of the finest teahouses," Tanaka finished.

"Noriko-san —"

"Was the most beautiful . . ."

"*Hai.*"

Hiroshi listened as they reminisced in abbreviated sentences, the way friends of many years often do. He immediately liked Tokohashi for his humor and candor. The two men paused in a moment of silence, giving respect

279

to Noriko-san's memory. Hiroshi glanced up at his stable master's cleanly shaven head, so like the monks he saw moving quietly through the Buddhist temples, a stillness emanating from within each one of them.

When Tokohashi was finished with his topknot, Hiroshi sat perfectly still and gazed into a mirror. His hair was pulled tightly back, folded back and over again, lying smooth and flat against the top of his head, just as samurai had worn their hair. His pulse quickened with pride. Without a word, it told everyone that Hiroshi Matsumoto was a *sumotori*. And for the first time, he felt like one.

12
A NEW WORLD
1947

Two years after the surrender, Fumiko watched Japan slowly waking to a new world. Shops began to reopen, food became more abundant, the rhythms of daily life returned to an almost normal pace. At moments, it felt like old times with the sweet smell of *sembei* crackers and incense wafting through the air as she walked past the Kyo-ou-ji temple on her way home.

So it was still a surprise for Fumiko one afternoon, when she looked up to see a *pan-pan* girl rushing down the alleyway toward her wearing dark glasses, Western clothing, and high heels, a cigarette burning between her fingers. All at once, she was reminded of just how much had changed. She felt her blood rise, the beat of her heart against her chest. On occasion, she'd seen these young women from a distance, gathered in twos or threes like a flutter of birds on the streets. She'd heard how they entertained soldiers, these "women of the night." But now it was broad daylight. She imagined how Yoshio would make that clicking sound with his tongue and tell Fumiko to remember that everyone had his or her own story. It was not for her to make judgments.

The clacking of the young woman's heels grew louder as she approached. Fumiko tried to avoid looking, but the bright red lipstick and nail polish drew her gaze. In an instant she spied something familiar in the woman's face that all her garish makeup and sweet perfume couldn't disguise. The *panpan* girl who passed by without so much as a fleeting glance was her neighbor Okata's oldest daughter, Junko-san. Fumiko touched her empty ring finger. Although Okata had been despicable as the head of their neighborhood association and had taken advantage of so many in the name of the *kempeitai,* Junko had always been a sweet, quiet girl who loved to read and studied hard. But a year after the surrender, rumors spread that Okata had fallen down while drunk, hit his head, and was never the same again. Fumiko knew he and his family were simply casualties of the war. She turned to watch Junko disappear down the alley, her hips swaying in her tight dress. Fumiko cringed with the knowledge that so many decent young women like Junko were reduced to this in order to survive.

It was the younger generation Fumiko worried about most. She breathed in deeply and exhaled slowly, terrified to think she could lose her own grandsons to this new world. Hadn't they already been lost once as babies, when their parents died? She remembered how her heart had raced with the responsibilities of raising two baby boys. She hadn't thought much about the difficulties they'd face as young men. So many young people were drifting away after Japan's defeat, wandering in the darkness and despair of surrender and occupation. They fed on escapism and decadence. Fumiko heard through neighborhood rumors that many pursuits weren't healthy, the drinking and drugs, the strip clubs, the aimless suicides. These restless young people called themselves the *kasutori* culture, after some kind of alcohol they drank. Fumiko sighed, relieved that Yoshio couldn't see what Japan had become.

Fortunately, Hiroshi had settled into his life as a *rikishi* apprentice. He had dinner with them at least once a month, and she smiled to recall how tall and strong he'd become. When he complained of the long hours and hard work, Yoshio was quick with an answer. "Do you think a champion is made out of thin air? It's through the hardships you endure that you'll gain real strength."

They were no less proud of Kenji the scholar, as Yoshio called him, who had been accepted into Tokyo University. Yoshio was thrilled that Kenji was studying architecture, though Fumiko was fully aware he had chosen it for their sake, not his own. She knew he'd have been much happier spending his life carving Noh masks, lost in the magical world of the theater. Still, it wouldn't harm Kenji to be an artisan with an education. For Yoshio and her, the past was past; the future belonged to their grandsons.

THE *RIKISHI*

Hiroshi helped Fukuda put the last of the equipment away, and then swept the practice room while his young friend gathered the rest of the towels. While Fukuda chattered on about what kind of stew they would be having for lunch later, Hiroshi still felt Tanaka-oyakata's impatience at practice that morning, his sharp, terse scolding that cut through the thick air of the room. "No, no, no, keep your knees bent!" he had yelled at Hiroshi. Even Daishima had kept a low profile.

The first postwar professional sumo match was held in the gardens at the Meiji Shrine in western Tokyo. Hiroshi had easily won his matches, though it felt no different from the practice rounds he'd been doing for the past year. The wrestlers were novices and young. The next major tournament of the year, the September *honbasho,* would take place in a few months' time. It was an important one for several of the young wrestlers, including

Hiroshi. If he fought well, he would be in line to advance to the next level, the Jonidan Division. But this particular tournament carried another kind of pressure: Hiroshi would be wrestling a young sumo named Kobayashi from the nearby Musashigawa-beya. As Tanaka-oyakata drummed into him during practice, Kobayashi was an up-and-coming wrestler who shared many of Hiroshi's distinctions: the same upper-body strength and the ability to move quickly. A wrestler of such caliber would test Hiroshi's skills and they would both be watched closely. Tanaka had barely paid attention to earlier matches, confident his *sumotori* would win. This time, Hiroshi felt his *oyakata*'s anxiety, tied to his own hopes of raising his ranking and making Tanaka-sama proud.

"What do you think?" Fukuda's voice interrupted his thoughts. As always, his conversation each morning was centered on food. "What kind of *chanko* do you think Haru-san has made today?" he asked again. He hadn't suffered as much from the severe food shortages during the war as everyone else had because his father was a farmer who had hidden away some of his rice crop when the war began. Every year, he stored away the same amount so the military wouldn't be suspicious. It was his hope that his son could stay healthy and strong and become a *sumotori*.

Until there were enough *sumotori* at the stable to do all the chores, Tanaka's older daughter, Haru, prepared some of the food. She was fifteen, very pretty, and already accomplished at the things her mother would have done as *okamisan* of the stable. After she cooked the *chanko* in the main house, Hiroshi or Fukuda would carry it over to the stable. Hiroshi would never forget the first time he'd seen Haru and her bandaged hands. Although she seemed fine now, she still hid her hands in the folds of her kimono or the pockets of her jacket. She always seemed shy around him.

"I think Haru-san's making you a special *Mizutaki chankonabe,* with lots of fresh fish and tofu, onions, cabbage, shoyu, sugar, and plenty of sake," Hiroshi teased, shaking away the morning's practice. Food was still scarce during the occupation and *Mizutaki* was Fukuda's favorite. Hiroshi remembered playing the same game with Kenji during the war when there was so little to eat that they filled their stomachs with talk and dreams.

"*Mitzutaki chankonabe* over steaming bowls of rice," Fukuda added, rubbing his round stomach.

Hiroshi threw a dirty towel at him and laughed. "You need to finish all the laundry first."

Haru chopped the last of the turnips and threw them into the *chanko*. Even in the heat of summer, she liked cooking for her father's wrestlers. And though it was only temporary, just during the school break until classes began again, it gave her something to do each day. She had volunteered for the job when the young wrestler who had done the cooking suddenly decided last month that the rigorous training and difficult life of a sumo weren't for him. Haru stepped in before her father assigned cooking duty to either Fukuda or Hiroshi, who both already had enough to do.

Haru looked down at her hands. The skin on her fingers and palms had thickened as they healed, and now the only sign of a scar was just below the thumb on her left hand, where the soft pad of skin and flesh puckered to a small rise. She couldn't help touching it with her other fingers. It was the only telltale sign of the fire, and barely noticeable if you didn't look closely, which only Haru did. She opened and closed her hands, felt the skin pull tight. She had to look hard to find the lines on the palms of her hands that should tell whether she had long life, good health, love, or fortune in her future. Sometimes she wondered if this meant her very life would be forever shrouded and obscure, unreadable by even the best of fortune-tellers.

At times, Haru still felt a sharp burning in her palms and the tips of her fingers, and suddenly the three years disappeared and she was twelve years old again, hooking her arm through Aki's as they ran and ran, their eyes stinging, lungs burning, running through the thick, acrid smoke back to the stable, running fast so that her little sister wouldn't see the burned bodies writhing in agony, pleading for water. Haru dragged Aki along, heavy as an anchor. All the while, the burns on her hands were so painful she could barely stand it.

When they finally reached the sumo stable, Haru slumped onto the step at the front gate, her raw hands raised as if she were begging. Yellow pus oozed from the burned flesh, caked with mud where she had soothed them in the dirt of the trench all night. Aki ran back and forth, trying to find something that might comfort her, water or a blanket. The fire had consumed part of her father's sumo stable, though the house and the building that housed the *keikoba* still stood.

"It's my fault, it's my fault," Aki repeated over and over, touching her singed hair, the raw patch on the back of her head.

Haru shook her head, her words stopped by unbearable pain, thinking, *How could this war be your fault?* But she didn't have the strength even to whisper the words.

When the smoke had cleared, Haru heard her sister cry out, *"Otosan!"* and run to him as he appeared through the wall of smoke. Haru looked up but she couldn't stand. So she waited, palms throbbing, and watched as her father, covered in black filth, picked Aki up and held her tight. Then he saw Haru and knelt down in front of her, his eyes like two bright stars in the dark night. "Haru-chan," he whispered, pulling her close. At last, Haru allowed herself to cry.

It took months for her hands to heal from infections, first on one finger and then another. By the time the bandages were removed, most of the nerves had been affected, leaving her hands numb. Since then, Haru had felt distant from everything in her life, with the exception of her father and Aki. The fire dulled her vision, too. Nothing would ever be as hot and bright again. Even though Haru excelled in her studies, she didn't really feel connected to the pencil that touched the paper.

Haru looked up when she heard Aki sliding the door open to let Fukuda in. She smiled to think how much food the *rikishi* consumed in one sitting: the *chankonabe,* which was a mainstay stew made from a variety of ingredients, as well as the many bowls of rice, the beer, the tea. Before the war and occupation, her mother had shopped with the wrestler on *chanko* duty, stopping at one market after another. Now, Haru went by herself or with Aki, buying whatever was most reasonably priced, mostly root vegetables and an occasional piece of salted fish. In earlier, more prosperous days, the stew pot was filled with generous pieces of beef, chicken, or pork; squid, crab, or shrimp. There would also be side plates of pickled vegetables, fried fish or chicken, *sashimi,* sweet potatoes, and salad. Today, however, they would have a broth instead of a stew.

Haru's hair clung to her sweaty forehead. She lifted the lid from the big iron pot and added a dash of shoyu for taste, and then hesitated before adding more. She watched as the vegetables bubbled in the thick, fragrant broth.

"Fukuda-san is here for the *chankonabe!*" Aki called out. Haru knew her sister would bow and smile and then return to their room, to flip through her magazines or read a book. At twelve, Aki had become too self-conscious to watch the big boys practice at the stable, and except for going to the market with Haru, she kept mostly to herself.

Haru turned back to the pot of *chankonabe* and dropped in a fistful of udon noodles to fill up their stomachs. In the past few weeks, food had become more abundant and reasonably priced. If she were lucky, maybe she could buy half a chicken, or perhaps even a whole one at the end of the week.

Fukuda came lumbering down the hall into the kitchen. The young wrestler filled the room with a playfulness long missing from the stable. Hiroshi, who was older and more serious, made Haru feel less comfortable than did Fukuda, who was closer to her age. Fukuda seemed more like a brother than one of her father's *sumotori,* more easygoing than the others.

"A *soppu dakki chankonabe,* with udon," she told him.

Fukuda bowed. "We're lucky to have you cooking for us, Haru-san," he said.

Haru smiled. She took down a bowl and scooped some noodles and broth into it. "Here," she said, knowing he would be eating last, after all the other *rikishi.* "Just a taste."

Fukuda bowed again, a smile on his wide, open face. He balanced the bowl in both of his hands, blew on it, took a few measured sips, and then slurped the noodles down.

Hair

Aki sat at her desk and touched the small bald scar on the back of her head where the hair no longer grew, a reminder of the firestorm that had caused worse hurt than this scar. No one ever noticed it now, since her long hair covered the spot, but to Aki, it was like an open wound. The imperfection felt hard and smooth, about the size of a small prune plum.

She turned the page of her magazine, unconsciously feeling for the hairless patch. Haru often teased her about the habit, saying that she'd only make it bigger if she continued to pick at it. But Aki thought otherwise. Despite its traumatic origin, the scar provided her a strange reassurance of her survival, and she couldn't stop feeling for it, making sure it was still there.

The summer heat was stifling. Aki wondered how Haru could stand being in the kitchen every day, cooking *chankonabe* for her father's wrestlers, but then her sister did everything without complaint. Aki could never keep up, *ichi, ni, san . . .* always three steps behind. She tried to quash the flicker of discontent and keep it from becoming a point of meanness. She loved her sister, she did, but with Haru busy every day with shopping and cooking for the sumo stable, the summer seemed endless, each day blending into the next. Sometimes Aki dreamed that her mother was still alive, that it wasn't her body that Hiroshi had found by the river after the firestorm. That it was all a mistake and her mother would one day return to them. It made Aki feel better to imagine that, to touch the smooth patch on the back of her head and hope that when her mother returned to them, her hair would grow back again in the same spot.

REBUILDING

September finally brought cooler days. With the windows open, a slight breeze moved through the long, narrow studio where the architecture students built their models. Kenji cut a piece of paper into small squares with a razor and drew dark lines to make a grid that resembled a shoji window. When the ink dried, he inserted it into the small wooden frame he'd built and pressed it tightly together with his fingers until the glue held. Later, he would fit it into the house along with the other windows he'd made. This was the one aspect of architecture he liked, creating small models of life-sized designs. It gave him satisfaction and came closest to creating something out of different materials, like the masks. He stood up from his worktable, tall and thin at eighteen. As he tossed his head to the side, a shock of hair fell across his forehead and he pushed it out of his eyes.

He heard laughter across the room from two young women, whom he recognized from his other classes. They looked away when they caught his gaze. While they'd never spoken to him, he always felt them watching him, or whispering whenever he walked by. He smiled to himself and looked down at his model. He thought of Hiroshi, who often teased him, saying, "I may have the strength in this family, but you, little brother, were blessed with the good looks." And though Kenji disregarded his brother's observation, some girls evidently agreed with him. Kenji had little experience with women and, like the frail boy called Kenji the ghost, still felt invisible. What was it now, he wondered, that made him suddenly so visible to these girls? His *obachan* said that he'd grown into his body. Then why wasn't he visible to the one person he hoped would see him?

She was a girl in his drawing class his first year at Tokyo University. Her name was Mika Abe, and though he'd never been formally introduced to her, he sat two chairs behind her in class and found himself watching her the way these girls watched him. He studied the way she walked, in lovely, even steps. He noted the way she dressed, mostly in Western clothing with little scarves and necklaces, but once she had worn a beautiful kimono to class, deep purple with a white chrysanthemum pattern on it, and the nape of her white neck was exposed when she bent down to draw. It took deep concentration on his own drawing to resist touching that small sliver of pale skin.

Little by little, he learned about Mika Abe

from other students and from a friend in admissions. He knew that before the war her father had been successful in the textile business, which explained the beautiful kimono she wore. She was born on October 15, four months after he, in Tokyo, and had two brothers. He also knew that she was an art major. At other times, he came to his own conclusions. She was studying art, which meant her family had marriage plans arranged for her, some rich industrialist's son most likely. Art wasn't a career as much as a pleasure for a young woman to study at a university. Kenji himself wondered how he would make a living. But what did it matter? Mika Abe was much too beautiful ever to pay attention to someone like him.

Kenji returned to his model and the pleasure of working with his hands. Every afternoon after his last class, he found himself back at the studio working on his model — a comforting reminder of when he had gone to the mask shop every day after school and felt safe from the outside world.

Now everything seemed in utter confusion. Every day Kenji walked past the burned shells of buildings, past loud American soldiers whose bodies blocked the entire sidewalk, past women and children begging on every street corner. He wondered when life would be better in this new Japan. Since his encounter with Okata, Kenji felt ready for anything.

Kenji pushed open the wooden gate of his grandparents' house and paused a moment in the courtyard. This was the kind of end-of-summer evening that he loved most, still warm, with a tinge of regret in the air.

After dinner he guided his *ojichan* out to the backyard. Where the watchtower once stood, his grandmother had planted a vegetable garden.

"Here, *ojichan,* I've brought you a gift."

His grandfather raised his face and smiled. "Some might say I'm too old for gifts, but don't believe them. What is it?"

Kenji put the metal pipe in his hand. "A souvenir. Something they're selling in the streets. It's called a defeat pipe, made of machine gun cartridges and anti-aircraft gun shells. I thought it might interest you."

Yoshio laughed. His fingers felt the small bowl where the tobacco was placed, the thin metal stem. "I can't imagine what your *obachan* will say if she sees me smoking this. She wants only to live in the present." He reached up and patted Kenji on the shoulder. "But I don't suppose there's any harm in keeping it as a reminder. We should never forget the past." He fingered the pipe again, smiled, and slipped it into his pocket. Then, as if reading Kenji's earlier thoughts, his grandfather asked, "And what is the world like out there today?"

"Complicated," Kenji answered.

His *ojichan* nodded. "Japan will face many complications before she can fully revive," he said, very matter-of-factly.

"How long will it take?"

"You can't expect Japan to find balance right away after so many years at war." He looked up at Kenji from his darkness. "We're stepping into a new world, and an entire way of thinking must be changed. But the old ideas can't be easily discarded. Like a pendulum, new ways must swing to the other side before returning. Don't worry, though, we'll once again find our place."

"Japan certainly seems to be swinging the wrong way now," Kenji said, discouraged. "It's terrible. There are homeless people everywhere. And where's the food they promised? Why do we still have to rely on those vultures that run the black market?"

"Just wait," his grandfather said. "Things will improve. It takes time to rebuild a nation. And you, Kenji-chan, will be part of the rebuilding," he added, smiling.

"Hai." Kenji swallowed the rest of his words. He wanted to believe his *ojichan,* wished for his patience and optimism, his hard certainty. But unlike his grandfather, Kenji viewed the world on a much smaller scale, intimate and orderly like one of his models. The idea of spending his life rebuilding a whole nation

was too large for him to fathom.

Kenji glanced around the backyard. In the waning light, it looked smaller and shabbier. Just after the war, he and Hiroshi had offered to rebuild his *ojichan*'s watchtower, but his grandfather had shaken his head. "What for?" he'd asked. "It served its purpose. Now we must look toward the future." Perhaps he and Hiroshi were the ones who really wanted the watchtower up again. It had been so much a part of their childhood. Only now, when they reminisced, did they understand how it had shaped their growing up in this house. The watchtower had stood all through their childhood, which ended when it fell. He smiled at the memory and turned back to his grandfather.

Upstairs, Kenji had grown used to having the small bedroom all to himself now. With Hiroshi at Katsuyama-beya, the house always felt quieter and emptier. His older brother still came home each month to eat with them, but it wasn't the same. Their lives were also more complicated now, and Kenji wasn't sure he liked it. He stopped studying and picked up *The Book of Masks,* carefully turning the pages and studying each intricate face. He never tired of them, seeing something different each time — the delicate strands of hair on the female *Zo-onna* mask, or the bold, wavelike brows on the *Fudo* spirit mask. He imagined that he might be carving one now if things had been different. As Kenji closed the book, Akira Yoshiwara returned to his thoughts. His sensei's absence still left an emptiness that lingered like a sentence never finished. He hoped Yoshiwara had survived the war and if so, that they would one day meet again. Kenji often searched the faces he passed along the alleyways, hoping that his sensei might be among them, but he knew that many people lost during the war would never be accounted for. His *obachan*'s closest friend, Ayako-san, had never returned from Hiroshima. Perhaps Akira Yoshiwara died there, too, and had disappeared like ash, like dust into the air. Kenji closed his eyes and placed his hand on the cover of *The Book of Masks*.

The next afternoon, Kenji walked past the old mask shop, expecting to see the same abandoned and forlorn storefront — the empty, dusty rooms he'd grown used to seeing every week. Instead, he was surprised to see a cart filled with flowers propped in front. Someone had claimed the small space as a flower shop. Bright purple and yellow irises, pink tiger lilies, and white chrysanthemums lit the window from inside. Such vibrant signs of life stunned him. What if Yoshiwara had returned? Digging in his pocket, Kenji pulled out all the money he had and bought irises for his *obachan* from the middle-aged woman who owned the shop. Akira Yoshiwara was nowhere in sight. Still, his *ojichan* was right; some things were changing for the better. Kenji smiled to think that his sensei would approve; in the midst of all the devastation and confusion of war and occupation, beauty flourished once again where his masks used to be.

THE TOURNAMENT

The months leading up to the September *honbasho* were filled with anticipation. During off-hours, Hiroshi and the other *rikishi* kept busy by helping Tanaka-oyakata rebuild his stable. The two-story dormitory, private rooms for upper-ranked wrestlers, and an eating area were finally rebuilt by the end of August.

Two weeks before the tournament, Tanaka-oyakata called Hiroshi into his office. Tanaka had relaxed, seeing how hard he and all the *rikishi* were training. Even Fukuda was making a conscious effort. The stable master was half-hidden behind stacks of files and papers and all that was visible was the shiny glint of his shaved head.

Tanaka-oyakata looked up. "Ah, Hiroshi, come in, come in." He pushed aside a stack of papers.

Hiroshi bowed.

"You've been here over a year now, and I'm pleased with your training, your hard work." Tanaka brushed the top of his head with the palm of his hand. "I've been thinking it's time for you to have a *shikona* before the *honbasho*. I'd like you to have the fighting name of Takanoyama," he said, sitting back in his chair. "Noble Mountain."

Hiroshi bowed again, surprised, but proudly accepted a fighting name that already lay heavy on his shoulders, testing him to live up to it. He wondered if that was why Tanaka-oyakata had given it to him. It wouldn't really belong to him until he had earned it. Hiroshi hesitated and asked, "Tanaka-oyakata, may I ask why you chose the name Takanoyama?"

A quick smile passed over Tanaka's face, as if he were revealing a secret. "The truth is, it's from a story I heard as a young boy," he answered. "When I was growing up, my mother told me a story about three majestic mountains — each named for qualities she hoped would be instilled in me as a man — Truth Mountain, Courage Mountain, and Noble Mountain. On each mountain was a village where the villagers worked to remain true to their mountain's name. And one by one, each failed the test. That is, until a young orphan boy came along who didn't belong to any of the mountain villages, yet held the characteristics of all three mountains."

Tanaka paused.

"How was that?" Hiroshi asked.

"My mother never ended the story." He laughed. "Each night she told me a different story which tested the boy's courage, his sense of truth, or nobility. I believe she wanted me to figure out for myself how one boy could possess all the attributes that the mountains had to offer. Within each story was a lesson. I understood what it meant to have courage and to tell the truth, but as a boy it was always the Noble Mountain that confused me the most. 'What does it mean to be noble?' I asked her."

Hiroshi cleared his throat.

Tanaka eyed him closely. "You didn't know I would be telling you a bedtime story, did you? But you must understand, Hiroshi, that there's a story behind everything. To be noble, my mother said, was to account for the life you lived, to always account for your mistakes, and to have dignity and worth. I later came to realize it has everything to do with what it means to be *sumotori*."

"*Hai*," Hiroshi agreed. "And did you ever figure out how the boy could possess all three traits?"

Tanaka paused and shook his head. "I suppose the boy wasn't hampered by the destiny of each mountain. He lived his life the best way he could, thereby achieving all."

Hiroshi knew he had a great deal to live up to.

■ ■ ■ ■

"Takanoyama," Hiroshi whispered under his breath. He sat quietly in the locker room before his long-awaited match with Kobayashi and closed his eyes, clearing his mind of all thoughts. When he opened his eyes again, Fukuda was playing cards with some of the other wrestlers. Their laughter and loud voices filled the stale air. Hiroshi pulled his *mawashi* belt as tight as possible, making it harder for Kobayashi to grasp. He slapped his muscular girth, increased by twenty pounds in the past six months.

The afternoon before, Kenji had paid an unexpected visit to the stable and given Hiroshi a book of poetry by the poet Basho. "You might find calm in reading his poems before the match," his brother suggested, slipping it to him quietly, unobtrusively. Kenji never did anything in a pushy way.

"Domo arigato." Hiroshi bowed, turning the slim volume over in his hands. Standing so close to Kenji, he was aware of their physical differences; he was now a good hundred pounds heavier than his slender brother. He pulled at his *yukata* robe. "Do you have time to come in?" he asked.

Kenji smiled. "I have the entire afternoon."

His brother had changed in the past two years; he was lighter in spirit and resembled their mother even more, with his deep-set eyes and the long hair he'd let grow out and tied back like so many of the artisans. Taller and more confident, he was no longer the little boy once taunted as Kenji the ghost.

He ushered Kenji into the training area, and, for the first time since arriving at the stable, Hiroshi saw everything from his brother's point of view. Kenji had moved forward into the modern world, while he'd stepped backward in time, living within the confines of ancient rituals and traditions. What must his brother think to see half-naked men training just for a few moments on the *dohyo* to prove who had the greatest strength? His brother moved slowly around the empty room, asking about Hiroshi's schedule, the training he undertook every day.

"Are you ready for the tournament?" he asked.

"Hai," Hiroshi answered, without a second thought. "How are your studies?" he asked. "Have you any time for making masks?"

Kenji hesitated. "Architecture is fine. For now," he added. "I haven't really had much time for the masks."

Hiroshi knew that Kenji found his greatest pleasure in the Noh masks, an art, much like sumo, that was ancient and revered. It was the masks his brother would always love most.

"Obachan always says you can't run away from your destiny."

His brother smiled. "No, I suppose not, perhaps just get sidetracked."

"You'll find your way back."

Kenji nodded. "I hope so."

The laughter from the other *rikishi* cut through the stagnant air of the locker room. Hiroshi stopped pacing and dug through his bag, found the book of Basho poems, and flipped through the pages. Each line was short and simple.

Winter solitude —
in a world of one color
the sound of wind.

He read the characters over and over until the words made him think of moments in time outside himself. He closed his eyes and repeated the lines like a chant until he could feel his heartbeat slow and his breathing become calm again. Even the raucous laughter of the other *sumotori* seemed far away.

When Hiroshi entered the sumo arena just before his match, he looked up at the bright lights and thought of "a world of one color." Unlike the original sumo stadium now occupied by the Allied troops, this sports arena was much smaller. Brightly lit, with a high ceiling, the open room hummed with voices, thick with the heat of too many bodies. He looked up at the blur of faces, too far away, knowing that somewhere out in the audience were his grandparents and Kenji. His heart pounded as he neared the *dohyo,* following Tanaka-oyakata and other members of his stable. For a moment, Hiroshi felt dizzy, as if he might black out, but instead, he breathed deeply and found his balance again.

Across the *dohyo,* Hiroshi searched for Kobayashi amid a group of other wrestlers waiting for their matches to begin. He'd only seen him once, from a distance, and guessed that he was the tall, round-eyed young sumo gazing back across the *dohyo,* watching him just as closely. They weren't even in the ring yet, but already the *niramiai,* or stare-down, had begun.

Just before their match was to begin, the *yobidashi* held up a fan and announced their names in the traditional high-pitched sing-song voice. Hiroshi relished the sound of the ring attendant's voice piercing the air, quieting the entire audience as it reached the highest seats. The five syllables of his new *shikona* rang out like a poem: Ta-ka-no-ya-ma. *A world of one color,* he thought, while he stood at the edge of the *dohyo.* To Hiroshi's surprise, the wrestler who stood across from him was not the one who had glared at him from the other side of the ring. The Kobayashi he faced was slightly shorter than the other sumo, but muscular and strong, with a good-sized girth that hung over his belt. He had a large, sloping forehead and narrow, piercing eyes that followed Hiroshi's every move. He and Kobayashi waited for the *yobidashi* to step off the *dohyo,* and then entered and bowed to each other before returning to their opposite sides. The air in the arena was warm, thick with the sweet scent of incense and the dank smell of the clay used for the raised *dohyo.* Sweat beaded on his forehead. The audience had quieted down to a whisper.

Hiroshi began the rituals he'd been taught from the day he entered the stable, and Tanaka's voice remained a constant echo in his head. First he clapped, and did two *shiko,* leg stomps to drive out the evil spirits, then he threw salt to cleanse the ring and again to drive out more of the spirits. At the east and west sides of the ring, Hiroshi and Kobayashi squatted down on their toes in unison, clapped their hands to let the gods know that a match was taking place, then held their arms out to show they had come without weapons and were ready to fight in fair play. After performing the prebout rituals, Hiroshi heard the *gyoji,* the referee, announce both names again as they stood and approached the center of the ring. Hiroshi and Kobayashi crouched into position at the starting lines, knuckles on the ground, facing each other in the *niramiai.* His heart raced as he locked his gaze on Kobayashi, at the edge of his forehead that dropped abruptly into his narrow stare, knowing that to flinch now could lose him the match even before it started. *"So much of sumo is concentration, in finding your opponent's weak spot,"* Tanaka had drilled into him. *"If you can do that, the match will be won."* Kobayashi squinted hard, too, giving no sign of backing down. For Hiroshi, everyone in the hall seemed to disappear and there was only Kobayashi, like a wall in front of him, staring him down, hoping to knock him out of the *dohyo* as quickly as possible. He felt his adrenaline rising, every muscle in his body ready to push forward, ready or not. *"Never give up, never,"* Tanaka had said. *"Use your instincts to find a way to win."*

The wrestlers repeated the *niramiai* two more times, rising to return to their corners, tossing a handful of salt into the ring, and coming back to the starting line, all the while turning back and never taking their eyes off each other. Hiroshi's mouth was dry. He pulled at his black *mawashi* belt, slapped his stomach, felt his sweat pool against the edge of the taut cotton material. It was like a dance, Hiroshi thought, like all the dances done before great battles.

He heard the *gyoji* call out, *"Matta nashi,"* it's time, holding his war paddle out vertically to signify the match was beginning. Hiroshi and Kobayashi crouched and locked eyes, breathing in and out in a unified rhythm. A thin line of sweat traveled down his opponent's round face like a drop of water on glass. Hiroshi's fists touched the ground for a few tense moments, just as Kobayashi's did, until the *tachiai* brought their bodies together in a sudden impact so perfectly synchronized that each remained standing. Before Hiroshi moved again, Kobayashi grunted and grabbed hold of his *mawashi* belt on both sides; he felt the hard slap of Kobayashi's body pushing against his, using all his weight to force him out of the *dohyo*. Just as quickly Hiroshi swung his body to the side, and grabbed the back of Kobayashi's belt, hoping to throw him down. Instinctively, Kobayashi thrust his weight in the other direction and at that moment, Hiroshi wrapped his leg around Kobayashi's and tripped him to the *dohyo*, using Kobayashi's own momentum against him. Kobayashi fell hard, with a low groan. It all happened so quickly Hiroshi didn't have time to think, but reacted just as Tanaka-oyakata had trained him.

From the moment Hiroshi had entered the *dohyo*, the world around him had stopped, only to start again when he heard the thundering applause and the cheering voices. It sounded like all of Japan had come alive just for him, and Hiroshi was determined not to let them down.

Tanaka-oyakata caught his eye as he came

off the ring, nodded his head slightly in approval. He didn't say a word to him until they were back in the locker room. Then Tanaka took him aside and told him, "You didn't move quickly enough after the initial *tachiai*. That's what wins or loses a match. You were lucky. Remember your weaknesses and learn from your mistakes."

Hiroshi bowed. He knew Tanaka-oyakata was right, but what did it matter if he was a split second late; he had won, hadn't he? What more did Tanaka want?

After the match, when all the other *rikishi* had gone to sleep, Hiroshi soaked in the *ofuro* for a long time, relaxing in the warm, steamy air. The victory played over and over in his head, each maneuver flickering through his mind like a movie. Most *rikishi* had particular wrestling strategies they favored, although it was important to vary them. To become overly dependent on any one tactic was a sure giveaway.

Hiroshi placed a wet towel over his face and leaned back. In the ring tonight, he hadn't really thought about any of the seventy *kima-rite* moves; his body just seemed to take over with an instinctive sureness that surprised him. Sitting up, he let the towel slip into the water.

Hiroshi lay down but couldn't sleep. He

imagined all the upper-ranked *sekitori* wrestlers laughing at him, so excited over one win, with so many tournaments still ahead of him. They'd slap him on the back, pull on his belt, and tease him, their voices low and rough. "Do you think one match makes you a champion?" Hiroshi knew it didn't. What Tanaka-oyakata had told him was true, his career was only beginning and the road was long. He must learn from his mistakes, grow faster and stronger if he were to become a champion. Yet this match was his first taste of real victory, and he drank it in. The other wins had been too easy, but Kobayashi was his equal.

As the snores of the other wrestlers grew louder, Hiroshi shifted on his futon. He would be up and training again in a few hours. He closed his eyes and saw again the smiling faces of his *obachan* and *ojichan* after the match. Kenji stood proudly beside them. Only then did Hiroshi fall asleep.

13
THE VILLAGE OF AIO
1948

By late March, the biting winds that whipped through the mountains had finally calmed, and ice thawed in pale rays of sunlight that made everything appear as fragile as glass. While the snow melted, Akira resumed his regular schedule, eager to see Kiyo waiting for him every afternoon on the rutted road that led up to the house. During the week and on Saturday mornings, she returned to school down in the village.

Akira walked up the sodden path, skirting the icy water that streamed down in muddy rivulets. The air smelled of fresh pine, wet earth, and the wood fires that burned nonstop in the big, dark, sloped-roof houses.

"Akira-san! Akira-san!" Kiyo called out to him on this clear Sunday morning.

Her voice echoed down through the trees and Akira smiled and waved. There was no one else to hear her on the mountain road today. Mostly, the people of Aio kept to themselves. Other than old Tomita-san, who had brought him up from the station in his cart, the couple he rented his room from, and Emiko and Kiyo, Akira had few friends in Aio. "That's just the way people are here," Emiko had told him. "They keep to themselves." Akira respected the wish to keep a polite distance. But Emiko and Kiyo had changed him. For the first time in years, he anticipated and worried about the needs of others. It was a responsibility he took for granted back in Tokyo. There were even moments when he felt he could love and take care of Emiko and Kiyo, just like any husband and father. But alone in his room, when Akira closed his eyes and his hand reached down to find release, the smiles he saw half-cloaked in an alley's darkness were on the faces of other men.

Akira watched Kiyo taking careful steps down the slope toward him, as she angled her body sideways along the narrow dirt path. This shortcut was steep and faster than walking around the curve of the main road, but now her *tabi* socks and sandals were covered in mud. For a moment he felt as a father might feel waiting for his child, that hard piece of ice in the middle of his stomach slowly melting.

"Come on, I have a surprise for you," Kiyo said, happy and excited as she reached him. "It's your turn to seek it out." She took

Akira's hand and led him away from the main road, along another muddy path that led up a steep incline toward the rocks.

"I should see if your mother needs more wood," he said, following her off the path. "Where are we going?" he asked.

"You'll see," Kiyo answered.

The path led up the hillside through a wooded area of tall pine trees that left the world in half-shadow. Patches of ice formed islands on the ground. Hot and sweaty with the climb, his feet slipping on the soft, muddy earth, Akira was glad when they came out of the trees at the top of the path into a clearing. It seemed the whole world was melting around them. He heard the crackling sound of ice thawing from above, water streaming. Akira looked up at the steep incline that led through the rocks. "And what will I see here?" he asked.

Kiyo laughed. "Just wait," she said.

Following, he noticed how much taller she'd grown during the winter months. Now that spring had arrived, her plain maroon kimono looked too short, exposing her ankles and wrists. It made him suddenly wonder what sort of a young man Kenji had grown into. He imagined him tall and thin, too serious and always capable.

"Over here!" Kiyo called out, all legs and arms as she hurried up the rocky trail. Akira must buy her a new kimono. There was still money in the tin from his years of mask making, and he required very little for his simple needs. Perhaps he could take Emiko and Kiyo shopping for a kimono down in Oyama, where he could also buy more charcoal and drawing paper. He looked up to see Kiyo impatiently waiting for him in the middle of the muddy path, the mountainside rising all around her. The sun beat down on them as he reached her.

"It's in there," she said, pointing down to a narrow, dark crevice between two large rocks. She appeared so slight against the towering mountain.

"What's in there?" he asked.

"A gift for you."

Akira smiled. In her excitement, she'd given away the hiding place. In all their previous games of hide-and-seek, Kiyo was always the one seeking the small gifts he delighted in giving her. All during the long, cold winter, he imagined her wandering around the house alone, with school so haphazard when it snowed. How did she contain her spirit? "All right," he said, bowing to her slightly. He walked up to the slim crevice between the rocks, knelt down, and squeezed his left hand into it, feeling for whatever Kiyo had hidden there. He faintly heard the sound of water running down the rocks above, the melting snow carrying stray stones, and as he felt the icy trickle against his hand, he imagined this was what darkness felt like. His fingers touched a piece of cloth, closed tightly around it, and pulled it forward.

At the same moment, he heard a rushing sound coming down the mountain, and looked up to see a river of water and mud, felt the rocks shift. It rushed over him so quickly that his head thumped against the ground as the mud and water drenched him. He shouted at Kiyo to run as a second wall of mud and rocks buried him. Akira struggled for breath, his arm twisted where he knelt against the rock, his left hand in terrible pain. He spat mud and tried to move, but his hand was pinned, the pain excruciating. He heard a scream not his own. It was Kiyo, somewhere beyond the mud wall, digging through the rocks and sludge.

In his darkness, his head began to spin. Akira found a pocket of air and took another deep breath, pressed his forehead to the rock, and closed his eyes. He saw his father's angry red face as he soaked in the *ofuro.* Then Sato, at the door of his shop, the slight smile on his lips the day he left, never to return. Now it was Kenji who peered through the darkness as through the shop window, a boy who loved the masks as much as he did. Didn't that mean something? Hadn't Akira done some good in his life? Would Kenji understand that he had had to leave, had had to flee the war, find his way to Aio to help

Emiko and Kiyo? There had been no other choice.

Akira's head rolled back, the pain cold and remote, his fingers numb. Later, he would remember hearing more voices, especially Emiko's as she tried in vain to dig away the rocks and mud from his pinned hand. She smelled of sweat and wood smoke, her breathing frantic. He looked into her mud-splattered face and saw her fear. Akira tried to smile and say something to put Emiko at ease, but the sound escaping his bared teeth scarcely sounded human. In response, she only grunted as she dug at the mud around him, pushed and pushed at the rocks. It should hurt more, he kept thinking to himself, but instead, it felt as if his entire body were going numb. Emiko screamed for Kiyo to run for help. He tried to tell her not to scream, for Kiyo was frightened enough, and the neighbors didn't like to be disturbed. But the air felt squeezed out of him and his eyes closed again before the words left his lips.

Akira awoke with a start, gasping for air. It took a moment for his head to clear, his heart to calm, his eyes to focus on the high dark beams and above them the steeply pitched roof, tipped together like praying hands. Daylight filtered through the windows and a fire was burning low in the hearth. He turned his head from where he lay in the corner of

317

the long room but saw no sign of Emiko and Kiyo.

Just before awakening, Akira had dreamed he was drowning in a lake. Every time he grabbed for the rocks right in front of him, he slid back into the cold water. When his breath gave out and water filled his lungs, his eyes snapped open to the dimness of the room. With relief, he gulped the smoke-tinged air, but when he tried to sit up, he screamed in pain. Something like fire shot through his left arm, up from the bandaged stump where his left hand had been.

The Meeting

Kenji had just stepped out of the architectural studio when he glimpsed Mika Abe walking across the campus. He hadn't seen her since last semester's drawing class. She was dressed in Western clothing and was with a girl he casually knew from another first-year class. His heart raced as he paused a moment to remember the other girl's name: Sachiko. The path they were taking led straight to a crowded, open plaza where students met after classes and hovered in small groups, dismantling their day, talking politics, planning where to meet in the evening. If he hurried and circled around them on an outside path, he could double back and walk toward them. Kenji hoped to find an introduction to Mika through Sachiko. He had nothing to lose.

As Kenji raced down the path, he remembered the alleyways he used to run down as a boy, past the rows of identical wooden houses that lined the narrow streets. The confused maze of winding alleyways wound around like a puzzle when he was younger, until he looked up to see his *ojichan*'s tall, narrow watchtower, and he was instantly comforted and never frightened of getting lost.

Now, he looked up and saw the tall buildings, cold and nondescript, a few flowering trees added for color, and he felt suddenly lost. In the distance, Mika and Sachiko walked leisurely, lost in conversation, allowing him to pass them with ease and circle back in their direction. Kenji sucked in several deep breaths and kept his gaze lowered as he walked toward them.

"Kenji-san?"

He looked up, heart beating, his neck sticky with sweat.

"Kenji Matsumoto?"

He was surprised to find it was Mika speaking to him. *"Hai,"* he said, bowing.

"We had a drawing class together." She smiled. "I'm Mika Abe. And this is Sachiko-san."

"Hai," he said, and tried to remain steady. "It's nice to see you both." He bowed again, unable to take his eyes off her face, her slightly high forehead, the straight bridge of

319

her nose, and her dark, challenging gaze.

"We haven't seen much of you in the art department," she continued.

"I'm over at the architecture department now." He pulled away to glance quickly at Sachiko, who appeared distracted.

Mika smiled. "Ah," she said. She looked over at Sachiko. "We should be going now."

"I hope to see you again," he stammered.

Mika smiled and nodded.

He watched them walk off until they disappeared among the flock of other students gathered at the plaza. But as Kenji walked back toward the studio, he only heard her soft, melodious voice say his name over and over again.

Mika Abe knew who he was.

LISTENING

In May, the street of a thousand blossoms came alive again, and the warm wind carried its sweet scent to Yoshio. Azaleas, lilies, and freesia bloomed in window boxes and gardens that once grew vegetables under the orders of the *kempeitai* until they were dug up and transformed into air-raid shelters. The same dirt turned over and over again, and still it produced life. Yoshio smiled at the thought. His family, too, had survived.

In the five years since he'd been completely blind, Yoshio Wada had discovered many other ways to see. Sitting in his old wooden chair in the courtyard, he faced the warmth of the sun and breathed in deeply. The thick, humid air tasted of lychee and lilies of the valley, the last sweet blooms of spring. His afternoons beside the old maple taught Yoshio to distinguish subtleties that others took for granted. He heard voices in the wind and saw tints of color in his darkness. As the day progressed, the air itself changed from fresh and sweet to heavy and tired. Even the swaying of Fumiko's kimono had significance. Only if she were rushed, in a hurry to go and stand in food lines, would her sleeves brush along the table, the soft sweep of cloth against wood. From memory, he could almost see the harried expression on her face, the quick shake of her head. Otherwise, she always held her sleeves close to her sides and kept them silent.

What Yoshio could no longer see in people's eyes, he now heard in their voices. Fumiko's was a soothing balm, a cool drink of water on a hot day, a calm hush in the dark. When she spoke, he saw her face, both young and old, with the same dark brown eyes that gleamed in the sunlight so long ago at the Bon Odori. I see you, he sometimes wanted to say, if only in memory.

The voices of his grandsons were as different as their personalities. Yoshio tilted his head to listen when they sat with him in the courtyard. Hiroshi's voice was strong and steady, black and white, his feet firmly planted on the ground. Hiroshi would get where he wanted to go, one step at a time. Kenji's voice was softer, more tentative and dreamlike. His younger grandson never sounded quite settled; he thought too much sometimes, and lacked the confidence of his older brother. But in his work, Kenji would find his way, of that Yoshio was certain. From the tone of each voice, he could always tell whether Fumiko and his grandsons were happy or sad, disgruntled or satisfied. Even their breathing gave them away, the slight pause, the heavy silence, a quick gasp of fear, a loud exhalation of disgust. And when Hiroshi and Kenji confided in him about a problem — a wrestling match lost or won, a class Kenji was taking, or news of the American occupation — Yoshio was happy to be sitting there in his darkness, listening.

Yoshio stood and moved his chair to catch the last slanting rays of sun. Hiroshi would be coming home in a few weeks, at the beginning of June. During his last visit, Yoshio had reached up and touched his face. "Let me see you," he said. He raised his hand to gauge his grandson's height and smiled when he felt the manly stubble on his cheek, the muscular arms and rock-solid girth. Hiroshi inhabited a body Yoshio no longer recognized. Then Hiroshi guided his grandfather's hand to the slick topknot on his head.

"What do you see?" Hiroshi asked, a smile in his voice.

Yoshio was reminded of standing up in the watchtower with a young Hiroshi asking him the very same question. "I see a champion," he answered.

During the past year, sumo competitions had been revived and matches were regularly broadcast on the radio again. Ecstatic, Yoshio tuned in religiously. The sumo tradition was one of the few surviving vestiges of old Japan that gave comfort throughout a difficult transition. Before and during the war, passion for sumo soared. Afterward, it was still held in such high regard that even the occupation forces came to know the sport, placing bets on tournaments, cheering their favorite wrestlers, especially Hiroshi, whose popularity was growing. Yoshio kept track of every step of his career. His grandson already had a reputation for quickness, for bringing an opponent down within seconds.

When he and Fumiko couldn't go to the arena, it seemed the entire neighborhood gathered at their house, or at the bar, to listen to the match on the radio. "Hiroshi will be on soon," or, "Did you go to see Hiroshi last time?" buzzed through the neighborhood. Yoshio heard and relished it all. This was when he felt the proudest. Sumo brought back hope. When Yoshio listened to a match, it was as if he could see again; the years that lined his face and clouded his eyes dropped away, and he was a young man once more, filled with joy and enthusiasm.

The sun on his face had shifted, filtering its warmth through the maple leaves, leaving cooler shadows in the courtyard. At last their daily life was returning to some kind of normalcy. He was alive and reasonably well. He didn't dare tell Fumiko about the dizziness he sometimes felt when he stood up too quickly, or the pockets of forgetfulness that seemed to come more often. She had enough to worry about.

Yoshio turned when he heard the gate whine open slowly, followed by the soft click of its closing. He could tell it was Fumiko by the lightness of her steps.

"It's a beautiful day," he said.

He heard her pause. "How did you know it was me?" Fumiko asked, a smile in her voice.

"Do you think just because I *can't* see that I *don't* see?" he asked.

Fumiko laughed. "No, I don't think you miss a thing, old man."

He held his hand out and felt a slice of warm sunlight fall upon it as she approached.

An unexpected summer storm blew all night, whipping rain against the side of the stable and sending sheets of water running off the roof and slapping onto the ground. Four-thirty always came too early, Hiroshi thought as he pushed himself up from his futon. He looked over at Fukuda, still asleep. His young friend seemed to become more lethargic each day, sloppy and slow during practice, barely trying. Lately, Hiroshi often saw Tanaka-oyakata simply shake his head and walk away without bothering to instruct Fukuda. To Hiroshi this was worse criticism than a barrage of angry words, for it meant that Tanaka was already letting Fukuda go.

And Daishima didn't make it any easier with his constant ridicule. His gruff, booming voice shook the stable as he chastised Fukuda in front of the other *rikishi*. "Can't you hear? I told you I wanted hot water!" Or, "You fool, I asked you to bring me the black *yukata* robe!" which sent Fukuda stumbling back upstairs as Daishima laughed. Hiroshi tried to anticipate all the *sekitori*'s needs before he asked. But even Hiroshi didn't have an easy time of it. Daishima was huge, demanding, and mean-spirited. Always, the *chanko* was too salty or not salty enough, the water too hot or too cold. Even though he had reached the upper ranks, Daishima didn't deserve such special treatment. His coaching methods were sadistic and always carried out at the expense of someone else when Tanaka-oyakata wasn't around. If Hiroshi learned anything from Daishima, it was this: if he ever reached the *sekitori* rank, he would never abuse his position.

Hiroshi shook Fukuda awake. His young friend stirred but turned away from him in sleep. Hiroshi winced at the sight of the red welts across Fukuda's shoulders and back, received at the end of yesterday's practice. Daishima had called Fukuda up to take part in the *butsukari-geiko,* an exercise in which one wrestler charged another, attempting to push him out of the *dohyo.* The defender, Akori, tried to hold Fukuda back or throw him down. As the two young wrestlers repeatedly slammed into each other, Daishima watched, slapping a bamboo stick against the palm of his hand, his raspy voice continually demanding, "Again!" until both wrestlers were so exhausted, Fukuda could no longer stand.

"Get up!" Daishima yelled. "Get up, you fool! How will you ever become *sumotori* if you can't stand on your feet?"

Fukuda lay on his side, breathing heavily.

"I said, get up!" Daishima slapped the bamboo stick against the ground next to Fukuda, and then kicked him in the thigh.

"Get up, or I'll beat you up!" he screamed.

Hiroshi watched, the blood rising to his head. It wasn't his place to say or do anything. Daishima's rank rendered him voiceless. *Get up. Get up,* he thought, willing Fukuda to rise from the *dohyo.*

The bamboo stick came crashing down on Fukuda's shoulders and back, one hard thwack after another, until Daishima was winded, while Fukuda lay on the *dohyo* receiving each blow without a sound.

Despite the consequences, Hiroshi stepped forward and grabbed Daishima's arm just as the bamboo stick was poised to strike Fukuda again.

"What?" Daishima turned and jerked away from Hiroshi's grip. "You son of a bitch!" he roared, raising the bamboo stick toward Hiroshi.

"Stop it at once!" Tanaka-oyakata's voice cut through the air. The *rikishi* stepped back as Tanaka grabbed Daishima's hand and pushed him away. "Explain yourself!"

Daishima panted. "I had to teach this fool a lesson. A wrestler must always rise up and fight!"

Tanaka-oyakata stepped close to Daishima and hissed, "I want you to leave! Now!"

Daishima threw down the bamboo stick and pushed his way out of the crowd, while Tanaka motioned for Hiroshi to help Fukuda. Already, angry red ridges were rising across his back.

Hiroshi shook Fukuda harder. "Wake up," he whispered, trying not to disturb the other wrestlers.

"I'm not getting up," Fukuda mumbled.

Only then did Hiroshi realize he was pretending to be asleep. "Please hurry," he urged.

Fukuda turned toward Hiroshi and opened his eyes. "I'm finished. I'm leaving the stable," he said. "This isn't the place for me." He sighed as he said the words, as if he were suddenly freed of some great restraint.

Hiroshi forced a laugh. "What are you saying? You love sumo."

Fukuda grimaced in pain as he raised himself onto his elbows. His large stomach rose and fell under the covers. "I'm no good at this, Hiroshi-san. What's the point in staying any longer?"

Hiroshi paused. It was true, Fukuda wasn't a natural *sumotori,* but he was only eighteen and there was still time to train and learn if he wanted it badly enough. In the past few months, he hadn't really tried.

"Being a good *sumotori* means we have to practice every morning," Hiroshi said, as if speaking to a child.

Fukuda shook his head sadly. "It wouldn't make any difference."

Hiroshi swallowed. Before his eyes, the boy Fukuda had become a man. "You've made up your mind?"

Fukuda nodded. "I'll talk to Tanaka-oyakata this afternoon. I'll finish out the week. I'm sure he'll be grateful he doesn't have to ask me to leave." Then he added, "There was a reason he never gave me a *shikona.*"

Hiroshi's fighting name, Takanoyama, provided him with a sense of who he was, and who he strived to become.

"What will you do?" he asked.

Fukuda smiled. "There's my father's farm, for now. Who knows, I may find something that I'm really good at. Better that, than to be less than mediocre at something else." Fukuda rubbed his eyes with the palms of his hands.

Hiroshi grabbed Fukuda's arm and gave it a squeeze. "But you made the past few years here bearable for me."

"I distracted Daishima," he said with a laugh. "Now, you'll have to deal with him alone."

"You've been a good friend." Hiroshi smiled sadly.

"I was never meant to be *sumotori,* not like you, Hiroshi-san. I've seen the concentration and determination you have on the *dohyo.* It's as if there's no other world. You're on your way to reaching the Sandanme Division, while I'd be lucky ever to make it to the Jonidan Division. And when you've risen to the rank of *ozeki,* champion, and *yokozuna,* grand champion status, I'll always be your biggest fan." Fukuda slapped his round belly. "As you can see."

"You haven't left yet," Hiroshi said, trying to sound lighthearted. "If you expect me to reach the rank of *yokozuna,* I'll still need your help."

Fukuda smiled as Hiroshi pulled him from his futon. Together they had endured all the rigors of being the lowest-ranked *sumotori,* all in a cloud of constant exhaustion. It was a bond Hiroshi would never forget. Now that Fukuda was leaving, he would do everything in his power to make his last week at the stable more bearable.

But Fukuda's last days as a *sumotori* were difficult ones. Daishima continued to ridicule him in front of all the other sumo. "So, where will you go if you can't even collect towels and wash my back clean?" While some of the other *rikishi* laughed, Fukuda took all the condescending remarks in good humor. He picked up the towels left on the floor after practice and said nothing, merely smiled good-naturedly, while Hiroshi held back his anger and waited.

The day before Fukuda was to leave the stable, he was optimistic and eager to finish his daily chores quickly so he and Hiroshi could sit down to eat. As they swallowed the last of the *chanko,* and drank down several bottles of beer, Hiroshi leaned toward his friend and said, "I'm going to break a centuries-old tradition and give you your new *shikona*. You will now be known as Takanowaka, Noble Youth. Don't ever let anyone make you think otherwise."

14
THE CHALLENGE
1949

With Fukuda gone six months, Hiroshi missed his young friend's company, his innocent exuberance that filled the hard, cold edges of stable life. His moment to strike back came during one morning practice when Tanaka-oyakata sent him into the *dohyo* with Daishima again. After watching the big, lumbering *sumotori* every day, Hiroshi knew all his moves, how he used his weight and strength against an opponent. Daishima, on the other hand, seemed too preoccupied with his own needs to have paid much attention to anyone else. While Hiroshi was still small by comparison, he had developed more muscle, strength, and speed over the years.

"Let's see if Matsumoto-san has learned anything," Daishima said to his small audience.

Tanaka-oyakata cleared his throat and clapped his hands. The other wrestlers gathered around the *dohyo* and formed a loose circle. Hiroshi took a deep breath and crouched down, his knuckles to the ground in the *niramiai,* the stare-down position. He looked hard into Daishima's eyes and didn't flinch when the big man grimaced at him. He'd won enough matches to detect what was behind the stare, and how much his opponent wanted to win. They stood up and went back to their sides, then returned for the start of the match. The room fell quiet. Everyone in the *keikoba* knew that this was something more than an ordinary practice. Hiroshi felt the air buzz, as if a bee were flying around the top of his head. Sweat dripped slowly down his forehead, a salty, sour tang in the air. As he crouched, he felt the muscles in his legs tense, ready to push him forward in an instant. He matched his breathing to Daishima's, making eye contact as they first touched their fists to the ground and then charged at each other in one synchronized motion. The impact of Daishima's initial strike was hard and violent as his upper body rammed Hiroshi in the chest. But Hiroshi was ready and held his ground. Daishima came at him again, using his bulk and strength to push him toward the edge of the *dohyo.* At the last moment, Hiroshi wrapped his arm around Daishima's neck in a headlock, and forced him down hard onto the *dohyo* with an inside leg trip. It all happened so quickly, Hiroshi scarcely believed it had really taken place. His heart raced. For a moment, the only sounds in the room were the labored breaths of the fallen *sekitori,* the air humid with sweat and dank earth, and then something unexpected, an animal-like sound that emerged from Daishima, who remained on the ground. At the edge of the *dohyo,* the other wrestlers stood back and could barely conceal their subtle smirks and low whispering. Daishima supported his shoulder, obviously in pain, as he was helped up by Tanaka-oyakata.

Hiroshi bowed low as they passed.

Daishima glared at him and said in an even tone, "Don't think what happened here will ever happen again. You were lucky, that's all." Then he turned and walked away, throwing his towel to the ground.

Hiroshi steadied himself. A *sumotori* must never dishonor the sport by showing his emotions. It was wrong to use sumo as a means of revenge, but he counted this practice win as a small exception. It was for Fukuda, and it meant more to him than any tournament match ever had, even defeating Kobayashi. He felt the blood pulse through his veins. Someone had to show Daishima that fortunes could turn, and if he had to dishonor the sport and himself this once to do it, then so be it. Hiroshi stepped out of the dohyo and felt Tanaka-oyakata's gaze heavy upon him.

Sho Tanaka sat at his desk after a long day. As evening approached he rubbed the top of his head and sighed. At least Fukuda-san had had the sense to know that the life of a *rikishi* was not his destiny. When the boy came to his office six months ago, bowing low and asking permission to leave the Katsuyama-beya, Tanaka felt both relief and sadness. He had liked the young man from the start for his easy personality and youthful enthusiasm. But he had already planned to dismiss him at the end of the month. Tanaka had never found the right *shikona* to give Fukuda. What fighting name could he possibly give to a wrestler who didn't want to fight?

To his request, Tanaka had replied, "I want you to know, Fukuda-san, that the *rikishi* life is not for everyone. Leaving Katsuyama-beya doesn't mean you've failed, it just means that you'll find your rightful place somewhere else." His words sounded ordinary, mechanical, uninspiring.

Fukuda stared down at his feet.

Then Tanaka stood up, went around his desk, bowed low to Fukuda, and tried again. "I believe, Fukuda-san, there are many here who could take lessons in how to behave from you. We'll certainly miss you."

Fukuda bowed back. When he stood straight again, there were tears in his eyes.

■ ■ ■ ■

Sho Tanaka never thought the words he had spoken to Fukuda on how to behave would apply to Hiroshi. What was Hiroshi thinking? Daishima would be out of the January *hon-basho* because of his dislocated shoulder. It was a selfish move that would only hurt the stable now that its highest-ranked wrestler could not fight. Had he been mistaken about Hiroshi? Given him the wrong *shikona,* Noble Mountain? Sho stood up and shook his head, then closed the door to his office and made his way back down the stairs to his house across the courtyard. His daughters would be there, waiting for him to have dinner. He had always tried to protect his family, but as with the war and occupation, so many things were beyond his control. And it was no different with his *rikishi.* In less than a year, he had watched both Hiroshi and Fukuda lose their spirit of innocence. This was nothing he hadn't seen before, yet it somehow saddened him. He looked up at the darkening sky. The snow had stopped, and the cold, fresh air revived him. Sho Tanaka breathed deeply, shook off the day's events, and walked toward the glowing lights of his house.

Loss

Almost a year after the accident, the mountain was thawing again in the April sunshine, but Akira still felt a phantom pain where his hand used to be. Kiyo helped him to split the wood now. It had taken months for his wound to heal, and for him to adjust to having only his right hand. The accident replayed repeatedly in his mind until it was simply a series of events; the sudden avalanche of mud and rocks that buried him under thick mire, his struggle for breath, his crushed hand, Kiyo's scream, Emiko's cries, the rush of footsteps and voices. They dug him out from under the mud, but his hand remained pinned. Shock numbed his body as he moved in and out of consciousness. There was no time to get a doctor from Oyama, so the quiet neighbor Kanuki-san, who made wood charcoal, took his axe and separated Akira's hand from his arm just above his wrist. When they held him down to cauterize the bleeding stump with fire, the burned smell of his own charred flesh was the last thing he remembered.

Akira imagined it was like chopping a limb from a tree. He wondered if the bones of his hand were still wedged between the rocks, fused and fossilized. Even if his left hand hadn't been amputated, it would have been crushed beyond use. His only luck was in being right-handed. Akira dwelled on this last

337

thought; at forty, less and less of his body was of use to him.

After the accident, Akira stayed with Emiko and Kiyo in the main house, until he was strong enough to move to the barn. They'd gone down to the village to retrieve Nazo and his things during those early days when he was still feverish. For a long while, he did nothing but sleep, waking only to eat the pickled turnips and rice soup Emiko fed him and then sleep again. As he convalesced, Kiyo stayed at a distance, a shadow flickering in and out of his vision until he was strong enough to sit up and call for her. She sat silently by him, her face a troubled mask, her eyes darting back and forth to his bandaged stump until Akira pulled the blanket up and over it.

"There's something I want to tell you." He smiled, seeking the vibrant thirteen-year-old girl he'd come to love. Instead, he saw traces of the woman she would become in the curve of her eyebrows, the thin, tragic lips.

Kiyo leaned in and then pulled away from him, her eyes brimming with tears. "It's my fault," she whispered.

She smelled of outside, of earth and trees and the cold. Akira lifted his bandaged arm from under the blanket and felt a sharp stab of pain. "This?"

She nodded.

"I didn't know you could cause an avalanche," he teased.

A small smile. "You know what I mean, Akira-san, if I hadn't brought you up there, then . . ."

"Kiyo-chan, I wouldn't have gone if I didn't want to. It was an accident. Avalanches can happen any time, at any moment. How could you or I have known?"

Kiyo lowered her gaze and hiccupped. She shrugged.

He touched her cheek with his right hand. "So, it was an accident. There's no blame. Do you understand?"

Another hiccup. *"Hai,"* she answered.

"There's only one thing I need to know. Then I hope we won't speak of this ever again."

"What is it?" she asked, wiping her nose with the sleeve of her kimono.

"What did you hide for me between the rocks?"

Kiyo looked at him, still teary. "It was *mochi* that I made myself. They were wrapped in a *furoshiki.*"

Akira remembered touching the cloth that contained the *mochi,* a sticky rice delicacy pounded soft by Kiyo, until it was as smooth as flesh, then shaped like small eggs and filled with red bean paste. When he was a boy, it was one of his favorite treats, and he tasted again the sweetness on his tongue.

■ ■ ■ ■

"Last one," Kiyo said, leaning over and placing the log squarely on the block.

Akira nodded. Concentrating all his strength in his right arm, he raised the axe and, with a calculated swing, hit the block of wood, splitting it in half. He stepped back, dropped the axe, and wiped the sweat from his forehead with the back of his hand.

"Pretty good," Kiyo said, collecting the wood to carry back to the house.

"Next time, *you're* chopping," he teased. He squatted next to her and stacked the wood against his left forearm, surprised as always that his hand was missing. At least the rest of his arm was still good for something.

"Then what will *you* do?" Kiyo asked.

"I'll supervise."

She laughed, and turned when Emiko called from the house. "I have to go. I have to study for a test tomorrow." Kiyo made a face.

He smiled. Since school had resumed in the village again after winter break, he saw less of her during the day. "Go then, I'll bring the rest up."

She bowed and hurried up the path toward the house.

At the door Emiko lifted some of the wood

from his arms and invited him in. Akira bowed and entered. Despite the months he had convalesced in her house, he once again acted with the formality of a guest. Those days when Emiko had bathed his face with cool water and sat with him until his fever broke now seemed far away. Her touch had been that of a mother with her child, a nurse, someone who healed. One night, he'd awakened to see her sleeping by the fire, her lips parted as if she had stopped talking in midsentence, and something close to love moved through him. Was it love? Or had he confused it with the comfort they found in each other's company? He closed his eyes and fell into a deep sleep.

Akira stacked more wood by the hearth and placed another log on the fire. His cot in the corner of the room had been put away, every trace of his three-months' stay gone.

"Kiyo-chan seems to be enjoying school," he said. In the flickering light of the fire, Emiko's face looked young again, still filled with hope.

"*Hai,* as much as she fights it, I believe she's also enjoying it." Emiko smiled.

"She's so bright," he said.

They heard Kiyo's footsteps and fell silent. A vegetable stew bubbled and sputtered in an iron pot above the fire, but Emiko poured his tea without asking if he would stay to eat with them. He had turned her down too many times, preferring to return to Nazo and the barn, fearful of Emiko becoming too attached, himself, too. Akira drank down the rest of his tea and stood.

He bowed. "*Domo arigato.* I must get back to the barn."

Emiko smiled politely. *"Hai."* She bowed back, without rising.

Walking down the path to the barn, Akira paused to watch the sunset. He'd been in Aio for almost five years. Another man might have already married Emiko, cared for her and Kiyo as a husband and father would, but he wasn't like other men. As the sun dropped below the mountains, the light fell to gray shadows. He walked quickly to the barn and swung the door open to a drafty darkness, the sharp smell of mold and decay. "Nazo," he whispered, and then waited in the dark. He had stayed in Aio because Emiko and Kiyo were the closest he'd ever come to a family.

KNOWLEDGE

Haru sat in the quiet library and flipped through the book of plants until she found what she was looking for. She laughed out loud when she spotted the drawing and realized it was little more than a weed, *Pteridium aquilinum,* a bracken fern. Haru glanced up to catch a warning frown from Miyayama-san, the school librarian. She bowed her head in quick apology then returned her gaze to the drawings in the book. With its triangular-patterned bright green leaves, the fern would always be the most beautiful plant in the world to her. After all, it was the first sign of life she saw pushing its way out of the ashes after the firestorm.

Haru excelled in her studies. Unlike Aki, she was curious about everything, other countries, politics, how books were written, what made plants grow through ashes. While most of her sixteen-year-old classmates focused on boys, Haru sat in the library during part of her lunch and read. Usually, she had the cool, dark room all to herself, along with Miyayama-san, who never seemed to leave. Haru looked up when she heard the whine of the door opening. One of her schoolmates, Setsuko-san, hurried in and took the seat across from her at the long wooden table.

"I have a report to finish," she whispered to Haru.

Haru nodded.

Setsuko laid her books out one by one for show, then leaned forward and asked, "I've always wanted to ask you, what's it like to have so many young *rikishi* right next door at the stable? They seem so . . . so *strong.*" She smiled, looking down at the books in front of her.

The question surprised Haru. She rarely thought about them in that way. For as long as she could remember, the *sumotori* her father trained were as much a part of her everyday life as her father and Aki were. Of course, she saw the *rikishi* more often than she admitted to Setsuko, mostly at a distance, coming and going, wearing *yukata* kimonos or, sometimes, just their *mawashi* belts. When she met a *rikishi* in the courtyard, or at the stable, she bowed quickly and was on her way. They were always her father's students. When her school resumed and she stopped cooking for the wrestlers, she saw less of them, especially Fukuda, who had since left, the only sumo she thought of as a friend.

She smiled at Setsuko-san and said, "We don't see them that often. Our lives are pretty separate from theirs."

"Are they as big as they look in magazines?"

"Some of them," Haru answered. "Some aren't that big, just strong."

"I don't know what I'd do if I ever met one," Setsuko whispered.

Haru shrugged.

"Do you think I could come over and meet a *rikishi* sometime?"

"I'm afraid there's very little chance. They keep to a rigid schedule of practice," she said, annoyed at Setsuko's persistence. She wanted to return to her reading.

"Girls, please be quiet!" Miyayama-san scolded.

For once, Haru was grateful for the scolding. She watched the light in Setsuko's eyes dim before she looked down at her books.

THE MASKS

The masks returned to Kenji at night. In his dream there was a bare stage, the wooden bridge to be crossed, and the pine tree painted on the backdrop. Then slowly, the beating of the drums, the high-pitched lament of the flute, the murmuring chorus, as one by one costumed Noh actors came forward until Kenji could reach out and almost touch their masks. Every time he tried, he awoke.

In his last year of college, Kenji was working part-time in an architect's office as an errand boy. Twice a month, he was sent out to pick up balsa wood for models at a lumber company not far from the university. Every firm was vying to rebuild Tokyo, which at last had regained her footing. Kenji scarcely noticed the American soldiers now, their presence blending into the new landscape of building and growth. Since the war in Korea began last month, in June, steel production had increased in the Japanese factories, and for the first time since Kenji was young, Japan was thriving.

While he waited at the counter of the dusty office for his order of balsa wood, he picked up a block of Japanese cypress the color of pale, dry grass. It was nearly five years since he'd held such beautiful wood, the kind Yoshiwara-sensei used for making masks. He ran his hands over its smooth planes, breathed in the subtle, sweet scent, and imagined the face trapped within. His life was so different now, studying architecture, which Kenji found abstract and distant. Lines measured and drawn on paper led to scale models constructed by others; he admired the finished structures, but had little part in building them.

Now Kenji smiled at the vision of a face slowly emerging from this cypress — brow, eyes, nose, cheeks — all shaped and defined by his own hands. The face looked like Mika Abe, the girl from his drawing class, a face he longed to touch, to hold, to —

The clerk returned with a wrapped bundle. "Shall I add that to your order?"

Kenji shook his head, replaced the block of cypress on the counter, and felt the dream of the night before descend on him again. Its weight made his shoulders slump. Like the Noh masks he could never quite touch, Mika Abe was beyond his reach. Yoshiwara-sensei had vanished. The war was lost. Four years wasted. And next year Kenji would graduate from Tokyo University with a degree in architecture. So what use was a block of cypress?

His throat ached as he signed for the balsa.

THE TRUNK

Aki was bored. Rain had fallen for three continuous days before turning into a thick mist of summer fog. As if trapped in a dense cloud, she spent the afternoons inside doing her chores, but, at twelve, her housekeeping skills hadn't improved. She halfheartedly swept the floors and dusted the tables before going to look for Haru, who always seemed busy with the household accounts, or helping her father with the stable, or reading book after book, even during these precious summer weeks when they were out of school.

This afternoon, Haru was in the dining room, the account books spread on the glossy black lacquer table. Aki stopped at the open door, but didn't speak. Why interrupt her sister's concentration? Haru would barely glance up, absorbed as usual by columns of black numbers, to say in her distracted voice that she would be just a little longer before finding something for them to do. But hadn't she been promising Aki the same thing since she was a little girl?

Across the courtyard, her father was in an

entirely different world, preparing his wrestlers for the next tournament in September. When Aki was little, she liked to watch the big boys practice. Even during the war, she followed her father into the vacant practice room and watched him stare at the empty ring. When she surprised him by inching up behind him and clapping her hands, he always smiled and picked her up. That precious closeness seemed a long time ago. Nowadays, she didn't see her father until dinner. Afterward, he went to visit friends at a teahouse, or crossed the courtyard to the stable, where the light glowed in his small upstairs office until late at night. Aki no longer followed him.

Instead, she turned back to her room and glimpsed the storage closet at the end of the hallway. Aki hadn't looked in it for years and wondered if she might find something interesting there. She felt the hairs prickling on the back of her neck as she slid the door open. On the two top shelves were remnants of their childhood, games and toys, and old clothes. Below the shelves, an extra futon sat on top of a red lacquered trunk. What was in there? She pulled the futon off and the silver and gold mosaic inlay of a phoenix immediately caught her eye and made her heart jump. It looked strangely familiar. She remembered seeing the same trunk years ago when her mother was alive. Aki was four or five and had found her mother looking through it, lovingly touching the things inside.

"What's in there?" Aki had asked.

"Memories," her mother had said, smiling at her.

"Can I see?"

Her mother closed the lid slowly. "When you're a little older, I'll show you and Haru-chan everything."

Aki knelt, running her fingers over the uneven surface of the mosaic tiles, imagining her mother doing the same. She tried to lift the cover, but it was locked and her anticipation turned to frustration. As she stole into her father's room to look for the key, a twinge of sadness filled the hollow of her stomach. She hadn't been here since her mother's death almost five years ago, but nothing had changed. Her eyes searched the room quickly until she saw a clay bowl on the second shelf of the *tokonoma*. Two keys lay inside. She grabbed them both and hurried back to the trunk.

It was the second key that turned the lock. Aki raised the cover. Under layers of milky rice paper lay the most beautiful kimono she'd ever seen. She lifted it out of the trunk to see white peonies soaring upward from the hem, their pale petals a stark contrast to the vibrant red and gold of the silk material. She felt its softness and tried to imagine her mother wearing it as a young apprentice geisha. Underneath more paper, she found the wide black obi. Beautifully embroidered with gold thread, it felt heavy in her hands. Beneath that were two more kimonos, green and blue, but neither as opulent as the red one, and a pair of tall wooden sandals. Aki reached for the sandals and stepped up into them, wavering unsteadily. She laughed and caught herself as she almost stumbled taking a step. She couldn't imagine how anyone could walk in them. In a separate wooden box were her mother's hair decorations, silver combs, and makeup. And, at the bottom of the trunk was a framed black-and-white photo of her mother as a beautiful young *maiko* wearing the very same silk kimono with peonies.

15
DAY AND NIGHT
1950

When Hiroshi stepped onto the *dohyo* during the last match of the January *honbasho,* he knew that winning the tournament would put him within reach of the Juryo Division and becoming a professional *sekitori* wrestler. The difference between upper and lower ranks was said to be day and night, heaven and hell. After the match, he remembered the smooth coolness of the clay beneath his feet just before he charged his opponent and shifted his body to the right at the last moment, hitting the wrestler hard on his left side to throw him off balance. Hiroshi quickly took advantage by charging again and knocking the wrestler out of the ring before he had time to right himself. Within seconds, he was assured the tournament win.

Two weeks before the Haru Basho, the spring tournament in March, Tanaka-oyakata called Hiroshi into his office. Piled on his desk and the floor of the small room were the bundled

351

stacks of tournament ranking sheets called *banzuke.*

"Ah, Hiroshi," Tanaka-sama said, looking up from the papers on his desk. "Here's something I'd like you to look at." He turned the ranking sheet around for Hiroshi and pointed down the side of one crowded column.

Hiroshi bowed. His heart raced as he leaned closer to the desk. His name, Takanoyama, written in small, perfect characters, was circled on the right side of the sheet, below the top level of wrestlers. Underneath were his hometown, Yanaka, Tokyo, and his rank in the Juryo Division. He had been promoted to a *sekitori* wrestler.

"Did you know?" Hiroshi asked. His gaze lingered on the ranking sheet in happiness.

"I thought the Sumo Association might promote you after your wins at the Hatsu Basho in January. But nothing is ever certain."

Hiroshi took a step back and steadied himself. At twenty-four, he had reached a rank many other *sumotori* only dreamed of. It left a sweet taste on his tongue.

Tanaka smiled, ran his hand across the top of his shiny head, and said nothing.

Hiroshi bowed. "I'm honored."

"You've earned it."

Hiroshi bowed to his *oyakata* again. "*Arigato gozaimashita.* If it weren't for your training —," he began.

Tanaka-oyakata cut him off. "My training wouldn't mean a thing without your skill and diligence. Remember, Hiroshi-san, success is not handed to you. You must work hard for it and you must never dishonor what you've achieved."

"*Hai,* Oyakata-sama." He bowed, remembering his less than honorable behavior with Daishima.

The benefits of his new rank included wearing a white *mawashi* belt during practice and a silk one during tournaments, and making *tegata,* the autographed handprints for his fans. As a Juryo-ranked wrestler, he would now fight fifteen tournament matches instead of seven. He could hardly wait to tell his grandparents that his *sekitori* salary came with bonuses that would also allow him to provide for them financially.

"And Hiroshi," Tanaka-oyakata added, "your apprentice will be the new boy, Sadao."

Hiroshi celebrated his promotion at the Sakura teahouse, hosted by Tanaka-oyakata. It was the first time he'd been in a geisha teahouse, and everything about it fascinated him, from the large *sakura* tree in the small courtyard to the front door and entrance hall, where a large brush painting hung. A maid led them past several immaculate tatami rooms of differing sizes to a larger back room with a long table surrounded by cushions.

The shoji panels were hand painted with scenes of Mount Fuji, and slid open to a quiet garden. Three other *sekitori* wrestlers joined them, but Daishima remained conspicuously absent. The door to the room slid open and two geishas, who had been kneeling just outside, entered, and bowed to them. Hiroshi had never seen a geisha up close before. He watched, fascinated, as they moved in small, graceful steps, carrying plates of yakitori, pickled cabbage, grilled fish, sake, and beer. They filled the room with their sweet perfumes and light chatter. A geisha named Momiko danced for them, telling a story with each movement she made. Afterward, when she leaned close to Hiroshi and poured him more sake, the sleeve of her purple and white kimono brushed against his arm and he blushed at her touch. The other *sekitori* watched and teased him. "It looks as if Sekitori Takanoyama has found himself a new admirer." Momiko glanced up at him and looked away. He gazed at her pale, white skin, her long, thin neck, and wasn't quite sure who admired whom.

THE BIRD'S BEAK

While Nazo dozed, sprawled out on the table beside him in the drafty barn, Akira finished the *Okina* mask with paints Tomita-san had brought back for him from Oyama. He'd meant to finish it before the accident, and was now more determined than ever to resume his life as a mask maker. The quality of the paints was poor but would have to do. Working one-handed made everything take longer, from mixing pigments to painting the exact curve of an eyebrow, but nothing could exceed the joy he felt painting a mask again, the gratification of completing it. Akira was so involved that he didn't hear the knocking on the barn door until it grew louder and more persistent, and he finally called out, *"Hairu,"* come in. As the door creaked open, he expected Kiyo returning from school.

At fourteen, Kiyo was growing up, spending more time with her friends down in the village. Still, there were afternoons when she came home early and walked with Akira high into the mountains, where the cool March air felt like breathing ice. They avoided the path that led to the rocks where Akira had had his accident. He would never be able to convince her it wasn't her fault. For months afterward, she had watched his recuperation from a distance. Even now, her eyes brimmed with tears when she looked at his arm and she grew quiet, while he spoke, filling the air with more words than he'd ever uttered in all his years in Tokyo.

Akira tried to imagine what his life might be like in Tokyo, occupied for the past five years by American forces. He heard some scant news on the radio when he went down to the village, and now and then he read a newspaper brought back by Tomita-san, who made trips down to Oyama for supplies. Tokyo seemed a world away.

When he and Kiyo reached the top of the path, they hiked up through the sweet, scented pines to the rocks and sat on a ridge that jutted out and curved down at the end, which Kiyo had named the Bird's Beak. From there, they looked out over the valley, down at the peaked roofs poking through the trees, thin wisps of smoke floating into the air. Then it was his turn to be silent while Kiyo told him about her day, her voice wrapping around him like a blanket.

"You're early," Akira said now. He was so sure it was Kiyo at the door of the barn that he didn't stop painting.

"*Sumimasen,* Akira-san. I hope I'm not disturbing you."

He looked up to see Emiko standing just inside the door. "Emiko-san," he said, putting down the paintbrush and bowing. "Please come in." In the almost two years he'd been living in the barn, she'd entered only a few times.

Emiko stepped forward as if pushed by the sunlight that gleamed in her hair. She stopped and bowed. Fine lines around her mouth creased in a tentative smile. "Akira-san, Kiyo-chan and I would be honored if you came to dinner this evening."

She stood straight and rigid as her gaze darted around the barn and he wondered what she saw, his makeshift living quarters in the corner, surrounded by rusty metal tubs, shovels, and hoes, the battered table and oil lantern where he worked, the otherwise dingy light that made everything appear tired and discarded. Nazo lifted his head and lay back down again.

It was such a formal invitation, Akira asked, "Is it a special occasion?"

Emiko smiled again and shook her head. "It's just an opportunity for us to have dinner together."

"Hai." He smiled back. "I would be honored." He saw her face lighten at his acceptance as her body wavered and relaxed.

"We'll expect you at six, then," Emiko said, and bowed. She turned to leave and walked back out into the sunlight, closing the door behind her.

By the time Kiyo arrived at the barn, it was too late for a hike up the mountain. Instead, Akira cleaned up before he walked up to the house. Kiyo ushered him in and they sat by the hearth and talked and laughed with Emiko as she cooked sukiyaki. They watched as the broth with carrots and turnips bubbled and sputtered when she dropped in the thin slices of chicken, cabbage, and rice noodles. Akira couldn't remember when he had last eaten so well. Afterward, Kiyo entertained them with a poetry reading, and when he rose to leave, it was not without a trace of regret.

"*Domo arigato,* Emiko-san, it was a wonderful dinner. I don't know how to repay your kindness."

Emiko blushed. "It's so little, compared to all you've done for us."

Akira bowed. "I've done little. I'm a very lucky man."

Emiko blushed again and bowed.

In half sleep, Akira heard the barn door creak open and he sat up as footsteps, slow and hesitant, approached his cot in the corner of the barn. He reached down for his axe, heavy and solid in his hand. As the footsteps grew closer, he clutched the axe handle tighter then took a breath. "Who's there?" he demanded. The footsteps stopped in the darkness.

"It's me, Akira-san," Emiko's voice answered.

"Emiko-san? Is everything all right? Is it Kiyo-chan?" He put down the axe and struck a match. The sudden glow of his oil lamp startled them both, as their shadows jumped on walls.

"Kiyo is fine. She's asleep. We're fine," she added. She stood where she stopped, wrapping her trembling arms around her dark cotton kimono. Her long hair fell over her shoulders. "I need to speak to you."

With her hair down, she looked younger, slender and vulnerable in the wavering light. For the first time, he saw something of Kiyo in her eyes, and around her mouth. Until then, he had imagined Kiyo resembled her father, whose legacy lived in his young widow, his inquisitive daughter, this mountain house. Akira stood up and gently guided Emiko to his cot, wrapping a blanket around her before he sat beside her.

"What is so important that it can't wait until morning?" he asked in a whisper.

"Please forgive me, but I wanted to speak about . . . about us." Emiko avoided his eyes but kept talking. "I've been alone for a very long time . . ."

Akira swallowed and looked away. He always feared it might come to this. And why not? Emiko was a desirable woman who deserved a good man to take care of her and Kiyo. "Emiko," he whispered. But she was already leaning toward him, her lips finding his. For a moment, he allowed himself to be kissed and to kiss her back, tasting a sweet softness he longed for himself. He did love her and Kiyo as much as he could, and wished it were enough. But when he felt Emiko's hand caress the back of his neck, he pulled away from her and stood. "I can't," he said, "I'm sorry."

Emiko stood, too, pulling her kimono tight. He saw pain and embarrassment flicker across her face, aging her again. She bowed and hurried toward the barn door. Akira watched her shadow hurry ahead of her and wanted to call her back but didn't.

THE APPRENTICE

After attending to Daishima and acquiescing to all the higher-ranked wrestlers for five long years, Hiroshi was now one himself. Sadao, his apprentice, was one of three new *rikishi* at the stable. He appeared young and hardworking, but, unlike Fukuda, who was open and playful, Sadao remained closed and guarded. For the first time in his life Hiroshi also had a room of his own. It was small but quiet. He gazed out the window to the courtyard below, relishing the thought of no longer sleeping in the same dormitory-style room with the other *rikishi*. He would have to reacquaint himself with the idea of privacy and the luxury of sleeping in late again.

Tanaka-oyakata now maintained two *sekitori*-ranked wrestlers at the stable, though Daishima had recently slipped down one rank to *komusubi,* while Hiroshi rose to the Juryo Division. They had remained at a polite distance after Hiroshi defeated him during the practice session almost two years ago. But

360

at thirty-three, Daishima had to entertain thoughts of retirement rather than falling out of the *sekitori* division and risking dishonor for both himself and the stable.

"*Sumimasen,* Sekitori Takanoyama." Sadao's voice broke into his thoughts.

"*Hai.*" Hiroshi turned from the window to see his young attendant standing at the doorway of his room carrying a wrapped package.

Sadao bowed low to him. "Excuse me, Sekitori Takanoyama, your bath is ready. Also, Tanaka-oyakata asked that I bring this to you." He bowed again and put the package on top of Hiroshi's *akeni,* the bamboo trunk in which he stored his personal belongings. On tournament days, it would be Sadao's job to transport it to the stadium.

"Thank you, Sadao. What is it?" Hiroshi unwrapped the package and was surprised to see an ankle-length maroon *kesho-mawashi,* the handmade silk ceremonial apron embroidered with white and gold and worn around the front of his waist to participate in the *dohyo-iri,* the ring-entering ceremony.

"Please tell Oyakata-sama that I've received the package."

"*Hai.*" Sadao bowed.

Hiroshi watched the boy leave the room, light and sure-footed. His fingers followed the intricate chrysanthemum pattern on the ceremonial apron. It was well made and costly, far more elaborate than any ceremonial apron he'd worn before. It was all part of the pageantry of sumo. His heart jumped to think how intricately the sport of sumo was tied to his life and his country. Despite Japan's defeat, sumo retained its history and honor, a tradition that the Japanese people could still cherish. It was a tradition given to very few men, and one Hiroshi felt privileged to serve.

After practice the next day, Hiroshi bathed himself on the low stool, rinsing off with bucketfuls of warm water. His arms and legs were heavily muscled now, his stomach solid. He had grown in size and strength but tried to keep his weight down. He slapped the towel against his back and waited for Sadao to return and scrub it. The boy wasn't sixteen yet, and already quick and attentive. But something about him made Hiroshi think he was younger, his thin, still-boyish face, the dark, inquisitive eyes that darted everywhere; a rare laugh still tinged with innocence. Hiroshi knew that his young attendant, like himself, was an orphan, his parents having died in the 1945 firestorm. And while Hiroshi was raised by his grandparents, he heard Sadao had grown up on the streets, where he had acquired the hard edge needed to survive. Hiroshi tried to get him to talk more. "And where did you live after the firestorm?" he asked, as the boy stood behind him and scrubbed his back. Unlike Daishima, who was either silent or belligerent, Hiroshi was curious to know more about the young attendant he would need to depend on.

Sadao paused for a long time. "I lived with friends," he said.

Hiroshi turned around and eyed the boy closely. He had the right body for wrestling, big-boned and sturdy, but he would need to grow taller, put on more weight in the coming years, and strengthen his leg muscles. But unlike Fukuda, he trained hard and wasn't easily distracted.

Sadao poured another bucket of warm water down his back. "Excuse me, Sekitori Takanoyama," he said, "I need to check if the water in the *ofuro* is hot enough. I'll return to wash your hair."

Hiroshi nodded. For now, the boy's story would remain untold.

THE GRADUATE

Nakamura Hall at Tokyo University was filled with the families of graduating architecture and design students. The buzz of excited voices cut through the hot, still July afternoon. Kenji was seated onstage with his graduating class as he looked out among the packed audience. He wondered if Mika Abe might be in another hall on campus at the same moment, graduating with the other art students. He glanced about for his family, worried that it might be too hot for his grandparents. He'd seen them shortly after they arrived and the happiness on their faces seemed to erase all the difficulties of the past years. Standing next to them, Hiroshi looked like a warrior from the past. But when the commencement ceremony began, Kenji relaxed, knowing his brother was taking good care of them.

After the graduation ceremonies, Hiroshi celebrated by taking them to dinner at the Katana restaurant. The alleyways were alive again with small shops and restaurants reopening. After so many years of struggle, Kenji could feel his grandparents' excitement at being at the Katana again. Before the war, they had eaten there once a month. It was a small, comfortable family-run restaurant that Kenji chose above all the other newly opened ones. He watched his *obachan* touch her teacup, her bowl, and the wooden chopsticks as if she were afraid they might disappear. Hiroshi stood and raised a toast. "To my college-educated brother, the scholar!"

Kenji studied Hiroshi's face, strong yet always forgiving. There were traces of their father in his brother's face; a strength and determination Kenji knew was tempered by his innate integrity. Hiroshi was quickly climbing the ranks in sumo, and his next big tournament would be at the new Kokugikan sumo stadium built in Kuramae.

Their arms were already lifted in a toast, when Kenji stood before he lost his nerve. He bowed formally to his grandparents. "*Ojichan, obachan,* I've been thinking about this for a long time," he began. "I'm sorry to disappoint you, but I can't . . . I don't wish to be an architect. Now that I've graduated, I hope to continue learning to be a mask artisan."

The only halfhearted argument he could make about returning to the masks was that the preperformance censorship implemented by the government during the war had been lifted from traditional theater. Actors would need masks again, and perhaps one day he'd make a mask that would be worn by the famous actor Otomo Matsui, just as Akira Yoshiwara had. Maybe Matsui would even know something about the whereabouts of his sensei. He would keep quiet and wait. In his moment of uncertainty, a thought rushed through Kenji. *If I were still Kenji the ghost, I would simply disappear.*

His *ojichan* lowered his sake cup soundlessly to the table and spoke softly, thoughtfully. "There are many ways in which to rebuild a nation," he said.

"There are many different kinds of scholars," his *obachan* added, for which he was grateful.

"Hai." His grandfather nodded. "It's what you've always wanted. We live a short enough time on this earth. A man should do what he loves."

Kenji swallowed. His heart raced with happiness.

His *obachan* smiled, raising her sake cup again. *"Hai,* your *ojichan* speaks the truth," she said.

"And when have I not spoken the truth?" his *ojichan* teased.

"When have you not spoken?" His *obachan* rolled her eyes and made them all laugh.

Kenji drank down the sake and felt the warmth spread throughout his body.

LEAVING

Haru was all packed. There was still a little time before she left for the train station. She stopped to look around the room and catch her breath. Weeks had led up to this moment in late September, but the reality of leaving had struck her only during the past week. Eight months earlier, when she received the letter from Nara Women's University, she had carried it with her for days without telling her father or Aki. It surprised her like an unexpected gift. Not that there'd been any reason, since her grades were good and her test scores high; still, Haru wanted to enjoy the feeling a little longer before she shared it with anyone else.

At seventeen, Haru could have just as easily been preparing for her marriage ceremony as going off to study at a university. She knew girls in her class who wanted nothing more than families of their own. But her father embraced Haru when she told him, smiling widely. "It's what you hoped for," he said, before letting go.

It took Aki more time to adjust to the idea that she'd be gone. Hesitating, Haru had questioned if she should go to Nara. She'd become both mother and sister to Aki since the firestorm, and she wavered at the idea of leaving her sister alone, dangling. But after a week, Aki had accepted her leaving and seemed happy again. She even spoke of visiting Haru in Nara. At fourteen, her sister was already a classic beauty, fair-skinned and delicate, resembling their mother more with each passing day.

Haru stopped packing, and glanced quickly at herself in the mirror. With her hair pulled back, she was darker complexioned and sharper featured than Aki, though she saw hints of her mother in the high bridge of her nose and around the mouth. She was dressed in her traveling kimono, a fine weave of silk embroidered with blue irises, an expensive gift her father insisted on buying for her. She looked older in the exquisite kimono. It was almost as if someone else were looking back at her in the mirror. She wondered what others saw when they looked at her. Just yesterday, she'd seen Hiroshi-san. She met him by surprise on her way home from picking up some last-minute daikon at the small shop down the road.

"Haru-san," he said, bowing to her.

"Hiroshi-san." She bowed back. When she stood straight, she barely reached his shoulder. Hiroshi was muscular but not as heavy as some of the other *sumotori*. He was wearing a dark blue *yukata* robe and looked quite handsome, older and more self-assured than the young *rikishi* who used to come to pick up the *chanko* she cooked. The sweet smell of *bintsuke* in his hair floated through the air.

"I understand that you're leaving for Nara tomorrow."

Haru paused. *"Hai,"* she said, realizing everyone at the stable must have known for months.

"Your father said you'll be entering Nara University a year early." Hiroshi smiled. "He's very proud of you."

Haru blushed.

He must have noticed, and added, "It's hard to keep any secrets at the stable."

Haru couldn't imagine anyone keeping a secret with all the *rikishi* living in such close quarters. *"Hai,"* she said.

"May I?" He offered to carry her *furoshiki*.

"Domo arigato, but it's not heavy." She

clutched the *furoshiki* tighter, grateful to have something in her hand.

"We'll be very sad to see you leave," he said, walking along with her.

She blushed again, pushed her free hand into the folds of her kimono. For a big man, he moved lightly as they walked in silence. Haru glanced up him. "May I ask you a question, Hiroshi-san?"

"Hai," he answered.

"How was it for you leaving your family and coming to the stable?" Haru had always wondered how boys as young as fifteen could leave home to train as sumo apprentices. She was older and going to university, but still she felt bereft.

Hiroshi cleared his throat. "I was a bit older than other boys when I came to the stable. I imagine the young ones are terribly homesick at first."

"Hai," she agreed.

He added, "But I've wanted to be a *sumotori* ever since I was a boy; most of us want the same thing. We all realize what an honor it is to be chosen. And we are fortunate; your father is a good man."

He hadn't said a good coach, she thought, but a good man, which somehow meant more to her. Haru already knew her father was a good coach, so it meant more that a *rikishi* also respected him as a person. "He thinks very highly of you," she said. She looked away, knowing that her father had spoken of Hirohsi-san just once or twice over the years, saying what a hard worker he was.

"Your father has been kind," he said. "I have a long way to go yet."

She smiled. "*Hai,* we all have."

"And what will you study at Nara?" he asked.

Haru looked up, pleased at how comfortable it was having this conversation with Hiroshi. "Science," she answered. "Botany, perhaps, the science of plants." She felt her heart beating faster. For months after the firestorm, she had searched for any signs of life and found it in a weed that refused to be smothered. Its endurance had inspired her studies, including Darwin's theories and books on botany. Still, she felt suddenly foolish and had no idea why she'd told him botany. "Or maybe not," she added.

Hiroshi laughed. "I believe, Haru-san, you would make a very good scientist."

"Why is that?"

"Science is very precise," he answered.

She waited for him to continue but he didn't. When they reached the front gate of the stable, Hiroshi bowed low and said, "Science is also full of surprises." He smiled. "I hope to see you again before you leave."

Haru bowed back. It was the longest conversation she'd had with a man, other than her father.

Haru stroked the smooth material of her kimono and returned to her packing. When she glanced up, Aki was standing in the doorway. "Don't forget to write me," she said, her voice sad, her face solemn.

Haru smiled. "How could I forget to write to you? Besides, we really won't be that far away."

"Yes we will," Aki said. "You won't be here at the house, or even in Tokyo, so it will be far away."

Haru didn't know what to say. "Just think, you'll have this room all to yourself," Haru said lightly. "Soon, you won't want me to return and disturb your things."

Haru watched her sister. Where had that vibrant young Aki gone? The little girl who once entertained and exasperated her was now a thin, sullen young woman, whose bright eyes had dulled even with all her beauty. Haru sometimes felt she'd lost more than just her mother five years ago. She cleared her throat, looked down at the thickened skin on her palms. "We'd better go," she said, grabbing her bag and Aki's hand. "*Otosan* is waiting."

Sho Tanaka paced back and forth in the courtyard, waiting for his daughters to come downstairs. Fall was in the air, the sad, lonely scent of summer fading. A lessening of light. Haru, spring. Aki, fall. Each daughter named for the season in which they had arrived into the world.

If they didn't hurry, Haru would be late catching her train to Nara. How had the time slipped away from him? When had she grown into a young woman? He smiled to himself at the thought. Was Haru ever a young girl? She always seemed older than her age. At seventeen, she had sacrificed so much of her youth taking care of the household. After Noriko's death, she became *okamisan* of the stable, taking care of Aki and helping him with the *rikishi,* and, strangely enough, the wrestlers always treated her with the respect usually given to a grown woman. Even Daishima, who thought of nothing other than his own well-being, respected Haru.

Sho couldn't imagine the Katsuyama-beya without her. What he would miss most was Haru's warmth and her nurturing ways. It was something he wasn't able to give to either of his daughters after Noriko's death. After Aki lost her voice, she became remote and difficult. If anyone questioned her too closely about the firestorm, she would cry and stay by Haru's side. Instead, he had remained at a distance and devoted himself to rebuilding the stable, watching the *rikishi* slowly return. He had survived the loss of his wife at the cost of his daughters. Sho shook his head and couldn't imagine what he and Aki would talk about every night with Haru gone. Her calm had tied their lives altogether.

There had been too many goodbyes lately. It made him wistful. He looked up to see if his daughters were coming. Other fathers might worry about finding their daughter a good husband. But Sho felt Haru deserved to find her own way. Any college boy with any sense would see Haru's value. He smiled to think how much she was like him, disciplined and organized. Thankfully, both of his daughters had resembled their mother, each a daily reminder of Noriko. Sometimes, when he caught a glimpse of Aki leaving the house in a hurry, he still saw Noriko rushing off to shop at the market.

At the train station, he would be saying goodbye again, this time to Haru. One by one, it felt as if everyone were leaving him, though it would never be as devastating as Noriko's sudden absence. He never had the chance to say goodbye — to whisper *sayonara* in her ear — a simple word that would have meant so much.

"There you are," he said, seeing Haru and

Aki step out of the house. Yes, it was true. They had grown up without his realizing it; he had been too busy training boys to become *sumotori* while his little girls had become young women. Even Aki wouldn't need him much longer. She was already so distant, keeping to herself and spending so much time in her room. What did a fourteen-year-old girl do in her room all day? he wondered. Then he smiled and touched the sleeve of Haru's kimono, taking the suitcase from her hand and, as he looked down, catching a glimpse of the small scar on her palm. "We must hurry, Haru-chan," he said, "or you'll miss your train."

The Road

It was still dark when Akira stepped outside and quietly closed the door to the barn, the October air cold and crisp. He knew winter wasn't far off and checked again to see that he'd stacked enough wood by the side of the barn. It was just before dawn and dark shadows moved with the wind, the rustling branches waving as he turned back once and headed toward the main road that led down to the village of Aio. Akira felt an ache in his chest that traveled down to where his hand used to be. He moved with slow, careful steps, as if the darkness and the rutted road were deliberately slowing him down. He saw the road that lay before him like his life, scarred by long winters, the harsh, dry summers. Akira swung the bag with his few possessions over his shoulder. He left behind a note, the cat Nazo, who was too old and settled to travel such a distance again, and the finished *Okina* mask. Kiyo would take good care of Nazo and the mask.

As dawn's light slowly brought everything into focus, Akira walked faster, knowing that each step took him farther away from Emiko and Kiyo. He stopped a moment when the sun rose to reveal a breathtaking sight; all around him the pine trees stood silent and the red-orange leaves of autumn blazed as they reached upward toward the light.

It was never the same with Emiko after her visit to the barn that night. They hardly spoke and danced around each other politely, acting like two guests at an inn. He kept to himself in the barn, cut the wood, and did the chores, but there was a lingering sadness to everything he did. What little hope he'd had for a family life had vanished. So many times he had wanted to give in to the comfort of Emiko and Kiyo and their praying-hands house. They might have been happy as far as lives go. But he couldn't stop asking himself, Wasn't there supposed to be more to life? Hadn't he felt it before with Sato? Only once did Emiko refer to that night. And even then she offered it as an apology, as if everything were her fault. "I'm sorry to have bothered you, Akira-san. It wasn't my place."

He bowed to her. "It *is* your place, Emiko-san," he said softly. The rest of his words sat on the edge of his tongue and never emerged. He saw her eyes imploring him to go on, and how the deepening lines that etched her face made her appear beautiful to him. "Thank you for allowing me to stay," he said instead.

Emiko smiled thinly and bowed back to him.

It wasn't long before Kiyo knew something was wrong. "Why are you both acting so distant, so strange?" she asked, stroking Nazo's stomach as he lay on the table in the barn. He was old and no longer spent his days chasing squirrels, or leaping at low-flying birds.

Akira laughed it off and went on cleaning out the barn. "What are you talking about?" he said.

She eyed him closely. "My mother seems so sad," she said.

He knew she was waiting for him to say something. "I'm sorry," was all he could think of.

"Did something happen?" she asked.

Akira shook his head. "We all get sad sometimes."

He watched her pick up Nazo, rocking him

back and forth in her arms. The aloof cat that once had hated to be carried was completely different with Kiyo.

"I hope I never get that sad," she finally said.

He didn't look at her then. There was nothing he could say. Kiyo was going to be fifteen and life was just beginning for her. Akira wanted nothing more than to protect her always from life's sadness, shield her from the hurt she'd invariably experience, but at that moment, he knew he wouldn't be the one to do that. These thoughts played over in his mind as he made his way down the mountain to the village of Aio. From there, he would find a ride down to Oyama and catch a train back to Tokyo. He would be there by evening.

MESSENGERS FROM GOD

From the moment she stepped off the train, Haru was in love with Nara. During the four-hour journey, she read about the city as soon as she was in the compartment by herself. All thoughts of loneliness disappeared in the pages. Nara was once the ancient capital of Japan, where Buddhism grew and thrived, and the Todai-ji temple housed the largest bronze statue of Buddha in the world. There was also Nara Park, which covered half the city, and was famous for the deer that roamed freely, deer once believed to be messengers from the gods. Most called it Deer Park. Nara was lovely in a way that she hadn't expected — much smaller and quieter than Tokyo — filled with temples and shrines, and in the middle of it all stood Nara Women's University. While Haru missed her father and Aki, even the sumo stable, she found a certain relief in being in a new place where the difficulties of the past were far away and she could glimpse her future right in front of her, spread out far and wide like Deer Park.

Haru spent the two days before the start of classes walking around Nara, visiting shrines and temples, looking forward to seeing Nara Park. Each morning, she was out of the dormitory before anyone else was up. It was late autumn and cool in the early mornings, the leaves falling all around her, blanketing her footsteps in a soothing quiet. She left visiting the park for last, the afternoon before her classes were to begin. A calm before what she hoped wouldn't be a storm. She had had enough storms in her life.

Haru wasn't disappointed. Nara Park was a world of its own. A wall of tall pine and oak trees protected it from the noise of the outside. Stepping into the park, she felt an immediate sense of comfort that swelled in her chest. There was a multitude of paths to follow. With every step, she discovered a new plant or unfamiliar foliage that she sketched quickly in her notebook. She hoped to see deer roaming in the park when she came to a flat, open expanse of green grass, where they were fed by visitors and taken care of by park attendants. But there wasn't a deer in sight. Haru followed the empty path and wondered where the deer were hiding. Were they tired of being put on show? From the corner of her eye, Haru saw shadows by the trees, a small group of deer standing perfectly still, watching her. She stopped and smiled, held out her hand to them. After all, she had entered their world, and she was the one on display.

Haru walked around the park until sunset, watching the sun disappear behind the tall trees before she returned to her dormitory, exhausted. After a quick meal, she fell into a deep sleep. Even the strange hollowness of the dormitory and the whispering voices of excited students all around her didn't wake her. Instead, she dreamed she, too, was a messenger from the gods, standing among all the deer that roamed freely through the park, their warm breath against the palm of her hand as she fed them deer crackers, made of plain rice flour. Haru stood with them, surrounded by the sheltering trees, waiting to hear what the next message was.

By November, with money he borrowed from Hiroshi, Kenji finally found a small shop with a two-room apartment over it that he could afford to rent. Many of the spaces he looked at were just small hovels, abandoned casualties of the war. This particular shop needed work, but it wasn't far from Akira Yoshiwara's old mask shop, and was quiet and unobtrusive with a sizable front window to display his masks. Kenji also liked the neighborhood, tucked away in an alley, so that the actors would have to seek him out, just as they had Yoshiwara. He would remain just invisible enough. Everything else would have to be a compromise. The front room was small, even more so when he built shelves to line the walls, but the back room provided ample space to set up the saw and two tables where he would work, much as Yoshiwara had. He felt a tug of sadness at not having his sensei there to give him the skill and technique to be a truly distinctive mask artisan. That Kenji would have to learn on his own.

Kenji bought blocks of Japanese cypress from the same lumberyard where he used to buy balsa wood for his architecture classes. He used his money sparingly, not wanting to take advantage of Hiroshi's generosity. A diet of noodles and rice and vegetables would suffice. If he needed more sustenance, he had only to visit his grandparents.

Slowly the shop was becoming his. When Kenji came downstairs every morning, the rooms held the subtle sweetness of the cypress wood and paints. But his shelves remained empty, one *Zo-onna* mask finally finished and waiting to be painted. It took him days to get through the simple steps his sensei had accomplished in hours. He couldn't afford to make too many more mistakes. His first cuts with the table saw were disasters, uneven or off the mark. A small tragedy every time he wasted any wood. As the weeks passed, Kenji learned to adjust his strength, guide the wood and not force it in order to get the shape he desired. He remembered the words Yoshiwara-sensei told him from the very beginning. "Think of the wood as a living thing, warm to the touch. Never push; let your hands guide the wood." As Kenji relaxed, the cypress wood came alive in his hands. He began to see the masks that would slowly emerge from the remaining blocks of wood.

Kenji went for a walk every evening, shaking off the stiffness of chiseling and sanding all day. The cold December air revitalized him. The alleyways were filled with people again and twice a week he went directly after work to visit his grandparents. On this particular evening, Kenji found himself jumping on a train and getting off near the university. When he was going to classes every day he dreaded the trip, but now that he had graduated, it felt somehow soothing to return to the familiar. He crossed one street and headed for the old architecture studio when he saw her, Mika Abe, dressed in dark, Western-style clothing, crossing the road and going into a small restaurant. Just by the way she walked, he knew it was her.

"Mika-san!" he called out, picking up his pace.

She stopped at the doorway and looked up. When he reached her, he was surprised by her red lipstick and dark eye makeup. She looked like one of those young followers of the *kasutori* culture his *obachan* talked about. According to his grandmother, they were to blame for the uncontrollable behavior and countercultural sentiments that had captured the thoughts and actions of so many of his classmates and contemporaries. He found Mika Abe as beautiful as before.

Kenji wasn't sure she recognized him at first. He hadn't thought about how he must look until that moment. It couldn't be much different from the first time he had seen Yoshiwara emerge from the back room, disheveled, wood dust all over his hair and kimono, appearing older than he was. It was too late for him to turn away.

He bowed. "Kenji Matsumoto," he said.

"*Hai,* I know." She bowed back. "It's nice to see you again."

"Please forgive my appearance. I've come from work."

Mika smiled. "Are you designing the houses, or building them?"

"Neither." He laughed. "I've opened a mask shop in the Yanaka district. It's the Noh theater I've always loved."

She watched him for a moment in silence. Was it curiosity or disbelief he saw flicker in her eyes? It felt like an eternity before she said, "I'm afraid I have to go; I'm meeting some friends. But I'd like to visit your shop sometime."

Kenji bowed. "Of course, I'd be honored."

"One day very soon," Mika said, smiling. She bowed and turned into the restaurant.

It wasn't until Kenji was halfway back to Yanaka that he realized he hadn't given her directions to his shop.

16
HISTORY
1951

Sadao scooped more coals onto the fire. The *ofuro* was almost hot enough for Takanoyama's soak, the steam rising like smoke. Every day the *sekitori* asked him more questions about his life before the Katsuyama-beya. It was just a matter of time before Takanoyama learned the truth about him. Sadao had lied to Tanaka-oyakata. He was only twelve when he came to the stable, though he could easily have passed for fifteen. He was already tall for his age and broad shouldered, the son of a butcher, his father a large man with the strength of a bull and nicknamed *buru* by everyone who knew him in their Tokyo neighborhood. Sadao, who had helped his father at the shop since he was a little boy, was called young *buru*. Those days seemed far away now, days when he was still very small and his father's shop was filled with the bloody carcasses of chickens and pigs, and an entire side of beef whose sheer size fascinated him. And once, someone had kept a dead ox in his father's meat locker until he could arrange for its burial. As the war progressed, the cement-walled meat locker was stripped bare by the *kempeitai,* and the only signs left of his father's once successful butcher shop were the remnants of dark bloodstains on the floor.

Sadao's parents had died in the firestorm when he was six years old. His father refused to leave his shop when the incendiary bombs were dropped, telling them not to worry, the Americans had never bombed so close to the city center before. Sadao and his mother had found protection in the meat locker, listening to the low drone of the approaching planes, waiting for his father to come. Instead, they heard his father's screams, and his mother hugged Sadao tight and told him to stay there, and not to leave until she returned. "Don't go, don't go, don't go," he'd begged. His mother touched his cheek, said she'd be right back. She never returned.

Sadao waited in the dark. He sat stone-still on the cement floor and used the matches and candles sparingly, as his mother had taught him. Outside, the roar of the angry wind was deafening and seemed to suck the air right out of the room. Sadao remembered crying until his stomach hurt from fear and hunger. He lay down then, covered his ears and closed his eyes. The heat wrapped itself around him like a blanket. When Sadao awoke, it was to silence. Rising from the floor on wobbly legs, he disobeyed his mother and opened the door of the meat locker, only to see that the world he once knew had been reduced to smoldering ashes.

After the death of his parents, there was nowhere for him to go, and no living relatives close by. Sadao walked down the devastated streets crying when a group of kids found him. They were all orphans, they said, and they stayed together in order to survive. They took little Sadao in, taught him how to live on the streets, and he remembered being afraid and biting his lip rather than asking them what the word "orphan" meant.

Later, it was just as easy to say he was fifteen rather than twelve when the man who had seen him fighting in the streets wanted to know how old he was. He could be any age they wanted him to be, if they paid. Hadn't he survived for half his life knowing how to read people? And where were his parents? the man had asked. He didn't have any, he answered. There was nothing for him to worry about. He saw the man's brow wrinkle, his hand running across his smooth, shaved head. Sadao wondered if it meant the deal would slip through his fingers. He was afraid that if he told him his real age the man might not be interested. He looked like a man who might like his boys older.

Instead, the man named Tanaka-san had

taken him to a place called the Katsuyama-beya, where he was the stable master and trained boys to be sumo wrestlers. It wasn't at all what Sadao expected when he arrived almost a year ago. It was a place where he could start over again, be someone he had always wanted to be.

After living on the streets for so many years, everything at the stable felt too big and too small at the same time. He wasn't used to sleeping in a warm room on a futon whose softness made him feel as if he were being held. It frightened him, a reminder of his parents and his lost childhood. He remembered his mother's voice, high and singsong, and his father's thick, strong hands, which could wrestle the animals he butchered to the ground by himself. But Sadao's biggest fear was that his parents' faces were slowly disappearing in a fog, slipping from his memory, while he tried without success to forget his life on the streets. Why couldn't he forget those faces instead? He recalled how he had prayed to an unknown god, the deity his mother worshipped, lighting incense and chanting, or the Buddha his father had perched in the back room of his butcher shop. But nobody had come to save him when they touched his body, when they did unspeakable things to him, laughing, leaving yen coins, leaving cigarette butts, leaving chocolate bars . . . leaving.

■ ■ ■ ■

Sadao gathered the towels and returned to wash Takanoyama's hair. It took at least three washes to get the *bintsuke* wax completely out. Sadao liked Takanoyama and thought he was fortunate to be his personal attendant. He had heard stories from other *sumotori* apprentices, whose *sekitori* took advantage of their positions, making life miserable for them. Sekitori Daishima was said to have ill-treated his attendants, including a young sumo who was a close friend of Takanoyama's when he was starting out. Perhaps that was why he was so fair and patient, and treated him like his younger brother. He began teaching Sadao to be a *sumotori* from the start. "Watch everyone and everything around you to understand the stable life," Takanoyama advised. Sadao soon learned the principles of honor and hierarchy that had governed the sumo world for hundreds of years. Takanoyama tried to draw him out, but Sadao kept to himself, something he'd learned on the streets; the less you made yourself visible, the better. After all, weren't all the rules of survival the same?

He liked it at the stable. Before long, he knew that most of the wrestlers maintained their own private rituals. Sadao sat in the locker room and watched some *sumotori* chant and meditate before a tournament, while others held talismans — a coin, an *omamori* bag with a special prayer in it, or beads — and still others played cards or read magazines and told endless jokes to relax. Sadao felt as if he could reach out and grab the energy, thick with the fear, excitement, and restlessness of pent-up animals.

Sadao had a few rituals of his own. Every morning when he awoke, he touched the futon he slept on and then he knocked softly on the floor three times, just to be sure he was really there. When he rose, it was still dark outside, and he heard the snores and grunts of all the sleeping wrestlers, and felt strangely at peace.

The steam from the bath rose around them, sweet and hot, as he lifted another bucket of water and rinsed Takanoyama's hair.

"What will you do with your free time this afternoon?" Takanoyama asked.

Sadao hadn't even thought about it. Most days he had no free time. He moved from one chore to the other, and his day usually ended with washing the dishes after their evening meal. He ran his hands over the *sekitori*'s hair to see if all the wax was washed out. "I'll sleep," he answered.

Takanoyama laughed. "It was all I wanted to do, too."

Sadao had finished washing his hair for the

third time when Takanoyama turned around and asked, "How old are you, Sadao?"

Sadao stopped for a moment, weighing the question. Takanoyama watched him and waited. Not the way other men had watched him, but as if he were trying to figure out a puzzle and couldn't. The words rose to his lips. In that split second he'd made the decision to trust the *sekitori,* even if it meant having to leave the stable. "I'm almost thirteen."

Takanoyama sat still and didn't turn to face him. "Why did you tell Tanaka-oyakata you were older?"

Sadao shrugged. "At first, I thought that's what he wanted to hear. After I came to the stable, I was afraid he would make me leave if he knew I was so young."

Takanoyama grunted. He could almost hear the *sekitori* calculating his age. If he were twelve when he entered the stable, and his parents had died during the firestorm, then he was only a little boy of six when he was left alone to survive on the streets. He didn't want Takanoyama's pity. He hesitated before asking, "Will you tell Tanaka-oyakata how old I really am?"

Hiroshi shook his head. "The decision is yours to make."

As much as Sadao wanted to forget his years on the street, old fears returned to haunt him. What if Sekitori Takanoyama told Tanaka-oyakata how old he was? Would he have to leave the stable? On the streets, stealing had been as natural as breathing for Sadao. The wrestlers at the stable had so much, and he knew they wouldn't miss a small item or two, untraceable things that could be misplaced. It would be his insurance, just in case he found himself out in the cold again.

While Sekitori Takanoyama soaked in the *ofuro,* Sadao sneaked back into his room to rifle through the green lacquered trunk with Takanoyama's name hand painted in red along the border. Surely, there must be something of worth in it, something small he could hold on to and sell if he needed to. He quietly lifted the top and rummaged through the trunk to find a *yukata* robe, a pair of *setta* tatami slippers, towels, a tatami mat, his cushion, a *mawashi* belt, his expensive silk ceremonial apron, and a few personal items. There was also a photograph of a young couple, another of an older couple, and his book of poetry. Sadao stroked the gold trim along the apron, his fingers following the pattern of the white crane on the front. It would bring a fair amount of money on the streets. He shook the thought away. As he carefully put down the lid, something else caught his eye. He reached down and picked up a silver hairpin, which he held for a moment before slipping it into his pocket. He doubted Takanoyama would miss it anyway; it was probably given to him by some geisha at one of the teahouses he frequented.

Sadao knew stealing from Takanoyama-sama was wrong, but he couldn't stop himself, especially now that the *sekitori* knew the truth about his age. He closed the lid quietly and hurried back to the soaking room.

THE GINKGO LEAF

After a long, hot soak, Hiroshi waited for Tokohashi to arrive. As an upper-ranked wrestler, he now wore his hair in a more elaborate *oichomage,* a topknot that resembled a ginkgo leaf, to all the major tournaments and on special occasions. The fan-shaped ginkgo leaf came from a species of tree that was more than a thousand years old. While Hiroshi's wrestling name, Noble Mountain, gave him a sense of dignity, his *oichomage* gave him history.

Tokohashi was one of only a handful of hairdressers who had trained for ten years to execute a perfect *oichomage,* styled with numerous combs and picks. Hiroshi looked up when the door slid open, happy to see the diminutive, good-natured Tokohashi enter. At sixty, the hairdresser was five years from retirement, and Hiroshi hoped to make grand champion before then so that Tokohashi would be the one to dress his hair. Over the years, the hairdresser had become just as trusted in his life and career as Tanaka-oyakata was. While Tanaka honed the fighting skills of each wrestler, Tokohashi spent hours getting to know his character.

"Hiroshi, if you think the women were crazy about you before, they won't be able to resist you with an *oichomage*," Tokohashi teased, just as he had five years ago when he first styled his *chomage*.

"I should be married within the week," Hiroshi quipped.

Tokohashi carefully laid out his combs and *bintsuke* wax. When he opened the tin of wax, the sweet, flowery scent filled the air. "Now that you're *sekitori*, it might not be a bad idea; a strong young man should have more than one way to expend his energy."

Hiroshi felt the heat rise to his face and was happy Tokohashi stood behind him working. "In good time," he answered, keeping his voice light and noncommittal.

His rise in rank to *sekitori* did free him to marry, a thought that had flickered through his mind in the past few weeks. Until now, he'd lived a life of endless routine, one filled with rigorous training and continuous responsibilities. Just to lie down and sleep at the end of the day was comfort enough. Now Hiroshi saw an entirely different world opening up to him. He sat with this knowledge and tried to imagine the touch of a woman's soft skin beneath his fingers. He thought of the geisha Momiko, how her skin must feel like a flower's petal, smooth and cool, silky and fragrant.

ANOTHER WORLD

It was the noise that bothered Akira Yoshiwara most since he'd returned to Tokyo five months ago. When he first stepped down from the train at the Shinjuku Station in Tokyo, it took all his willpower to keep from getting back on the next train to Oyama. The noise was like a wild wind pushing him back, a nervous, frantic chorus filled with shrieks and cries that shook through his body. He missed the silence of Aio, the quiet whistle of the wind sweeping through the trees, the quick snap of a branch breaking, or the trickling water that ran down the river. Emiko had once pointed out to him that it was simply nature whispering secrets to them. Akira pushed his thoughts of her and Kiyo out of his mind.

The noise was unbearable, but so was the crush of the crowds that surged toward him as he gripped his bag tighter and walked toward the nearest exit. And what then? Akira no longer had any place to go. After almost seven years away, Tokyo was now a stranger. Or perhaps he was the stranger. He sidestepped the bodies rushing to get to their trains when someone knocked hard against his left shoulder. He looked directly into the face of a beggar standing in front of him, reeking, still wearing the tattered jacket of an army uniform, his hair and beard long and matted. *"Dozo,"* he said, holding out his filthy hand for money.

Instinctively, Akira raised his left arm as if to wave the man away. His arm was suspended in the air between them and his sleeve fell back to expose the angry scar where his hand once was. The beggar stepped back and mumbled, "Ah, my brother, you've already given enough because of the war." Then he quickly turned away from Akira.

Outside the train station, it was like another world. People were scattered everywhere but it was quieter. He squinted against the sunlight, then kept his head down and didn't dare look the patrolling American soldiers in the face. Akira walked for hours that first day, trying to acclimate himself to this new, brash Tokyo. The streets he once knew had vanished, along with the buildings that stood among them. Empty lots were everywhere. In some parts of the city, he saw the skeletal frames of new buildings going up. As darkness fell and the air grew cool, Akira found a small hotel on the outskirts of the downtown area where he could stay while he learned to navigate this suddenly alien city all over again.

It was weeks before Akira finally took a train back to Yanaka, walking from the station through the downtown area. He didn't want to face the devastation, the remnants of his past. But unlike downtown Tokyo, Yanaka remained remarkably untouched; many of the alleyways were exactly the same as when he left, new shops peppered among the old. There were fewer American soldiers patrolling the Yanaka area. Akira relaxed and followed the familiar route he had walked every day for fifteen years. It wasn't until he turned the corner just before his old mask shop that he felt suddenly nervous again, his heart racing. Part of Akira still hoped the shop stood empty, waiting for him to return and pick up the pieces of his former life. But just across the narrow alleyway was his shop, now filled with blooming flowers in the window. He thought of Kenji and wondered if he'd ever stood in the very same spot, contemplating what had happened to him. Akira cleared his throat and smiled. Life had gone on in Yanaka without him or his masks.

Escape

More than a year after Haru left for Nara, Aki still felt empty and lethargic. It wasn't just because her sister was away at school; it was the growing realization that people would always be leaving her, first her mother, and now Haru. One day, her father would die and leave her, too. If Aki thought too much about it, she'd fall into a deep, dark cavern she couldn't climb out of. So she pushed the bleak thoughts out of her mind and tried to concentrate on other things. Seiko-san came to mind. She was certainly someone Aki wished would leave her life, but every day she returned to torment her.

Of all the housekeepers her father had hired, Aki hated Seiko-san the most. Not only did she wear the same dark green kimono every day, she kept a vigilant eye over her, kneeling outside her room after school, rapping on her shoji door and trying to coax her to come out, reporting everything back to her father. Aki thought her old and creepy the way she hovered, her eyes always watching, telling her to do things when she had no authority. At fifteen, Aki didn't need anyone looking after her.

Like clockwork, Seiko-san knocked three times and Aki pictured her kneeling at the other side of her door.

"Wouldn't you like something to eat?" she asked.

"No."

"To drink?"

"No."

"Why don't you come out of your room for

a while? It's not healthy to be by yourself so much."

She remained silent.

"Perhaps later, then."

Aki knew she was being difficult, but Seiko-san was getting more and more insistent, and her first impulse was to snap back at her. She listened until she heard Seiko-san mumble something under her breath, heard her knees creak as she stood up slowly and padded back down the hall.

Haru always knew how to handle these housekeepers, while Aki invariably became too stubborn and ran into trouble with them and their rules. Her sister had quietly obeyed them, only to escape as quickly as she could. Now she was in Nara, having gotten away, leaving Aki with a series of housekeepers who disliked her as much as she disliked them.

Aki stood up from her desk and moved quietly to the window to open it, letting in a mild April wind. Just below was the flagstone courtyard, and a plot of dirt where her father wanted to plant a cherry blossom tree. She leaned out to check if anyone was around. If she were careful, she could lower herself down onto the tile roof of the *genkan* and slide down the support beam to the courtyard. She dropped her sandals first, which clattered as they hit the pavement below. Aki turned back, hoping Seiko-san hadn't heard. Then she lifted her kimono and swung her legs over the window ledge, lowering herself slowly onto the roof of the *genkan,* careful to make sure it could support her weight. From there, she just needed to slide down the beam to be free of Seiko-san. Carefully, she inched her way to the edge of the roof and held on as she wrapped her legs around the beam. She was halfway down when a splinter jabbed into her palm and she lost her grip, falling the last few feet onto her back, her head thumping against the patch of dirt.

There was the sound of footsteps. "Are you all right, Aki-san?" She looked up to see the towering figure of Hiroshi standing over her, dressed in a white *yukata* robe. She always remembered him as the tall one who'd found her mother's body at the river. Now Hiroshi knelt beside her, his large shadow covering her like a blanket.

"Hai," Aki quickly answered as she tried to sit up, embarrassed beyond words. She felt dizzy and stayed seated on the ground.

"Shall I get your father?" Hiroshi asked.

"No," she said. "I'll be fine, I just need a moment."

Hiroshi leaned closer and put his large hand on the back of her head. "Does your head hurt?" he asked.

She shook her head slowly and felt a slight throbbing. No one had to know. She was just grateful to have hit the dirt instead of the pavement.

He extended his hand and she felt him gently pull her up. His hand felt warm and comforting and she didn't want to let go. She bowed and brushed at her kimono. "I'm fine. *Domo arigato goziamasu.*"

Hiroshi smiled. "Trying to get away?"

Aki looked down, so he wouldn't see her smile. "Almost," she answered.

"I won't tell," he said.

She bowed again. *"Domo."*

"Just be careful," he added.

"Hai."

"And use your legs more the next time you decide to slide down that beam. That way, if you lose your grip . . ."

"Hai. Domo arigato."

They stood a moment longer before Hiroshi bowed and said, "I'd better return to the stable before your father finds me out here chatting with you. No more climbing today," he instructed, as he turned away.

Somehow, Aki didn't mind Hiroshi telling her what to do. She watched him walk back to the stable and remembered hearing her father say he'd just been promoted to the *sekitori* rank. She wanted to call out her congratulations, but instead, she watched as he moved quickly across the courtyard. Perhaps it wasn't a bad idea for her to help her father more at the stable. She brushed off her kimono and touched the back of her head to feel her scar. Right near it was a small swelling where her head had hit the ground.

THE *KASUTORI* CULTURE

Kenji walked down a street in the Shinjuku district. He knew that a number of new bars and strip clubs had opened in recent years. Every time he walked back from picking up paints, a new brush or chisel, he was drawn by the laughter coming from the dark, cool bars. It was a warm afternoon and he was pleased to have finished a new *Ko-jo* mask, the old man with distinct, high cheekbones and a flowing white beard. It was his first big commission and his most complicated mask yet. In the tight-knit community of the Noh theater word of his artistry was spreading. To celebrate its completion, he decided to follow the noise into one of the bars he had passed by so many times. His eyes adjusted to the dimly lit room, the wooden tables and mismatched chairs, the dark paintings that lined the wall. He brushed his hand against something sticky on the bar where he stood and wiped it onto his pants. It wasn't even dark outside yet and already the place was crowded.

Kenji ordered a glass of *kasutori shochu* — the alcohol of choice for all the young men and women who embraced the *kasutori* culture. Since the occupation, artists and writers had been finding solace in the powerful

401

alcohol. Kenji knew it was a culture that had grown out of guilt and grief, and the lies of a weak government that had led the nation into a disastrous war, only to accept the humiliating presence of occupation forces in defeat. While he hadn't participated, he didn't disagree.

The strong, foul-tasting alcohol provided instant gratification. It burned going down Kenji's throat, harsh and smelling like some kind of fuel. He coughed once or twice and felt the blood rush to his head. Within moments, his entire body grew warm. He ordered another drink. Hiroshi would never believe he was in a bar drinking alone, just as he wouldn't have believed the incident with Okata.

Kenji stood steadfast at the bar and swallowed another sip of the *kasutori shochu* to see what all the controversy was about. He felt the burning warmth again and remembered that two years before at the university, word had spread across campus that the writer Okoto Tamida and his girlfriend had committed suicide. His book became an instant success and Tamida became a symbol of the *kasutori* culture, fanning the feelings of displacement and rebellion that so many of his classmates embraced. Kenji remained at a distance and thought Tamida's death had more to do with drugs and alcohol. He wondered if Mika Abe had whispered among her friends and had been devastated by Ta-mida's death.

Japan had changed. Kenji took another sip. Just the other day, when he stopped at a store to buy miso, he'd seen the explicit covers of the pulp magazines sold in respectable shops his *obachan* went to, paired lovers, or women in sensual, scantily covered poses. *Panpan* girls were one thing, but it seemed a nation steeped so long in reserve and modesty had suddenly left its kimono wide open. He smiled to himself at the thought.

Kenji drank down the last of the *kasutori shochu,* which seared his throat. Two drinks and he felt light-headed; the room was spin-ning. He'd never been a big drinker and hadn't eaten all day as he rushed to finish the new mask. The alcohol burned down to his stomach. The room felt hot and crowded and he began to sweat as his stomach churned, then subsided. Kenji steadied himself and turned away from the bar. He needed to get something to eat. Everything looked bleak, from the shadowy bar to the customers dressed in black clothing, many wearing sunglasses in the already dark room. He walked toward the front door, unsure of his footing as he passed several tables of young people talking and laughing too loudly. Their faces blurred past him as he hurried toward the front door.

Once outside in the cool spring evening,

Kenji felt better. He took a deep breath before his stomach churned again. Then, just as quickly, he felt a sharp clenching pain in the middle of his abdomen. His head began to pound and his heart throbbed. He stumbled forward and had barely made it to the end of the street before he doubled over and vomited.

Kenji couldn't remember how he'd gotten back home. Hours later, lying on his futon with a cold towel over his eyes, he was startled to suddenly recall that he'd seen a face he thought he knew. He had stumbled past a table in the bar where two couples sat, and only now did he realize that one of the young women resembled Mika Abe. He couldn't help but feel slighted that she had never visited his shop. All she'd had to do was inquire. There were only so many mask shops in Tokyo. Now it bothered him to think that it was Mika sitting at a bar with a group of people who had no direction, who went to excesses in the name of art. He wished he could return to the bar to see if it was really her, but he could barely sit up without the room spinning, his head still throbbing. It couldn't be Mika, he convinced himself. As far as he knew, she wasn't part of the *katsutori* culture. But what did he know anyway? Besides exchanging greetings, he'd never really talked to her, and it wasn't any of his business how she lived her life. Still, it left an unpleasant taste on his tongue that wouldn't go away, no matter how much water he drank.

He returned to the same bar several times afterward, but the woman he thought might be Mika never reappeared. He began to get used to the taste of *kasutori shochu* and welcomed the light-headed feeling it gave him. When his head began to throb and his stomach burned, he always managed to find his way home to collapse on his futon.

Kenji awoke. The rhythmic pounding sounded like the drum used by the *yobidashi,* the ring attendant at Hiroshi's sumo tournaments; one, two, three . . . one, two, three . . . At first, he thought it was the throbbing in his head, the *katsutori shochu* still playing havoc. Kenji opened his eyes slowly and didn't know what time it was. He turned toward the window, sunlight slicing through the parted curtains, and realized then that the pounding was coming from outside.

Very slowly, Kenji pushed himself up from his futon and shuffled to the window. He didn't have the strength to face whoever it was. He leaned against the windowsill and raised the window with all the energy he could muster. Someone was still knocking on the door of the mask shop downstairs.

The window scraped open. He closed his eyes against the sound and sunlight. "What is it?" his voice growled, his mouth filled with wool, as his *ojichan* would say.

"Hello?"

It was a woman's voice. Kenji leaned forward and cleared his throat. It took a moment to focus on the young woman looking back up at him.

"Can I help you?" he asked.

The young woman, dressed stylishly in Western clothing, lifted her dark glasses and stared up at him. "I've come to see how you're feeling this morning," she said. She bowed formally to him.

Kenji rubbed his eyes and looked again. It was Mika Abe standing at his front door.

17
Resurrection
1952

Fumiko Wada stepped out of the kitchen and into the courtyard. It was her favorite time of day, a clear, balmy May morning before the heat of the afternoon became too oppressive and suffocating. She breathed in the fragrant scent of her spring garden. Her beloved lilies of the valley were in full bloom, their sweetness a conjurer of memories, a reminder of a lifetime of living, resurrected every spring from the same earth they were almost buried under.

She knelt beside the lilies she had also planted in the front courtyard where Yoshio spent most of his days. In no time, the white bell-shaped flowers would turn into hard red berries. One life would evolve into another. She had a great deal to be grateful for. Her family was now thriving in a world free of war. Not only had they survived the devastation of the war itself, but also the seven difficult years of American occupation that followed. It had finally ended last month, in

April, just as the green quill-like shoots of her lilies pushed their way to the surface.

Unlike Yoshio, sixty-nine-year-old Fumiko had had her doubts as to whether she'd live to see Japan find her footing again. The devastation wasn't just of their country, but of their hearts and minds. How could they ever find their way back? But Japan did survive, moving quietly and steadily forward, limping along after the war. The Japan she saw now was no longer steeped in militarism, but strived for economic stability and for a life of abundance. It wasn't unlike her garden, which Fumiko had slowly resurrected from the ashes. Each year the lilies returned, the stems grew stronger. After all, it was the cycle of life and something Yoshio had always tried to place her trust in.

For Fumiko, it was time to move on with their lives, though regaining their independence had not been without more violence. From the radio blared the news of the May Day rally, which had left hundreds dead and injured, but this time, the Japanese people were fighting among themselves, divided over the U.S. seizure of Okinawa, remilitarization, and the U.S. military bases, which would remain in the country. After all they'd been through, it was yet another tragedy. Still, a great weight had been lifted from Fumiko's shoulders, and in its place was the light breeze of freedom, which left her buoyant, lifted from the ground.

Her grandsons were the future. She saw Japan's rebuilding and Hiroshi's sumo career rise simultaneously. She and Yoshio never dared to say anything, for fear of bringing bad luck. At twenty-five, he had just reached the esteemed rank of *sekiwake,* only a year after becoming a professional, upper-ranked wrestler in the Makuuchi Division, and he was rumored to be the next *sumotori* to reach the champion rank of *ozeki.* Hiroshi's name was becoming indistinguishable from the sport of sumo itself. Every time Fumiko saw him in the *dohyo,* so big and powerful, she could hardly believe he was once the little boy who sat so still next to her, listening to the stories about his parents. During every tournament when Hiroshi walked down the *hanamichi,* the flower paths leading from the east and west down to the *dohyo,* he looked up into the audience, his way of acknowledging them. The first time Fumiko stepped into the new sumo stadium in Kuramae, she was filled with pride. Above the *dohyo* hung a Shinto-style roof, and even higher still were the large portraits of past tournament champions. It was an amazing spectacle she wished Yoshio could see. "I can see it all," he'd told her, "through your descriptions."

She was equally proud of Kenji, who had opened his small mask shop two years ago, not far from the one that once belonged to

Akira Yoshiwara. While his first two years were difficult, the past few months had finally brought her younger grandson some success as a mask artisan, along with a new friend, Mika-san. He now made masks for several up-and-coming Noh actors. He was still very young, and like that of all good artists, she knew his reputation would grow with time. She looked forward to the day when both her grandsons would be settled and have families of their own.

Fumiko stood up slowly, brushed the dirt from her kimono. She'd lost track of time as she worked in the garden. If she hurried, she could still make it to Ino-san's to buy miso for Yoshio's lunch. They'd become minor celebrities along the bustling streets and alleyways of Yanaka. "Tell Hiro-chan we know he'll be the next champion!" storeowners and neighbors alike would yell out to Fumiko as she walked down the street. She smiled and bowed, both proud and honored by her grandson's accomplishments.

Fumiko weaved down the crowded alleyways, voices coming from every direction, women carrying baskets filled with fruit and vegetables. Stores once again had merchandise on their shelves, as the smell of dried fish and fresh *sembei* rice crackers wafted through the air. Fumiko paused when she came to the storefront that used to be Ayako's bakery. In old times, she would be visiting her friend, stopping in for a cup of green tea and the latest news. Fumiko glanced in the window. A bakery again, with lovely smells drifting through the air. The door opened and closed, a warm fragrant air embracing her, but she couldn't bring herself to step inside. So many years gone, and Ayako-san's absence still felt like a raw wound, a throbbing just under her skin. She would never get over the loss. Having so many innocent people simply disappear would always be the cruelest aspect of the war for her.

She looked around the busy street. Remnants of the war and the suffering were slowly disappearing. Still, she couldn't imagine how anyone who lived through it would ever be able to forget. In her heart, Fumiko hoped the war and devastation would never be forgotten, so that future generations would learn from the futility of it all.

THE MASK MAKER

As Kenji guided the chisel across the wood, he saw the contours of a face take shape, each defining feature slowly emerge from the depths of the wood. He carefully hollowed out the eyes to the *O-akujo* demon mask. Soon he would fill the sockets with brass eyes, flare the nostrils, and paint the teeth a gleaming gold. In the dark theater, it would frighten and mesmerize. In the quiet of his shop, each mask made Kenji feel more alive in the world, the ground at last solid where he stood. Could the boy ghost have finally materialized into a man? He smiled to think so, his gaze moving toward the empty doorway.

His thoughts turned from the masks to Mika. The events of the past few months were like miracles to him. He woke up every morning hoping it wasn't all a dream — Mika Abe knocking on his door, saving him from the *kasutori shochu,* which he might easily have come to depend on. Unlike those restless, lost souls who replaced art with alcohol, the sharp, burning warmth that flowed down his throat gave him courage and made him forget his loneliness, his fear of failure. Kenji heard again his *obachan*'s constant worries. He was too thin, his hair longer than she liked. He tied it back like those artists did. He needed to get out more. She always said he looked like one of those displaced young people of the *kasutori* culture. But Mika had roused him from his stupor, made him get up, open the door, and let her in.

"I decided it was time to visit your shop," she had said, her voice calm, matter-of-fact.

He remembered squinting to see the perfect lines of her face. His head pulsated with a dull pain. All she had to do was look at him to see he was hungover, his thoughts

412

scrambled. Had Mika been at the bar? He wanted to ask what made her decide to visit him that morning. But Kenji felt as if his head would explode. Instead of answering, he leaned against the table and struggled not to close his eyes against the glare of the sunlight. What if he opened them again and she was gone? He nodded his head without saying a word.

Since November, Kenji had been seeing Mika Abe steadily for six months. He had gladly traded the *kasutori shochu* for her. And apparently she was more interested in him than the dark bars and strong liquor. Now it was her touch that spread warmth throughout his body, thawing every last fear.

Kenji heard the front door open and close but took his time in the back room, making the last few strokes of the large chisel before he moved to a smaller one for the more intricate details. He didn't expect Mika until late afternoon. When Kenji stepped into the outer room, he saw a man examining one of his masks on the shelf, his back to Kenji. He was dressed in an expensive silk kimono with a white diamond pattern, which seemed faintly familiar.

"Konnichiwa," Kenji said.

It wasn't until the man turned around that Kenji recognized it was Otomo Matsui standing before him. He'd aged in the past ten years, his hair all gray now, which gave the

413

great Noh actor an even more distinguished presence.

Kenji bowed low. "Matsui-sama, I had no idea it was you. I'm honored to have you in my shop."

Matsui smiled, still holding the *Okina* mask in his hand. "I've heard of your workmanship. Many say it has all the earmarks of a Yoshiwara mask."

He bowed again. "I would be honored to be half as good as Yoshiwara-sensei."

Matsui held up the *Okina* mask. "It seems I have the proof right in my hands. I also recall that we've met before."

"Hai," he said. "Almost ten years ago. I attended a performance with Yoshiwara-sensei."

Matsui nodded. "Backstage. You were the boy with Akira-san."

"Hai."

"Akira said then you'd be the next great mask maker. It seems he was right." Matsui placed the mask back on the shelf. "I've come to see if you'd like to make a mask for me?"

"You honor me, Matsui-sama." Kenji bowed. "It would be my greatest honor to have you wear one of my masks."

Matsui smiled. He placed a package on the table. "I'll leave an old mask with you for measurements. It was one of Yoshiwara's best. I'll need a *Warai-jo* mask. It's sad but fitting that I should play an old man now. I'll send

414

someone to pick it up at the end of the month."

Kenji bowed. "It will be waiting."

The actor turned to leave, his movements still fluid and elegant. It was Kenji's last chance to ask Matsui about his sensei.

"Matsui-sama, may I ask if you've heard anything about Yoshiwara-sensei?"

Matsui turned back. "I'm afraid your sensei has disappeared into thin air. Perhaps he's dead like so many others. And if he isn't, no one will find Akira unless he wants to be found."

Otomo Matsui smiled sadly, bowed his head, and turned to leave. Even as the door opened and closed behind the great actor, Kenji stood wishing for more.

THE RED COLLAR

At sixteen, Aki was restless and unable to concentrate on anything for long, including her studies. Unlike Haru, who loved Nara Women's University, she had no interest in pursuing such dry ambitions. In her mind, life was too short to sit in classrooms, laboring over words and numbers in books. She preferred to live the experiences herself, not just read about them. She flipped her schoolbook closed, the quick thud making her smile.

Since their mother's death, it was Haru who had assumed most of the household responsibilities of the *okamisan,* the stable master's wife, from the day-to-day details of running the stable to helping with the accounts. Sometimes, Aki hated how easily it all came to her sister, how organized and efficient she was. She knew her father was grateful to have Haru do so much. But now, with her sister away at school, the household responsibilities fell to her. With Seiko-san, their housekeeper, finally gone, there was just their cook, Suniko-san, who came daily to prepare their meals, while Aki was responsible for keeping the house in order. More often than not, she knew, her housekeeping skills were a disappointment.

Aki leaned back, opened her desk drawer, and pulled out the photo of her mother dressed as a young *maiko* that she'd found in the trunk. Her mother looked beautiful. She wasn't much older than Aki, though she appeared considerably more elegant. She fingered the bright red collar of her mother's vibrant silk kimono, the bold white peonies on the red background, the long scroll sleeves that hung almost to the ground. The black obi was tied higher than usual, reaching up under her arms. She looked just a little off balance, standing tall on wooden sandals and smiling shyly. It was Aki's favorite photo of her mother, who appeared both fragile and strong in it. Aki stared at her own face in the mirror. She looked older, her face was slimmer, her eyes deeper. It reminded her of a story her mother used to tell her and Haru when they were little girls. "The Mirror of Matsuyama" had been one of her favorites. "*Okasan,* tell it again, tell it again!" she often pleaded. She remembered how her mother's thin, arched eyebrows rose in flight. They reminded her of two wings that rose when she was exasperated or amused.

Then her mother would smile and Aki knew she would hear the story again, the soothing wave of her mother's voice rolling over her.

"A long, long time ago, in a very remote part of Japan, there lived a husband and wife, who had a little girl whom they loved very much. When the little girl's father went away on business, he promised to bring her back a present if she were good and dutiful to her mother."

Aki's mother had paused and looked at them, a smile in her eyes, like the two of you, she said, without saying.

"When her father returned, he brought his little daughter a beautiful doll and a lacquer box of cakes. He gave his wife a metal mirror, a design of pine trees and storks etched on the back. The little girl and her mother had never seen a mirror before."

Her mother always paused while telling the story to remind them that they lived way out in the countryside, where there were few luxuries.

"When the little girl's mother looked into the mirror, she saw another woman staring back at

417

her. She gazed with growing wonder until her husband explained the mystery — she was looking at herself. Not long after, the little girl's mother became very ill. Just before she died, she told her little daughter to take good care of her father. Then she gave the little girl her mirror, telling her to look at it whenever she felt most lonely, and she would always see her there.

"In due time, her father married again, and her stepmother wasn't very kind to the little girl. Remembering her mother's words, she took to hiding in the corner and gazing into the mirror, where she saw her dear mother's face, not drawn in pain as it was before she died, but young and beautiful again.

"When the stepmother found her crouching in the corner looking at something and murmuring to herself, she ignorantly thought the little girl was performing some evil spell against her. The stepmother went to the little girl's father and told him of her wickedness. When her father confronted his daughter with the tale, he took her by such surprise that she slipped the mirror into her sleeve. For the first time, he grew angry with her, and feared there was some truth to his wife's story.

"When his daughter heard the unjust accusation, she was so hurt by her father's words it was as if he had slapped her. She told him she loved him too much to ever kill his wife knowing that she was dear to him.

" 'What have you hidden in your sleeve?' said her father, still not convinced.

" 'The mirror you gave my mother, which she gave to me before she died. Every time I look into its shining surface, I see the face of my dear mother, young and beautiful again. When my heart aches, it helps me to bear the harsh words and cross looks by seeing my mother's sweet, kind smile.'

"Only then did her father understand that it was her own face she was gazing at, thinking it was her mother's. He loved his daughter even more for her filial piety. Even the girl's stepmother was ashamed and asked forgiveness. And the little girl, who believed she had seen her mother's face in the mirror, forgave her stepmother, and trouble departed from their house forever."

Aki looked closely at her mother's youthful face in the photo, and then gazed into the mirror to scrutinize her own reflection. She saw similarities in the oval shape of the face, the curve of her lips, and especially in the black pearl eyes. She leaned back. From a distance, there might be confusion, a young Noriko returned to the living. Aki imagined herself in the photo and tried to remember the light, graceful steps of the *Tachikata*, the traditional Japanese dance her mother had learned as a young apprentice geisha and taught her as a little girl.

■ ■ ■ ■

A low rumbling of voices outside led Aki to peer out the window to see her father talking to Hiroshi-san in the courtyard. She was too far away to hear what was being said. It appeared to be a serious discussion because neither of them looked happy. She knew her father could be harsh with his *rikishi,* often getting irritated and yelling at them for the smallest mistake. But wasn't this perfectionism the reason he was considered the best *oyakata* in Japan? She shaded her eyes from the sun. She thought Hiroshi's fighting name was appropriate, he resembled a noble mountain standing next to her father. He was big and muscular — but not like some of the other wrestlers, whose enormous stomachs spilled over their *mawashi* belts. She watched them move through everyday life with slow, laborious steps. But once on the *dohyo,* they were transformed into wrestlers who moved with such force and agility, she forgot all about their size.

When Aki was a little girl, she thought the *sumotori* were special men that the gods had created. How else could they be so big? "That would make me a god, Aki-chan," her father said, laughing. "You'll see when you grow older that they're just ordinary men. It's only through training at the stable that they become so big and strong. Otherwise, they wouldn't be able to fight the other big men and win."

Aki nodded. Even so, she always saw them as something other than ordinary men.

Hiroshi stepped back, his hands on his hips, a stance that seemed to her to be defiance. After her fall from the *genkan,* Aki had never had the opportunity to speak at length with Hiroshi. When their paths crossed occasionally, she bowed politely and remained quiet. She was grateful to him for keeping his word not to tell her father about her fall. She waited all that evening for her father's reproach, which never came. Now, as she watched Hiroshi with her father, Aki reminded herself that she must thank him again.

The voices abruptly stopped. She looked out the window and saw Hiroshi bowing to her father. When he stood again, they were the same height, but her father looked like an older, smaller version of the young *sumotori* standing across from him. Her father's pale, shaved head gleamed in the sunlight, the brilliance of it stealing her attention. At that moment, Hiroshi's gaze caught her watching them from the window, his eyes meeting hers for just an instant. Aki stepped quickly back, startled, her heart beating fast, just the way her mother's heart must have raced when she finished dancing — the young *maiko* wearing the red collar — with all eyes watching her.

THE RETURN

Akira Yoshiwara waited across the alleyway
from Kenji's mask shop, shading his eyes
against the sunlight. A rush of thoughts filled
his mind as he walked slowly toward the
shop. He had imagined taking these steps for
weeks now. Akira had caught his breath the
day he saw Otomo Matsui round the corner
and enter the shop. The great actor still
moved with grace and presence. Akira wanted
to follow him in, but decided against it. Kenji
deserved the honor of facing the greatest living Noh actor alone. Through the window,
he saw the two men talking and he felt the
same pride and joy he'd experienced so many
years ago when Matsui first entered his shop.
Perhaps it was a sign, the right moment for
him, too, to make his reappearance. He and
Kenji had followed different paths and had
come full circle back to the mask shop. Only
this time, Kenji was the mask artisan.

The door of the shop whined open when
Akira stepped in. The room was immediately
familiar; the same warm smells of sweet
cypress and the sharp, tinny paints. He
almost expected Nazo to come bounding out
of the back room. He was simply dressed, in
an old gray kimono, and for a moment
wondered if he were presentable after all

these years. Akira smiled to see all the masks on the shelves, and instinctively picked one up to examine the workmanship. He smiled even wider to see how well crafted the mask was, and how right he had been about Kenji's skills.

"May I help you?"

Kenji's voice came from behind and sounded almost irritated at being taken away from his work. It wasn't unlike a greeting he himself might have given.

"I believe you are the mask maker?" Akira turned and asked in his soft and steady cadence.

"Sensei?" Kenji recognized him immediately.

Akira smiled. Kenji was a tall and fine-looking young man. He wore his hair long and tied back, while his own was now cut short and streaked with gray. His mustache and beard were also softened with gray, and they both carried the same lean frames.

"I knew if I waited long enough, Otomo would find his way to you. After all, there are only so many brilliant mask makers. Your shop wasn't difficult to find."

Kenji looked stunned. "Where have you been?" he asked.

"Far away," Akira answered.

"How long have you been back in Tokyo?"

"For almost six months."

"And you didn't come sooner?" A slight

rise of accusation rang through his voice.

Akira looked away. "I had to decide if I would stay in Tokyo or not. There was no reason to disturb you until I came to a decision."

Kenji paused a moment. "And will you stay?"

He nodded.

Kenji didn't move. He appeared suddenly nervous and unsure, his long fingers tapping the edge of the table. "I've dreamed about this day," he said. "I've imagined it like a scene from a Noh play, how you, in the form of a man or a ghost, would return."

"I'm happy to say it's the man who has returned."

Kenji smiled and bowed, offered Akira a chair before disappearing to make tea. Years ago, he'd been the one to wander in from the cold, beaten and alone. Akira knew so many questions would come later, many he no longer cared to answer. When Kenji returned and poured him a cup of tea, he saw the first questions poised on his lips: *Why did you leave?* *"Where did you go?"* But the words were silenced when his gaze fell on Akira Yoshiwara's empty sleeve.

THE BAMBOO STALK

Hiroshi awoke with an unsettled feeling, a rumbling beast in the middle of his stomach.

424

It was the second Sunday of May, and the Natsu Basho would begin that afternoon. If he did well at the tournament, he was almost assured promotion to the champion rank of *ozeki*. Hiroshi was always mindful of his good fortune. Still, for the first time, he couldn't shake his anxiousness the entire morning.

During the last two-week tournament in March, he'd won thirteen out of his fifteen matches; he'd nearly lost another when his foot slipped and he almost went down. But Hiroshi caught his balance and recalled Fukuda once telling him that he had the strength of a bamboo stalk. "It leans forward and backward in the wind, but it always stays upright, Hiroshi-san, just like you." He often thought of Fukuda, and tried to imagine him a farmer toiling on his father's land; he hoped his young friend had found his way in life.

Hiroshi stood up from the futon and winced when his feet touched the wooden floor. His soles were tender and raw. The night before last, using a sharp pocketknife, he had lanced the blisters on them, developed from the constant rubbing against the dirt floor of the practice room. He squeezed out the pus and hoped his feet would heal before the tournament, but saw instead that they resembled two scarred battlefields. He gingerly walked back and forth until the tenderness dulled.

By the time Hiroshi reached the stadium

mid-afternoon, Sadao had his trunk ready for him in the locker room. While he waited for his first match, he read from his book of poems to relax. His anxiety had eased by the time he walked down the *hanamichi* aisle from the east side. The arena was filled and he transformed his worries into pure energy as he stepped into the ring.

During the first three days of the tournament, he won each of his matches. By the fourth day of the tournament, Hiroshi was completely relaxed when he stepped onto the *dohyo*. The roar of the crowd quieted. The air was thick and smoky. He and his opponent, a wrestler named Nakamura, moved flawlessly through the opening rituals before they knelt at the starting line and their eyes locked. The sudden, hard impact of their bodies felt no different from so many other bouts he'd fought. A split second afterward, Nakamura grabbed his *mawashi* belt and quickly wrapped his leg around Hiroshi's in an effort to trip him. He twisted away and felt a sharp, sudden pop in his knee, followed by an excruciating pain that traveled up through his leg to the top of his head. Hiroshi hung on to Nakamura's *mawashi* belt and struggled to drive him out of the *dohyo* before he collapsed. Sweating from the agony and effort to stay upright, Hiroshi tasted sweat as he held tightly on to the belt, and summoned all the strength he had to throw his weight against Nakamura. In the next moment, amid the daze of voices and bright lights, he experienced a moment of stunning weightlessness as both their bodies fell hard against the clay surface.

RECOVERY

Hiroshi dreamed he and Kenji were boys again, running down the Yanaka alleyways. He felt the heat of the sun pushing against his back like a warm hand. *"Faster, faster,"* he heard Kenji's laughing voice call out. His brother was just ahead of him, but no matter how fast Hiroshi ran, he couldn't catch up. Their old neighbor Harakawa-san, who had died during the war, was alive again, eating a bowl of steaming hot udon noodles. He lifted his chopsticks in a wave as they ran by. When Hiroshi looked ahead, he saw that it was now a young woman he was chasing, and when she finally turned back, he glimpsed Aki-san just before he jerked awake.

For the rest of the night, Hiroshi couldn't sleep and lay uncomfortably on his futon, his knee secured by a brace that kept him flat on his back. Unlike other wrestlers, whose point of force was amassed in their stomachs, his strength was concentrated in his legs, iron hard and muscular after years of training. The weeks after his injury, Hiroshi had an operation to mend the torn ligament in his knee. Each day since, he struggled through therapy and exercise, which was as rigorous as the early days of sumo training, when every muscle in his body ached, and sleep was his only refuge. Now, he wished sleep would overtake him again. Instead, there were moments of dreaming and then sleeplessness.

Every morning, Sadao helped him up from his futon like a helpless child. Once standing, Hiroshi could move around slowly by himself on crutches. He winced now to recall how he'd taken his frustrations out on Sadao more times than he wanted to remember, like the morning he accidentally hit his knee as the boy was helping him up from his futon. The pain had surged upward to the tip of his tongue, and he'd blurted out without thinking, "Be careful! Didn't your *okasan* teach you anything?" The word "mother" slipped from his lips before he could catch it. Sadao bowed and apologized, then quickly left the room, with Hiroshi standing amid his own shame.

Now, as he lay wide awake, Hiroshi's mind raced. His thoughts revolved around the match, how he might have prevented the injury if he'd just turned his knee into, instead of away from, Nakamura's leg trip. Afterward, all he remembered was the impact of both their bodies falling and hitting the *dohyo,* while the pain in his knee raged like a spreading fire and forced him to stay down.

The audience had quieted as Tanaka-oyakata hovered over him. He was finally ruled the winner, the judges being in agreement that Nakamura's elbow touched the *dohyo* first. It was a short-lived victory. Due to his injury, Hiroshi had to forfeit his remaining matches, having won only four out of fifteen, his first tournament lost in almost five years. Tanaka-oyakata quickly applied for an injury exemption from the Aki Basho in September so Hiroshi wouldn't risk a demotion. An exemption allowed him to miss one tournament, leaving him seven months for his knee to heal before the Hatsu Basho in January. He knew that many sumo careers ended just as quickly as they'd begun because of lesser injuries. He saw again the grim look on Tanaka-oyakata's face when he told him, "Hiroshi-san, I won't tell you otherwise. Few wrestlers are able to fight professionally again after an injury like yours."

Hiroshi's emotions shifted several times a day since his injury — the slow, uphill climb from disbelief to acceptance — followed by a growing frustration that swelled into a heated anger. At night, it transformed itself into the acidic taste of fear that ate away at him in the darkness of his room. It took both intelligence and strength to climb the ranks. From the time he was a boy, his *ojichan* had told him, "To have strength without knowing how to use it means nothing." All his life, his mind and body had worked in unison. If pain was a means of getting there — the sore muscles, pulled hamstrings, the dislocated shoulder — it was all part of being *sumotori*. At twenty-six, sumo had been his all-consuming passion. Like the daily bowls of rice, the *chanko-nabe* stew filled with chicken, beef, fish, shredded crab, or fist-sized shrimp, it sated his appetite, gave nourishment to his life. There was never a need for anything else, until now.

By the beginning of June, a few weeks after his operation, Hiroshi began to exercise outside in the courtyard, walking in slow circles with the help of the brace and a cane. It was a warm afternoon when he looked up to see Haru standing by the front gate.

"Hiroshi-san won't be winning any races at that speed." She smiled.

"I'm afraid even a snail could beat me now," he said.

She laughed. "Only for the time being."

"Haru-san, are you home for long?"

"Just for a few weeks," she answered. "Then I'm returning to Nara to do some research."

Hiroshi smiled. "Ah, the scientist."

"Hai." Haru blushed. At nineteen, she was a lovely young woman, dressed in a blue and green lightweight summer kimono. It was evident the years away had given her more self-assurance.

"I hope everything is well in Nara," he said.

"Everything is very well, thank you. I'm enjoying it there." Haru paused then added, "I was sorry to hear about your injury. It must be very difficult."

Hiroshi tapped his cane against the flagstones, green veins of moss between them, as he walked in the courtyard. He thought of his *ojichan.* How quickly he'd acquired an old man's habit of tapping. "It is. I'm afraid I'm not very good at remaining immobile."

She pulled at the collar of her kimono. "My father says your knee will gain strength in time, but you'll have to be patient," said Haru, watching him closely.

"Also something I'm not very good at."

Haru paused for a moment. "Perhaps things happen to help us learn about ourselves."

Hiroshi smiled. Haru had always seemed so much older than her age — even when she was a young girl — taking the place of her mother as *okamisan* at the stable. "*Hai,* perhaps," he answered.

"I believe you'll beat that snail in no time," she quickly added.

"In another month or two." He laughed. The sun had shifted and was shining directly down on them now. He saw a thin film of sweat form on her forehead. "I've heard there's a large park in Nara."

"It's a very beautiful place," Haru said.

"Perhaps you can show it to me one day."

She nodded and smiled. "I think you'd like it there."

Hiroshi tapped his cane against the flag-stones again. "It's hot out here, Haru-san. I shouldn't keep you any longer."

She bowed. "I'm sure I'll see you again before I leave."

Hiroshi bowed back. He watched her walk quickly to the house, disappearing into the cool darkness, even as the echo of her voice still lingered.

Hiroshi saw Haru once or twice afterward, but only in passing. And then she was gone again. By mid-June, the brace was off. Every afternoon, he went for longer and longer walks to strengthen his knee. He moved un-hurriedly down the crowded Tokyo streets and saw the distinct colors of the world around him; the sun-washed green of the leaves, the sharp reds and yellows of the kimonos, and the dull whites of the sleeping neon lights. Hiroshi reflected on the realities he'd have to accept; if he couldn't fight until the March Basho, he would likely be demoted to the *komusubi* rank, and if his knee never were to heal properly, he would have to do the honorable thing and retire from the sport he'd loved since he was a boy.

CIRCLES

From her window, Aki watched Hiroshi walk slowly around the courtyard in circles. It reminded her of some childhood game she and Haru had once played. She'd been watching him every day for weeks, ever since his knee injury when he first hobbled out to the courtyard, leaning heavily on a dark wooden cane. Each day he appeared to move with greater ease, and she was careful never to let him see her watching. It was another one of her small secrets, like the treasures in her mother's red lacquer trunk that she held so close.

Until Aki saw Hiroshi's slow, struggling steps, she had never believed anything could defeat him. He always seemed so tall and strong to her. Everyone else paled in comparison. For the first time, she considered what it meant to be a *sumotori* and how desolate it must feel to be injured and unable to compete. She wondered if Hiroshi had ever thought about his life beyond sumo. They had lived across the courtyard from each other for so many years and she didn't know a thing about him.

Aki was tempted to climb out of her window again, slide down the support beam, and land squarely before him, but she knew he would think her still a child, not the seventeen-year-old young woman she'd become. Before Haru left again for Nara, Aki had seen her talking to Hiroshi in the courtyard. He spoke to her sister the way she hoped he would one day speak to her, gentle words filled with interest and admiration. Haru commanded more attention than she realized just by the way she listened to people. If she weren't her sister, Aki might have been jealous. Instead, she wished for her calm.

Aki leaned farther out the window, the branches of the *sakura* tree blocking her view. She knew Hiroshi would soon be within sight as he circled around the courtyard again, his cane clicking dully against the flagstones. Then, as if keeping pace with her thoughts, his imposing figure slowly rounded the corner. Aki's heart jumped when she thought he might glance up and see her, but he limped by, his concentration on each careful step. Only after Hiroshi was out of sight again did Aki step away from the window and pick up the photo on her desk of her mother as a young *maiko*. Without thinking, she found herself moving in the same circular pattern as Hiroshi around her room.

WARMER DAYS

When Hiroshi was a boy, the longer and warmer days seemed to strengthen his mind and body, enter his blood and muscles. It felt as if the air were animated and came alive. There were actually moments when he could feel his limbs growing, a dull ache in his knees and elbows. It triggered memories of wrestling in the park, of running down the alleyways playing hide-and-seek, the sweaty, dank, sour smell of the boys, the *ting, ting, ting* of the metalsmith, and of eating his *obachan*'s red bean rice cakes with Kenji until his stomach hurt. Now, the ache in his knee was due to the healing process, but the advent of summer still had the same physical effect on him, the need to be in motion.

Hiroshi limped slowly down the alleyways of Yanaka. It was his first time back since the operation on his knee six weeks ago and he wanted to surprise Kenji and his grandparents. He was wearing a black silk kimono, his hair still styled in a fancy *oichomage*. It was warmer than he expected and he felt large and conspicuous walking down the narrow lane. Men and women stopped and bowed to him. Children wanted to touch his kimono for good luck. The reserve and propriety of his countrymen seemed to fall away when it came to sumo. It still surprised him when people shouted out his wrestling name during matches and in the streets: "Takanoyama! Takanoyama!" Hiroshi thought back to when he and his *ojichan* used to listen to the radio, yelling and cheering when their favorite wrestler won a match. He felt proudest of his country then. Now, it was startling to hear his own fighting name called out with the same pride and enthusiasm.

Hiroshi turned the corner and entered Kenji's mask shop. It was small and crowded and he always felt too big and clumsy in the fragile space. Masks were lined up on the shelves like faces watching him. It sent a quick shiver down his back. He once asked Kenji if all the staring masks didn't spook him, like *obake*, conjuring up the childhood ghost stories his *obachan* had told them. But his brother smiled and said they were like old friends. Hiroshi reached up and took down a demon mask, painted bright red with gold horns. He fingered the details, the upturned eyebrows and grooved cheekbones. Kenji's work was flawless, every detail accounted for. He raised the mask to his face and the world narrowed to the two eyeholes, confined and manageable. Hiroshi stepped back and bumped into a table, grunting in irritation, guarding his knee. He had offered many times to finance a larger shop for his brother, with a bigger workshop and a decent showroom, but Kenji always smiled and politely declined. "I like my back against the wall. It gives me a sense of security." Perhaps he felt the same about his masks.

"I thought I heard someone." Kenji entered from the back room, holding a block of wood in his hands. "How did you get here?"

"My driver let me off a few blocks from here. The doctors want me to exercise."

Kenji nodded. "It's good to see you."

Hiroshi bowed and squeezed his brother's shoulder. He was a few inches taller and at least a hundred pounds heavier. At twenty-three, Kenji had put on a little weight, which suited his too slender frame. He had his hair tied back, the sparse growth of a mustache on his upper lip.

"Is it true?" Hiroshi asked.

Kenji laughed. He appeared so much lighter than when he was young, so much happier. "You've spoken to *obachan?*"

Hiroshi nodded. "When will I meet your Mika-san?" he asked.

Kenji smiled. Happiness. Hiroshi was glad that his brother had found joy, something that seemed to elude him during their childhood.

"Right now," he said. "Mika, my brother, Hiroshi, is here!" he called out, and then in a softer voice, he added, "She came to return a book I lent her."

Hiroshi put the demon mask back on the shelf. He turned around and there she was — the young woman who had captured his brother's heart — clutching a book in her hands. She was slim and pretty, dressed in Western clothing, a modern young woman, quick and confident, as his *obachan* had told him. Her dark eyes were searching and

437

inquisitive — observing his size, the silk kimono, his *chonmage,* where her eyes lingered a moment longer on his ginkgo-leaf topknot. She bowed low, and then moved closer and extended her hand. "I've heard a great deal about you, Hiroshi-san. It's a great honor to finally meet you."

Hiroshi bowed and took hold of her hand, which seemed so small and delicate in his. "It's nice to meet you, Mika-san. There's a rumor you've made my brother very happy."

Mika blushed and bowed her head again. "Your brother has brought me much happiness," she said, glancing at Kenji.

For a moment, she sounded formal and old-fashioned. When she put the book down on the table, he saw that it was Kenji's beloved *Book of Masks.*

Hiroshi walked slowly to his grandparents' house. He knew Kenji would marry Mika Abe just by the way they looked at each other, the quick glances and shy smiles that no mask could hide. Hiroshi's life as a *sumotori* left little time for anything or anyone else. Sumo had been his sole mistress and he felt it acutely now limping down his childhood streets, filled with families and children.

Hiroshi turned the corner and shook his thoughts away. He slowed as the sweet aroma of grilling yakitori and *sembei* crackers set his stomach growling and made him once again nostalgic for his childhood. Hiroshi walked slowly on, oblivious to the stares of recognition, to the young children who stopped and pointed at him, to the shouts of "Takanoyama, Takanoyama!" None of it mattered at that moment. He felt a dull ache in his knee as he walked toward the street of a thousand blossoms, to the house of his grandparents, where his dreams of sumo had first taken root.

18
OF GREAT BEAUTY
1952

Yoshio sat in the courtyard and heard footsteps moving toward the front gate. The chimes rang as the wooden gate was pushed open, the long whine followed by someone stepping in. He leaned forward toward the sounds and couldn't quite place the movements. Fumiko would have helped the gate along impatiently. Kenji would close it slowly, meticulously, while Hiroshi, who had paid them a surprise visit last week, would have let the gate slam behind him. The steps he heard didn't resemble any he'd already memorized.

Yoshio had become more fragile in the past year, venturing out less and less. His body was slowly disobeying his wishes, slight tremors and persistent headaches arriving more often, along with an increasing loss of balance. Sometimes he wavered from side to side, as if he were standing on a boat in the middle of some endless sea, his body following the motions of the waves. Most of the time, Yoshio was content just sitting in a quiet place for most of the day, out in the sunny courtyard or in the warmth of the kitchen.

Again, Yoshio heard the footsteps moving toward him. Was it simply the wind playing tricks on him? He listened. Usually, his impulse was to call out, but Yoshio remained silent, waiting. He concentrated on something else, a memory. The first time Kenji visited with Mika. Yoshio still remembered the smile he heard in Fumiko's voice greeting the young woman. "Welcome, welcome, Mika-san! Kenji-chan has told us you met at the university." Fumiko had stood beside him and brushed her hand against his. Light, like a butterfly's wings. Kenji was twenty-three, and he knew she thought it was about time one of her grandsons had a girlfriend.

He heard Fumiko inside cooking dinner, the scent of rice wine and sugar in the air letting him know that he was still alive. He tilted his face up toward the warmth of the setting sun and closed his eyes against the dull throbbing in his head. He hadn't forgotten the footsteps, feeling someone standing right there beside him, even if he refused to acknowledge their presence. Yoshio wasn't ready to go yet. Life was too long and too short at the same time. He hoped to be there for Hiroshi's return to sumo, and Kenji's marriage to Mika, whose voice sounded earnest and intelligent. And there was still so much he hadn't said to Fumiko, one last dance around the circle. He sighed and relented. He'd have to wait for her wherever spirits went. The pain increased and spread to the top of his head, unbearable, like a vise squeezing from both sides. He reached out and fell to the ground. So this was how it felt to have his life drained from him, leaving the weight of your body behind. Yoshio opened his eyes again, and for a moment he saw everything around him as clear as day. He looked up to see his daughter, Misako, standing near him, smiling quietly. Behind her was a very blue sky. He wished for Fumiko to walk out just then so that he might have one last glimpse of her. Instead, her last fragrant lilies were right in front of him, the tiny white bells balancing on thin stalks above green, green leaves. Like Fumiko, they, too, were of great beauty. Yoshio smiled at the thought before his body shuddered one last time.

■ ■ ■ ■

PART THREE

■ ■ ■ ■

The flowers whirl away
in the wind like snow.
The thing that falls away
is myself.

— Prime Minister Kintsune

19
OUR LADY'S TEARS
1953

Fumiko carefully clipped the thin stems of the lilies, their heavy fragrance a reminder of joy and sorrow. It was on a windless day in May a year ago that she'd found Yoshio's body lying so peacefully among them, his eyes open and his lips parted in a slight smile. In his gaze she saw that he wasn't afraid and it somehow calmed her. She called out, *"Yoshio,"* just once before kneeling beside him, leaning over to close his eyes, and then taking his still-warm hand in hers. In their final moments together, Fumiko closed her eyes and saw the graceful steps of his youth, moving in the circle of the Bon Odori. It was his dancing that she loved first, the lightness of his steps as he moved toward her. The rest came so easily, a lifetime that passed too quickly. Her heart raced. What hadn't she told him? She couldn't think then. She couldn't think. And so, she let Yoshio go.

She tasted the sourness that rose up to her throat and swallowed it back down. Her grief had changed with age, dull and flat now like an ongoing hum, no longer the loud, frantic scream of youth. In the end, the body betrayed everyone. Fumiko pushed back a strand of gray hair, smiled, and leaned against the wooden bench to push herself up. Her knees ached and were giving her trouble, her movements slower and requiring more effort.

She gathered the lilies that lay beside her into a bouquet and carried them into the reception room, placing them in a vase on the *tokonoma* beside the photos of Misako and Kazuo, and one of Yoshio. Then she knelt on the tatami and bowed to them. Her words came easily now as she gazed up into their frozen smiles. She stood straight and returned to the low dining room table, where her paper and fountain pen waited. Fumiko lowered herself onto the cushion and began her weekly letter to Yoshio. If she set her thoughts down in words, they wouldn't disappear. Where had she left off? There was so much to say.

TIME

Time was running out. Hiroshi was forced to withdraw from the Hatsu Basho in January and the Haru Basho in March when his knee became tender and swollen again, just days prior to each tournament. Two weeks before the March tournament, he'd been officially demoted to the *komusubi* rank. According to the doctors and Tanaka-oyakata, his knee had healed and his exercise regimen of leg lifts and weights went far beyond what he was doing before his injury. There was no physical explanation as to why his knee swelled before each tournament. After the swelling went down the second time around, Hiroshi began training for the Natsu Basho in May.

A year had passed since Hiroshi's injury and the death of his *ojichan*. His grief found itself in sleeplessness, in the words stuck in his throat, in the swelling of his knee. Since then, time moved forward according to the tournament schedules and never paused long enough for him to catch his breath. Sometimes he actually heard his grandfather's voice telling him to "slow down, life isn't a race." But wasn't it in the sumo world? There were only so many good years. Hiroshi struggled hard to stay in shape, only to lose, instead of gain, weight. Now, on the eve of the May tournament, he knew that stepping back into the *dohyo* meant everything; if his knee failed him again, his sumo career would be over.

In the dressing room before Hiroshi's first match, Sadao helped him to put on his silk *mawashi* belt. He felt the belt tighten around his crotch and wind tautly against his hips. They'd said very little to each other as they moved through the same routine they followed before each tournament. The boy bowed and handed him his book of poetry. He liked Sadao, who was reliable and intelligent, even if he remained cautious and spoke sparingly. He continued to work and train hard and Hiroshi hoped that in time he would relax and have some fun. A lost childhood was hard to recapture in a sumo stable, but he saw Sadao most relaxed when he stepped onto the *dohyo*, leaving the memories of his past behind.

Hiroshi didn't have the patience for poetry today. Instead, he paced back and forth trying to keep his knee warm and flexible. The trick was to keep moving. Unlike before the last two tournaments, this time his knee didn't swell.

A medley of voices had returned to him in a dream the night before; his *ojichan*'s, low and raspy with age, like gravel in water. "You don't have to prove anything to anyone. You'll always be a champion." He saw again his grandfather's familiar smile. His *obachan* looked on, worried, and said in a soft blanket of a whisper, "The sumo life is short. It's the rest of your life that you must think about." Hiroshi couldn't imagine any other life than sumo. When he tried, there was only a feeling of emptiness in the pit of his stomach and the sound of dry leaves being crushed. Kenji, who sat across from him, appeared content and happy as he quietly said, "Don't worry, you'll fight again."

Hiroshi walked down the *hanamichi* aisle and looked up to where he knew his *obachan,* Kenji, and Mika were sitting. He couldn't see beyond the glaring lights, but he knew they were there. He only wished his *ojichan* were with them. When his name, Takanoyama, was called out, the audience roared as he stepped onto the *dohyo* for the first time in a year. The clay felt comforting against the battered soles of his feet. Hiroshi was nervous and his knee felt stiff as he moved through the opening rituals, a tight knot resisting every move he made. Slowly, it began to loosen with each leg lift and every squat. He suddenly felt in control of his body again. *"Matta nashi,"* the referee called out. *It's time.* The words rang through Hiroshi's head like a chant. *It's time to fight,* he thought. It's time to win this tournament for his grandfather. It's time to rise up in the ranks and step toward his destiny. *It's time.* His stare locked onto the eyes of his opponent, while all the noise seeped away except for the beating of his own heart. When his body sprang forward and slammed into his opponent, he felt all the pent-up fear and energy of the past year take over.

Their marriage was to be without fanfare, a simple civil ceremony. It was what he and Mika wanted, even though his *obachan* and Mika's parents were unhappy about it. Kenji wasn't interested in all the complicated wedding rituals. Theirs was a marriage of love, not defined or determined by a matchmaker and outdated customs.

"Wasn't it the same for you and *ojichan?*" he asked his grandmother.

His *obachan* watched him for a moment. "We still waited and had a customary *yunio.* You of the younger generation might think it's all nonsense, but an engagement ceremony with all the traditional gifts is a centuries-old tradition. Why do you and Mika-san think it should be broken now?" She poured him a cup of green tea at the low dining room table.

"Mika and I don't need those things to know we'll have a good marriage," he said carefully.

"There's nothing wrong with tradition," his grandmother said, so softly that he couldn't help feeling bad. Her gaze moved toward the reception room where the photos of his parents and grandfather sat on the *tokonoma*.

"No," he said, trying to soothe her. "There isn't. There'll be more than enough for you to do when Hiroshi marries. The great Sekiwake Takanoyama's wedding will be a public event," he added. His brother's successful comeback had made him an even more beloved *sumotori* than he already was.

"But Hiroshi's wedding isn't yours," his grandmother said. "It isn't so simple. The rituals are a symbol of your commitment. You act as if they'll steal something away instead of adding to your life together."

His grandmother's gaze fell upon him. He could almost feel it burning into his skin. "Mika and I prefer to have a modern marriage," was his only answer.

His *obachan* sipped her tea and didn't say another word.

Life *was* never simple. Kenji knew his was filled with contradictions. Wasn't mask making for the Noh theater one of the most traditional Japanese art forms? He wasn't deferring to Hiroshi or his grandmother as he might have when they were young; he just preferred to live his life as quietly and inconspicuously as he could. Marriage was between Mika and him, and he knew his grandmother would be speechless if she found out Mika was the one who had proposed to him.

They were returning from a Noh performance of *Aoi no Uye,* about the demon of jealousy tormenting Princess Rokujo. Kenji had been given his first big commission to make several of the masks, including the *Han-*

nya, the demon mask. Mika had worn a kimono that evening, orange-red with a beige wave pattern made of silk material from her father's textile company. Afterward, they were walking back along the Ginza in Tokyo when Mika paused.

"Is something wrong?" he had asked.

She had looked him directly in the eyes. "Kenji-san, will you marry me?"

He thought she was joking at first, teasing him out of his seriousness. "*Hai,* tomorrow," he answered, joking back — until something in the way she looked at him told him otherwise. "*Hai,*" he said again, without a moment's hesitation. He felt the heat rise to his face.

Mika reached for his hand and didn't let go all the way back to Yanaka.

His *obachan* did insist on Mika respecting the tea-pouring ceremony in both households, and she gave Mika all the traditional gifts wrapped in rice paper — the dried cuttlefish, the *konbu,* or kelp for child-bearing, the long linen thread to symbolize their old age together, and the folded fan to represent growth and future wealth.

POETRY

Hiroshi entered his *obachan*'s courtyard, the chimes setting off the familiar ringing from his childhood. So often, he had entered to see his *ojichan* sitting by the maple tree, his head tilted to the side, seeing through each sound. His grandfather always knew who stepped in. The memory made Hiroshi smile and a sudden longing rose up inside of him. His *ojichan*'s presence wrapped around him.

Hiroshi knew his grandfather would be proud. He'd won twenty-seven out of the thirty bouts he fought during his last two *bashos*, regaining his *sekiwake* rank. He once more stood to be promoted to the rank of *ozeki* champion. Every night during a *basho*, Sadao brought him ice to wrap around his knee, hoping it would keep any pain subdued until the tournament was over. His injury was a constant reminder of his vulnerability, of how each small step could trip a person.

He looked up when he heard his grandmother move carefully down the steps of the *genkan* to greet him.

"Hiro-chan, I was just thinking about you," she said, smiling.

Hiroshi watched his *obachan,* who had become so thin and fragile since his *ojichan* passed away. The bigger and stronger he grew, the smaller she appeared. Hiroshi instantly wanted to protect her, to recapture all the years he had been away training.

He and Kenji saw her more often since his grandfather's death. They worried about her being alone. But she adamantly refused to live with Kenji and Mika, who had moved to a small house near his mask shop, while Kenji's partner and sensei, Yoshiwara-san, lived in the rooms above the shop. "This is where I will always live," his *obachan* told him, her voice sharp and definite. He knew better than to ask again.

"I thought you might like some company," he said, bowing low and then giving his grandmother a hug. She used to pull away quickly, excited with questions about the stable or upcoming tournaments. Now, she remained as light as a feather in his arms.

When his grandmother finally pulled away, she stepped back and watched him closely. "It's about time you spent your free afternoons with someone younger than your old grandmother."

"I can't find anyone more beautiful," he teased.

She shook her head. "You haven't even tried."

Hiroshi laughed. He wanted to tell his grandmother there was someone, someone he'd known since she was a little girl, who was still young, seventeen, almost nine years younger than he was, and his *oyakata*'s daughter. Instead he said, "When I find the right woman, I promise you'll be the first to know. There'll be time enough after the Aki Basho."

But just saying her name made him pull at

the collar of his kimono and wonder what she was doing at that moment. Hiroshi couldn't say when it began, this distant courtship between Aki and him, perhaps the day a few years ago when he looked up at her window and glimpsed her peering down at him, half-hidden behind the shoji screen that covered her window. She stood motionless, with a flicker of innocence that only came with youth, a restlessness that was inherent, so different from her sister, Haru. He only wore a *mawashi* belt and felt naked. A noise, a dog barking, made him turn away. When he glanced back, Aki was gone.

At first, Hiroshi thought it nothing more than a coincidence, but in the days that followed, he felt her lingering presence at the window when he walked through the courtyard. Then again, her gaze was a constant shadow when he exercised his injured knee. He was always careful not to look up, not to frighten her away. Only a quick glance, a fleeting look — the skip of his heart — a momentary connection before it was broken like a string pulled taut and cut. Then she was gone, the black-pearl eyes and soft white of her cheek disappearing behind the shoji window. Over the months it became a dance, and he was reminded of his grandparents dancing at the Bon Odori, moving slowly around and around the circle, taking cautious, measured steps toward each other.

Aki was in her last year of high school and Hiroshi feared she might go away to study at a university like Haru. If so, she might be lost to him forever. Most evenings he stared up at her room, a light shimmering in the darkness, hoping to catch a glimpse of her, the faint outline of her shadow. If not, he restlessly wandered from one teahouse to the next pursuing other shadows.

"Something tells me you've already found the right woman." His *obachan*'s voice brought him back.

She was smiling, that knowing glance he'd seen ever since he was a little boy. He almost expected her to touch his cheek and tell him to go outside and play.

"How is it that you know so much?" he asked.

"Ever since you were a boy, Hiro-chan, I could understand you better by the expressions on your face than the words you spoke." She laughed. "Don't you think every face tells its own story?"

"Like a book?"

"More like a poem. If you study it long enough, you'll soon find its meaning."

He was always surprised by his *obachan*'s ability to see through all of them, especially his *ojichan*. Hiroshi followed his wiry grandmother into the house. He was mistaken. She was still as strong as she always was.

THE SURPRISE

Haru rushed to her class, her books heavy in her arms, her cotton blouse wet against her back as she hurried across the square. She'd lost track of time reading in the library, and now her botany class had begun and she would have to sneak in quietly, again. Now in her third year at Nara Women's University, Haru was certain that she wanted to study botany. It was the persistence of plants that had won her over, how they persevered under the most difficult situations. She thrived in their tenacity. She smiled to herself thinking how she'd told Hiroshi-san she would study science, even before she realized what she was saying. Perhaps her mind knew before her heart did. And what had he said — that science was full of surprises? He couldn't know how right he'd been. Hiroshi seeped into her thoughts during the quiet moments. He was becoming quite the sumo star. The times Haru returned home to Tokyo felt different now. She'd begun to worry about her father, and especially Aki. While her father remained preoccupied with his work, her sister grew even more restless. When she'd asked Aki what was wrong, she only shrugged and said, "I can't wait to grow up." She hated school and couldn't wait to graduate. But the biggest change Haru saw was in her sister's appearance. Or did the distance simply make her see it more clearly? Each time she left and returned, Aki seemed to resemble their mother even more.

Haru slowly opened the door to the lecture hall, cringing at the sharp whine. A few students turned her way as she scrambled up the steps to a seat in the back row.

"*Domo arigato,* Miss Tanaka, for joining us this afternoon." Professor Ito's voice accosted her just as she reached her seat. She felt the eyes of the entire classroom on her.

"*Sumimasen,*" she apologized, the blood rushing to her head. "I'm very sorry to be late." Haru bowed quickly, and didn't dare look up at Professor Ito with his rumpled suit. She put down her books and slid into a chair.

For the rest of the lecture, she heard very little of what was being said, ashamed that Professor Ito had singled her out, even when another student rushed into the lecture hall after her with no consequences. For the first time since coming to Nara, Haru wished she were somewhere else.

"Miss Tanaka, I'd like to see you a moment after class," Professor Ito called up to her as they were leaving. Haru rolled her eyes and stepped aside, letting the other students pass by. First, he embarrassed her in class, and now he wanted to lecture her more. She watched him bow his head to each of the departing students, thinking how his Western-style gray suit looked too large on him, noticing that his hair was already thinning on the top of his head, and that his dark eyes weren't as penetrating as the other girls had remarked. The only thing she did agree with them about was that Professor Ito didn't look older than thirty-five.

When the room emptied, Haru made her way down to him in careful, measured steps. He was putting the last of his papers into a briefcase and closed it just as she reached his desk.

"Ah, Miss Tanaka," he began, looking at her from behind rimless glasses. "I was wondering if you'd be interested in assisting me in the class next term. Mainly reading papers, checking notes, that sort of thing? It pays very little, but I believe you're one of the few students who can actually comprehend what I'm saying."

Haru hadn't expected a compliment and a job offer. She held her books tightly against her chest as she ruminated over the question.

"You needn't give me an answer now," he added.

"No," Haru blurted out. "I'd like the job very much. I'm very grateful for the opportunity." She bowed low and rose to meet his gaze.

Sho Tanaka drank down the green tea. The Sakura teahouse was quiet; it was too early for customers to trickle in and fill the rooms with their loud laughter and errant voices that grew edgier as more sake was poured and the night wore on. He liked the stillness of late afternoon, the emptiness of the banquet room as he sat alone at the long table. His thoughts fell into order and made more sense. It was at the Sakura he first saw Noriko, in this very same room where he still felt her presence. He grasped at memories that blurred around the edges, not recalling the exact words or the season in which they'd taken place.

Through the shoji window a slant of sunlight had fallen across the tatami and the entire room felt aglow. He looked up when Yasuko-san, the mistress of the teahouse, entered wearing a dark cotton kimono. Toward evening, she would change into a colorful silk embroidered one and assume her hostess role. She'd known Sho since his sumo days, and Noriko even longer, since she was a young *maiko* who came from Kyoto to entertain at the Sakura. In many respects, she had been Noriko's elder sister and had grieved as a family member at her death.

As an old friend, Yasuko never questioned why Sho arrived early and sat in the banquet room alone. She always brought him tea and left him to his thoughts. Only this afternoon, she paused and knelt down beside him. "Perhaps you'd like something stronger?" she asked.

Sho smiled and shook his head. "I still have work to do later."

She made a soft sound. "But I have just the thing to go with your memories."

He watched as she rose and left the room. For so many years, Yasuko had remained his closest confidante, and so much of his own history began here. The teahouse had belonged to Yasuko's family for generations, and just after the war when her mother passed away, Yasuko had taken over running it. While the war years were desolate, the occupation years were prosperous for her, with American soldiers frequenting her teahouse nightly. After the occupation, when Japan began to prosper again, Japanese businessmen returned to their old ways of relaxing at teahouses and Yasuko's business soared.

The Sakura was also the place where Noriko returned the one and only time she was so angry with him she abruptly left the house. The girls were little and already asleep. Rather than wake them, she simply walked out the door when he came home late again after a night of drinking. He sobered up quickly and worried as the hours passed and Noriko didn't return. It began to rain heavily and he couldn't leave the girls alone and go search for her, so he waited and was given a humbling lesson. When she finally did return in the early hours of the morning, Sho, who was half-asleep in the reception room, quickly stood up as he heard the front door slide slowly open. Noriko stepped in quietly, her kimono soaked. He learned later that Yasuko had wanted her to stay until the rain stopped, but she insisted on returning home.

She bowed quickly when she saw him. "*Sumimasen,* I'm sorry, I needed to —" she began, shivering from the cold and wet.

But he didn't allow her to say another word. He bowed low to her, wiped away the water that dripped down her cheek, and took her hand.

"Ah, here we are," Yasuko said. She returned holding a bottle, which she placed in front of him with two glasses. "Some expensive American whiskey," she said, smiling. "It was given to me by the famous general himself!"

Sho looked at her and laughed. "*Iie,* no!"

"Is this not the most famous teahouse in Tokyo?" She knelt down beside him and poured the whiskey into the glasses. "To friendship!" She lifted her glass against his and drank.

He followed.

"And how are the girls?"

Sho drank down the rest of his whiskey before he answered. "Haru-san is doing fine in Nara." He paused.

"And Aki-san?"

"She thinks she's in love with Takanoyama," he blurted out. It had been troubling him for weeks and he felt better saying it aloud. Did they think he didn't notice the little dance that was going on between them? However harmless, Hiroshi was on the brink of becoming the next *ozeki* champion, and he didn't want anyone or anything to disturb his concentration, not even Aki.

Yasuko laughed. "Is there anything wrong with that? Aki is becoming a young woman and has always been so different from Haru. She's better off married early so she can settle down. Takanoyama is already a big star."

"It isn't the time," Sho said, too abruptly. "She's too young."

"You of all people should know that love doesn't pick a time. It comes when it comes." She smiled, filling their glasses again.

"Maybe I should ask Haru to return?"

Yasuko-san shook her head. "And what, make both of your daughters unhappy? Take Hiroshi-san aside and talk to him. Remind him what this upcoming tournament means. After he becomes champion in a year or two, Aki will be waiting for him." She sipped from her glass and watched him.

"When did you become so wise?" Sho asked.

Yasuko sighed. "You think I haven't heard

this story before? Every night, it's a different story. I've lived my life saying the right things and look where it has gotten me."

Sho leaned closer to her and breathed in the sweet scent of narcissus. He felt the heat of the whiskey move through his body. "Yasuko-san, it has made you one of the most powerful women in Tokyo."

"And what does that mean to me?" she asked. "In the end, I'm alone."

He heard the weariness in her voice and it filled him with sadness for both of them. She was still a very beautiful woman. There was once a moment when he and Yasuko had found comfort together. They had Noriko in common, which in the end became the reason they didn't stay together. He watched her drink the rest of her whiskey before pushing herself up from the cushion.

"Have as much as you like," Yasuko said, gesturing toward the bottle. "It only makes me feel melancholy to drink such expensive liquor. Don't worry, everything will work itself out," she consoled him with a quick smile.

Sho stood and bowed to Yasuko, then watched her leave the room, a strand of hair trailing from her chignon.

The Visit

Hiroshi had expected it to be Sadao when he heard a knock on his door, only to see Tanaka-oyakata waiting when he slid the shoji door open. Hiroshi bowed low to his coach.

"Hiroshi-san, I was wondering if you had a moment to talk. There's a private matter I'd like to discuss with you," he said, bowing back.

"Yes, of course, Oyakata-sama," he said, stepping aside. The two of them filled the small room. He watched his coach brush the top of his head with the palm of his hand.

"I wanted to talk to you about Aki-san," he said, his voice deep and steady.

"About?"

"About your interest in her," he answered.

Hiroshi looked away in embarrassment. Had his feelings been so obvious? He hadn't thought further than wishing for a quick glance of her each day. He hoped for more in time. "Aki-san is a friend," he finally said.

"*Hai,*" Tanaka said. "And I hope it will remain that way for a little while longer. Hiroshi-san, you've worked hard to reach this point in your career, more so after your injury. You've achieved what most *sumotori* only dream about. Sponsors are eager for the outcome of your upcoming *basho*. It's an opportunity I'd hate to see you lose because you were distracted."

Hiroshi cleared his throat. "And you believe I've been distracted?"

Tanaka paused before he said, "As your coach I'm here to remind you that if you're to become *ozeki*, champion, and perhaps even *yokozuna*, grand champion, your mind and body must be focused on only the tournaments. Do you understand?"

Hiroshi looked his coach in the eyes. "*Hai*, I understand," he answered.

Tanaka-sama nodded, bowed, and turned to leave. But he stopped long enough to add, "Hiroshi, just remember, if and when you become champion you'll be able to have anyone and anything you want."

Hiroshi bowed again. If he once thought of sumo as a way to restore pride to his defeated country, he now also saw Aki as part of the prize. He trained hard and stopped his daily walks through the courtyard. As the days passed, he focused on the flow and strength of his moves. The only eyes he allowed himself to concentrate on were the hard, narrow ones of Kobayashi and the other wrestlers he would face during the stare-down.

20
NEW TRADITIONS
1954

Kenji loved spring best. It promised the warmth of summer, yet still held the freshness of winter. When he was a boy, it was always the season of anticipation for him, one in which his limbs seemed to stretch out after a long sleep. He smiled at the thought. Since Yoshiwara-sensei's return, followed by his marriage to Mika almost a year ago, Kenji felt as if he'd finally materialized, Kenji the ghost disappearing for good. For the first time in his life he felt anchored.

Kenji awoke just before dawn and couldn't sleep. He watched Mika, the dark outline of her body illuminated by the moon. She turned over, murmured in dream state, and then fell back into a deeper sleep. He rose quietly from their futon into the dark early-morning chill and made his way back to the mask shop as he always did when an idea kept him awake.

The sweet smell of the cypress wood rose in the sawdust as he guided the wood against the blade of the saw and shaped the curve of the forehead, something he did with the ease of repetition. He paused and glanced up at the ceiling, afraid the quick drone of the saw might have awakened his sensei upstairs. Kenji felt the clean edge of the wood and blew the sawdust away. Very carefully he began to chisel out her eyes, the deep, dark pockets and thin brows he loved. He smiled, still not quite believing that he and Mika were married, that the smooth touch of her skin was his alone. There was one ritual he would always keep — every year of their marriage he would carve a mask of Mika — slowly capturing each nuance of her face as it changed from year to year. One day their children and grandchildren would be able to see her gradually age before their eyes, even after she and Kenji were long gone from the world.

Kenji stopped working when the milky first light of dawn entered the shop. He stretched and yawned, finally feeling tired as he carefully wrapped the mask in a piece of cloth and tucked it away in a cabinet. If he made his way back home, Mika might not even know he was gone. He smiled to think of her dark hair spread out like a fan against the white pillow, her eyes dazed with sleep, taking a moment before they focused and really saw him. Or perhaps she was already up, waiting to welcome him back to bed.

"I thought I heard someone down here." Yoshiwara-sensei startled him.

"*Sumimasen,* I'm sorry, I couldn't sleep." He bowed. "I thought I would come back and finish some work."

Yoshiwara smiled, waved his arm in the air to dismiss his apology. Kenji still expected a hand to emerge from his sleeve like the magic tricks he'd seen as a boy. A year after his return, his sensei had finally said, "It was an accident of nature." The explanation came from out of nowhere and Yoshiwara never looked up from the mask he was working on. "It was a bright and beautiful day after the snows and she just wanted to play an innocent game. But nature and fate had other plans." Kenji listened intently. He wondered who the "she" was but kept quiet. Before then, he had had his own explanations, that it was a war wound, a stray bullet, an explosion or fire that took his sensei's hand as he fled from the *kempeitai* or the American planes. Only once did Yoshiwara tell Kenji anything about his whereabouts during the years he was gone. "In the village of Aio, all the wood was made into charcoal. The masks felt very far away." In time, Kenji thought, he would hear the entire story. Until then, he was grateful for the bits and pieces Yoshiwara shared with him. His sensei's past was like a puzzle that would eventually all fit together. For now, the most evident change in the once taciturn Yoshiwara was how his words flowed more freely. His calm voice filled the room in unexpected bursts, as if to cover up some need or loneliness. Kenji recognized the hard kernel of grief and how, strangely enough, they had traded places over the years.

Since Yoshiwara's return, Kenji had listened and learned more about the masks, corrected the bad habits he had developed on his own: how he gripped the chisel too hard, or didn't step away from the mask enough to gain perspective. "See with the eyes of the audience," Yoshiwara told him. Kenji was an apprentice in training all over again. While his sensei could no longer chisel out the details of a mask with only one hand, he directed, taught, criticized, and still painted each mask with the precision and artistry that had made him the best mask maker in Japan.

SENSEI

After Kenji left the shop to go home, Akira Yoshiwara stayed to watch the morning light fill the mask shop and set it aglow. He was proud of the man Kenji had become, traces of the boy he once knew almost gone. His marriage to Mika-san had given him the courage and security he'd been searching for. Akira smiled to think that sometimes life was generous.

It was still early, but he'd been wide awake

470

for hours listening to Kenji's dull movements downstairs, punctuated by the short, sudden bursts of the saw. As he lay on his futon, he saw in his mind's eye the curves and lines that took shape from a block of wood and felt a dull ache at the stub of his wrist where his left hand had been. He longed to guide the wood through the whirling blade again, feel the drone move from his fingertips up through his body. No one could understand — except for Kenji — how alive it made him feel.

When Akira walked into Kenji's shop two years ago, he was still determined to make a mask from beginning to end. He worked late at night after Kenji left, or early in the morning before he arrived. But one-handed, the balance wasn't there. His forearm couldn't replace his hand making the precision cuts, chiseling in the rough facial features, and hollowing out the back of the mask. Piece after piece of cypress wood was ruined and discarded. Kenji stacked new blocks of wood every day without saying a word. After a few weeks, Akira gave up. It was one thing for a man to want something; it was another to admit he couldn't do it. Hadn't desire and regret colored so much of his life already?

From the shelf, Akira took down an unfinished devil mask. He neatly lined up the jars of paint he needed across the table and concentrated on the things he could do. He devoted himself to sanding each mask until it acquired the smoothness of skin. Then he lacquered the back and made sure each intricate feature was painted. Yesterday, he had applied six coats of whitewash to prepare the devil mask for painting. His finger swept across the raised cheek to make sure the whitewash was dry. He would also need the box of brass balls used for eyes and teeth to complete the mask. The quiet of the room was soothing. As Akira opened each jar, the sharp smell of the paints greeted him like old friends. It was always the time of day he loved best, when work allowed his thoughts to roam without judgment or recourse.

He reached for the red paint. Akira's sleep had been troubled lately, dreams he barely remembered when he awoke, though he carried lingering memories of Emiko and Kiyo into the day. Kiyo must be a young woman of almost eighteen now, someone he might not recognize, perhaps thinking of marriage and a child of her own. He smiled and carefully mixed the red paint with just a touch of brown, though it still appeared as bright as blood. And what of Emiko, had she found someone to share her praying-hands house with? He dipped the brush into the paint and spread it quickly and steadily across the mask, in even strokes. Aio was so remote. He imagined Emiko sitting by the hearth, accepting her life as it was. The red paint covered the ghostly pale wood, bright and glossy. When it dried, Akira would outline the eyes, lips, and horns in black and gold, draw in the intricate dark eyebrows with a fine brush. He stepped back to see the mask from a distance. In Aio, he used the hair from a horse's tail to fashion the eyebrows and a beard for the *Okina* mask. He'd left Emiko and Kiyo a note saying he had to leave, that something urgent had called him back to Tokyo. He was grateful to them for his life in Aio. Even as memory, the words returned to him empty and hollow. He looked up when he heard the faint stirrings of noise coming from the alleyway. The day was beginning. He found solace in knowing that Emiko had Kiyo, someone who would always care for her. Akira sighed, carefully picked up the red devil mask, and set it on the shelf to dry.

The Great Barrier

Hiroshi, still sweaty from his morning practice, sat on the tatami mats and watched Sadao pour him another cup of green tea. He rubbed his knee out of habit and leaned toward the low table where a bubbling pot of *chankonabe* waited for the upper-ranked wrestlers. He ladled spoonfuls of the chicken and vegetable stew over his bowl of rice. Hiroshi felt stronger than ever, having gained muscle weight while maintaining his speed. Even his skin felt different, stretched tightly across his hard stomach and the taut muscles of his thighs and calves.

"Are you ready to scale the great barrier?" Nishagawa asked. He'd just been promoted to a *sekitori* wrestler in the Juryo Division. The term *ozeki* meant "great barrier" and it was a formidable obstacle every *sumotori* hoped to conquer.

"As ready as I can be," Hiroshi answered, swallowing rice from his bowl. "The rest is up to fate."

"Ah, our elusive fates, the perfect remedy for avoiding upset," Nishagawa said and laughed.

Hiroshi grunted in reply, trying not to give in to what he really felt, the uncertainty of his future. "Until you can think of another," he added.

If Hiroshi could scale the great barrier and reach *ozeki* rank, sumo life would become easier. He'd no longer be demoted with just one tournament loss and could win and lose with a greater margin, while still maintaining his champion rank. The decision for promotion was made by the Sumo Association based on a wrestler's winning record from recent *basho,* along with his moral character and sense of sportsmanship.

"I propose a toast to overcoming the great barrier, the dream of so many men!" Nishigawa raised his glass of beer.

Normally, Hiroshi would raise a glass in a toast. It was already a warm day and he would have usually downed several beers with his meal, but through the years he had developed certain rituals he followed as the *honbasho* days approached. Three nights before each tournament, he ate only chicken *chankonabe* and drank pots of green tea and no alcohol. He recalled the story his *ojichan* told him, how no wrestler ate beef before a match. "And do you know why?" his grandfather had asked. "Because cows walk on four legs and chickens walk on two legs. And a *sumotori*'s goal is to always remain standing on two legs." He could hear his *ojichan*'s voice as if he were in the room, see him stroke his chin and smile. It was a gesture he'd seen since he was a little boy and he deeply missed it now.

Hiroshi raised his cup of tea and drank it down.

Three days later, the crowd roared when Hiroshi entered the arena at the May Basho. When he stepped onto the *dohyo,* he felt an energy surge through his body as he knocked the first wrestler out of the ring within seconds of their initial contact. Hiroshi climbed over the great barrier one match at a time, losing only twice, and on the day of the final match, he stepped back, threw the salt into the air, and watched it scatter on the *dohyo*. With the first impact of his body against his opponent, he felt completely focused, knew he would have to move quickly and use all his strength to win the match. He clipped the wrestler's shoulder, grabbed him under the armpit, and threw his weight backward, forcing him down to the *dohyo* before he knew what had happened to him. When the *gyoji* declared him the winner, Hiroshi knew that whatever barrier he had scaled, it had been accomplished in order to get to Aki on the other side. He raised his eyes to the audience, wondering if she was somewhere up there in the haze of lights, looking down at him as she had from her window.

STAR FESTIVAL

With exams over and all the papers graded for Professor Ito's class, Haru could finally relax. The next year would be her last, though she'd already made up her mind to return for graduate school. She looked forward to returning to Tokyo for the summer to see her father and Aki, but first she would stop at Hiratsuka for the afternoon to attend the Star Festival, called the Tanabata, which was held every July 7. Classmates had told Haru the festival was lively and colorful. When she stepped down from the train and walked to the center of town, huge Tanabata decorations lined the main street. Crowds of people pushed slowly ahead, admiring the long red, green, pink, and blue streamers that hung from bamboo branches along both sides. She was told the streamers represented the weaving of threads, based on the tale of the weaver princess named Orihime and a cow herder prince named Hikoboshi who lived happily within the universe. But they had angered the king by spending too much time together and not doing their jobs, so he banished them to separate sides of the Milky Way. They were only allowed to meet one day a year, on July 7. And it was a tradition to make wishes on the colorful streamers and hang them on the bamboo branches.

Haru had always loved the story, an ongoing romance floating through the universe. She felt sorry for the weaver princess and cow herder prince, relegated to meeting just once a year. When an older woman stopped her and handed Haru a piece of pink streamer for her to write a wish on, she held the lightness of the paper in her hand before she wrote down the name Hiroshi and slipped it into her pocket.

21
COURTSHIP
1955

It began to snow just after the New Year. Even so, Hiroshi lingered in the courtyard after practice hoping for a glimpse of Aki. He was the first *sumotori* to reach the rank of *ozeki* since the occupation and in the light of a newly recovered Japan. He immediately captured the public's imagination as the orphan who had risen from the ashes of the war to become a champion. He read it over and over again in newspaper and magazine articles, which Kenji and Mika would tease him about relentlessly. "Even the emperor isn't as revered," his brother added. Hiroshi smiled. He wondered if Aki felt that way about him.

In the four months since rising to the rank of *ozeki,* Hiroshi's schedule had become impossible. Following practice in the mornings, there were interviews, appearances, and dinners that filled most of his afternoons and evenings. Wherever Ozeki Takanoyama went, fans mobbed him, sponsors courted him for his endorsements, and his photo graced the front pages of newspapers and magazines. He presided over New Year's festivities and was photographed carrying one baby after another. A child held by a *sumotori* was good luck, sure to grow healthy and strong. A child held by a champion was even more auspicious. It was a world Hiroshi had only just begun to taste as an *ozeki*. He couldn't imagine what it would be like if he were to reach the rank of *yokozuna*.

Hiroshi shivered in the cold and pulled his thin cotton *yukata* robe tighter. He looked up at Aki's shoji-covered window, closed against the sharp winds, and wondered where she was and if she had returned to Nara with her sister for a visit. He'd only fleetingly seen Haru during her holiday visit home the week before; he'd always been too busy with appearances. He was fortunate to have had one brief conversation with her when he saw her waiting in front of the stable.

"Haru-san." He bowed, pleased to see her.

She bowed even lower. "Ozeki Takanoyama, I'm honored to see you," she said formally, though she smiled up at him. "How does it feel to be a champion?" she asked.

He laughed. "How does it feel to be teaching?"

Haru smiled. Hiroshi thought she looked lovely in her quiet, careful way, a beauty so different from her sister's. She was no longer self-conscious, but an intelligent young woman who was already teaching a class at Nara Women's University. Rumors around the stable were that she would continue her education and study for her graduate degree.

"We're both accomplishing our goals," she said.

He wanted to say more, but the car sent to pick him up had arrived and he was already late for an interview. "We'll speak more about this later," he said and smiled. Hiroshi bowed quickly and stepped into the car. He turned to see Haru standing there, the hand she always hid from him raised in a wave.

Two days later, she left again for Nara before they had another chance to speak.

Hiroshi felt foolish standing out in the snow, which began to fall again in soft, almost translucent flakes. Aki had obviously given up waiting by the window for him. He rubbed his eyes as if awakening from a deep sleep. He was twenty-eight years old and had spent most of his young life in training. Hiroshi only realized now that all the control and strength that governed his mind and body had nothing to do with the power of his heart.

"Hiroshi-san?"

He turned to see Aki standing near the *sakura* tree planted where she'd once fallen. She wore a heavy winter kimono the color of new leaves, and appeared out of nowhere like a beautiful spirit in one of Kenji's Noh plays. He bowed. "Aki-san, what are you doing out in the cold?" He felt his blood race as warmth slowly spread throughout his body.

"I was hoping I might speak to you," she said.

Hiroshi heard the quiver in her voice as she glanced down and then back up at him. A flicker of snow had fallen onto her cheek, melting when it touched her skin. He took a step toward her, buffered by the snow blanketing the world around them, and reached out to wipe away the falling tear.

Radiance

Fumiko hadn't expected visitors on such a cold, snowy day. She was in the kitchen making tea when she heard the muffled sound of the chimes and stepped into the *genkan* to see who was entering the front gate. It had stopped snowing and the world outside was a soft white blanket. Soundless. She was happy to see it was Hiro-chan entering, but stopped short when she saw someone was with him, a young woman. Fumiko stepped back in the *genkan* and watched them for a moment. The young woman was wearing a dark maroon winter kimono with her hair beautifully dressed. She walked slowly with Hiroshi, looking up and listening to him as he pointed toward the bench by the maple tree. Yoshio.

He was telling her about his *ojichan*. They paused for a moment and the young woman stopped and smiled at him. She held a wrapped gift in her hands. *Mochi* with red beans, she suspected, or petit fours, which also made a good first-acquaintance gift to her. When she turned, Fumiko was given a clear view of her face and saw why her grandson was taken with her; she was beautiful in a classical way, with porcelain skin and fine, delicate features, a young woman who might have stepped out of a woodcut from the Edo period. If Kenji's Mika-san was outgoing, self-assured, and represented the modern world, Hiroshi's young lady appeared more self-contained.

There were things Fumiko sensed immediately while watching them, the radiance of happiness, the small, intimate gestures, the faint air of not belonging in this time and place. Fumiko smiled and stepped down from the *genkan* to welcome them.

FATHERHOOD

It was mid-April and the rains had finally paused. Kenji stopped sanding the mask he was working on and peered out the front window. People rushed down the alleyway, hurrying to get somewhere else before it began to rain again. A part of him wanted to step outside and be carried along with the wave of bodies, as if he were flowing down a river to a new destination. Kenji shook his head. He would never leave without Mika. He returned to the worktable and slowly began to sand the mask again.

He and Mika had been married for more than two years, and in early February, she began suffering from terrible morning sickness. Every day he returned at lunch to check on her, bringing biscuits or rice crackers and making her tea to settle her stomach. After more than a year of trying, Mika was finally pregnant. Kenji couldn't get over the fact that he was going to be a father. Akira teased him about the silly smile he constantly had on his face, openmouthed, like an *O-tobide* mask. "Let's hope the child takes after his mother," his sensei said.

But their joy was short-lived when the doctor told them Mika wasn't pregnant, that her symptoms might have been a result of her desire to have a child. He reassured them everything was fine and they should keep trying. But something had changed after the week they thought she was pregnant; the overwhelming elation had turned into an uncomfortable silence. Soon, Mika began to spend more time working at her father's textile company. Kenji knew working made her happy and took her mind away from having a child, which was the best thing for now. He wondered if everyone had to try so hard.

■ ■ ■ ■

Kenji heard the front door open and close. He stepped out from the back to see Hiroshi filling up his small shop. He was dressed in a formal dark blue silk kimono with silver clusters of a diamond-shaped pattern.

"I've come to see how the famous mask maker is doing," Hiroshi said.

Kenji laughed. He was glad Hiroshi had come to spirit him away from his morose thoughts. "And what really brings the revered Ozeki Takanoyama to my humble shop?"

Hiroshi bowed. "I've come with some news."

"Which is?" Kenji asked.

"I wanted you and *obachan* to be the first to know about my engagement, before you heard of it on the radio, or read about it in the newspapers."

"Aki-san?" He had met Aki a few times, once at his *obachan*'s house, and later, while attending one of Hiroshi's tournaments. She was very beautiful in a fragile, distant way, with eyes that watched everything around her. She spoke very little, as if she were fearful of saying something wrong. Mika thought she was lovely, simply young and shy, she said, talking him out of his cynicism.

Hiroshi smiled. "We hope to marry next year."

Kenji paused too long and caught himself. "Well, it's about time!" he said, and stepped up to hug his brother, something they rarely did. "This calls for a toast!" Kenji disappeared to the back room and returned with a bottle of whiskey.

"What's this? My little brother drinks?" Hiroshi teased.

"Only on cold, rainy days," he said. "Or special occasions, such as this." Kenji poured them each a glass and raised his in a toast. "To marriage!"

"To marriage," Hiroshi echoed.

The amber liquid burned going down Kenji's throat and spread comforting warmth throughout his body. He no longer thought about Mika's becoming pregnant. Across the room, a row of masks gazed back at him. Kenji was in no position to make judgments about Aki or anyone else; he spent most of his days away from the world, making masks. Wasn't he the one who, as a boy, stood to the side watching, invisible to everyone? All that mattered was that Aki made his brother happy. And Hiroshi's happiness was very important to him. Besides, she was the daughter of Tanaka-oyakata; she knew what being the wife of Ozeki Takanoyama must entail. Their privacy would always have to be balanced against his public life. Kenji swallowed the rest of his whiskey, along with his apprehension, which felt small and hard and was something he couldn't quite name.

The Path

Haru saw signs of spring everywhere in Deer Park, from the budding leaves that clung to branches like small knots to the thin whisper of ice melting on the ground that cracked beneath her steps. There was only a trace of winter left in the sharp April air. Her warm breath trailed like smoke, and a fine vapor still hovered above the path. She'd long since traded her kimonos for Western-style clothing, which was more suitable for her countless forays among the plant life. Haru felt most alive in the world during these early-morning walks in the park before her classes began. She remembered it all, the slant of rain that fell through the mist in winter, the heat of the sun that filtered through the trees during a summer heat wave, the buds of the cherry blossoms that unrolled like tiny fists opening every spring. She saw all of life revolve within the park, changing in its own intimate and subtle ways.

So early, the park was almost deserted; there was only an elderly man walking a good distance ahead of her, deep in his own thoughts. The pale gray light turned brighter and she heard the rustling of the deer in the trees but hadn't seen any yet.

Haru touched the letter from Aki in her

pocket, which had arrived yesterday bearing unexpected news. She could feel the heat emanating from it, as if it might catch fire at any moment. It was little more than a month since she'd last heard from Aki, and she'd been eager for news from home. What she hadn't been prepared for was the news of Aki's engagement to Hiroshi, and her sister asking her to return to Tokyo for her engagement ceremony in June. "It happened so suddenly," she wrote in her quick, large characters. "We're to be married next year."

Next year. Haru picked up her pace, so that her breathing grew rapid and her heart raced as she ran down the path. She'd almost caught up with the elderly man walking in front of her when she suddenly veered away from the main path, where it branched off onto several smaller trails. Like the park's arteries, they led in different directions down through the trees, toward the lake or to the old temple. It gave Haru choices, for which she was grateful. *Aki is marrying Hiroshi.* She took a moment to catch her breath and chose the path through the trees, careful of the uneven ground so she wouldn't fall. She picked up speed on the downslope. Her heart pounded harder in her chest and she tried to keep her breathing steady as she struggled to keep up the pace.

Haru's four years at Nara Women's University

had passed in a blur. At twenty-one, she would graduate in July with an honors degree in botany and a chance to keep teaching, while she was pursuing her graduate studies. Professor Ito had become her advisor and valued advocate. There were moments when she thought Ito-san might have an interest in her, other than as a student or colleague, but aside from having tea with her and discussing students, he always kept a proper distance. She'd had a male friend or two who flitted in and out of her life, but Haru was happiest with her work, looking for new species of plants, cataloguing and inspecting them with wonderment. There would be time for a relationship later. In the back of her mind, she had always thought there was Hiroshi-san. Until now, he had been the shadow standing at the end of the path.

Haru ran faster when the trail leveled, weaving in and out of the trees until she grew dizzy, her heart about to burst as she finally slowed to a stop and dropped to the damp grass. She lay there panting like some wild animal, surrounded by the tall, silent trees as she gasped for breath. She felt sweat pool at the base of her throat, under her arms, and between her breasts. Her heart pounded against her rib cage as she stared up at the clearing sky, the bloom of life all around her. Up until now, Haru had thought her life in Nara was extraordinary, but as the beating of her heart calmed and the sharp pull in her lungs subsided, she realized that gaining one thing meant losing another. Wasn't that the way it always was? It was that simple: her mother's life for that of Aki and her; her life in Nara for that of marrying Hiroshi.

Her breathing calmed and she began to feel cold. She lay silent and small among the maple and wisteria, oak and cedar trees, finding comfort in the knowledge they'd still be standing long after she was gone.

22
YOKOZUNA
1956

The start of the Aki Basho fell on the second Sunday in September. The moment Hiroshi had waited for all his life had finally arrived. He rubbed his knee, touched the soles of his feet, and stood up. He laid his ceremonial apron carefully in his *akeni* trunk and closed the cover. The warm, thick air of nervous tension had permeated the stable all morning as they trained before going to the stadium. The quick, terse commands that came from Tanaka-oyakata had already begun in the days leading up to the tournament. The stable master paced the floor and seemed agitated from the start, snapping at the younger *rikishi* who didn't move fast enough or hit hard enough. It hadn't been that way a year ago when the messenger came with the news from the Sumo Association that Hiroshi was promoted to *ozeki* rank. Tanaka-oyakata calmly accepted the news as if he already expected it. This time was different. The chance for Hiroshi to reach the highest rank of *yokozuna* left everyone at the stable on edge. If he could win this tournament, capturing at least thirteen of his fifteen bouts, his promotion to grand champion was almost assured; the final decision would be made by the Yokozuna Council. And still, like Tanaka-oyakata, Hiroshi knew anything could happen, a single wrong move could end even the most illustrious career. He leaned over to rub his knee again.

Hiroshi untied his *yukata* robe and looked down at the green silk kimono Sadao had laid out for him to wear to the stadium. His muscular girth protruded like a solid mountain through the opening of the robe. From the courtyard, he heard the rustlings of the lower-ranked *rikishi* as they hurried back and forth, preparing to move trunks and equipment to the stadium. Sadao would be coming for his trunk soon and he listened for the boy's breaking voice among the others.

Hiroshi felt unsettled in the charged air. Sponsors and fans alike were waiting for his last bout to take place late that afternoon. He was to fight against the wrestler Kobayashi, whom he'd first defeated years ago. Since then, their rankings had risen side by side. They'd won an equal number of matches against each other, and, like him, Kobayashi had risen to the rank of *ozeki* and was a popular wrestler among the fans. It was their matchup that made this tournament so eagerly anticipated. The outcome would most likely determine which wrestler would reach the rank of grand champion.

Hiroshi breathed deeply and felt ready for whatever the fates dictated. More than anything, Hiroshi wished his grandfather were alive to see him reach *yokozuna*. It had always been their shared dream, and one he hoped to achieve now in honor of his grandfather. There was a knock on his door and he slid it open to see Sadao waiting on the other side. The boy bowed. "I've come to take your trunk to the stadium," he said, his voice rising.

"Right there." Hiroshi pointed. He could feel Sadao's energy and tried to play it down. "Be careful with it."

Sadao bowed again. At seventeen, he continued to show signs of becoming a fine young sumo. He was smart and listened well. Already quick and strong, he'd grown taller in the past few months. Hiroshi watched him and resisted the urge to smile at his young apprentice.

But Sadao remained serious and hesitant. "Ozeki Takanoyama, may I speak to you for a moment?"

Hiroshi nodded, distracted, wondering if he hadn't forgotten something that he needed brought to the stadium. He noticed the boy held something in his hand that he rubbed nervously against his kimono sleeve. "What is it?"

"I want to give you something" — Sadao hesitated — "give you back something."

"It can't wait until after the *basho?*"

Sadao shook his head and bowed low. Without looking Hiroshi in the eyes, he held out the silver pin. "I took this from your trunk not long after I arrived here," he said quickly.

Hiroshi turned the pin over in his hands. It felt small and delicate between his fingers. He hadn't missed it until now. "It belongs to my *obasan.* One of the few pieces of jewelry she hid away during the war." He paused and waited, forcing Sadao to look up at him before he asked, "Why?"

Sadao bowed low again. "Back then, I thought I might need to sell it in case I'd have to leave the stable. I was wrong, Ozeki Takanoyama, and I hope you'll forgive me."

Hiroshi fingered the pin. "Why return it now? You could have easily slipped it back into the trunk or sold it. I would have never noticed."

Sadao cleared his throat but didn't look away. "Because I hope to become a *sumo-tori,*" he said.

Hiroshi nodded. "Then you'd better get my trunk to the stadium."

After Sadao carried out his trunk, Hiroshi watched from his window as, moments later, his young attendant moved across the court-yard and out the front gate. The boy was learning the meaning of honor and that pleased Hiroshi. He paused a moment longer at the window, still foolishly hoping for one quick glimpse of Aki before he left for the stadium. However the tournament played out, he found comfort in knowing that nothing would stop him from finally marrying Aki.

The White Tiger

Aki sat alone in her father's private tatami-lined box at the stadium, which seated up to four people on flat cushions. She wore a lightweight yellow kimono with a delicate willow pattern, which had once belonged to Haru. The squared-off privacy of the box allowed her a clear view of the *dohyo* with just enough distance. She was grateful for the luxury of having a little room to breathe, while still being surrounded by a packed stadium full of fans, fans who had come to see the great Ozeki Takanoyama fight his final bout of the tournament, while she had simply come to see Hiroshi-san.

She'd hardly seen him during the past few months. While Aki knew he was busy training for the tournament, she despaired at times to think he might have lost interest in her. But it was her *otosan,* seeing her unhappiness, who told her not to worry, that the impor-

494

tance of the upcoming tournament demanded all of Hiroshi's attention. In those rare moments they shared, she remembered the closeness she once had had with her father as a little girl.

Aki glanced around the crowded arena, ablaze in hot white lights, the air thick with anticipation. Large portraits of past sumo champions hung from the walls and each peered down at the crowd with their dark, powerful gaze. Aki knew that one day Hiroshi's portrait would also be hanging there and she was filled with pride. Her eyes settled on the thick tassels that hung at each corner of the Shinto-style roof suspended high over the *dohyo*. Each was a different color, to represent the four seasons. While the green and red tassels symbolized spring and summer, the white and black ones signified autumn and winter. When she and Haru were young, her father told them that each color also represented an animal: the green dragon, red sparrow, white tiger, and black tortoise. This was the Aki Basho, or the "white tiger" *basho.* As a girl, she spent hours making up stories in her head of how the four animals came together to help those in need. Even now, she imagined them peeking out from the tassels, looking down on the crowd below.

Aki was as eager as the audience to see Hiroshi fight. Just a year ago, she also attended the tournament in which he won and was promoted to the *ozeki* rank. She smiled to think that she was somehow connected to his promotion, like an *okame* who brought good fortune. She had witnessed how hard he'd worked after his injury to fight again, and it only made her admire him more. Across the short distance that separated them, Aki saw Hiroshi's strong, dark features and his ginkgo leaf topknot as he stood on the sidelines. She always found him handsome, she thought as she watched him from afar, bigger than life to her. Hiroshi looked imposing — tall and muscular — his weight nicely distributed, his stomach and chest thick and solid over his *mawashi* belt.

In a high-pitched voice, the ring attendant sang out the names of the next wrestlers. With the sudden roar of the crowd, she looked up to see Hiroshi step forward and bow to his opponent, Kobayashi, before they returned to their respective corners.

This was the match everyone had waited months for — the two great *ozeki* vying to become the next *yokozuna*. Aki leaned forward as both the wrestlers clapped, did their leg stomps, rinsed their mouths with power water, and threw salt onto the *dohyo* before they entered the ring. She watched Hiroshi closely, looking for any signs of pain or weakness in his knee as he moved to the east and Kobayashi to the west side of the ring. They squatted down on their toes in unison, clapped their hands again to alert the gods, and extended their arms out to show they fought fairly and hid nothing. It would have looked silly if she were doing the same thing, but Hiroshi and Kobayashi appeared noble and graceful as they moved through the rituals that were derived from Shinto beliefs. They stood and returned to their corners, threw salt in the *dohyo* once again to cast out the evil spirits. Aki watched how each quick gesture revealed something about the sumo. Kobayashi slammed his fistful of salt down on the ground with a quick, hard toss, while Hiroshi threw his salt upward through the air so that it fell like rain.

They approached the center of the ring and squatted down at the starting lines, knuckles touching the ground for the stare-down. Kobayashi was the heavier of the two as they stood head to head. They looked out of balance in Aki's eyes, though she knew there were no weight classifications in sumo; a smaller wrestler might fight a larger one and win through speed and skill. Still, Aki watched and worried that Hiroshi might be defeated. The wrestlers rose, slapped their stomachs, and returned to their corners, then threw salt into the *dohyo* again, motions that were repeated two more times. Sweat glistened on their backs. They looked back and glared at each other, and Aki saw the transformation from the Hiroshi-san she knew to that of Ozeki Takanoyama. An intense concentration had taken over his entire body. The absolute silence of the arena was broken when the referee held out his war paddle and called out, "It's time!"

After several false starts, Takanoyama and Kobayashi lunged toward each other with an impact she could only imagine. Aki watched spellbound as Takanoyama moved swiftly and forcefully. There was precision in Hiroshi's every move, never a sloppy or careless step when he wrestled; his intensity was so focused it sent a shiver down her back. Aki could hardly believe she was watching the same man who had once limped around the courtyard.

Kobayashi slapped at Hiroshi's body and pushed him backward. The crowd turned silent when Takanoyama was pushed to the edge of the *dohyo* by Kobayashi's bulk. Aki's heart raced and she half-stood in fear that he might lose. Then, in one desperate move, as Kobayashi moved forward to push Hiroshi over the edge, he swung around and tripped Kobayashi out of the *dohyo* first. The crowd exploded as Aki let out a small scream. She sat back down, exhausted.

Without displaying any emotion, Hiroshi and Kobayashi bowed to each other before Kobayashi departed from the ring. Hiroshi squatted in the *dohyo* as the referee extended his *gunbai* to him with envelopes of winning money on it. Takanoyama made three chopping motions with his right hand in thanks, from left to right, and then in the middle over the envelopes of money. The roar of the crowd was thunderous. But unlike when Aki was little, it no longer frightened her.

After the tournament, Aki filtered out of the stadium with the crowd. Colorful banners were posted outside the stadium naming all the sumo who participated in the tournament. She moved along with the jubilant crowd, feeling both happy and sad. Her father and the upper-ranked *sumotori* would return to the stable much later, after a night of drinking and celebrating at a geisha teahouse. Hiroshi had lost only two bouts out of the fifteen during the two-week tournament. He was almost assured the grand champion title. Would he still want to marry her with all his fame and fortune? If Aki were a white tiger, she would go after her prey, circle around and around him until he took notice of her.

Aki returned home and wondered what it was like at a geisha teahouse, entertaining important guests with music and dance, humor and conversation. "You must begin the conversation, but always let the guest finish it," her mother once told her. It was at a geisha teahouse that her father met her mother on a night they were celebrating his rise to the *sekitori* rank. Her mother entered the banquet room and stole her father's heart. Aki wondered if another geisha might be stealing Hiroshi's heart at that very moment, with her face painted in a perfect white mask, hovering over the table with her beautiful, studied movements. Aki sat down in front of the mirror and stared at her own face, at the same dark, luminous eyes that belonged to her mother, wondering if she, too, could walk into a room and steal Takanoyama's heart.

THE SACRED ROPE

A few days after the September tournament ended, two messengers sent from the Japan Sumo Association arrived at the Katsuyama-beya, to officially notify Hiroshi and Tanaka-oyakata of Ozeki Takanoyama's promotion to *yokozuna.* Hiroshi's head was still throbbing from all the drinking he'd done at the geisha house after the tournament, and his knee ached as he paced the floor of his room. That morning, a crowd of reporters and photographers had gathered to wait for the impending news. When the messengers arrived, they pushed into the stable courtyard where Hiroshi knelt and bowed low, formally accepting the promotion. "I humbly accept. I will do my best to uphold the honor and tradition of the rank of *yokozuna.*" Hiroshi looked up at the sea of flashing camera bulbs and felt weightless, suspended in the bright lights.

That afternoon was the *tsuna-uchi,* the braiding of the sacred rope. Fifteen young, white-gloved wrestlers from the Katsuyama-beya and other affiliated stables came together to twist and braid Yokozuna Takanoyama a sacred rope made of a hemp cloth stuffing and a special cotton and silk fabric. They wore white gloves to keep from soiling the rope, which would then be wound around Takanoyama's waist before he performed the *yokozuna* ring-entering ceremony. Guests were invited to witness the event. His *obachan* sat to the side on the raised tatami viewing platform, along with Kenji and Mika. The extra length of the belt was then cut off into measured pieces and given to his grandmother and his many sponsors.

Wearing an elaborate ceremonial apron adorned with Mount Fuji and trimmed in gold that had once belonged to the great Yokozuna Kitoyama, Hiroshi felt the heaviness of the sacred rope as it was wrapped around his waist, thirteen feet in length and weighing more than thirty pounds. It took at least three wrestlers to help coil it around him. Tanaka-oyakata instructed him to practice the less common *shiranui*-style ring-entering ceremony, with two loops formed on the back of his sacred rope, as opposed to the *unryu* style, which only had one loop.

Before Hiroshi started, he glanced at his *obachan,* whose eyes told him how proud she was. He wished his *ojichan* had lived to see this day. Then, with both of his arms outstretched, Hiroshi squatted down and began the dancelike steps. The stable door creaked open and he glanced up to see Aki slip in, dressed in a beautiful rose-colored kimono with a pattern of white cranes on it. She looked up and met his eyes, gazed directly into them, and didn't look away.

Two days later, Hiroshi's *suikyo-shiki,* his grand champion installation ceremony, was held outside at Tokyo's Meiji Shrine. After receiving a new sacred rope and his *yokozuna* certificate, Hiroshi performed his first *dohyo-iri* as grand champion in front of thousands of fans. A warm rain fell steadily as he stepped forward. He looked up to the gray sky and felt his *ojichan*'s presence smiling down upon him. Tears of happiness. To either side of Yokozuna Takanoyama stood his two attendants, upper-ranked wrestlers from the stable, one called the "dew sweeper," who cleared the path for him, while the other, the "sword bearer," protected him. They symbolized ancient times, with the sword representing the *yokozuna*'s samurai status. Blinding camera lights flashed like small explosions. Hiroshi took a deep breath as the rain ran down his shoulders and back. He moved quickly, effortlessly, through the steps he had dreamed about in his sleep. At the end of the dance, Hiroshi squatted down and clapped loudly to let the gods know of his arrival.

Later, after most of the crowd had dispersed, including the press and photographers, Hiroshi looked for his family. Instead, he found a familiar face waiting for him. He recognized Fukuda-san immediately, even though he hadn't seen him in years. "I told you you'd reach grand champion," Fukuda said, smiling. Hiroshi was delighted to see his old friend, who hadn't become a farmer, but a successful businessman, opening noodle shops all over Japan. He invited him to the celebratory dinner Tanaka-oyakata was giving in his honor, knowing his coach would be pleased to see Fukuda again.

The rain had become a hazy mist and Hiroshi could barely see three feet in front of him before everything disappeared into dark shadows. For just a moment, he turned and thought he saw Aki, dressed in a formal kimono, moving carefully across the grounds in *geta* sandals. But he only had to look again to see that it wasn't her.

MAJESTY

The afternoon of Hiroshi's grand champion ceremony, Kenji sat between Mika and his *obachan* in the front row of the Meiji Shrine, watching the majesty of his brother's moves as he performed his first *dohyo-iri* as grand champion. He felt the tears welling up in his eyes. Hiroshi had always been a champion to him, and now all of Japan would celebrate the fact. When they were boys, he and Hiroshi often played at being *sumotori,* his brother always careful not to get too rough. Kenji knew there were times he disappointed Hiroshi, backed down when he should have stood tall, whimpered when he should have raged. He was grateful when it began to rain and no one could distinguish his tears from the drops falling from the sky.

When they arrived home after dinner, Mika couldn't stop talking about Hiroshi. "Hiroshi-san truly fits the image of a perfect *yoko-zuna,*" she said, as she slowly undressed, reaching back to unfasten her obi.

"And what's that?" he asked.

"He's someone larger than life." She turned and asked, "Can you help me with this?"

Kenji walked over and stood behind her, unfastening each small hook of her obi. She looked very beautiful in the purple kimono; the subtle texture of leaves was woven into the material with fine gold thread. Kenji could recognize a piece of his father-in-law's material anywhere. In the past year, Mika had taken an even more active role in helping her father get his textile business back up and running at full operation.

"And what about me?" he asked, suddenly embarrassed at sounding too much like a small boy competing with Hiroshi again.

"What about you?"

"What am I like?"

"You're my real life," she said, glancing back at him and letting down her hair.

Kenji unhooked the last clasp and dropped the obi to the tatami.

CEREMONY

An auspicious day in early October was chosen from the Japanese almanac for Aki and Hiroshi to marry. His *obachan* had selected favorable dates for both their engagement and marriage. Aki liked Hiroshi's grandmother, though it frightened her that the slight, gray-haired woman could see so much without saying a word. Her grandparents on both her mother's and father's sides had died when she was still a baby. And she would never be able to see her own mother grow old. So she had been instantly drawn to the older woman even when Fumiko Wada gazed intently at her the first time they met, as if drawing out all her frailties.

Aki stared into the mirror the morning of her marriage ceremony and couldn't recognize herself. Behind her, Haru smiled reassuringly as she watched the hairdresser comb her hair back in an old-fashioned up-swept style, similar to that of a geisha. Bright *kanzashi* ornaments then decorated her hair, which would later be covered by a *tsuno kakushi,* a white cloth hood for the ceremony. It was worn symbolically to hide the *tsuno,* or horns, and to show obedience. She willed herself not to reach up and touch her small hairless spot hidden beneath all the ceremonial objects. Their wedding would be in the traditional Shinto style, closed to everyone but family and close friends. Aki thought of how she had very few of the latter, except for Haru and Hiroshi. A large reception would be held at a hotel afterward where the media would be allowed. It frightened her to think how the marriage of Yokozuna Takanoyama had become a national event. For weeks leading up to the ceremony, they were pursued wherever they went by media and fans alike.

She looked into the mirror and caught Haru's eyes. "I'm so glad you're here."

Her sister smiled. "Where else would I be on your wedding day?"

Aki tried to smile. The words were a comfort, if only for a moment. She felt helpless among all the grandeur. After Aki's hair was styled, Momoko-san, an older woman who specialized in preparing brides for the traditional wedding ceremony, arrived. She knelt in front of Aki and evenly applied a creamy white makeup all over her face, so that she appeared to be wearing a thin, white mask. Momoko-san then darkened her eyebrows and Aki felt like a ghost, with only her eyes and lips appearing natural. Just after, her lips were painted a bright red and she was reminded again of the photo of her mother as an apprentice geisha and just how much she resembled her.

On a stand near a full-length mirror was Aki's white silk wedding kimono with elaborate embroidered cranes stitched into the material. Underneath it, she'd have to wear several underrobes and another white kimono. This way of dressing carried on a tradition begun by the brides of the samurai. White also symbolized the beginning of her new life as Hiroshi's wife and the end of her old life as Tanaka-san's daughter. It was a complicated ritual, which she was just beginning to understand. Aki would be changing two more times, from her wedding kimono to an ornate red and gold flower-decorated robe, and finally, to a deep purple mixed-pattern kimono usually worn by a young, unmarried woman. Afterward, as a married woman, she would no longer be able to wear such a bright kimono. The idea of not being able to do something turned over in her mind. It was followed by a sudden, sharp pain that gripped at her stomach and made her hesitate. Aki quickly glanced into the mirror again, but Haru was no longer there.

THE *Sakura* TREE

While Aki was being helped into her wedding kimono by Momoko-san, Haru slipped out to the courtyard for some fresh air. It was the first time she'd been alone since returning to Tokyo; she found the constant buzz of voices almost too much for her to bear. Each time Haru returned home from Nara, she noticed that even the air was different, heavier with fumes that made her head dizzy. Upon arriving home, the first thing she saw was the *sakura* tree her father had planted in front of the house, along with a few new shrubs by the front gate. It brought her a measure of calm to see them.

Haru walked across the courtyard to the stable, knowing it was most likely empty, the wrestlers having been given the day off to attend Hiroshi's wedding. She'd made the trip across the yard hundreds of times as a girl, but in this instance it felt strangely unfamiliar, as if she were crossing new territory. The wooden door creaked open and she had the impression of being young again, sneaking a peek at her father's *rikishi.* Only this time, Haru was looking for a place to be alone for a few moments. She stepped into the practice room, the dirt floor soft against her wooden sandals. The room was dim, smelling of damp earth and sweat; the bold white line of the *dohyo* almost glowed. She walked to the edge of the circle and stopped. Ever since they were little, she and Aki were told repeatedly that girls were never to touch the *dohyo*. As an adult, she thought, *If it's so sacred, why can men touch it?*

Haru suddenly felt the weight of all the things she should and shouldn't do upon her shoulders. During Aki's engagement party in June, she had borne the whispers of women dressed in expensive kimonos, who openly wondered why Haru, the older daughter, wasn't marrying first according to tradition. She felt their furtive glances when they thought she wasn't looking and their false smiles as they bowed to her. She'd had enough of their narrow-minded, old-fashioned thinking and had only wanted to leave.

Haru looked down at the simple round of dirt and felt a quick, sharp urge to step over the line and onto the sacred ground. After all, it wasn't made of clay like the real tournament *dohyo*. She glanced around the dim room to make sure she was alone before her bare foot slipped out of her sandal and balanced just over the white line. In the next moment, Haru's foot brushed and then rested on the cool dirt. Just as quickly, she pulled it back and into her sandal. Her heart raced as she stood perfectly still and waited for the roof to collapse or for the gods to strike her down, but neither happened. Haru turned around to see the practice room unchanged, even if something small and hard inside her had.

It would always remain her secret, her first step toward an unknown direction, and Haru found solace in knowing that tomorrow she would be on the train back to her life in Nara. She couldn't think beyond that. She closed her eyes for a moment and took several deep breaths until she thought she heard Aki calling for her. They were to leave for the Shinto shrine within the hour. Haru glanced at the silent room and then hurried back to the house to get dressed.

MARRIAGE

Hiroshi stood next to Aki at the altar in the middle of the temple's ceremony room. He wore a black silk kimono, the Matsumoto family crest of two pine trees emblazoned at five different areas in white. Under his kimono, he wore a *hakama*, a pin-striped pleated skirt. Aki resembled a beautiful light in all white. She kept her gaze lowered and glanced shyly up at him once before the ceremony started. When the priest began his chanting, the austere formality of the ceremony filled the clean, spare room. They stood before their family members, who sat in two rows to each side of them, facing each other. Hiroshi's *obachan* sat to his right, and next to her were Kenji and Mika-san, chanting silently along with the priest. He glimpsed Haru sitting next to Tanaka-sama on Aki's side and caught her eye for just a moment before she looked away. After the purification ceremony, the priest called upon the gods to bless them, ending the ceremony with the *san-san-kudo,* the ritual of sharing sake. Hiroshi held the first of three flat cups and sipped from it three times, handing it to Aki, who took three sips from the same cup. This was repeated with the second and third cups, and then sake was offered to their families. Hiroshi thought of how similar these wedding rituals were to a sumo match, the preparation taking much longer than the ceremony itself.

After the private ceremony, Yokozuna Takanoyama and his new bride, Aki-san, stood and smiled for a multitude of wedding photos, including the press waiting outside of the hotel. Their guests dined on a lavish eleven-course banquet, with each dish symbolically representing felicity, prosperity, and longevity. These delicacies included abalone, *konbu,* a fish with its head and tail turned up to form an eternal circle, clams whose two shells symbolized a couple, and lobster with its lucky red color. After dinner, they lit a candle at each table to symbolize their new life together, and Hiroshi hugged his *obachan* and bowed low to his father-in-law, Tanaka-oyakata. At the end of the evening, Hiroshi and Aki bowed to their families and friends before they retired upstairs to an awaiting suite.

The suite was large and inviting, with a balcony overlooking the lights of Tokyo from the sitting room. On the table were gifts, bottles of sake, champagne, and wine, bowls of rice crackers, edamame, and seaweed. In the bedroom, two large futons were laid out side by side on the tatami. The newly married couple stood silently on the balcony, breathing in the cool, fresh air, until Hiroshi excused himself to bathe. When he finished, he waited on the balcony for Aki to bathe.

It felt as if words would be an intrusion. They'd said very little since coming up to the suite and moving silently into the bedroom. Hiroshi had spent so much of his life learning the detailed rituals of sumo, each step with its own meaning and purpose. Now, as he loosened the sash of Aki's silk kimono and it slid away from her body like water, he felt as if the rules he'd learned would be of no help. She'd just finished bathing and he felt the heat of her skin against his own as they lay facing each other on the futon. He would always remember the softness of her skin and its pale, creamy color, not unlike the white of her wedding gown. She'd seen him near naked in his *mawashi* belt during practice and on the *dohyo,* but her body opened up like a flower to him as he moved toward her slowly, gently. She was so lovely, and his fingers traced the rise of her hip as she shivered under his touch. He slowly undid her hair, which spread across the pillow like black silk, the tips still damp from her bath. He kissed her lightly and his fingers found the nape of her neck, caressing it slowly, sending a shudder through his own body. Hiroshi looked into her eyes and saw that she wasn't afraid. Aki was waiting for him. She smiled and raised her hand to stroke his cheek as he pulled her toward him.

OSHIMA

It was December and cold as Haru packed quickly. Her small room looked as if a typhoon had blown through. She opened another drawer and took inventory. There was no need for a bathing suit in winter, even if Oshima was well known for its long stretches of sandy beach and summer tourists, but Haru folded it neatly into her bag anyway. They would be taking a train to Yokohama, and from there they'd catch the ferry to Oshima.

Haru could hardly believe it when Professor Ito pulled her aside a few weeks ago and unexpectedly asked her to join his research group traveling to Izu Oshima, the closest of the seven volcanic islands known as the Izu Archipelago. They were to stay on Oshima for the weekend, collecting specimens on the less populated west side. She would return to Tokyo afterward for the New Year.

The ferry only carried a handful of passengers, their research team of five, which included three fellow graduate students, Professor Ito, and herself. There was also a younger couple who kept to themselves and an older man who sat alone and read for the entire trip. It began as a calm day, cool and gray but mild. Toward the last hour of the trip, Haru left the small group and went upstairs to the top deck to watch the ocean. The ferry rose and fell against the waves, leaving a trail of milky froth behind. She felt as if she were moving on the water with nothing but the sky above and the sea below her.

"Are you enjoying the ferry ride?" A voice rose above the hum of the ferry's motor and the rush and splash of the water below.

"Yes," she said, at first quietly. Then she raised her voice when she saw it was Professor Ito. "Yes, I am," she said, again.

"I've taken this ferry many times, and still I enjoy it, provided the weather is agreeable like today."

Haru smiled. It was the first time they'd

spoken of anything but plants or students. "Do you go to Oshima often?"

The professor nodded. "Usually once a year. Ever since I was a graduate student like you, and then afterward when I began to teach. It's being in the field that I love best. It breaks the monotony of the classroom."

The wind had started up, and Haru found it more difficult to keep her footing. *"Hai,"* she said. "It's something I hope to do more of."

Professor Ito smiled. She thought he must be near forty, and age was just settling in nicely onto his face. At twenty-three, she was surprised at how easy it was to talk to him now that they were away from the university.

"I'll keep an eye out for you," he said. "Perhaps we'll go on another research trip together."

Haru blushed. "I would be honored," she said.

"See over there?" He squinted and pointed to the far distance.

She saw the endless sea, a glassy mirror.

"We may be too far away yet, but just keep focusing and it'll eventually come into view."

"What am I looking for?"

"You'll see very soon." He smiled.

They stood on the deck in silence, lost in the lulling motion beneath their feet and the salty fish smell. The winds had picked up, blowing the strands of her hair away from her face. Haru felt like a young girl again, excited with anticipation. Her eyes watered. Then, as if time had stopped, she could just make out the vague outlines of something large and menacing in the distance, reaching upward toward the sky.

"There it is," Professor Ito said softly, almost lovingly, still pointing. "Right there in the center of Oshima is Mount Mihara. It's still an active volcano that possesses a long and terrible history."

She shaded her eyes and looked hard to see the blurred lines of the volcano. "How so?"

Professor Ito stared straight ahead. "Back in 1933, a young high school student committed suicide by leaping into the volcano. That same year, another one hundred and twenty-eight people jumped to their deaths. Can you imagine? Many thought it was Mihara that lured all those people to their deaths."

Haru shook her head and stared down into the water. She couldn't imagine so many suicides. Lives swallowed by the dark shadow of a volcano. She wondered if they'd died from the fall, or if it was the heat that killed them first. Haru felt a chill as she recalled the bodies she'd seen right after the firestorm, charred black and stiff, a scream frozen onto their faces. They had had no choice, while others chose to jump into the smoldering lava, which burned hot white and didn't leave a trace of anyone ever having been alive. "It's such a tragedy," she said, in a voice barely audible.

The sea had turned choppy. The boat lurched and she grabbed on to the wet rail, her hand slipping as she fell toward Professor Ito. He raised his arms to catch her and pulled her against him, holding her tightly until the boat calmed again.

"Perhaps we should go back downstairs," he suggested, becoming more formal again.

Haru nodded and followed the professor back down. From behind, she focused on his patch of thinning hair that scarcely hid the perfect *O* on the back of his head.

They'd discreetly begun seeing each other when she returned to Nara after the New Year. The first time Professor Ito kissed her, he told her to call him by his given name, Ichiru. She whispered it once before he leaned forward and kissed her again.

23
LIFE STORIES
1957

On most afternoons Akira Yoshiwara excused himself from the mask shop to take a long walk down by the river. He walked along the alleyways of Yanaka and cut across the park and through the wooded area to where the river narrowed and stilled. In another life, he might have ventured there for other purposes. Rumors were rampant that men met other men there in the dark of the woods, the silent trees masking their veiled lives.

At forty-seven, Akira was there for other reasons. There were fewer people walking the dirt path and the trees muffled the noise from the city. Time seemed to pause. He could get closer to the river, take in the sounds and scents down by the water, the calm trickling, the faint breeze of dank earth on the warm, muggy summer afternoons, or the cold air of winter that whistled through the trees as the water rushed by like cracking ice. All of it soothed him, carried with its currents the memories of Aio and brought down his fever of restlessness. Like him, the river was full of secrets. It wasn't that he didn't cherish his work at the mask shop, or his time spent with Kenji. Unlike the complications he'd had with Emiko, Kenji was like a son and he felt closer to him and Mika than any of his own bloodline. Yet there was a part of him no one would ever know or understand. Sometimes Akira still thought of Sato, at other times of Emiko and Kiyo, wondering if life had been kind to them. But their faces had faded in the past few years like an old photo or a fairy tale he had heard a very long time ago. The memories came to him in bits and pieces but no longer as a whole.

"It's your turn to hide," or "It's your turn to seek," he still occasionally heard Kiyo's voice telling him. Akira didn't hide or seek in the years since he'd returned to Yanaka. He simply returned to the masks.

Akira walked slowly along the riverbank. It was a mild April and already turning to dusk. It was usually quiet this time of the day. He wandered along a path winding around the river's edge, a section that remained un-touched by the encroaching building and construction that had enveloped Tokyo since the occupation ended. On the other side of a stone walk, it sloped down to the water, a murky green in the afternoon light. He noticed everything, even the slimy moss that grew along the edge of the river like strands of a woman's hair. If he closed his eyes and listened to the listless drift of the water, he might be in Aio again, sitting by a mountain stream created by the melting ice. Sometimes, as he watched the river flowing, he wondered what it would be like to move in the same quick, fluid motion, never setting down roots, never staying in one place to develop attachments. Yet, Akira came to the river for exactly the opposite reason. He came to recapture his memories so he wouldn't lose them all. He felt them return to him most intimately down by the river, as if they were ghosts that hovered just above the surface, inviting him in.

GIFTS FOR THE YOUNG

Fumiko slowly lowered herself onto a cushion at the dining room table. Before she began to write, she stretched her fingers to loosen the dull ache in them that now plagued her almost continuously. She was seventy-five years old now, and arthritis made her once straight fingers look like the crooked roots of ginseng, the stubby knobs of fresh ginger root. It was increasingly difficult and painful to form her once fluid characters. Her calligraphy was something Fumiko had always taken great pride in, having won awards and ribbons when she was a little girl in Sapporo. Now, she could barely stand the sight of her shaky writing. But it was summer again and the warm weather soothed her joints, made her feel brave.

Fumiko knew Yoshio would understand why her letters to him only came occasionally now. Who knew better how age stole away all the gifts given to the young? She smiled at the irony of her writing to him; if he were alive, his blindness would keep him from reading it. But wherever he was, writing was her way of communicating with him. Fumiko put down her pen. Her thoughts flowed too quickly and she couldn't keep up. She flexed her hand and her fingers felt weak. She looked down at her shaky writing and frowned at the uneven lines of a child. She would certainly win the prize for the poorest calligraphy in the class now.

She heard the front gate whine open and pushed herself up from the table. She was expecting Hiroshi and Aki, who had recently bought a new house in Shoto, an exclusive area in Shibuya Ward, but when she stepped out to the *genkan* she only saw the imposing figure of her grandson laden with packages.

"Ah, there you are," he said, bowing.

"Aki-san?"

"She had hoped to come with me. She sends her apologies but was feeling a little under the weather this morning."

Fumiko drew in a breath and stepped down. It was a beautiful day in early July and she'd been looking forward to their visit. She had hoped to get to know Aki better. Unlike Mika, Aki-san always appeared uncomfortable around her no matter how she tried to put the young woman at ease. Fumiko always felt there was something unreachable about her; she could see it in her eyes. "I hope it isn't anything serious."

Hiroshi smiled widely. "It should be resolved in just over six months."

It took Fumiko a moment to understand what Hiroshi was saying, that Aki was with child. For the past few years, she knew Kenji and Mika had been trying, and she always expected to hear the news from them first. "Hiro-chan, a baby?"

He nodded like a young boy. "Your first great-grandchild."

For a quick moment her heart fluttered; as delighted as she was for Hiroshi and Aki, she felt a sharp sting of grief for Kenji and Mika. Still, Yokozuna Takanoyama must have carried more than a hundred babies this year; young mothers stopped him in the streets so that his strength and good health would rub off on their children. It was time he carried his own child for a change. Fumiko stepped toward her grandson and reached up to touch his cheek.

Alone in the *keikoba* before morning practice, Sadao gripped the long wooden bow in his hands and swung it from side to side, up and down, then in slow circles that grew faster and faster, disrupting the still July air. He was delighted with the force of it, at the power he felt between his hands as the whistling sound of air vibrated around him. At the age of eighteen, Sadao wasn't as tall as he had hoped, but he did live up to his father's nickname of *buru*. He was powerfully built and very strong and had been given the fighting name Takanoburu. During his six years at the stable, he had quickly learned the intimate rituals of sumo and had risen to the Makushita Division, just below that of an upper-ranked wrestler. He knew both Tanaka-oyakata and Yokozuna Takanoyama expected him to move up in rank after the upcoming tournament in September. Then, by the newly added Kyushu tournament in November, Sadao hoped he would have reached the rank of *sekitori.* It was something he dreamed of, but, before then, there was one ritual he loved best and hoped to perform before he advanced in rank. Only a wrestler in the Makushita Division could perform the bow twirling ceremony, which represented a token of gratitude on behalf of the winning wrestlers of the day. It was the only time a lower-ranked wrestler was given the honor of wearing a *kesho-mawashi* apron with the chrysanthemum emblem of the sumo association on it. He would have his hair styled in an *oichomage,* that of the ginkgo leaf, and receive a cash bonus.

But they weren't the reasons Sadao hoped to perform the bow twirling ceremony; if he rose in rank, this tournament would be his last opportunity to show his appreciation for the home Tanaka-oyakata and sumo had given him. He also knew Yokozuna Takanoyama could easily influence his selection as the bow twirler. Sadao decided to talk to him about it, knowing the best time to approach the Yokozuna was after his long, hot soak, when he was most relaxed.

The soaking room was still thick with steam when he brought in clean towels. Sadao bowed. "Excuse me, Yokozuna Takanoyama, I was wondering if I might speak to you for a moment."

Takanoyama reached for a towel and dried off. "Of course, what is it?"

Sadao paused, and then said in one quick sentence, "I was wondering if you might mention my name to perform the bow twirling ceremony during the fall tournament?"

Takanoyama paused and looked at him. "I didn't know you were interested in performing the ceremony."

"I am."

"And have you heard the superstition attached to performing it?"

"*Hai,* I've heard what the other *rikishi* say. I don't believe it's anything more than stories to pass the time." Sadao swallowed. He'd heard that most of the wrestlers who performed the bow twirling ceremony were rarely promoted beyond the Makushita Division afterward.

"Some look at it as a curse," Takanoyama added. "Do you want to take the chance?"

"Does the Yokozuna believe in such tales?" Sadao asked lightly.

Takanoyama smiled. "Let's just say, I certainly wouldn't challenge such tales, real or not."

"I'm willing to take my chances," Sadao answered. He wasn't superstitious; he didn't believe in curses or bad luck, just as he didn't believe in good luck. He'd sat on the floor of his father's bloodstained meat locker, while the world as he knew it at the age of six disappeared. He believed only in the moment, nothing before or after.

"And it won't take away from your own training?"

Sadao smiled and bowed, "No, Yokozuna, I'll train for the ceremony before or after practice."

Takanoyama cleared his throat and gave his wet towel to Sadao. "We'll see, then."

Sadao didn't look up when he stepped up on the *dohyo* and the referee handed him the bow, as Yokozuna Takanoyama had instructed him. "Concentrate on the task at hand." In the first row were all the wrestlers from his stable, as well as Tanaka-oyakata and Yokozuna Takanoyama, who had stayed to see him perform. Sadao moved to the center of the *dohyo* dressed as an upper-ranked wrestler. He was already perspiring and his stomach churned. He knew that if he dropped the bow, it would not only bring him shame but he would have to pick it up with his feet. To touch the *dohyo* with his hands would mean defeat. He'd memorized the steps in his sleep, and now he grasped the bow tighter as he swung it in front of him and over his head in swift circular motions that grew in speed as he relaxed. He was in control, with the blur of motion in front of him and the whistling sound of air filling his ears like locusts. Earlier in the day, Sadao had won all his tournament matches and was likely to be promoted to the upper ranks before the November tournament. He was determined to prove the curse wrong. Sadao felt the bow vibrate in his hands and travel throughout his body. More than anything, he wished his parents could be there to see him. It was a moment he hoped would last forever, a moment that belonged entirely to him.

ANSWERS

It began one morning with a queasy feeling in her stomach that quickly rushed up to her throat. At first, Haru thought it was something she'd eaten but it persisted each morning throughout the early weeks of July until she could no longer ignore the fact that she was pregnant. She knew it was true by the way her body felt, a heaviness growing inside of her, a constant reminder that she was no longer alone. Haru moved through each day, both frantic and fearful. After Oshima, she and Professor Ito had seen each other for more than six months. They'd only been intimate a few times, enough for her to have to pay for her indiscretion. It didn't take her long to realize loneliness and admiration weren't good substitutes for love. So they had parted just before the waves of morning sickness began.

Haru leaned over the sink. She didn't think there was anything left inside of her to come out. She would be returning to Tokyo at the end of the month. She could still easily disguise her pregnancy, but it would be just a matter of time before her family found out. If she calculated right, there was a certain irony in the fact that Aki's baby was due at about the same time as hers; only her sister was happily married to Hiroshi. For just a moment, Haru's stomach roiled at the thought. She wished, too, that she were the one married and looking forward to something as miraculous as a child growing inside of her.

Haru shook the thought away and tried to clear her mind of worries. She wondered if their children would like each other. When they were young, Haru was always secretly jealous of Aki's resembling her mother in appearance, with her black-pearl-colored eyes and fair complexion. She was always beautiful. Her own likeness to her mother came in smaller, subtler ways that grew with age; in her mannerisms and the way she carried herself. She leaned away from the counter and caught her reflection in the window, seeing a face she was just growing comfortable with, wondering which of her features she'd find in her own child.

Haru felt another wave of nausea come over her and still couldn't believe this was happening to her. She swallowed saliva, took a deep breath, and washed her face with cold water. There were ways to take care of an unwanted pregnancy, but none she could bring herself to do. She had to decide if she wanted to keep the baby or not. Until then, Ichiru didn't have to know, and might never need to know if she just returned to Tokyo to live. Her thoughts ebbed and flowed all morning as she ate rice crackers to settle her stomach. It was finally mid-afternoon by the time she dressed and dragged herself to the university to clear out her office.

Two nights later, the answer to all Haru's questions arrived in the middle of the night. She awoke with a dull cramping in her lower stomach and back, which gradually intensified. Her fear tasted bitter. She dragged herself to the bathroom and doubled over in pain. There were spots of blood, and then more, followed by a cleansing flow that washed away the life growing inside of her. Haru spent three days in bed afterward, sleeping and waking, feeling numb to the world around her, as she had after the big firestorm when her hands were burned. She was alone again and felt nothing.

24
THE ARRIVAL
1958

Aki couldn't wait for the baby to arrive. She moved around her bedroom slowly, feeling heavy and clumsy. Her legs were swollen and her back hurt. Everything made her feel sick, from a taste of the cook's seaweed soup to the sweet straw smell of the damp tatami mats from the continual February rains. At twenty-two, she already felt old and tired. Did her mother feel like this carrying Haru and her? For Aki, this last month of pregnancy was nothing but a torment, and she could barely remember what it was like not to be pregnant.

The New Year holidays had come and gone and Aki felt as if she had missed everything, refusing to lumber along after Hiroshi as he went from one celebration to another. At first, she felt hurt and angry that he'd leave her behind, even when she knew it was always more business than pleasure. Dinners were arranged by the Sumo Association almost a year in advance, and wives didn't accompany their husbands to these business dinners, which she had to remind herself was what sumo had increasingly become, a business. Hiroshi was the great Yokozuna Takanoyama and everyone wanted to see him. They had a roomful of gifts from sponsors and fans alike who'd never even met him. Sometimes, she looked at her towering husband and willed him to stay home with her for just one night. At other times, she saw Hiroshi for only moments in a day as he hurried from one meeting to the next.

It seemed the entire world had left Aki behind. She knew Haru was busy with her life researching and teaching in Nara. She'd written to her several times in the past month, but still hadn't heard back. So Aki waited alone for the baby to arrive. She was uncomfortable both day and night now, and she sometimes felt as if this baby were squeezing the life from her. Aki carefully lowered herself down on the futon, lying on her back, loosening the tie of her cotton kimono, and rubbing the globe of her stomach. The baby's weight pressed down against her lower spine, and she couldn't imagine ever being able to get up again.

The room was dark when Aki awoke. She had no idea what time it was. The pain took her voice away and her arm flailed to Hiroshi's side of the futon only to find herself still alone. She grabbed at the futon until the pain subsided enough to call for their housekeeper, Tamiko-san, once, twice, louder, until she heard a door sliding open and footsteps rushing up the stairs. Then Aki took deep breaths through the next wave of intense pain, which steadily increased and brought a moan to her lips. She closed her eyes and began to count, just as she had when she was a little girl and couldn't fall asleep, or was frightened, *ichi, ni san, shi* . . .

A NEW LIFE

When classes convened after the New Year, Haru moved to a small apartment near Deer Park, not far from the university. She did her own research early in the mornings before teaching; then there were classes to prepare for and papers to correct when she returned home exhausted in the evening. On weekends, there was the new apartment to settle into. Slowly, she was finding her way again.

On a cold, snowy morning in early February, Haru rushed to her office and looked down to see a note slipped under the door. She was late again; her decision to walk that morning had been unwise. She had a class to teach in five minutes but stooped to pick up the thin sheet of paper. "Your sister's baby has arrived. Please call." The baby was a week early. Haru had hoped to be there before Aki delivered. A flood of emotions rushed through her; a tender new life, a child to hold in her arms, and the fear of not being able to let it go. She could only hope the thoughts of her own unborn baby would lessen now that one child had made it safely into the world. There was no time to call just then as she rushed off to teach her botany class. Haru returned to her office to call during her class break. She phoned the house first, waited a long while for the connection, only to have Tamiko-san tell her that the baby had arrived just after midnight and Aki was in the hospital. "It's a boy," she said, her voice rising with the joy of it. Haru thought of how proud her father must be to finally have a boy in the family. Tamiko-san added that Yokozuna Takanoyama had instructed that if she were to call, to ask that she come to Tokyo as soon as she possibly could. All afternoon, Haru was unable to reach Hiroshi or her father, leaving messages for both.

On the evening train to Tokyo, Haru felt the heaviness of guilt resting on her shoulders. Aki had written her three letters in the past month and she hadn't responded to any. The miscarriage had left Haru feeling distant from everything and everyone. Even Aki felt too far away. Every day she could barely get through her classes. But her excuses stung now, like the flames had against her palms.

Haru knew her sister better than anyone. Aki was lonely and frightened and needed her words of encouragement.

The train rumbled on. She looked down at the thickened skin on the palms of her hands and wondered what she would find if she peeled away each layer. All the nerve endings hadn't been destroyed, because little by little she felt a tingling in the tips of her fingers and on the pads of her palms. She rubbed her hands together and blew warmth back into them.

Haru turned at the sound of snow whipping against the window, tiny particles of ice clinging to the glass as the train swept through the moonless night. She hoped that her new nephew would live his life with the same tenacity. Haru wasn't sure how she'd react at seeing him. Would the sight of him be a constant reminder of what she had lost, even if he was the only ray of light in an otherwise horrific winter? She caught her own depthless reflection in the pitch-black window, a slim, unsmiling face that had spent far too much time in classrooms. Haru closed her eyes and saw beyond the window's darkness, to the mountains and trees, the flickering houses with people inside, entire lives being lived on the other side. For the first time in months, she felt more like herself again.

He was named Takashi, which meant "emi-
nence." Hiroshi chose it on the baby's seventh
day of life at his naming celebration, called
the *Oshichiya*. Takashi was dressed in white
with a name plaque hanging on the wall
above him, his name inscribed in beautifully
written calligraphy. Hiroshi thought it important for his son to enter the world with a
name that already predicted his future. He
imagined great things for his son. When he
was awake, Takashi's bright eyes seemed to
follow all the movement around him. "He
doesn't miss a thing," his *obachan* said. "He
reminds me of your *ojichan*." Hiroshi knew it
was the highest compliment she could give.

Even if he had come into the world early,
Takashi was long limbed and good-sized.
When he was placed in Aki's arms for the
first time at the hospital, she looked like a
frightened child. Hiroshi watched her relax
the longer she held the baby and felt the
small rhythms of his body adjust to hers. He
saw Aki smile, enchanted with the child in
her arms. Hiroshi knew at that moment that
nothing could possibly bring him greater joy.

At the naming ceremony, his *obachan* and
Tanaka-oyakata talked over each other in
excitement. Kenji and Mika were delighted
with their new nephew, taking turns to carry
him, while Haru appeared pale and tired, but

stayed to enjoy the ceremony; she would return to Nara the following day. The first time she held Takashi, he saw a moment of sadness in her eyes before she smiled and kissed him tenderly on the forehead. Hiroshi was grateful she could stay with them. Haru's calm presence anchored Aki, gave her weight and security so she wouldn't fly away. It troubled him that even after two years of marriage, it was something he couldn't give her. He was partly to blame, away so much of the time at tournaments and sponsor events. Aki grew increasingly morose each time he left the house. But what was he to do? It was both an honor and the duty of being a grand champion. Now, with the new baby in her arms, he saw the light return in Aki's eyes each time she looked at Takashi. It brought Hiroshi an overwhelming joy to see how his son was already living up to his name.

IN LIGHT

Aki stood by the window and held Takashi in her arms. It was cold and she wrapped him tightly in a silk quilt. She found herself checking on him two or three times a night, even when he didn't cry, still surprised that he was now a part of her life. She tried to remember all the folktales her mother had told her when she was young, tales like "The Two Frogs" and "The Little Peachling," which she would soon be telling Takashi. As the pale light of the moon touched his face, she thought of how beautiful he looked asleep even if she knew it might conjure up bad omens to think such things. She quickly whispered aloud to the gods. "But look, look, his eyes are too small and his nose is just a bit too flat." She glanced down at Takashi, nestled in her arms, and felt content for the first time in her life.

Aki was nine years old when she lost her mother to the firestorm. Growing up, Haru had stepped in to fill the void of her mother's absence until she left for college, after which a growing disquiet began to fill Aki's days. She took refuge in the contents of her mother's trunk, as if some small part of her had returned. Her subsequent marriage to Hiroshi had brought her some calm, but not long after, he was away much of the time at tournaments or at dinners with sponsors held by the Sumo Association. She couldn't go out without the reporters and photographers that hovered around their house, frightening her. The birth of Takashi had saved Aki. What she felt for him had taken on a physical sensation, one that provided nourishment and courage. She held Takashi close and whispered, "I'll never leave you."

It was May and the alleyways outside the mask shop were filled with people enjoying the warm sunshine. Yanaka was once again the vibrant place of Kenji's childhood. He picked up a block of cypress wood and watched it slowly take shape as he guided it through the saw. In the straight, clean lines, he began to see the shape of the truck he envisioned. Afterward, he would sand it down and paint it a bright blue and green with red wheels. In a couple of years, he imagined his nephew, Takashi, pushing the truck around in the shop on his hands and knees, atop tables and up and down stairs, its wheels rattling across every surface. Kenji smiled at the thought, wishing at the same time he were making the truck for his own son.

Kenji looked up to see Akira Yoshiwara standing in the doorway watching him. His sensei's movements were still as quick and quiet as always, though his hair and beard were almost all gray, and as he squinted against the morning sun he appeared older than his fifty years.

"It's quite a nice piece you're making there." Yoshiwara smiled. "Are you thinking of expanding our business?"

Kenji laughed. "I think we'd do quite well making toys. This will be the first of many for my nephew, Takashi, when he's old enough to play with them."

"Not to mention the toys you'll be making for your own children," his sensei added.

Kenji nodded. There was always that hope. His respect and friendship for his sensei had continued to grow over the years. "Yoshiwara-sensei, have you ever thought of having children of your own?"

Yoshiwara laughed. "Who would want an old, one-handed mask maker who can barely take care of himself?"

In all the years Kenji had known his sensei, he'd never seen him interested in a woman. He never appeared interested in anything but the masks. But since his return to Yanaka, Kenji had seen a softer, gentler side of his sensei that made him feel strangely sad for him. "I imagine there's a whole world out there who would be fascinated with Akira Yoshiwara."

"You always had a vivid imagination, Kenji-san," his sensei said, shaking his head. "I'll leave you to your dreams and get back to work."

Kenji watched Yoshiwara disappear into the front room. He picked up the wooden truck and quickly made the last cut. He wondered what Mika would think of his toy making. He blew away the sawdust clinging to the wood and ran his fingers across the smooth cut before he placed it safely on the top shelf. It would be ready for painting by the week's end.

In Darkness

Four months after Takashi's birth, in February, Hiroshi came home late after an evening with sponsors. Aki's futon was empty and he assumed she'd gotten up to feed Takashi. A dim light filtered through the shoji door to Takashi's room and something pulled him toward it to check on his wife and son. He stumbled toward Takashi's room, where he heard a faint, low humming and smiled to think Aki was singing their son back to sleep. The floorboards creaked under the weight of his steps, and when he slid the door open, the singing stopped. "Aki-chan," he whispered, but she didn't answer. Perhaps she was afraid to wake Takashi, or angry with him for staying out late yet again. He reeked of stale smoke and liquor, which filled the small, warm room. Hiroshi stepped closer to where she sat in the chair by the window and heard a low moan come from her. "Aki, what is it?" he asked, his own heart suspecting now that something was terribly wrong. He turned up the electric lantern and saw her sitting with the baby in her arms, slowly rocking back and forth. He leaned over and stroked her warm cheek then lowered his hand to his sleeping son. Only when he touched Takashi's cold, lifeless body under the quilt did he know his son was already dead.

REQUIEM

The night after Takashi died was the first time Aki had seen Hiroshi cry. In the darkness of their bedroom, they lay side by side on their futons, neither of them sleeping. The muffled, throaty sounds came gradually so that she didn't quite realize he was crying until it was clear and unmistakable. Aki hoped it might strike some deep reservoir in her so that she could cry, too. But as she lay listening to his weeping grow louder, she only felt grief like a seed growing inside of her, stealing away all her tears. It was as if everything else inside of her had dried up. Aki tried to say something to comfort him, to at least turn over and embrace him, but she didn't want to embarrass him. So she lay still, as a coldness spread through her body like a thin layer of ice across Lake Biwa, fragile and precarious.

The first week after Takashi's death was like a swarm of voices and faces, some Aki recognized and some she didn't. Haru had returned from Nara for the Shinto ceremony. She remembered the sharp smell of incense, the soft chanting of mantras, the ringing of the altar bell, holding Haru's hand at the temple and refusing to let go. Her sister had led her out of the firestorm; she could lead her out of this death storm, too.

Reporters and fans descended on the great Yokozuna Takanoyama's house, the death of his son a tragedy that made the headlines. All the doctors could tell them was that Takashi had simply stopped breathing during the night. There were no other signs of illness, no fevers or rashes, no excessive crying or marks on his body that would suggest anything else. It happened to some babies without explanation. Aki had promised Takashi she wouldn't leave him, and so he was taken from her. All Aki could think was, what kind of demon would steal the breath from a baby? And how was she supposed to accept that her son died for absolutely no reason at all?

The days passed like dark shadows, ghosts that lingered in every room. Months after Takashi's death, Aki's grief was still something tangible. Even now, she could feel his tiny body in her arms after she found him lifeless in his crib, cradling him, praying he'd just fallen into a deep sleep from which he would awake. She sang to him "The Lullaby of Edo" as she did every night.

Sleep, baby, sleep,
Oh, my baby, sleep,
How lovely, how lovely,
How nice you are!

But his body only grew colder, almost waxy to the touch, like a bad dream. Not until Hiroshi came into the room did Aki realize Takashi was really dead, and that she'd awakened to the real nightmare. For days after, the nursery rhyme she sang to him played over and over in her head. When she finally stopped hearing it, the silence filled every crevice of the house. It wasn't the same as with her mother's death, when Aki had had no voice. This time she chose not to speak; she was too frightened of what would come out if she did.

25
GRIEF
1959

During the four months after Takashi's death, Hiroshi watched helplessly as Aki grew increasingly remote from everyone and everything around her. She wouldn't leave the house, fearful of the throng of reporters that waited for her outside the gates. Hiroshi tried to reason with her, his calm words growing steadily angrier, while she sat day after day, blank-faced, staring, his words vanishing into air. She had long ago stopped listening. As much as Hiroshi tried, he knew only Haru could find a thin thread of connection. But her life was in Nara now, and how could he ask her to return yet again?

As Hiroshi lay on his futon, a rush of blood colored his face when he thought of his behavior the night before. He'd drunk too much sake at the Sakura teahouse and returned late to find Aki sitting silently by the window in their room. Only this time he didn't have the patience to put up with her silence. *"Talk to me!"* he had said, at first quietly, then growing in volume when she turned away and ignored him. *"Look at me!"* he demanded. He realized he was reduced to seeming childish when he grabbed her arm and practically lifted her from the chair. Hiroshi knew he was hurting her, but he wanted a reaction, any reaction. He was the grand champion and her husband, and Aki owed him a small gesture of respect; and still, she remained silent, looking at him with such blank indifference in her eyes that a great roar rose up in him and he pushed her away, watching her fall to the mats, her shoulder hitting hard against the chair. She was as light as a feather, and it frightened him to think how little it would take for him to really hurt her. Hiroshi left the house and didn't return until the next evening, wondering if she would still be there. He entered the house, embarrassed and filled with shame. His stomach lurched to think Aki might be gone, but there she was, sitting silently by the window as if nothing had happened.

In the early morning light, Hiroshi lay sleepless. His thoughts spun over and over. As *yokozuna,* if he could give strength and good health to all the other babies he carried, why hadn't he been able to do the same for his own son? On the futon next to him, Aki lay quiet. He turned to see the purplish-blue bruises on her arm and shoulder, the fingerprints of anger. He realized then his grief was no better than hers — he had been compelled to strike out whereas she had turned inward. The bruises appeared like scattered islands and he leaned over and kissed her shoulder gently, her skin soft and warm against his lips. Aki turned slowly toward him, her hand rising up, and for a moment, Hiroshi thought she might slap him, but instead her pale fingers traced the scar on his forehead and came to rest on his cheek. When she opened herself to his embrace, he wondered if for just a moment they could forget their loss together.

Afterward, they'd come to an unspoken truce, the stare-down broken. Hiroshi moved through the house quietly, his steps as calculated as in the *dohyo.* He no longer wished for an awkward word or two. Like Aki, he preferred a silence that wouldn't lead to any more hurt or misunderstandings.

SALVATION

Since Takashi's death, Hiroshi had missed three tournaments. With the Nagoya Basho added in July, there were now six major tournaments held each year. Though he was secure in knowing he would never lose his *yokozuna* rank, Hiroshi knew that if he stayed away much longer, he would have to do the honorable thing and retire. But at thirty-two, he wasn't ready to give up the *dohyo*. In mid-January, seven months after his son's death, on a pewter-gray morning that felt too cold to snow, Hiroshi left the house with Aki still asleep.

It began to snow as Hiroshi entered the front gates of the Katsuyama-beya and he felt the strange sensation of stepping back into the past. In the courtyard, he glanced up at the window in which he and Aki had first begun their courtship. It was empty and quiet now. He hurried toward the stable to begin training for the Haru Basho in March.

Hiroshi pushed open the wooden door and the familiar stench of sweat and musk, the dank, earthy smells laced with the sweet *bint-suke* hair wax, rushed at him. All activity in the *keikoba* paused at his entrance. Tanaka-oyakata and Sadao were the first to welcome him back. A group of lower-ranked wrestlers already in the midst of practice stopped and bowed low. There were new, younger faces Hiroshi didn't recognize and he searched for traces of greatness in each one of them. Who would be the next grand champion?

Thirty minutes later, Yokozuna Takanoyama stretched his tight muscles with the series of exercises he'd practiced every morning for the past thirteen years. The pain pulled at the back of his thighs as he leaned forward doing leg splits. He welcomed it all, as if the sheer physical pain could make him forget everything else. He'd lost weight and would have to train hard to catch up with all the aspiring *rikishi*. Tanaka-oyakata welcomed his return and watched from a distance, allowing him to train at his own pace. He sensed his father-in-law moved around the stable with a quick, busy determination to deaden his own sorrow at Takashi's sudden death. When Hiroshi finished warming up, he stepped onto the *dohyo,* his feet touching the cool, smooth dirt for the first time in months. The memory soothed.

Following him onto the *dohyo* was Sadao, whom he'd chosen to practice with. Sadao was a *sekitori* now, thereby refuting the bow twirling superstition, and had risen in the ranks to become a good, strong wrestler. They moved quickly through the preliminaries and squatted down at the starting lines. Hiroshi felt a knot of anxiety in his stomach as his knuckles touched the dirt. He slowed his breathing, his gaze intent. The sudden impact of their bodies was quick and violent. Sadao's blow to his chest was solid and hard, knocking the wind out of him. There was only a moment before the young wrestler's next move, but Hiroshi's instinct and experience kicked in. He moved just out of the way as Sadao charged, grabbing him in a headlock and forcing him to the ground before he knew what had happened. Sadao rose and bowed low to him.

Hiroshi would later replay those moments on the *dohyo,* when his mind was fixed on only his opponent and all other life had ceased to be. He was thankful for the respite; those moments of concentrated will that allowed him to forget. But in the midst of his small victory, Hiroshi learned that grief was an opponent he would never be able to defeat.

Birthday

It was February again and the wind was blowing. It gusted through the house with a sigh as Aki lit a stick of incense and bowed to a photo of her baby son. Family photos filled the *tokonoma* as she knelt before them, but only Takashi had been granted so little time on earth. She bowed low to the ground and struggled in her grief to push her body back up, as if all the strength were drained from her. She relented and lay prostrate on the tatami, which was rough and cool against her cheek, the old grassy smell a reminder of when she was young and tumbling on the floor with Haru.

Time was playing tricks on her. Finally, eight months after the death of Takashi, on what would have been his first birthday, Aki relinquished herself fully to the sorrow of it. While Hiro-chan returned to sumo, she had chosen to remain silent and alone most days. She knew it wasn't healthy. She would have gladly traded her own life for that of little Takashi. At least she had made some memories in her twenty-three years, while he was never given the chance. Her tears came freely, silently, for all that might have been. She closed her eyes and the wind seemed to turn to voices, soothing her.

Aki put on a silk padded coat over her kimono, picked up the *furoshiki* in which she carried fruit, red bean cakes, and rice crackers to place at Takashi's grave. She had hoped to leave quickly, before their housekeeper, Tamiko-san, had time to talk her out of going, but it was too late.

"Please, Aki-san." Tamiko bowed. "Yokozuna Takanoyama will be home shortly. He asks that you wait for him to go to the cemetery with you."

"Tell Yokozuna Takanoyama that I'll be waiting for him at the cemetery."

"Then I'll go with you," Tamiko said. Her voice rose in fear.

"No. I'll go alone," Aki said with a sharp finality. She saw the distress on Tamiko's face, and softened. "Don't worry, I'll be fine."

"It's too cold to walk," the housekeeper pleaded.

"I'll be fine."

Aki slid the front door open and braced

herself against the shock of the cold wind. She looked back once and smiled to reassure Tamiko that all was well with her. Then she hurried out to the courtyard and through the front gate without looking back.

The wind was icy and her face numb by the time Aki reached the cemetery. Even her tears felt frozen. She walked down the stone path to the large, fenced-off plot Hiroshi had chosen, and where they would all rest one day. Now, there was only the tall, white marble marker with Takashi's name, followed by his birth and death dates written in bold, black characters. Aki stood before it and bowed. "Look what I've brought you, Takashi-chan." She brushed away the leaves, opened the *furoshiki,* and carefully placed the fruit and food at the foot of his marker. Then she stood and bowed again. It calmed her to think that her mother, Noriko, and his great-grandfather, Yoshio, were watching over little Takashi. Sometimes, his spirit was so alive in her that Aki still felt the warmth of his small body in her arms. She sat down and laid her head against the cold marble and began to softly sing "The Lullaby of Edo" to him, the words lifted and carried away by the wind.

Kenji walked quickly down the alleyway, pulling the collar of his kimono tighter against the sharp February wind. He looked up at the darkening sky, which was sure to bring rain before nightfall, and shifted the package under his arm as he walked. Had his nephew Takashi lived, he would have celebrated his first birthday today. Kenji wanted to stop by the cemetery before going home. He recalled the morning he and Mika heard the news of Takashi's death. If it hadn't been Hiroshi's choked voice over the phone, he might have thought someone was playing a cruel joke on him. A stunned silence followed before he was able to take a breath again. After he told Mika, she began to cry, her tears flowing translucently down her cheeks, and he couldn't help wondering how he could capture those tears on a mask. She leaned against him, and he held her, smelling the lovely scent of jasmine, lilac, lilies; a bouquet of flowers in her hair. He made a pitiful attempt to console her.

"Maybe it was his time," Kenji whispered.

He wasn't prepared when Mika glared up at him with an angry look he'd never seen before. "What time? He wasn't given any time!" She pulled away, her voice hard and final.

■ ■ ■ ■

Kenji knew she was right, but it made him feel better to think otherwise. There were no guarantees in life. Wasn't everyone given only a limited time on this earth? Like his parents? Like his *ojichan?* But in his heart, he couldn't understand the dictates of any god who would take a baby away from his parents so soon. And he couldn't imagine how Hiroshi must feel, all the lost moments with his son. There was so little he could do to ease his brother's pain. For the rest of his life, Hiroshi would wear grief like a scar, not unlike the one that marked his forehead; stricken and furious, helpless to save his child no matter how strong he was. Kenji remembered them as little boys, his brother the strong one, rock solid like the earth, while he was a leaf that could be blown away in the wind. Only Hiroshi protected him from nature's forces. Now, he would do the same for his brother; open his arms wide to protect him from the coming winds.

By the time Kenji reached the cemetery, the world around him was steeped in gray shadows. The white marble of Takashi's headstone stood out like a beacon. Around it were the neatly arranged food offerings that he knew Aki and Hiroshi must have left earlier. He

553

bowed to his nephew, before he knelt to rearrange the offerings, placing them to one side. From the package he carried, Kenji pulled out the brightly painted wooden truck and placed it next to Takashi's headstone.

DIRECTION

The knock on her office door startled Haru. She didn't expect any students and hoped for some quiet time to grade papers and study for her own final exams. It was hard to believe she would have her graduate degree in June, only three months away. Haru had no idea what she'd do afterward. Since the miscarriage she'd had difficulty concentrating. Now, the sudden interruption irritated her. She cleared her throat and said abruptly, "*Hai,* come in," without looking up from the paper she was correcting. The door whining open was another irritant she'd have to take care of.

"Haru-san, I hope I'm not disturbing you?"

She looked up at the sound of his voice, a knot instantly forming in the middle of her stomach, not knowing what might have brought him to Nara. "Hiroshi-san," she said, surprised. She quickly stood. Then, "Is it Aki?" The loss of Takashi last year was devastating. Haru spent the weeks after his death taking care of her sister, who had retreated inward again. Haru eventually returned to Nara drained — grief a weight she could no longer carry, not for Aki, not for Takashi, and especially not for herself. She had hoped her work and teaching would provide distraction, but since she'd returned, even that didn't help.

He bowed. "Aki-chan is as well as can be," he said, trying to put her at ease.

"My father?"

"Tanaka-oyakata is fine." He bowed again. "I'm sorry to arrive unannounced. I'm on my way to Osaka to meet with some sponsors before the *basho* there, and thought of stopping in Nara to see you."

Haru never imagined seeing Hiroshi in her office at the university. He filled the already small, overflowing space that she shared with another lecturer with his sheer size, with the flowery scent of *bintsuke*, with his deep, steady voice. He was dressed elegantly in a dark kimono, standing awkwardly before her. There had to be something terribly wrong to bring him to Nara. "Is it Aki-chan?" she asked again.

He nodded and swallowed. "Since Takashi's death, she barely says a word. She hardly eats and sleeps very little," he said, his gaze turned downward, staring at the scuffed wood floor. "I'm afraid she's drifting into her own world. I'm at a loss as to what to do."

He appeared tired and defeated. There were dark bags under his eyes and he'd lost weight.

She knew through her father that he'd returned to sumo and that things were still difficult with Aki. Haru sat back down in her chair. "What can I do?" she asked, more to herself than to Hiroshi.

Hiroshi sat in the chair across from her. "Haru-san, you're the one person Aki-chan has always felt the closest to. She's the most comfortable with you. I see it every time you return to Tokyo. I wouldn't be here if I didn't think she needed you now." He paused, took a breath, and the chair squeaked when he leaned back against it.

It was a kind of curse, she thought, but wiped it quickly from her mind. "Are you asking me to return to Tokyo?"

Hiroshi paused. "For just a short time, until Aki-chan is better."

Haru looked down at her hands, feeling a tingling at her fingertips as they lay on top of the papers she'd been correcting. She turned and gazed out the window for a moment, out at the willow tree that she loved, already missing the sight of it. Tiny buds were just balancing on its limbs. She'd loved Nara from the moment she arrived and once dreamt of spending her life here. But after the miscarriage, everything had changed. Haru was no longer sure what she wanted. Even with an opening in the department, she hesitated applying for it. She'd go home to Tokyo in June after she finished her degree, and return to

Nara when Aki was feeling better. It would give her time to decide what direction she wanted to take. She swallowed her thoughts and turned back to Hiroshi. "I won't be able to return until the term is over in June."

He stood up and bowed low to her. "I will always be indebted to you, Haru-san."

"Aki's my sister," Haru said, looking up at him.

He smiled sadly.

She stood up from her desk. "Shall we take a walk? Perhaps I can finally show you our famous park."

"It's a beautiful day for a walk," he said, smiling. "My train for Osaka doesn't leave for another few hours."

It made Haru happy to think she'd be in the park with Hiroshi. The great sumo champion would step into her realm and see how small they really were in the natural world. It would, at the very least, give him a glimpse into her life in Nara. Haru stood and steadied herself. She stacked the papers she was grading and grabbed her sweater. "Shall we go?" she said.

FEVER

Over the years, Akira Yoshiwara had found ways to compensate for having only one hand. A vise secured on the table now helped him to keep the masks steady and in place, so that Akira could even chisel out some of the features one-handed. It meant more to him this second time around. He became so adept that it was even difficult for the actor Otomo Matsui to tell the difference between a new mask and an old one Yoshiwara had made.

Just after his fiftieth birthday a fever stirred inside of Akira Yoshiwara, unexplained warmth that made him feel as if his skin were too hot to touch. All through the week, he felt his temperature rise most keenly in the early afternoons as he worked on the masks. By evening, the October days would grow cool and windy. The fever ebbed and flowed and he knew he was ill, but dusted the notion off like wood dust during the moments he felt better. All his life, Akira had rarely been sick, even as a boy in Yokohama. He hadn't felt this way since Emiko cared for him after the loss of his hand. A fever had taken over, and in his delirium, Akira forgot everything and only recalled his sense of release. Now, the thought calmed him. He wavered, and leaned against the worktable before he reached for a bottle of whiskey he kept atop the shelf. The sharp sting of liquid felt almost cool going down his throat, quenching the growing heat of his body. Akira looked up at the shelves to see the masks watching him and felt strangely at ease.

By the end of the week when Akira tried to get out of bed his body refused. The fever flushed through him as he lay back onto his damp sheets. Akira drifted in and out of sleep until he heard the door of the shop unlock downstairs. He trusted that Kenji would eventually come up to see why he wasn't already downstairs with the door unlocked and the tea made. Finally, he heard Kenji's footsteps, light and tentative on the stairs as they approached. He felt his fever rising, his body growing heavy. Akira didn't wait for Kenji to knock but called out for him to come in, though he wasn't sure if he'd spoken the words aloud before he closed his eyes and slept.

Days later when his fever broke, Kenji helped Akira outside to sit in the warm sun. His body felt weak, cleansed by the fever. "What did I say to you when you found me delirious with the fever?" he asked.

Kenji smiled. "That it was the second time you were being saved."

THE LAKE

Hiroshi watched Aki slowly become herself again with Haru back in Tokyo. Her voice grew stronger and she spoke more with each day, as if she were slowly awakening from a deep sleep. Listening to Haru's and Aki's voices reminded Hiroshi of his *obachan* and her friend Ayako-san together when he was a boy. It was the same sweet, carefree tone that he always loved and envied. He paused at the kitchen doorway and listened to their melodious words ring through the air like music, never once like the gruff staccato words and grunts that men often used to address each other.

He studied the similarities and differences between the sisters; although they had the same inflections when they spoke, the slightly taller Haru, with the always inquisitive eyes, who never cared if her skin was tinged darker by the outdoors, was the opposite of the more fragile, black-pearl-eyed, creamy-skinned Aki, animated again in her sister's company. Occasionally, Aki would still lapse into staring vacantly out the window, or down at the floor, lost in her own world. Moments later she would return as if she'd just stepped out. Hiroshi wondered where she'd gone and what she was thinking, but held his breath until she was herself again.

By the end of July, Hiroshi returned to Tokyo after the Nagoya Basho. He'd been away since early July. A heat wave simmered throughout most of Japan and the air remained so hot and stagnant that each breath was a gift. Even a thin cotton *yukata* robe felt heavy against his body. As he watched Haru and Aki try to remain comfortable in the sweltering heat, Hiroshi made arrangements to take them and his *obachan* to Hakone, where the cooler mountain air of Lake Ashino and the hot springs had long been a favorite spot. But only he and Aki finally boarded the train to Hakone. His *obachan* hadn't wanted to travel in the heat, while Haru chose to return to Nara for a visit instead.

When they stepped out of the car at the train station, a crowd immediately surrounded them. There were few places Yokozuna Takanoyama wasn't recognized. On most days, photographers were waiting outside their home for a quick snapshot. The rush of strangers and flashing lights terrified Aki. While Hiroshi's driver stepped forward to clear the way, he gently took hold of Aki's arm as they hurried along to catch their train.

When they arrived in Odawara, they transferred to the mountain-climbing train, which wound its way up the lush mountain slope by the side of a flowing river. The higher they climbed, the cooler the air became. Away from the hot press of people and the media, he saw Aki find calm and her body relax as she watched the trees flicker by. From the train, they would ascend farther up the mountain in a cable car. Aki grasped his arm and Hiroshi pulled her close as the car swayed to the side when he stepped in. It was the first time they had laughed freely together after Takashi's death, just over a year ago. He sat down and was careful to stay centered on the seat to balance the car as it moved slowly upward.

"Oh, look!" Aki said, pointing below.

Hiroshi looked down on views of the natural hot springs as whiffs of sulfur vapors floated upward and he felt as if they were being transported to another world.

They stayed at a famous *ryokan* at the edge of Lake Ashino. The inn was built over three hundred years ago and was often visited by the imperial family, as well as many famous artists and writers. Yokozuna Takanoyama was given the special cottage behind the inn, surrounded by trees, with a hot spring bath and a veranda that overlooked the lake from each room. The smell of the pine trees and fresh air was a welcome change from the stifling world of Tokyo. Hiroshi and Aki were slowly getting to know each other again and he was thankful the fates had led them to Lake Ashino by themselves.

The next morning, after they finished a breakfast of miso soup, fish, rice, and pickled vegetables, they walked down a dirt trail from the inn to a wooden dock to embark on a ferry ride across the lake. When Hiroshi stepped onto the boat, the rocking motion gave him a strange sensation, as if he'd been there before, but he shook it off and helped

Aki step down onto the deck. It was a pleasant excursion; the boat was filled with other guests from the *ryokan* who tried not to stare at the famous *yokozuna*. At one point, the ferry slowed down and shut off its rumbling motor so that the passengers could enjoy the majestic view of Mount Fuji that rose before them like a towering god. It wasn't until they had docked again that an old man, with a wrinkled face and thinning gray hair, approached Hiroshi and bowed very low, introducing himself as the captain of the boat.

"*Sumimasen,* please excuse me for bothering you, Yokozuna Takanoyama. Never in my life did I think we would have this opportunity."

Hiroshi bowed back. "How may I help you?"

"I would like to apologize, Yokozuna-sama. I have met you once before a very long time ago."

Hiroshi tried to place the old man's face. Was he a friend of his grandparents'? If so, he had no memory of the man at all. "I don't understand," he said. Aki had stepped back on the dock and waited for him.

The old man fidgeted with the soiled hat in his hands. "You see, I've lived with the guilt for the past thirty years, of how I left all my passengers in the water after the boat had sunk." He shook his head and tears brimmed in his eyes.

"What are you saying?"

"That I'm the one responsible for the deaths of your mother and father when you were just a baby." He took a deep breath and continued. "When I read the story of how you were orphaned, I knew it was my boat that had struck the rocks and left you without parents. I would give anything to take that evening back." He bowed low again.

Hiroshi stood in disbelief as the other passengers milled around them. "It can't be . . . ," he said.

"We had drunk too much sake that night. We had no business taking passengers out to sea. I have lived each day trying to forget. And when I saw you board this morning, I knew that the gods had given me a chance to apologize to you."

"Why did you leave?"

"I was frightened. I swam away."

Hiroshi remembered all the stories his *obachan* told him as a boy, and how she had always wished the captain of that boat dead. Now, here he was standing before him, a small, withered man who looked no more a killer than his own grandfather had. "And what do you expect of me now?" Hiroshi asked, his own voice sounding strange. "Forgiveness?"

The old man shook his head. "It will never be my place to ask that of you. It was simply my way of finally accepting the guilt, to say it out loud to the one living person whose life I altered that night."

Hiroshi swallowed but didn't say a word. He didn't feel the anger he always imagined as he pushed past the old man and stepped out of the boat without turning back.

"Do you know him?" Aki asked when he joined her back on the dock.

He hesitated and shook his head. When he was a boy, Hiroshi always believed he would track down the man who had left him and Kenji orphans. As a man, he knew the past was best forgotten. What had it to do with his life now? He would never say a word to his *obachan* and stir up such painful memories. "He wanted to know if I enjoyed the boat ride," he finally told Aki.

She smiled and touched his arm lightly with her fan.

26
INDEPENDENCE
1960

At sixty, Sho Tanaka was slowing down. He entered the sumo stable and stopped to watch two young recruits at practice, wondering if he still had the energy to take them up the ranks. As a stable master, he'd already produced two grand champions, with young Sadao on his way to reaching *ozeki* rank. All around him was the hum of activity he'd heard for over forty years, the grunts and groans, the slaps and thuds of men pushing their bodies to the furthest limits. Sho walked through the training room, and bowed quickly back to all the wrestlers before he made his way upstairs to his office. He knew he'd find Haru there, going over the books, making sure that everything was in order. Ever since she'd returned to Tokyo, Haru had been taking care of Aki, handling most of the household matters, and spending a few days each week helping him with the stable accounts. He glanced through the open door to see her sitting at his desk, concentrating on the books spread out in front of her. For a split second, he saw Noriko again in her profile. Had Noriko lived, he wondered what she would think of him now — stoop-shouldered and sagging, without a hair on his head. He knew many women still found him attractive. Even Yasuko-san called him "Yul-o Blenner," after the famous American movie star, when she saw him at the Sakura teahouse. He smiled to think Haru never realized how much like her mother she was. In fact, Sho thought his older daughter grew lovelier with age.

"I thought I'd find you here," he said.

She looked up and smiled. "Is everything all right?"

"Everything's fine." In that moment, he also saw her as a wonderful teacher, someone who listened as well as instructed. Noriko would have been so proud of her. Sho sat in the chair across from his desk, his hand running across his smooth pate. He had never regretted keeping the original building of the stable that had survived the firestorm. He had built from the past like new branches sprouting from a proud old tree. His small, cube-shaped office had remained unchanged for both practical and sentimental reasons. It was the first time he sat where his *rikishi* usually did, facing his desk. "I was thinking," he said thoughtfully, "that it's about time you returned to Nara and to your teaching."

Haru put down the pencil. "And who will

take care of you?" she asked.

He laughed. "What makes you think I can't take care of myself? I've been doing it for years."

"Ah, that's why it's taken me almost a year to straighten your books out."

Sho smiled. "I happen to understand my accounts perfectly, and that's all that matters. Besides, if it'll make you feel better, I'll hire a professional to do it for me." Since Hiroshi had reached the rank of *yokozuna,* the stable had benefited from sponsor money. Sho had even been thinking of building a new wing to the stable, along with a large new office for himself. But in the end, he had decided to keep things the way they were.

"And Aki-chan?"

"She can take care of herself. Besides, Aki-chan has Hiroshi to care for her. She isn't your responsibility. I want you to return to Nara and be happy."

Haru nodded. *"Hai,"* she said.

But he wasn't sure she was convinced. Even as a little girl, she'd had a mind of her own. Tanaka stood up and paced the floor. "Haru-chan, you've made me very proud with all your accomplishments. Now it's time for you to enjoy all that you've worked so hard to achieve. Go back to Nara and your teaching."

"What makes you think that's what I want?" she asked.

He stopped. "Isn't it?"

"I thought it was."

"Then go back and see if it is. If it isn't, return to Tokyo because it's your decision. Not because of Aki-chan or your old, failing father, but because it's what you want."

He watched her glance down at the open accounts book; the dark quick scratches were a blur from where he sat. When she looked up again, there were tears in her eyes.

Homecoming

When Haru stepped off the train in Nara, she felt the first trace of fall in the air, lighter and sweeter, not the crowded, hot breath of Tokyo. As she walked down the street toward her apartment, the waning light set everything aglow; even the trees seemed ablaze. She had been hesitant to leave Tokyo, unsure of what there was to return to in Nara. But even Aki seemed resolute that she should return. Just the day before, Haru had been combing out her sister's hair, trying to put her at ease, when it seemed just the opposite was happening.

"You must be excited to be returning to Nara." Aki glanced up at her in the mirror.

Her sister had been calm and playful all morning. There was a healthy color to her cheeks again, nicely offset by her kimono with magenta flowers. "I'm not sure," Haru said.

Aki raised her hand and caught her wrist as the brush stroked downward. "Don't you want to return and teach?"

"I'm not sure," Haru repeated.

Aki turned around to face her. "Is it because of me? Please don't worry, Haru-chan, I'm all right now."

Haru smiled, and her gaze found an unexpected contentment in Aki's eyes. It startled her at first. She had noticed something different about her sister since she returned from Lake Ashino, a tangible joy. She *was* free to return to Nara.

Haru had left Tokyo with a heavy heart. She missed her father and sister and the life she knew so well, filled with voices and childhood comforts. Was the ghost of her unborn child still haunting her? Did she really want to stand in front of a classroom of students? She felt a cool wind blow as the trees rustled and waved. As she rounded the corner and her apartment building came into view, she saw the brightness of Nara again, a place she loved. Haru smiled and walked faster, more lightly, as if toward the open arms of an old friend.

The Secret

Aki was pregnant again. Even before she saw the doctor, she felt the baby growing inside of her, a faint, fragile pulse of life. She thought back to their week at Lake Ashino last August and smiled. Ever since, she and Hiroshi had found happiness again. She rubbed her stomach; she couldn't be more than two months along, still barely showing. The idea that she could keep this secret to herself for a little while longer calmed her. No one had to know just yet.

Ever since she was a little girl, Aki had loved secrets. "If I tell you my secret," Haru once said to her, "you have to hold it inside and never let it out. If you do, it won't be a secret anymore." Aki was five and nodded enthusiastically. She remembered how the fullness of the secret filled her body, weighed her down with importance. She was the keeper of Haru's secret, even if she could no longer remember what it was.

There were very few secrets in Aki's life now. She was married to the great Yokozuna Takanoyama, and any opportunity for a private life was confined behind the gates of their house. Once they stepped outside, their every move was scrutinized and followed by reporters and photographers. She hated the flash of their cameras, which temporarily blinded her as if she were caught doing something wrong, her eyes wide with fear. She felt the panic as voices shouted questions at her: "Where is Yokozuna Takanoyama?" "When will you have another child?" "Do you think the Yokozuna will win his next tournament?" She began to think that they waited outside just to torment her, and as much as she tried to ignore them, Aki couldn't just walk by bantering with them as Hiroshi did. Her pregnancy would simply be another headline in the newspaper, which she wasn't ready for. She rubbed her stomach, the slightest rise only she felt. The baby was hers and would remain her secret for as long as possible.

PURSUIT

By late November, the weather was unusually mild, cool and comfortable with a hint of wetness in the air. The first time Kenji followed Mika was just a few weeks before. It was unexpected and on sheer impulse. He was on his way to the mask shop when he caught a glimpse of his wife's back, the blue-green of her kimono as she made her way down the alleyway and through the crowd toward the train station. She was even more beautiful now, ever since she'd begun to wear traditional kimonos again. In the past few years she'd become even more involved in her father's textile business, designing fabrics in bright, vibrant colors that he could see from afar. He found himself following the blue-green of her kimono as if it were a mirage he was trying to get to, a calm, placid lake he could swim in.

The next day, and the day after, when Kenji followed her to the train station, it was with a calm awareness that there was something desperate in his pursuit. Yet, he felt strangely closer to her from a distance, similar to when they were university students and he sat behind her, loving her from afar. It became more and more difficult for Kenji to keep up with her schedule, all the meetings and travel. At the same time, their marriage had come to a standstill and he searched his mind to find movement again. He wondered if it would have been different if they'd had a child, something they no longer talked about. Their evening conversations were reduced to a minimum of words until Mika looked up and said, "I'm going up then," and went upstairs, his gaze following. It began to sound like a refrain from a Noh play each night. He felt her slipping away from him and sometimes thought it better if they'd yelled and screamed, giving voice to their frustrations.

Each morning for weeks, Kenji pursued this same pattern. He waited for Mika to leave the house and followed her down the alleyway at a careful distance. Just once, early on, did he venture too close and thought Mika might have seen him, his heart drumming as she moved quickly along, lost in her own thoughts. He stood across the road and watched her enter the swarming station and hurry down the stairs to the train, disappearing from sight. Only then did he wind his way back through the crowds, already late for his morning tea with Yoshiwara-sensei.

By December, when Kenji stepped out into a cold wind, Mika was wearing a saffron-colored kimono with a burgundy obi, which made it easy for her to stand out in the crowd. She walked at a brisk, confident pace, and each day he seemed to notice something new about her; how she fixed her hair in a chignon, or tied it back away from her face, sometimes in a braid, sometimes not. She stared straight ahead and never looked back, never curious about the people around her. And she always seemed to be carrying something. Some days, she was weighed down with material samples and he wanted to rush forward and take the weight from her shoulder. But he held back.

Kenji didn't know what made this morning any different from the others, but the same impulse that had made him pursue Mika now brought him to a standstill. He saw her receding into the crowd, her head bobbing up and down in the vast sea of people, her saffron kimono disappearing down the alleyway until she rounded the corner and was gone. Then he turned around and walked the other way to the mask shop.

■ ■ ■ ■

Kenji had just poured a cup of tea when he heard the front door of the shop open. He stepped out of the back room, surprised to see Mika standing there, flushed and breathing hard as if she'd been running.

"Is everything all right?" he asked.

"You stopped following me," she answered, and dropped her material samples to the floor.

"You knew?"

"From early on."

"Why did you come all the way back?"

She paused to catch her breath. "I came back for you," she finally answered.

27
WITH CHILD
1961

From the moment Hiroshi found out Aki was expecting another child, a flicker of apprehension stayed with him. What if they should lose this child, too? His uneasiness grew each day leading up to the tournament, and as he stepped up to the *dohyo* for the first match of the spring *basho* in Osaka, he remained unsettled; the glare of the lights felt suffocating, the roar of the crowd too loud. Usually, when something bothered him, Hiroshi trained hard and concentrated all his worries into winning. But even the cool clay of the *dohyo* felt foreign to the hardened calluses on his feet. When he locked eyes with his opponent, he felt nothing of the fighting instinct that had helped him to reach grand champion. Moments later, Hiroshi felt his leg tripped out from under him as his back slammed hard against the *dohyo*. The entire stadium went silent in disbelief, and it took him a moment to realize that he'd lost the match, until the *gyoji* declared the winner by pointing his war paddle toward his opponent. All he wanted was to lie there for another moment, forgetting.

He won his match the next day and the day after, nine out of fifteen bouts and his lowest numbers since he'd reached the rank of *yoko-zuna*. Still, he gained another tournament win. Hiroshi was on his way to becoming one of the most successful sumo wrestlers in Japan's history. Not since before the war, during Futabayama's reign, had a wrestler been so popular. His anxiety calmed and turned to exhaustion by the time he returned to Tokyo and waited for the birth of his second child.

Aki's pregnancy and delivery went so smoothly, he thought it was a gift from the gods, a small token after the death of Takashi. His daughter, Takara, which meant "treasure," was born in April. She had Aki's fair skin and her black-pearl-colored eyes. The first month after Takara's birth was happiness. Aki took to motherhood with the ease and calm that came with a second child. When Haru returned to Nara, Hiroshi moved nervously through the house, checking on the baby while she slept, placing the tips of his fingers lightly over her stomach to make sure she was still breathing. He watched her with an intensity he sometimes felt the baby understood, though she couldn't possibly at such a tender age. Still, Hiroshi felt her eyes following him as he hovered near during her feedings. He began to believe that if Takara survived through her first four months, the length of Takashi's short life, she would live a long, healthy life.

A month after Takara's birth, Aki suddenly stopped breast-feeding her and a nurse was brought in. Over the next few months, Aki slowly retreated into her own world again. She sat silently in her room, not wanting to see anyone, paying less and less attention to the baby, or him, hardly sleeping, and no longer caring about her appearance.

Hiroshi was lost as to why Aki would withdraw from life now with a healthy, beautiful new baby to care for. His *obachan* and Mika tried to give him answers when they came to visit.

"Aki-san just needs a little time to herself," his grandmother said.

Mika nuzzled little Takara. Hiroshi knew how much she and Kenji had hoped for a child. "I've heard that some women are in tears for months after childbirth," Mika said. "It's hard to control your emotions. Aki-san should be fine in a little while."

As the weeks wore on, Hiroshi tried to take their words to heart. As July approached, nothing had changed. It was late morning and the air already hot and sticky when Hiroshi carried the baby over to where Aki sat and stared out the window.

"Aki-chan, look who I have here," he said, keeping his voice calm and direct.

Aki remained silent, her gaze directed out the window.

"Aki-chan, Takara needs her mother." He leaned closer to her with the baby.

She turned and looked down at the mewing baby for just a moment before closing her eyes and shaking her head. "Take her away," Aki said, at first quietly. Then she seemed to rise out of her lethargic state, her eyes wide, almost fearful, as she screamed, "Take her away! Take her away! Take her away!"

Hiroshi quickly turned away from Aki, holding their crying daughter close. He couldn't tell if it was anger or disgust that guided him back to the baby's room. That afternoon, he talked to the finest doctors in Tokyo, hoping they could help Aki.

Hiroshi began to spend more and more time at the Sakura teahouse, where he was treated with the respect a great *yokozuna* commanded. The alcohol dulled his pain, while the voices and laughter made him forget his troubles at home. Sponsors were more than happy to take good care of him. Geishas were there to meet his every demand, and one new geisha in particular, Meiko, made him especially happy. He knew that Yasuko-san, the mistress of the teahouse, was an old family friend of the Tanakas' and disapproved of his growing friendship with Meiko. She'd known Haru and Aki since they were babies, and even the great Yokozuna Takanoyama, with all his fame and wealth, couldn't stop her from making sure Meiko was often called away to other parties at rival teahouses.

On a particularly still, humid night in August, Hiroshi arrived at the Sakura with a party of ten, already in a sullen mood. Aki had been particularly unresponsive that evening. They were ushered into the banquet room with the large, low table where geishas attended to their needs, and Hiroshi drank his sake down quickly. He already felt slightly drunk as he watched the geisha who served him pour more sake into his cup. Suddenly, he asked loudly, "Yasuko-san, where's Meiko-san? Why is she never here anymore? Are you hiding her from me?"

Yasuko smiled and walked over to Hiroshi, kneeling beside him. "And why would I do that?" she said softly.

Hiroshi drank down another glass of sake. "Perhaps you're jealous of our friendship."

Yasuko laughed and leaned closer. "Perhaps you should rethink your friendship with Meiko-san."

Hiroshi smiled at first before he suddenly slammed his glass down, sake splattering on the low table and on him and Yasuko. Angrily he yelled, "Who are you to tell me who to be friends with?"

The entire room stopped talking and looked their way. He glared at them, not seeing anything until the murmur of voices and laughter returned.

Yasuko remained calm. She leaned over to him and said discreetly, "Perhaps, Hiroshi-san, I'm your only real friend here tonight." From her obi she extracted a handkerchief to wipe away the sake that had splashed her cheek.

Hiroshi cleared his throat and remained silent. Of course, he knew she was right. He didn't know anyone in the room well; they were all business acquaintances, no more. He watched Yasuko-san stand and move away from him, stepping lightly out to the hall and kneeling as she closed the sliding door to the banquet room. Voices continued to buzz around him as he watched her slowly disappear before his eyes.

ANOTHER WORLD

Aki couldn't sleep. It was August, hot and muggy. She lay on the futon next to Hiroshi, glad for the cover of darkness. From the other room, she heard the soft mewing sounds of her daughter, Takara. She was four months old and had already outlived her brother Takashi by three days. As much as Aki loved

581

her, she couldn't bear the thought of losing Takara to some silent death, as well. Was it possible to love a child too much? The feeling came to her gradually; a growing anxiety that spread through her veins like a poison and caused her to begin trembling with fear. Aki couldn't control her own limbs. And over and over in her mind was the question, Was it her fault that Takashi had died? Had she put him down or picked him up wrong? The doctors had found no evidence that it was anything but an unexplained defect that made him stop breathing. They gave her useless words and medication to help her calm down. Nothing helped. How could Aki ever be sure? She couldn't let it happen again. Only when she stepped back and watched her baby daughter from a distance did she feel calmer. She finally relaxed when Hiroshi hired a woman, Mitsuko-san, to come in to feed and look after Takara.

Hiroshi's sleep was full of noise and movement. He'd been drinking. She watched him and dreaded the daylight, when she'd have to get up and face another day. The doctors poked and probed, asked her questions as if she were a child. Mostly, she kept silent. How could she tell Hiroshi that her head ached and her hands trembled so much she didn't dare pick up Takara for fear of dropping her? It was better to separate herself from the baby before anything happened.

Out of the darkness, sounds arrested her. She heard the frogs singing in the black night, the swish of a branch against the side of the house, and the clock's relentless ticking, which echoed too loudly in her head. Aki covered her ears and stayed in that hollow vacuum for as long as she could. In it, she felt safe from the world and from herself.

THE HOUSE

September still smoldered. Fumiko arrived at Hiroshi's house early in the morning, before it became too hot and she was forced to stay indoors. She smiled to think of what Yoshio used to say, that it was like touching the coals of the *ofuro,* it was so hot. Even with the heat, she was determined to visit. She'd come to see her great-granddaughter, Takara-chan, but more important, she came to see Aki.

Fumiko pushed open the wooden gate and marveled at the size of Hiroshi's beautiful garden. The paved walkways were lined with *sakura* and pine trees and stone benches nestled between the trees, providing a quiet spot of beauty and a cooling shade. A small stream trickled down through rocks into a large pond shaded by a large pine tree, and over it was a bridge constructed from beautifully aged wood and iron braces. Against the fence were rows of black bamboo. Irises, azaleas, and peonies bloomed in spring, the garden ablaze with color. It was a testament to Hiroshi's success as a sumo and a business-man, though Fumiko paused in the quiet garden and thought it unfortunate her grandson spent so little time enjoying the garden himself.

The great *yokozuna* was away more than he was home, whether at tournaments or sponsor-related dinners and travel. If he were to sign on with his latest offer, the Mitsuki Tire Company, he would have to travel even more. Marriage was difficult enough without having to spend so much of it apart, and she wondered now if it affected Aki more than anyone realized.

The housekeeper, Tamiko-san, answered the door and bowed low when she saw that it was Fumiko. She ushered her into the reception room and hesitated before she went to summon Aki. When she returned, it was to apologize and tell Fumiko that her mistress couldn't be disturbed at the moment.

"Nonsense!" Fumiko said. She paused for just a moment and looked around the elegant room with its silk scrolls and expensive vases sitting in the *tokonoma.* Then just as quickly, she walked past Tamiko and up the stairs toward Aki's room.

"Please, please, she's very busy," Tamiko repeated, following her.

Fumiko had been in the house many times before. Hiroshi had bought the house just after they married and she still wondered why he needed so many rooms. She stopped at Aki's room and rapped on the shoji door. Without waiting for an answer, she slid it open. She'd never been in their room before and hadn't expected to be greeted by such darkness. The windows were still shuttered and the large room was hot and airless. Tamiko mumbled something, bowed, and quickly excused herself.

She kept her voice calm and firm. "Aki-chan, I've come to speak to you about Takara."

As her eyes became accustomed to the darkness, she saw Aki kneeling quietly at the other end of the room, dressed in the same cotton *yukata* robe she must have slept in. When she didn't answer, or glance her way, Fumiko walked over and knelt in front of her. She reached out and stroked her cheek. "Aki-chan, what is it that you're hiding from?" she asked gently.

For the longest time, they remained silent until Aki looked up at her, tears filling her eyes. Fumiko leaned forward and took her into her arms. "There's nothing to be afraid of. Your baby needs you now."

Aki didn't pull away and said flatly, "Takara-chan is better off without me."

"How can you say such a thing? There's no one more important to her now than you." Fumiko smiled, tried to keep their conversation light and focused.

Aki pulled away. "I'm afraid . . ."

"We're all afraid, even after our children have grown and gone. It's part of motherhood. Children are more resilient than you believe them to be, Aki-san."

"Then why isn't Takashi still here?"

For the same reason Misako wasn't, she wanted to say. Don't you think I've asked myself all the same questions? Instead, Fumiko reached for Aki's hand. "Once in a while, life plays tricks on all of us. You have a lovely daughter who needs you now. You mustn't dwell on the past."

Aki bowed her head. *"Hai,"* she whispered, in a voice so small Fumiko leaned forward to hear it. She felt Aki's hand slip away from her own as the young woman stood, slowly and unsteadily, and bowed low to her.

ICE NEEDLES

The fall semester ended in December. Tokyo was very cold when Haru stepped down from the train for the holidays. Her father had written of the heat wave during the summer and fall, which she could hardly believe now. The air was sharp and stinging, what she and Aki used to call "ice needles" when they were little girls. She smiled now to think how the winter wind left their faces raw and flushed as they ran down the Ginza during the holiday season before the war. The air carried the smoky scent of roasting chestnuts and she looked forward to drinking *ozoni,* a New Year's soup that contained *mochi,* the sticky rice pounded into soft cakes, chicken, spinach, daikon, potato, and carrots. She remembered the crowded street of shoppers, the blur of lights, and the chorus of sounds and horns that excited them as their mother's voice rose above it all to warn them, "Don't wander too far away."

Here she was, home again.

The train arrived late, and the usually bustling station felt too quiet in the dark of night. It held a hollow feeling that made her shiver now as an adult, and part of her longed for the warmth of her early childhood, of Aki's sticky hand clinging to hers.

Haru wasn't expected back until tomorrow morning, but at the last minute she decided to take the night train instead, with no time to let her father know. After teaching the semester in Nara, she had traveled to Kyoto for a few days' research before returning to Tokyo for the New Year's holidays. She had secured a position as a full-time lecturer in the botany department at the university. For the first time in her life, Haru looked down at the palms of her hands and felt free and happy. If she looked long and hard enough, she could almost see the faint lifelines emerging through her thickened skin.

Haru looked up when she heard the hurried footsteps of someone behind her. The click-clack, click-clack came closer and echoed off the high ceiling of the station, something she'd never noticed before, because it was always muffled by the daytime noise and crowds. For a moment, she wished for the crowds and chaos that daylight brought, not the few passengers who scattered like ants into the darkness. It was something she'd never felt in calm, quiet Nara. The footsteps grew closer then passed her by. She smiled at her own silliness. Haru drew a breath and walked out of the station. Having finally arrived in Tokyo, she discovered her tiredness was overtaken by the excitement of seeing her family, especially little Takara. She hailed a cab and gave directions to the Katsuyama-beya.

Each time Haru returned home, the stable appeared smaller than she remembered. The courtyard was lit with lanterns that gave off a hazy glow. Though winter, it was still crowded with a shadowy plant life, an array of shrubbery, the bamboo and pines, the branches of the *sakura* tree that reached out and now blocked the view of the house as she entered the front gate. She remembered the courtyard barren after the firestorm, burned hot white by the heat and wiped clean. She had waited day after day for any signs of life to reappear, and when they did, she had felt a sudden flush of happiness move through her.

"Haru-chan! Is that you?" Her father's voice floated out into the night.

"*Hai,*" she answered.

He stepped down from the *genkan* to greet her, dressed in a dark cotton *yukata* robe. "Why didn't you tell me that you were coming earlier?"

Even in the muted light, she saw the joy on his face, a face that had aged since she'd last seen him, the welcoming shine of the light off his pale, shaven head. "I only decided at the last minute." She smiled.

He took Haru's suitcase and led her back into the house. It, too, felt smaller when he slid the door closed behind them. Once inside, the floating presence of her mother surrounded her for a moment. And then she was gone.

"You might have telephoned from the station," her father added.

"It's late," Haru said. "I thought you might be asleep already."

"I don't need much sleep these days," he said.

"Perhaps you were just waiting up for me, after all."

Her father laughed. "I believe so."

They stood a moment in silence, which was broken when Haru took off her coat and turned toward the kitchen. "I'm going to make some tea for us." Her father picked up her suitcase and headed down the hall toward her old room.

"Haru-chan, I'm glad you're home," he called out.

"So am I," she answered.

In the kitchen, Haru felt at home again. It was the one room she felt comfortable in after her mother died in the firestorm. Unlike his office, in the house her father was a meticulous man and everything was as neat as when she'd returned to Nara, so many months ago. He looked tired. Even far away in Nara, she'd heard his concern for Aki between the lines in the letters he wrote to her, always careful to keep from suggesting she return to Tokyo again. In turn, she wrote to Aki religiously every week, though this time, her sister rarely wrote back. Haru let herself believe that Aki was busy with Takara, that she'd gotten over this bout of depression and all had fallen into place. Was she so wrong to want a life of her own? The blood rushed quickly to her head. She took a deep breath and reassured herself that she'd see Aki tomorrow and there would be time enough to speak in the days to come.

Haru sprinkled tea leaves into a pot when the hot water boiled and let it steep. Her father shuffled back down the hall and stood in the doorway just as he had done when they were little girls doing their schoolwork in the kitchen, while her mother prepared dinner. "My three stars," he used to call them. She remembered peering up at the night sky and wondering which star he thought she was. Now, her father standing in the doorway and the long-ago memory it conjured up comforted her.

The next morning Haru had just finished her breakfast when she heard voices in the courtyard. She hurried into the *genkan* and slipped into her sandals to see that it was Aki and her wet nurse carrying a bundled-up Takara. Her sister's appearance frightened her. Aki was so thin. In the nine months since the birth of Takara, her sister looked like a different person, hollow-eyed and skeletal. The kimono she wore had been hastily put on and without much thought, the brown obi mismatched against the blue and green flower patterns. Her hair wasn't properly combed. Not until Aki bowed and impulsively threw her arms around her did she feel any resemblance of this person to her sister.

"I look a mess," Aki whispered into Haru's ear. Her breath was sour, her voice high and tight, as if it might shatter like glass.

Haru held her tight then gently pulled away, happy her sister was at least out and communicating. "You just need to put on some weight, that's all."

Aki forced a laugh. "I wish that were all I needed," she said.

"Well, now that I'm back for the holidays, we'll work on fattening you up."

Aki brightened. "I've been waiting for you to come home."

She sounded like a young Aki again. "You'll be fine, you'll see," Haru said, smiling. Her words rose into the air and seemed to vanish like smoke.

Haru turned to the nurse and her little niece. Takara was a beautiful child, with large, inquisitive eyes and fair skin like her mother. She saw traces of Hiroshi in her eyebrows and around her mouth. "And look at you," she said. Haru took the squirming child in her arms and hugged her tightly. Another little star. Takara looked at her and calmed in her arms. A few moments later, she laid her head on Haru's shoulder as if it were the most natural thing in the world.

28
PAST AND PRESENT
1962

Kenji walked quickly down the alleyway to meet Hiroshi. It was a warm fall day and the passageways in mid-afternoon were still manageable. It was before the teeming crowds could make the walk to the old bar near his *obachan*'s house a stop-and-go process that he found increasingly unbearable.

Ever since Takashi's death, Kenji had tried to meet Hiroshi at least once a month. More often than not, one of them had to cancel. This time, Hiroshi asked that they meet at the old bar his *ojichan* used to frequent, a place Kenji took for granted no longer existed. He assumed it had closed down during the war. He hadn't thought to ask his eighty-year-old grandmother what had happened to it. After his *ojichan* died, the bar had in many ways died along with him. But there it was, a piece of the past right in front of him; small and run-down as he always remembered it, the faded wood and stained shoji windows unchanged. Anywhere else but in Yanaka the smallest ember during the firestorm would have set it ablaze. He stepped through the door and the familiar dim, damp, bitter smell confronted him. It took a moment for his eyes to adjust, to see that Hiroshi was already waiting for him.

"Hiroshi-san, I had no idea the bar was still here," he said, walking toward his brother.

Hiroshi smiled. "I passed it for the first time in years last month. It reminded me of *ojichan*."

Kenji looked around the empty room, at the sticky table near the bar where his grandfather and his friends had sat for so many years, and to the corner bar stool where he perched, watching them. He heard again their low, gruff voices and their laughter as they teased and argued. They had been a comfort in his loneliness back then. "Is there anyone here?"

"She's in the back. She should be out any minute."

Kenji sat in the chair across from his brother. "How's Aki-san?"

Hiroshi shrugged. He looked older, even in the dim light, the pale scar on his forehead strangely noticeable. He was dressed in a dark silk kimono, still every bit the famous sumo, strong and impressive. How could he not have aged, with Aki unwell and Takara to care for? He heard her sister, Haru, had returned in June and once again proved indispensable.

"Takara?"

"Growing." He smiled.

Kenji felt a stab of jealousy. She was a beautiful little girl. A woman emerged from the back room, middle-aged and tired-looking in a soiled cotton kimono. On a tray she carried two beers and a plate of edamame. It was far from the elegant geisha houses his brother usually frequented.

"I ordered for us," Hiroshi said. And then, "Aki seems to be getting worse. She hardly says a word."

Kenji drank from his beer. "She'll get better again," he said, though he wasn't sure he believed it.

"It seems a long time ago, the life we had here." Hiroshi looked around. "Simpler."

Kenji glanced at the lone bar stool in the corner, heard again the low drone of voices that had blanketed his loneliness. His brother had no idea how many hours he'd spent in the old bar. "It wasn't really," he said. "Everything seems simpler from a distance."

Hiroshi shrugged and unconsciously fingered the slight rise of his scar.

He looked tired — no, sad, Kenji thought. The moment of jealousy had disappeared and in its place was the love and admiration Kenji had always felt for his brother. He wasn't in any hurry; he could stay and talk to Hiroshi for as long as he needed to.

Aki dreaded the shadows that hovered over her, leaving everything in darkness. As the fall days shortened, the nights lengthened and she knew when the shadows were waiting by the stillness in the air and the breath they stole away from her, a squeezing, suffocating hand around her neck. She had long ago quit fighting them outwardly, and tried to remain as quiet and still as she could. That way the shadows might miss her; leave her alone when they saw she had very little life left to take. Aki sat now in the quiet semidarkness of her room, and felt the air begin to stir again.

Outside, in the garden below, she heard Haru asking, "Takara-chan, what kind of tree is this?"

Aki leaned toward the window, the warmth of the sun grazing her cheek, and saw her eighteen-month-old daughter, arms held out at each side for balance, as she walked toward her aunt: dark-eyed, full-lipped, round-faced, shiny black hair that gleamed with youth as she tumbled toward Haru.

"*Kae-de,*" Takara said. Ma-ple. Her voice sounded like a bell.

"*Hai!*" Haru clapped her hands. Happiness.

A small pinprick of envy pinched Aki in the arm. It should be her down in the garden, holding out her arms to catch the weight of her daughter, pulling her close. But Takara was happy and healthy this way. And she couldn't trust herself yet. Something could still happen to Takara. Just like Takashi, who died in his sleep, sleep death, death. Aki looked away, knowing that it was also Haru's just reward to have Takara. She'd given up everything she'd worked for in Nara to stay in Tokyo and care for them.

Sometimes, Aki fell asleep on the tatami mats trying to fool the shadows. Occasionally, she would dream of walking through a tall, wooden gate to a small house surrounded by light. She raised her hand against the glare and stepped into the beautiful garden filled with maples and willows, azaleas, Japanese quince, and irises that stood straight up in shades of blue-purple, reaching for the sunlight, the moonlight. She walked through the thick, fragrant garden, surrounded by sounds, the rustling in the grass, the hum of life buzzing around her legs, and up the stairs to the veranda where she waited for Hiroshi and Takara, knowing they were coming, filled with happiness, bursting with it.

ADRIFT

Haru put little Takara down for her nap, stroked her cheek, and waited until she fell asleep. She was still surprised at how easily she had adapted to caring for her. Like the

597

plants she studied, Takara grew toward the light, while Aki retreated from it. Haru knelt by the futon and watched her niece as her breathing grew measured and calm and she drifted off to sleep. She imagined the child her own.

During these quiet moments of the day, Haru worried about Aki, whose bouts of silence and depression lasted longer with each episode. The doctors couldn't seem to help and Aki refused to leave the house. Lately, Haru had another worry; she'd heard rumors that a young geisha had captured the interest of Yokozuna Takanoyama. Was Hiroshi so foolish as to think the press wouldn't hear about it? When she finally couldn't stand it any longer, Haru confronted Hiroshi as he was walking out of Takara's room.

"Are they true?" she asked. The words came out more abrupt and accusing than she intended.

"Is what true?" he asked back, walking slowly down the hall, Haru keeping pace.

"The rumors."

He seemed to puff up and grow bigger before her eyes. Haru imagined it was something similar to when he entered the ring, ready for a fight. "What rumors? I can hardly keep up with them." He forced a laugh.

"The geisha, Meiko." Haru watched his face, saw his lips purse in thought. She knew it was true from the pause.

"You know how things are bent out of proportion. The press will pick up on anything to sell a paper or magazine."

Haru stopped walking. "So, there has been something for them to pick up on?"

Hiroshi turned. "And now it's you, Haru-san, who are twisting my words around. I'm in your debt for all you've done for Aki and Takara, but my business isn't yours."

Haru held back her anger and tried to remain calm. "My concern is for Aki-chan and that these rumors don't reach her. I would hope that's where your concern lies, too." She stood for a moment, holding his gaze, before she turned and walked back down the hall, quietly slid open the door, and disappeared into Takara's room.

She hadn't seen Hiroshi since.

Haru paced from the sleeping child and back to the window. It was already October and becoming cold. She stared down at the immaculate garden below — ablaze with the last colors of fall, the red maple leaves, the round-faced cosmos she had planted, and the crimson veils of grassworts that surrounded the pond. She especially admired the *sakura* and maple trees that lined the winding paths and led to the large old pine and bridge-covered pond. Hiroshi had had it beautifully landscaped, each detail thought out so that she and Takara could spend hours in this small park of their own. How easy it was for her to make plants grow, and yet . . .

At twenty-eight, Haru looked down at the blooming garden that didn't belong to her and at the sleeping child across the room, who didn't belong to her, either. She felt a burning emptiness in her stomach where her own child once had been. But the decision to stay in Tokyo with Aki and Takara had been hers alone. And much to her surprise, she only occasionally missed her life in Nara, her days filled with students and research, wandering down the dank paths of Deer Park, correcting papers late into the night.

But each afternoon, standing by the window of the silent and lovely house, and taking care of a child she adored, Haru still felt adrift. Her life was neither here nor in Nara. She was like a buoy in the middle of the sea. Much like the ferry going to Oshima, there was only the sky above and the sea below, with no land in sight.

THE GRAND CHAMPION

Hiroshi swiveled from side to side in the chair and stared into the large mirror that filled the wall in front of him. The image gazing back was a thirty-five-year-old sumo grand champion, wearing a blue cotton *yukata* over his *mawashi* belt. He suddenly felt self-conscious, enormous in the chair and in the small, sterile room where he waited to shoot a commercial at the television studio. His left knee felt stiff from sitting too long. In the past year, it had become an increasing problem. Earlier, a young makeup man had dabbed makeup on a sponge and patted it across his shoulders, his stomach, his forehead and nose, the parts of his body that might shine on camera, he said. When Hiroshi looked in the mirror again, he expected to look changed. Instead, he looked the same but felt somehow diminished.

The makeup man left Hiroshi to practice his one line, while he waited for his cue. "Mitsuki Tire Company makes tires that last!" He read the entire script again and committed it all to memory. He was to pick up a tire in each hand and raise them both in the air, holding each up until he gradually appeared to weaken, his arms slowly lowering with the weight of the tires. Across the screen the audience would see the characters "Hours later . . ." and by then his arms would tremble with exhaustion, while he fought to hold up the tires. On the director's command, Hiroshi was to collapse to the floor, while the camera pulled back and the audience saw the tires rolling down a busy street followed by the voice-over, "Mitsuki Tires, the real grand champion of tires!"

Hiroshi squirmed in his chair. It was no better or worse than other commercials he'd done. His strong, chiseled features graced a thousand billboards selling everything from soft drinks and tires to candy and laundry detergent. "All Around Detergent can handle a sumo-sized load," a slim and beautiful Japanese woman exclaimed, holding up one of his oversized *yukata* kimonos. Since the advent of television, promoting products had taken on a new dimension. Not only was he a sumo grand champion but also a celebrity, better known than many movie stars. He couldn't walk down the street without being mobbed by fans. For the most part, the ads and television spots were silly and childish, but they paid him handsomely and he knew his wrestling career was fleeting. He already anticipated the time when his fans would no longer stop him on the street to ask for his autograph. Hiroshi's retirement from the *dohyo* seemed to inch closer each year and he thought of the old saying "Even a snail will eventually reach its destination." Other *rikishi* who retired in their mid- to late-thirties went on to careers as stable masters, or businessmen, many opening their own restaurants. Hiroshi recalled Fukuda's success with his noodle shops. But he couldn't see himself doing any of those things. He had his chance now to make his family and future comfortable while he could, and he wasn't about to waste the opportunities given him.

Little Takara was almost two years old. Just thinking of her made him smile. The fear that something might happen to her was a small stone that rubbed against his foot. On the nights when he was home, he watched her sleep and memorized any new changes that might have occurred during the days or weeks he was away. He saw her tiny fingers open and close in sleep as if she were trying to grab on to something. He heard again the steady rhythm of her breathing and the soft whistling sound that let him know she was asleep. She was already a beauty, resembling Aki. Yet, even though he knew Aki and Takara were thriving under Haru's care, he still worried that something might happen to them. He cleared his throat and pushed the bad omens out of his mind, just as he did in the *dohyo,* using all his strength and cunning to defeat his opponent.

His thoughts returned to the angry words he'd had with Haru a few months earlier. Was it still bothering him? How dare she question him? He hadn't felt right ever since, angry and ashamed. He'd avoided both Haru and the Sakura teahouse. He glanced up at the mirror again. He'd done one thing right in the past month, using his influence to secure Haru a teaching job at Tokyo University in the spring. It was the least he could do for her after she'd given up so much.

There was a sudden knock at the door and he turned to see a young woman peek in and bow. "Yokozuna Takanoyama, they're ready for you now."

He nodded, pushed himself up from the chair, and followed her out.

29

THE RETURN

1963

By the end of the summer of 1963, Akira and Kenji were busily preparing for the fall schedule of the Noh theater. Otomo Matsui was staging his last season before he officially retired, and they were commissioned to make all the masks. September would begin with his revival of *Aya no Tsuzumi,* or *The Damask Drum.* It was a story that Akira especially loved, about an old gardener who catches sight of a princess taking a walk around the laurel pond at the Palace of Kinomaru and falls immediately in love with her. When she hears of his love, she sends him a message to beat the drum that hangs on the laurel tree by the pond. When the sound of the beating drum reaches the palace, he will see her face again. The old gardener beats the drum to no avail, as no sound emerges. Finally, in great despair, he drowns himself in the pond, only to return as a ghost to torment the princess and discover the truth of the drum.

Akira worked on the old gardener and ghost

masks, which would both be worn by Otomo Matsui. He maintained his habit of working in the early hours of the morning when the shop was quiet. He picked up the ghost mask, which felt light and almost fragile in his hand. Everything would have to be perfect. He knew Matsui wasn't well and had especially chosen to play the old gardener and his ghost, roles he hadn't played since he was a young man. After thirty years of making masks for the great actor, Akira felt they'd come full circle together. He held the mask up and peered out through the eyes, his vision narrowed to what was right in front of him. He turned the mask around and could almost see traces of the actor himself in the carved features, the impressions of his high forehead and deep-set eyes.

He and Kenji had worked through the summer trying to finish all the orders. It was a great honor and a lucrative commission for them. Only now, after months of work, did he see that they would make their deadline. Akira felt his entire body relax. He glued the last of the beard onto the old gardener mask and gently returned it to the shelf to dry. He unlocked the front door. Kenji would be in at any moment by the looks of the lightening sky, and he returned to the back room to make hot water for their tea. Over the years, it had become a ritual for them to sit down, sip their tea, and discuss the coming day, a specific mask they were working on, or any problems. Akira felt fortunate to have this time with Kenji each morning.

He was relieved Kenji was content again. There were a few difficult years when he and Mika remained childless and he'd been upset with Mika away so much, traveling all over Japan for her father's growing textile business. Akira would appease him by saying, "A marriage isn't like water that slips through your fingers. It's solid and hard like stone and can be grasped on to. Don't let your pride get in the way." Then slowly, Kenji would relax and smile, talk about the masks they were working on, and forget his loneliness.

When Akira heard the front door open, he called out to Kenji. "Ah, you're just in time."

But it was a woman's voice that answered him. "I'm sorry, you must be mistaken."

Akira stepped out of the back room to find a young woman dressed in a plain green kimono. "I'm sorry," he apologized, "I thought you were someone else. How may I help you?"

"Akira-san," she said, as if she knew it would be him stepping out of the back room.

Her voice carried the same inflection he'd never forgotten. Suddenly, one of the ghosts that hovered on the surface of the river was standing right before him, full of life, flesh and blood, traces of the young girl from the mountains of Aio instilled in the young woman standing before him.

"Kiyo-san," he said, without a second thought.

She smiled and bowed low to him.

They stood for a moment, frozen in time. Akira cleared his throat and suddenly felt shy.

"I hoped you would be here," she said.

He invited her into the back room for tea and offered her a stool. "How is your mother?" he asked.

Kiyo hesitated. "She died last year."

The news was like a blow to him. And Akira wondered how he could still be standing when his legs felt so weak. He could no longer think of Emiko-san in the same way, sitting by the hearth in the praying-hands house, stirring the contents of the black iron pot. His grief was as dark as that pot.

"It was so unexpected," Kiyo continued. "She developed a cough that wouldn't go away. Within months, she could barely get out of bed. It wasn't much longer after that." Kiyo looked down at her hands.

"I'm sorry," he said. He saw more and more of the young girl he'd left behind.

"She spoke of you," Kiyo added.

Akira didn't ask of what she spoke. He felt as if his throat had closed. Instead, he heard the water boiling and thankfully turned away.

THE GUEST

Unlike other mornings when Kenji entered the mask shop, it was unusually quiet. Not the hissing of hot water, the sharp shrill of the saw, nor even Yoshiwara-sensei's low humming emerged from the back room. For a moment he wondered if something had happened to him; perhaps he was ill again and hadn't come downstairs. Then, from the back room he heard soft and teasing words, followed by Akira's voice calling out, "Kenji-san, is that you?"

Who else did he expect at this time of the morning? Kenji walked to the back room, surprised to see a young woman perched on the stool next to Yosihwara. He lowered his eyes to keep from staring.

"Hello." He bowed.

Yoshiwara stood up. The young woman did, too, bowing low to Kenji. "This is Kiyo-san," his teacher introduced. "She and her mother were very good to me when I lived in Aio."

Kenji paused a moment. As much as he always wanted to know about Yoshiwara, his sensei hardly spoke of his private life, and Kenji had always respected his wishes. But to see him sitting with a young woman so early in the morning felt unexpected and out of place. He bowed back to Kiyo-san and noticed that up close she wasn't as young as he first thought. She was in her late twenties, very pleasant looking with a slim, wiry build and large, expressive eyes. Her long black hair was tied back in a thick braid. She was dressed simply and it was her hands he noticed, worker's hands, tanned and veined, yet not unattractive.

"Are you visiting Tokyo?" Kenji asked.

She nodded shyly. *"Hai."*

Yoshiwara-sensei added, "Kiyo-san is in Tokyo for just a short time. She returns to Aio in a few days."

"I was hoping to find Akira-san," she said.

"You didn't know he was here?" Kenji asked. He wanted to ask so many more questions but swallowed his curiosity.

She looked at Yoshiwara-sensei and then back at Kenji again. "Over the years, I lost track of Akira-san," she said. "But it seems he left a trail for me to follow."

His teacher cleared his throat and his fingers tapped playfully against the table.

"And what was that?" Kenji asked.

"He left me a mask," Kiyo said.

Noh

It wasn't until the theater lights dimmed that Aki leaned back in her seat and relaxed. The low beating of a drum filled the cool, high-ceilinged room and calmed her. She hadn't been outside of the house and garden for almost a month, not since the middle of

610

August, and it made her nervous to be among so many people, so many different scents and sounds. She sat protected between Haru and Hiroshi in front-row seats. His brother, Kenji, had given them tickets for the Noh production of *The Damask Drum* with Otomo Matsui, and Haru insisted it was time she stepped out of the house. The famous actor was to retire at the end of the season and all of Tokyo wanted to see him in his last performances. Haru took such good care of her and Takara that Aki couldn't say no to an evening at the theater.

She closed her eyes and let her mind follow the rhythmic beating of the drums. When the courtier began chanting the story, Aki opened her eyes to the light-filled stage as Otomo Matsui dressed as the old gardener entered, circled the stage as if he'd walked a great distance around the pond, and stopped to stare offstage. His mask tilted up in surprise when he glimpsed the princess, and the courtier told of his instantaneous love for her. From that moment, Aki couldn't take her eyes off Matsui. Each move he made was like a slow dance and the mask he wore took on a life of its own, changed expressions with the simplest movement of his head. She saw both Otomo Matsui and Kenji-san's great talents at work. The tragic story mesmerized her, the drum hanging from the laurel tree that the gardener banged to no avail, his subsequent suicide over his unrequited love for the princess, followed by his return as a ghost. It all left her breathless.

"Are you all right?" Hiroshi leaned over and asked her.

Aki swallowed and nodded. She smiled at him reassuringly and felt a warmth move through her body. The truth was, she hadn't felt so well in a long time. She turned to see Haru just as deeply involved in the story.

When *The Damask Drum* ended and the lights came on during intermission, Hiroshi was called away by some business associates, while Aki felt freed from the dark cloud and the shadows that lingered around her. The Kyogen would be next; a comic piece that would balance the more serious Noh plays. But it was *The Damask Drum* that would stay with her, that provided the answer to stopping the shadows from overtaking her. Aki turned to talk to Haru and then stood up and gazed across the room until she found Hiroshi.

NOVEMBER 9, 1963

The train rattled on toward Tokyo as Mika sat next to her father, exhausted, thrilled at the textile designs she'd seen in Kyoto. She couldn't wait to tell Kenji of the rich colors, the vibrant reds and startling greens, her mind alive with designs and patterns. At last they'd reached a comfortable point in their life together and she longed to be home. She might even bring up the idea of having a baby again, though it no longer governed her world. Now that Otomo Matsui had given his last performance, they were finally taking a long-planned vacation to Toya-ko Onsen, the hot springs resort on the shores of Lake Toya in Hokkaido. Mika could already feel the initial shock of stepping into the heated water, the moment of hesitation before her body adjusted to its warm embrace.

There was a low drone of voices all around them. The train was filled, but they'd booked early and had good seats in the first car. Her father was reading the paper, nodding off behind his glasses. Mika glanced down at her watch; less than an hour to go. She closed her eyes as the train rocked her gently from side to side and a childhood lullaby filled her head.

Mika's eyes opened instantly at the shriek of the brakes, metal grinding on metal, the lights flickering on and off, the frantic voices. She had awakened to a nightmare. There was no time to do anything; to be frightened or react, to turn and see if her father was still sitting beside her. Instead, in the split second before the crashing impact, Kenji flashed through her mind as she watched the entire car crush inward toward them; like an accordion, she thought, like a silk fan closing.

WAITING

Kenji walked through the courtyard and let himself into the dark house. Mika still wasn't home and he felt the cold of her absence as soon as he slipped out of his shoes and stepped into the hallway. There was already the damp-tatami smell of winter, though they were barely into November. She'd gone to Kyoto for three days with her father, visiting other textile designers. "To see what the competition is doing," she teased. Once in a while, he still felt hints of the boy Kenji the ghost resurfacing, all those unsubstantiated fears. He swallowed that part of his childhood back down. Her trips away no longer bothered him. Kenji knew how happy she was learning her father's business, and how successful her fabric designs had become. He smiled to himself. Theirs was a marriage of equality and Mika wouldn't have it any other way. She'd be home any time now.

She was scheduled to return on the evening train so Kenji had purposely stayed late at the shop, eaten a bowl of noodles with Yoshiwara-sensei, talked about the masks in hopes of containing his anticipation. He hoped to return and find her already home. In a canvas bag, he carried all the masks he had carved of her during the past ten years.

Until now, he'd kept them to himself. He wanted to enter the warm house as if he'd been the one away, to show her he was fine with her gone, as long as she returned to him.

Instead, the house stood dark and empty. He moved quickly from room to room, turning on all the electric lamps so that the house blazed with a warm light. *"I'm here, I'm here,"* each one seemed to say as he snapped the lamps on. And just as his fingers found the switch on the last lamp in an upstairs room, he heard the gate creak open. Kenji stood a moment and thought he heard her wooden sandals click-clacking across the courtyard. He imagined the smile on her lips at the sight of all the bright lights guiding her home, and he could already hear her rush of words telling him about the trip. He thought about the sound of her voice, the smooth song of it, and hurried downstairs to meet her.

30
THIRST
1964

Kenji sat at the kitchen table in the dark. He only drank after work, wrapped comfortably in the darkness, not so others couldn't see him but so he wouldn't have to see himself. He reached for the bottle of whiskey and almost knocked it over, catching it before too much spilled. He laughed to himself and the raspy sound resonated through the cold, silent room. He stopped to listen when he thought he heard someone entering the courtyard, but it was only the wind. The wind. Just like the night three months ago when he thought it was Mika coming home, only it wasn't, because she and her father were 2 of the 161 passengers killed in the train crash at Tsurumi, outside of Tokyo. Kenji drained the glass in his hand and stood up, grabbing the edge of the table for support, wavering.

He arrived at the shop later each morning, his head throbbing through the afternoon. He'd been working on the same mask for weeks. He saw the worried look in Yoshiwara-sensei's eyes, while Hiroshi made daily visits. He hated the way they spoke to him, in quiet tones as if he were a child to be soothed. "Come stay at the house with us," Hiroshi pleaded. Yoshiwara-sensei agreed and added, "You shouldn't be alone now." They meant well, but he knew it wouldn't change anything. His life was like a landslide that he couldn't stop from slipping away, taking everything along with him. Only when he sat in the dark, drinking, did he feel better. For a short time, he stopped thinking Mika was dead and that he would never see her again in this world.

But tonight Kenji couldn't forget. The power of memory even brought back Mika's sweet jasmine perfume, which still lingered upstairs in the closet filled with her kimonos, sewn from the brilliantly colored fabrics she had designed. Sometimes he stood looking at them, breathing in her scent, stroking the silk and cotton fabrics, the particular spiral patterns that came to define Mika's designs. He knew the colors would remain, but soon her scent would fade and the thought of her leaving him again brought tears to his eyes.

Kenji grabbed the bottle and walked unsteadily down the hallway, pausing every few feet to grab on to something to stay upright. He needed to get to the lacquer cabinet where he had stored the canvas bag the night he came home to wait for Mika. He'd just remembered it, like a child who suddenly remembers hidden candy. When he finally swung the cabinet door open, there it was; the canvas bag with Mika's masks in it. He grabbed the bag and stumbled out to the courtyard, a dim light shining from the house next door. The cold February air was icy and sharp, which revived him a little. He smelled the wetness in the air.

Kenji took each mask out, one by one, his fingers moving over Mika's still features as he stacked them on the flagstones. His eyes burned and he wiped his nose on his sleeve. He drank down a mouthful of whiskey from the bottle and poured the remainder over the masks. There wasn't any reason to keep them. Mika was gone. There would be no children or grandchildren to show them to. And he didn't need the masks to remember her face; she was burned into his memory.

From his pocket, he retrieved matches, lighting several before one caught; the small spark of flame was warm against his fingers. He looked up to the sky and let the match slip from his hand onto the masks. But instead of igniting, the flame went out by the time it touched the wood. He knelt, trying to keep his balance, and struck another match, which the wind blew out. Then another. And another. When he struck the next match, he blocked the wind with his hand and the alcohol caught fire. Within seconds the fire erupted, the courtyard alight as Mika's face came alive in the flames. It was as if she were staring up at him accusingly. In that moment, Kenji awoke from his stupor and realized what he was doing. "No! No! No!" he yelled, his hands smothering the fire without thinking, smoke rising to taunt him as he stood, barely feeling the sting of his singed palms. He stepped back and lost his balance, falling backward to the ground, the back of his head slamming against the flagstones. He lay there stunned, his head throbbing, moving in and out of consciousness. For an instant he was Kenji the ghost again, invisible, not of this world. His eyes fluttered open and he felt a raindrop on his cheek as soft as a kiss, and for a moment it returned him to the real world. Then Kenji closed his eyes, only wanting to sleep and never wake up.

CLARITY

Aki relished the moments when the world around her was as clear and lucid as glass. For the past ten months, ever since she'd seen *The Damask Drum,* she'd felt lighter and more in control of her life. She spent more and more time with Haru and Takara, and had even taken her daughter to Kenji-san's mask shop in Yanaka to see her uncle. Kenji looked tired and had lost so much weight since Mika's death, she hardly recognized him. Since his accident, he remained quiet and subdued. But he always smiled widely when Takara was visiting, and it was the least she could do for him. And there was also her selfish wish of wanting to see firsthand how the beautiful masks were made.

While Kenji stayed with Takara, she wandered into the back room and stood quietly to the side watching Akira Yoshiwara paint the intricate features onto a mask. With bold, confident strokes, he transformed the static into the living.

"Have you always wanted to be a mask maker?" she asked. Her voice sounded timid and childlike.

Yoshiwara-san stopped painting. He looked up at her and smiled. "I believe so. I can't imagine what else I'd be good at."

"Your masks are beautiful," she said, hoping to keep his attention a moment longer.

The mask maker bowed to her. "Kenji-san and I are honored that you would think so."

Takara's and Kenji's voices filtered in from the front room. Aki felt fortunate to be spending time with Akira Yoshiwara. He had the reputation of being the greatest living artist of the Noh theater. Aki never imagined she would be having a conversation with him one day.

"Actually, Akira-san, I was wondering if I might buy a mask from you."

He paused for a few moments in thought. "I don't sell my masks outside of the theater," he said.

Aki blushed, afraid she had offended him.

But Yoshiwara continued, "I do give them to friends." He went to the shelf and stood a moment until he reached up and brought down an *Onna* mask, a young woman mask. "I would be honored if you'd accept this mask as a gift from me."

Aki paused, not knowing what to say. "I can't accept such a valuable gift. It's too much, Akira-san."

Yoshiwara laughed. "It's only an illusion, a finely shaped piece of wood, but still a piece of wood." He placed it in her hands.

Aki marveled at its lightness, at the careful details that made the mask come alive when she held it up. She marveled to think how real it could appear with an actor wearing it, and how lucky they were to be able to transform themselves into someone else, if only for a short time.

THE LETTER

Akira carefully opened the envelope and pulled out the letter. Every month or so, he received a thin, blue-colored envelope from Kiyo-chan, who still lived in the village of Aio with her husband and three children. Since her visit last year, their years apart had been gradually recaptured. He smiled to think of the restless young girl he'd known now having a growing family of her own. Her husband, Toroshi, was a builder and she had two sons and a daughter. After Emiko-san passed away, she was left the praying-hands house, and Toroshi had done a wonderful job repairing and remodeling it. "You wouldn't recognize the old place now," she wrote. "The main room is filled with light from all the windows Toroshi has put in." Akira tried to imagine the light-filled praying-hands house, but he somehow found more comfort in remembering the dark, safe, high-ceilinged room where he'd spent so much time sitting with Emiko-san by the hearth.

He skipped to the end and read the familiar closing. Kiyo-chan never failed to end her letters with an invitation for him to visit. "My family would be honored to have you visit. After all the stories I've told them about you, they keep asking when they'll meet you. Needless to say, your visit would bring us all much happiness."

Akira put the letter down. He had never thought of himself as bringing happiness to anyone. There seemed so little to show for a lifetime lived. He picked up a block of wood and held it in his hand, mulling over whether he should start another mask or wait until tomorrow. He smiled to himself and put the piece of wood down on the table.

He still walked down to the river several times a week. He loved the water in the same way Kiyo loved the mountains. They both held something sacred. He cleaned up, put on his jacket, and locked the door to the mask shop. As he sauntered down the alleyway, a cold wind blew and he drew his jacket closer. Winter was just around the corner in Yanaka, and Akira's memories returned to springtime in Aio and how the ice appeared like glass when it began to melt, cracking like a heart breaking, the entire world fragile and beautiful in the sunshine. Streams of wood smoke rose from the hearths and tinged the thin, sweet air. It caught his breath, even now, to think about it. Perhaps it was time for Akira to step out of his safe, dark room and into the light, after all.

31
DECISIONS
1965

Every morning a car picked Hiroshi up to train with the other *sumotori* at the Katsuyama-beya. At thirty-six, he had to work harder before each tournament, willing his body to do the things he could so easily do fifteen years ago. No doubt he had slowed, but his strength and experience still made up for it. Most of all, he hoped to set a good example for the younger *sumotori*.

As Hiroshi prepared for the May Basho, he found it difficult to concentrate, to stay focused on winning. It was as if his eyesight had dulled; no match was as sharp, as important. The past year had been difficult. He worried about Kenji, who was finally on the mend after staying with their *obachan* until he had gained back his strength. Hiroshi still believed something ghostly had brought him to Kenji's house that night. He wasn't expected to visit, but it was as if a voice had led him there. It was raining when he entered the gate and found his brother lying in the courtyard next to a pile of masks, a few charred. He couldn't begin to understand what had happened. Hiroshi carried Kenji back into the house, lifeless, his skin cold to the touch, and called a doctor. There was a bump that swelled on the back of his head, but fortunately, though the burns on his hands would hurt for a time, no major damage was done. Hiroshi remembered thinking of Haru, of how her hands had been so severely burned during the firestorm, and how she always hid them beneath the folds of her kimono. It was one of his first memories of her. He had stayed that night with Kenji, refusing to leave him alone, even when his brother awoke, his hands bandaged, embarrassed about the condition Hiroshi had found him in. Kenji stopped drinking after that night and went to stay with their *obachan*.

Hiroshi's thoughts wandered as the car moved slowly through a crowded intersection. Thankfully, Aki had been doing so much better this past year. He found himself wanting to spend more time with her and Takara; he was tired of training and traveling for tournaments and for business. Most *sumotori* would have already retired, but though he knew the time was right, he wanted one more year. He was still doing reasonably well and had won seventy-six of the ninety bouts he'd fought last year. It was an impressive and hard-earned achievement. Takanoyama would go down in history as one of the greatest sumo wrestlers after World War II. Japan was again strong. He was adored by fans and the media and no longer had to worry about money. Wasn't that what he had always wanted? It was by all accounts a full, fruitful life. The gods had been good to him.

These thoughts raced through his mind as the car turned down the road toward the stable. By the time they stopped in front of the gate, his thoughts of retiring were put aside. Hiroshi stepped out of the car just as Haru emerged through the front gate, wearing a Western-style skirt and jacket.

"Haru-san," he said tentatively. While he saw her often at the house because of Aki and Takara, they had rarely spoken for more than a few minutes since the geisha incident, neither of them ever mentioning it again.

Haru bowed. "I was just leaving to see Aki-chan and Takara before my class."

"Thank you for taking such good care of them." He bowed back. "Let my driver take you."

Haru bowed again and accepted his offer.

"Can we speak for a moment?" he asked.

"Yes, of course." Haru stopped.

Hiroshi hesitated, not knowing where to begin. A cool April wind blew. "Aki-chan seems to be doing better."

"She is."

"And Takara is growing like a weed," he

said, only to laugh at the bad example he'd chosen.

Haru smiled, relaxed. "She's flowering."

He missed these conversations with Haru, the only person who understood his family, perhaps better than himself. "And you, Haru-chan, how are you?"

"I'm doing well, happy to be teaching again at the university."

"Good, good."

She looked past him at the idling car. "I should go, or I'll be late," she said with a smile.

Hiroshi wanted to say more, but knew she was in a hurry.

Haru walked toward the car, paused, and turned back to him. "Thank you, Hiroshi-san, for arranging for the teaching position at the university for me. It feels good to belong somewhere again." She bowed low and disappeared into the car.

THE RUTTED ROAD

The air was still thin and cold in late April as Akira Yoshiwara walked the last stretch up the mountain from the village of Aio, following the deep ruts in the road that would lead him directly to the praying-hands house. The road was saturated; the last remnants of the melting snow ran down in smaller rivulets that would be etched into the dirt road come summer. It felt wonderfully prehistoric; nothing had changed, the same pine trees watched ominously over him as years before. He stopped to catch his breath, a sharp, quick burning in his lungs as the smell of wood smoke drifted over the top of the trees and Akira watched it rise into the sky and disappear.

Just around the bend and up the road, Kiyo and her family waited for him. But it was Emiko-san he longed to see step out on the road to greet him. It was her calmness that was so similar to his, the need and loneliness that lay just beneath the skin, that had drawn them together and then apart.

"Akira-san!"

He looked up at the sound of his name and squinted against the light to see Kiyo standing there, holding the hand of a little girl. He waved to them.

"Akira-san, we've been waiting for you," she said, her voice rising in delight just as it had when she was a girl and had found some small gift he'd hidden for her.

He smiled and walked faster up the road toward them as if each step brought him back in time. Over twenty years later, a mother and daughter once again waited along the same rutted road to greet him.

Kenji swept the last of the wood dust from the floor of the back room, covered the saw, and stored away all the paints. With Yoshiwara-sensei away for the next few weeks visiting Kiyo in the mountains, he thought it was about time to do some traveling himself. At thirty-five, Kenji had barely been out of Tokyo, only to the countryside during the war. It was something Mika had wanted them to do, travel more, and now that she had been gone for almost a year and a half, he finally found himself wanting it, too. Her shadow was always there, trailing him, pushing him forward. Now, she was the ghost.

It was a difficult year after Mika's death. The drinking, the burns on his hands, the few months he stayed with his *obachan,* healing. He smiled to think of her. At eighty-three, his grandmother was fragile but still formidable.

On his first morning staying with her, she brewed a strong tea and set it down on the table before him. "Drink this, you'll feel better."

Kenji didn't dare look directly into her eyes, afraid of what he'd see. So instead, he watched her hands, thin and heavily veined; the hands that had carried him as a baby and picked him up when he fell. He lifted the cup of tea with his bandaged hands and sipped; it was bitter on his tongue, hot and soothing down his throat. His neck was sore and the back of his head ached where it had hit the flagstone.

His *obachan* sat down across from him and said softly, "Do you think Mika-chan would want to see you this way? There was no one who loved life more. Don't dishonor her memory by giving up on the very life she treasured."

Her words echoed through the small kitchen. He looked down at his bandaged hands. His mouth tasted sour. *"Yes, yes, yes,"* he wanted to say, but why then had Mika simply disappeared, leaving him behind with all this sorrow? How could he explain the gaping hole where his heart was? So he nodded to appease his grandmother. *"Hai,"* he whispered, thinking that all lives eventually ended. And wasn't sorrow a kind of slow death anyway?

The year's distance had softened his outlook. Kenji glanced up at the canvas bag with Mika's masks in it sitting on the top shelf. Hiroshi had given the bag to Yoshiwara-sensei to keep. His teacher had put it out of the way, yet always within sight. It was up to Kenji as to when, and if, he looked at them again. On impulse, he walked over and reached up for the watermarked, soot-stained bag and swung it down to the worktable. He looked at the palms of his hands, which had completely healed, and tentatively opened the bag. One by one, he lined up the masks across the table and Mika was suddenly in the room with him again. A moment's agitation before he felt strangely calm, comforted. Kenji examined each mask closely; only two were really damaged by the fire. The others could be cleaned and easily restored. He reached into a drawer for sandpaper, a fine grade that wouldn't scratch the wood. Then Kenji gently, lovingly, began sanding away the scorched areas around her nose and along her cheek. He blew away the black dust and smiled to find that there was new life underneath.

THE CHALLENGE

It wasn't the challenge of winning or losing, but of standing up on her two feet that brought her such joy.

"You see, Yoshio," Fumiko said aloud. "I haven't forgotten." She reached up and placed the small bouquet of lilies in a vase by his photo. The past few weeks she'd remained bedridden, the constant pain in her hip making it difficult to walk. She'd fallen and broken it at the end of last August, just after Kenji had returned to his own home, and now, almost eight months later, it still gave her trouble. But this morning, Fumiko didn't care what the doctor said; she was lured by the sweet fragrance of the lilies in bloom and she was determined to put some by Yoshio's photo.

"Fumiko-san, what are you doing out of bed?"

She quickly turned around at the sound of Kazuko's voice, the live-in housekeeper Hiroshi had hired to take care of her and the house after she fell and broke her hip. She refused to move in with either of her grandsons, and only agreed to Kazuko's coming when she was bedridden. Fumiko felt uncomfortable with another woman in the house, doing all the simple things she'd done for more than sixty years. It irritated her to see the middle-aged, heavyset woman who stayed in her grandsons' room and moved through her house as if it were her own. And now, she had the nerve to confine her to bed.

"And why can't I be anywhere I wish to be in my own house?" she said.

"Fumiko-san, you know you're supposed to be resting."

Kazuko's voice dropped a few octaves. She was always too loud for Fumiko's taste. She imagined her as a child in school, always the one who spoke the loudest and knew the least.

"I'm fine," she said.

"That's what Sayo-san said," Kazuko went on about the mistress at her last position. In her stories, she was never the one who was wrong. "She thought everything was fine until one day she strained her back. I took care of her for months and I'm sorry to say that she never rose from her futon again."

Fumiko shook her head. She noticed that Kazuko never spoke of her personal life. Was she ever married? Did she have any children? Most likely she had scared them all off with her attentiveness. "If you're so sure I'll hurt myself doing the smallest task, then you'd better carry me back up the stairs to my room," she said, amused. Lately, their verbal sparring had become a game they played with each other.

"You're too funny, Fumiko-san. I can see you'll live to a fine old age."

Fumiko smiled. "I've already reached a fine old age, and I mean it. I believe it would be best if you carried me back up," she said. "I'm afraid my grandsons won't be happy to know that I've used up what little energy I have left climbing the stairs!"

Kazuko paused for a moment and studied her face. "I see, Fumiko-san. Do you think I'll give up working here because of your petty and difficult behavior? Well, I've seen it all." She walked over to Fumiko, turned around, and leaned over. "Get on, then," she directed. "Let me help you up the stairs."

Fumiko couldn't back away now and let Kazuko get the better of her. She had only meant to reclaim her position in the household, to give Kazuko a small reminder that she couldn't direct her every move; she hadn't expected Kazuko to really carry her up the stairs. Fumiko *had* acted childish, and now regretted it. Why was getting old so much like going backward? She hesitated before climbing onto the wide back. Slowly, she lifted her leg and a sharp pain instantly paralyzed her entire body. She stumbled back and a high-pitched cry emerged from her.

"It's okay now, just come closer," Kazuko instructed and she stepped backward to accommodate her.

It took Fumiko a full minute to catch her breath and allow the pain to move through her leg and out the tips of her toes. She took a deep breath and tried again.

Kazuko squatted yet lower. "Put your arms around my neck and lean forward onto my back."

She didn't argue and did as she was told. A child again. Fumiko leaned forward onto the big, broad back as if she were being sacrificed; her thin arms grasped tightly around Kazuko's red, blotchy neck like a winter scarf. It brought back a long-ago memory of once taking a walk with her father and her thirteen-year-old brother, Isamu. She was just a bit older than five-year-old Takara was now. It felt as if they'd walked half the day away. And even when their house was finally in sight, she simply couldn't find the strength to walk anymore, much less make it up the hill. Her father paid little attention to her and marched on in quick, long strides, his sandals click-clacking even as she fell farther and farther behind. It was Isamu who finally stopped and waited for her, teasing her into moving faster. "Hurry or even the tortoise will beat you home, Fumi." Then he leaned over so she could scramble onto his back, her arms wrapped around his sweaty neck, his slightly sour boy smell making her turn her head to the side. He carried her all the way up the hill and to the front door.

Kazuko took one stair at a time, a small grunt emerging with each step, careful not to drop her load. She was from the Niigata prefecture in central Japan, raised in a family of farmers, and as Fumiko suspected, was used to carrying much heavier loads than her. Fumiko turned her head and rested it for just a moment on Kazuko's thick, soft shoulder. She was tired, and the weight of life suddenly felt pressing. If Fumiko were to die right at that moment, she'd be more than ready.

The Wako Department Store

As soon as they stepped out of the darkened train station and into the bright daylight, Haru felt the July heat rising from the pavement, a mixture of afternoon boil and exhaust from the crowds and cars. The shrieking buses stopped and started along the teeming Ginza shopping district, lined with a multitude of tall buildings and expensive shops. After the war, soldiers and foreigners had brought the area back to life. Pale, sleeping neon lights shimmered in the sunlight. At night she envisioned them coming alive, the side streets aglow in the hypnotic flashing of lights. But in the blinding, mid-afternoon light of summer, Haru followed just a step behind Aki, who held Takara's sweaty hand as they walked down the congested sidewalk. Every once in a while, Takara turned back to make sure she was still behind them. Haru smiled and nodded in reassurance, part of her wishing she were holding the small, slippery hand in hers.

Since Aki was feeling better again, they went on more outings on the days she didn't teach; to the park or the market, even to the zoo, where Takara was fascinated with the giraffes, their height and, even more so, their long eyelashes. She thought giraffes were all girls, even if they weren't, because of their long, rolled eyelashes, which she called seaweed lashes, like the strips of dried seaweed rolled into sushi.

Haru smiled to herself and breathed in the warm, stale air. She'd found happiness in her life after all; teaching in Tokyo and watching Takara grow up. The Wako Department Store was just down the block and her heart raced at the thought of entering the tall doors and walking into the cool, open, high-ceilinged room. The Wako had a long history of selling watches and other luxuries from all over the world. When she and Aki were young girls, their mother took them to look at all the lovely things at least twice a year, and Haru grew dizzy from the powerful scent of new leather and sweet perfumes. She'd always felt as if she were stepping out of their scentless life and into the rich aromas of another. It would forever remain her favorite store and she hoped Takara would feel the same one day. The Wako Department Store was also one of the few buildings in the area to have survived the bombings at the end of the war. During the occupation it was used as the army PX, but was fully restored to its former glory when the occupation ended. She looked up to see the watchtower that defined the famous building, with its curved granite façade sitting on one of the most exclusive corners in the Ginza. Now that Aki-chan was finally better, returning to the Wako felt like a glorious moment — they had all somehow survived, to varying degrees, the madness of the war.

It was the last thing Haru thought about before an explosion ripped through the air, a noise so loud and familiar to all who had lived through the bombings during the war that she saw people around her instinctively dive to the ground, hands over their heads, as they were taught to do during the bombing drills. Haru moved forward without thinking, her arms going around Aki and Takara, trying to protect them. There was a general confusion, and while some ran, most stayed right where they were, too stunned to move. The twenty years between war and peace disappeared in an instant, as fragile as flesh. Moments passed before Haru heard voices of reassurance. "It's all right! It's all right!" someone shouted. In the far distance, sirens blared, coming closer. She looked up to see a great plume of smoke rising from the ground floor of a tall building just across the street. Only then did people slowly get up, dust their clothes off, and quickly continue along their way.

She saw how remnants of the war would always haunt those who had lived through it. Haru held on tightly to Takara, only to realize that Aki had slipped from her grip. Where was she? She looked frantically around, holding Takara's hand. "Aki," she yelled. "Aki!"

It was Takara who pulled at her sleeve and pointed down the street. Aki was cowering in a doorway, her hands over her head. Haru rushed over, pulling Takara along.

"Aki-chan, it's all right, it was only some accident across the road," Haru coaxed. She saw her sister's entire body trembling as if she'd lost control. "Stay right here," she said to Takara. Very slowly, she approached Aki and put her hand on top of hers. "Come now, everything's going to be fine."

"Okasan," Takara said.

Aki looked up.

"Everything's fine," Haru repeated.

She stepped out of the way so Aki could see for herself, as she glanced fearfully through her fingers like a child. The steady beat of life had returned to the Ginza, the heat and noise embraced them again. Slowly, so did Aki. Her hands slid away from her face and wrapped around her body as Haru helped her up. Her unsteady steps soon grew steadier as they walked back to the train station. Takara pulled at her sleeve, and when Haru bent over, she whispered, *"Okasan* is tired again." Haru held on to Aki's arm with one hand and Takara's hand with the other. Aki remained silent on the train, having retreated again into a world where she felt safe and comfortable. When the train pulled into their station, she looked over at Haru and asked, "Are we home?"

They never set foot in the Wako Department Store again. It wasn't until much later that they learned an old boiler had blown up in the building across the street, leaving one man injured.

32
August 6, 1965

From the window, Aki watched Tamiko-san leave the house with the bamboo basket she carried every morning to the market, the wooden gate slamming closed behind her. When she returned, Aki could usually tell by the contents of her basket what they'd be having for dinner; potatoes, carrots, and turnips meant a sweet vegetable stew, along with fish or pork tonkatsu. A whole chicken meant teriyaki or sukiyaki. She put such thoughts out of her mind; she didn't need to guess what Tamiko would have in her basket when she returned today.

Aki glanced at the clock to see that it wasn't quite ten. All morning, the radio had blared news of the twentieth anniversary of the bombings of Hiroshima and Nagasaki. Hiroshi had already left for another meeting with sponsors. She no longer cared who his meetings were with, whether they represented cold drinks or snack foods or tires. Takara was out with Haru and she smiled at the thought of her little daughter, so bright and curious at age five. She carried their best qualities, Hiroshi's strength and her once youthful inquisitiveness. With Haru's nurturing care, Takara would always be safe and secure. She didn't allow her thoughts to wander any further.

Aki knew she had no more than two hours before Tamiko returned. She stood up and went to the hall closet. Her mother's lacquer chest with the phoenix on top was stored there. She knelt and opened it, removed the tissue paper and the red kimono with the white peonies her mother wore as a young *maiko,* along with the red undergarments and her black-colored obi, which was interwoven with gold thread, her wooden sandals, makeup case, and her elaborate hair combs. Aki carried them all back to her room, where the photo of her mother as a young geisha apprentice, dressed in the very same kimono, sat squarely on her desk. She laid out the kimono on her futon and sat down to slowly begin applying her makeup first. From the green leather makeup case, she took out a glass container with a powdery white makeup. Then, with a flat brush, she mixed some of the makeup with water until it became a smooth, white paste. Aki studied her mother's photo before applying the makeup to her own face and neck. From the dark, waning moons of her eyebrows to the bright red of her lips,

Aki painstakingly copied each detail from her mother's photo. Her hair wasn't right but she pulled it back and pinned it up in a chignon. Then she placed the bright flower combs to each side of her hair. When she finished, Aki leaned back and stared into the mirror, at the face that could almost be her mother's staring back at her.

Aki's heart raced. She was almost there. She turned around to look at the kimono on her futon. The most complicated part of dressing would be tying the wide obi around her waist by herself. It was long and awkward and had to be wound around several times, a difficult task with the long scroll sleeves of an apprentice geisha's kimono hanging down. She tried a number of times and finally settled on fastening the many cords in the front, instead of in the back. It would never look as though a professional had dressed her, but it would have to do. She stepped up into the three-inch-high wooden sandals and felt as if she were rising out of herself.

Aki looked into the mirror and glanced at the photo one final time. She smiled and bowed to the geisha she saw reflected back at her.

The kimono was heavier and more cumbersome than Aki thought as she made her way through the garden. She carried rope and a wooden stool from the kitchen. The wind was blowing warm and muggy, the underrobe clinging to her back. The click-clack of the *maiko* sandals made it even more difficult to walk on the uneven stone path. But there was no hurry. No one would be home for at least an hour and she had plenty of time to walk through the garden. She stopped for a moment and looked up. The sky was a clear blue, the color of a calm sea. Aki remembered clear, hot days like this when she was a little girl, and how she was the first one up and out of the house to stand in the courtyard and stare up at the sky. She sometimes imagined it was the sea above her. She closed her eyes and heard the roar of the waves breaking and smelled the salt-fish breeze. She was that same little girl who had wanted to know if it rained because holes were poked in the sea sky. Was the sea sky crying? These thoughts felt like a lifetime ago.

Aki walked slowly down the path, hoping to choose a tree whose limbs were strong enough. She couldn't afford any mistakes. She began to worry that none of the trees in the garden could support her weight as the laurel tree had supported the old gardener in *The Damask Drum*. The *sakura* weren't fully grown and the willows and maples were too fragile. Aki's thoughts moved quickly back and forth until her gaze rested on the old pine tree near the pond. Much of the garden had been planned around the existing pine, and now she smiled to realize why. She looked back toward the house one last time, but didn't allow herself to think of Takara or Hiroshi, Haru or her father. It was better this way.

She threw the gardener's rope over the sturdy tree branch and watched it whip around once and come back to her. She did it again a few more times and pulled it taut against the branch before she moved the wooden stool underneath and set it steady. The area beside the pond was still cool from the shade of the tree. She carefully stepped up onto the stool, balancing herself with the help of the rope. Then she carefully placed the loop of the rough rope, thick and heavy, around her neck. Could it be as simple as this? She closed her eyes and saw her mother again on that awful day of the firestorm so many years ago, pulling Aki in one direction, while she fought to go in another, back to where they'd lost Haru. "This way," her mother's voice screamed above the roar, but Aki dug her feet squarely in the dirt where she stood and refused to move. The world was dark smoke around her when she suddenly turned at her mother's scream to see her back engulfed in bright flames like some strangely beautiful bird. She saw again the look on her mother's face, her eyes wide in pain and surprise as she pushed Aki roughly away from the fire. Afterward, all that she'd lost was her voice; along with the memory that it was her fault the fire had devoured her mother. She saw it all so clearly now as her mother's flaming body turned away from her and disappeared into the thick, choking smoke, leaving her alone and directionless.

Aki balanced unsteadily on the stool, lifted her arms so the long sleeves of the kimono hung down and fluttered in the warm wind like banners. She looked up at the blue sky that filtered through the branches of the pine tree like pieces of a puzzle, and relaxed at the thought of being reunited with her mother. Aki closed her eyes and counted, *ichi, ni, san, shi . . .* , before she kicked the wooden stool away.

AFTER

Hiroshi's meeting had ended early. From the moment the car dropped him off at the house and he stepped through the gate and into the garden, he felt something was wrong. The wind blew hot and then stilled; everything was too quiet. When Hiroshi found the house empty, he walked through the garden, following the path down to the pond. Immediately, it felt cooler in the shade of the willow trees and shrubbery. He began to understand why Haru and Takara spent so much time in the garden, squatting over some plant, delighting in every new discovery. The rustling birds sang out in the trees. He had just rounded the corner toward the pond when he stopped. At first, it appeared to be an *obake,* a ghost, wearing a bright red kimono, dangling in the air. His heart raced as he drew closer, recognizing it was Aki wearing the red kimono with white flowers hanging limply from the tree branch, her head cocked to one side. There was a stool turned over, a wooden sandal on the ground. Closer, he saw Aki's bloated and distorted face, as her protruding eyes peered down at him accusingly, and Hiroshi felt his legs go weak. His voice was a strange, stunned moan as he called out, "No!" before his breath caught in his throat. The air was suffocating, or was it grief pressed heavily against his chest? He wrapped his arms around Aki's legs and lifted her up, loosening the taut noose from her beautiful neck. The red, leathery rope burn had left an ugly necklace against her soft, pale skin. Her head fell forward and the past returned with its relentless power as he saw again Aki's mother down by the river after the firestorm.

33
CHANGE
1966

Hiroshi had skipped both the September and November Bashos following Aki's death. Afterward, he began training again for the January tournament knowing it would be his last. His lack of focus, along with a waning desire to fight, had begun last year, even before Aki's suicide. After her death, he had to transform the lethargy into something else; a way to get past the despair. Hiroshi always assumed he could make up the lost time with Aki when he retired, and now it was too late; all his unfulfilled promises had dissipated, leaving a lingering guilt. He somehow needed to put all his energy and concentration into this one last tournament before retiring.

After a morning of training, Hiroshi found Tanaka-oyakata upstairs in his office. Before, when he thought of retiring from sumo, the idea would lodge in his throat. Now he swallowed it with ease and sadness. He knocked. Tanaka looked up and motioned for him to come in. How many times had he sat in the small, crowded office across from Tanaka? His desk was buried in contracts, schedules, and a pile of *tegata,* the red ink handprints on *shikishi* white paper of his most popular wrestlers. Once they dried, each *sumotori* autographed his handprint. On top were Hiroshi's; over the years his handprints had become as popular as those of Yokozuna Futabayama.

During the almost eight years of Hiroshi's marriage to his daughter, Tanaka-oyakata had never changed, never showed any partiality in their working relationship. Only when they were with family did Hiroshi see Tanaka-san the father and grandfather. A tired smile crossed his father-in-law's lips. "Hiroshi-san, what can I do for you?"

Tanaka was much thinner and older than the man he first met in his high school gym, almost twenty years before. Hiroshi bowed. "May I speak with you for a moment?" he asked.

"Of course, of course." Tanaka pointed to the chair opposite his desk.

Hiroshi sat down and cleared his throat. The small office was warm and airless, a welcome change from the winter winds that whistled through the practice area downstairs.

"Is everything well with Takara?"

"She's very well, thank you. Haru-san has been wonderful with her," Hiroshi answered.

Tanaka nodded with a smile.

"I've come to speak to you about something else."

Tanaka stacked his papers, leaned back, and gave Hiroshi his full attention. "What is it?"

"I've been thinking that it's time for me to retire, what with Aki's . . ."

Tanaka-oyakata ran his hand over his pate in thought. "Of course," he said.

"And Takara's growing up so quickly."

"Hai." Tanaka grunted then looked away. After a moment, he continued. "You've been one of the greatest *yokozuna* in the history of the sport. You've stayed longer than most *sumotori.* You've made the Katsuyama-beya very proud. You've made me very proud. I know Aki-chan was, too."

When he finally looked at Hiroshi, his eyes were red-rimmed and moist. These were more words than Hiroshi had heard Tanaka-oyakata say in a long time. The room suddenly felt too small, suffocating. In that moment, the question Hiroshi had tried so hard to avoid all these months resonated through his mind. If he had retired earlier, could he have saved Aki?

He rose from the chair and bowed to Tanaka. "This will be my last tournament, then. The retirement ceremony can be held at the *hanazumo* in February."

"Hai," Tanaka-oyakata said. "It should give us enough time to prepare."

His father-in-law stood up and bowed low to Hiroshi.

It snowed on the second Sunday of January, the start of the Hatsu Basho. Hiroshi awoke to the soft, tapping sounds and a whiteness that covered the earth like feathers and muffled the world around him. He might have fallen back asleep if he hadn't heard Takara's excited voice already at the front door, imagining Haru not far behind his young daughter. His first match was that afternoon and he was due at the stable for a short workout before going to the stadium. But for the moment, he lay perfectly still and listened.

When Hiroshi stepped onto the *dohyo,* frenzied shouts from the audience filled the stadium. He bowed low and automatically moved through the opening rituals. His opponent was the up-and-coming wrestler Ogawa, young and large, his girth spilling over his *mawashi* belt. Hiroshi knew he'd never win the tournament, much less the match, unless he found a balance within himself; the concentration and harmony that felt very far away since Aki's death. He glanced up at the audience as he stepped toward the center of the ring and crouched down for the first round of stare-downs. He concentrated his stare on the fatty pockets just below the young wrestler's eyes. Ogawa didn't flinch, his eyes narrowing with determination.

The initial impact of his opponent's body was hard and solid. Hiroshi stepped back but didn't charge as he normally would. He felt lost in a haze and couldn't move. The next hit from the young wrestler came quickly and sent him precariously close to the edge of the *dohyo.* Along with the sudden silence of the crowd, he heard Aki's voice whisper in his ear, "What are you waiting for?" Hiroshi looked up and felt she was there. He had let her down so many times in life. It was, in the end, the last thing he could do for her in death, to win this tournament. When Ogawa charged at him again, Hiroshi reacted quickly and grabbed the wrestler's *mawashi* belt, twisting around and pushing him out of the *dohyo* first.

The roar of the crowd was deafening.

THE WIND

The wind blew sharp and cold as Haru walked in the garden with Takara. It was always the wind that carried the past back to her — unexpected and surprising each time — an icy whisper on her cheek that came with a winter breeze or a blustery day that sent leaves falling to the ground. Sometimes, it was a hot breath blown against the back of her neck, like a teasing voice or just a hint of the winds that had carried the inferno which had killed her mother and devastated her country so many years ago. It was an unforgiving wind that had left her hands without sensation and ended her childhood; a wind that had eventually taken Aki. However the winds came, they were invisible and eternal, something she'd never be able to grasp. The sharp winds now carried the scent of her mother's narcissus perfume and a faraway trace of wood smoke. It wasn't a sentimental wind but a clear and telling one.

Like her, Takara came alive among the plants and trees in the garden. The little girl ran down the path ahead of her. It felt as if the world around them were yawning awake, the garden filled with *ume* blossoms, the first blooms bursting white and pale pink against the blue sky. The new house Hiroshi had bought looked large and commanding. After Aki's death, he sold their house in Shoto in the Shibuya Ward and returned to Yanaka and a traditional Japanese-style house using wood posts and beams, with overhanging eaves and a wraparound veranda. It was a lovely piece of property, tucked away from the noise of Tokyo, yet near enough to the heart of the city by train or car. When Haru stayed to help raise Takara, one wing of the house had been set aside for her. Hiroshi also left the details of the garden up to her, and she chose *sakura,* maple, and wisteria trees for both their beauty and intimacy. She and Takara wandered down long winding paths through a variety of bamboo, irises, and lilies surrounding the pond. She saw hints of Deer Park in every corner. In the distance, willows moved in the wind like young geisha in dance. Each turn brought a new surprise; everything discovered to be seen and enjoyed.

She knew Aki would have loved this house and garden, and the thought brought a sharp ache. She couldn't imagine the pain Aki must have been in to leave Takara. She remembered the way her own grief after her sister's death was filled with movement, in tending to Takara, in teaching her classes, and in taking care of the mountains of details. It was the details that saved her, storing Aki's kimonos, packing her possessions, putting away her life.

And while Takara understood that her mother wouldn't be returning, death was still too large a concept for a five-year-old to grasp. At first, Takara remained quiet, not voiceless as Aki had been after their mother's death, but subdued, a stillness within her that was just as frightening. Haru saw her bewilderment. She stayed with her niece, slept in her room at night, and watched her carefully as the passing months gradually brought back her playful self again. Haru had always been a constant in Takara's young life, both as aunt and mother, and she struggled with the pleasure and the guilt. Was Takara her second chance? Did it have to come at Aki's expense? She flushed with the anger and the remorse of it; she hadn't been able to pull Aki through the fire this time.

Still, Takara never ceased to surprise her. The other morning she heard her niece talking to someone in the garden, but there wasn't anyone in sight.

"Who were you talking to?" she asked.

Takara looked at her, wide-eyed. "I was talking to *okasan.*"

"Was your mother here?"

Takara looked around the garden and answered, "She's everywhere."

Haru breathed in the cool, sweet air. She loved the approaching spring for all its possibilities. "Over here, over here!" she heard Takara call out. Haru pushed away her complicated thoughts. For today, she fully intended to live her life as it was given. She watched Takara examine the emerging blossoms, the newly unfurled leaves with a gentle, knowing hand. She stroked and held, never pinched or pulled. There was certainly something of Haru in Takara that would live on, and the thought brought her such happiness.

FUMIKO

At the February *hanazumo*, Fumiko shifted in the seat of the tatami-lined box, which provided a small shelter from the crowds who had come to see Hiroshi's retirement ceremony. It was hot and stuffy, and for a moment she was reminded of sitting in the cramped, airless bomb shelter her grandsons had dug during the war. Only it was too bright and she closed her eyes for just a moment, the noise and glare of the lights in the stadium forcing her to retreat within. Next to her, she felt Kenji's body lean closer to her, the fall of his silk kimono sleeve against her hand. He was making sure she was all right. Across from her, Haru quieted Takara. "Come and sit down," she said. The warm air stirred against her cheek when her great-granddaughter was pulled back into her seat. As always, they thought she had dozed off, and Fumiko understood now what Yoshio meant by seeing without seeing. Even with her eyes closed, she saw Takara's smiling face and heard the low purr of Haru's voice whispering for her to keep still. She resisted the urge to smile.

Ever since her grandsons were babies, Fumiko had endlessly worried that something might happen to them. They were so young and fragile when they came to her, and the ghost of Misako had lingered in every corner of her life. But Hiroshi and Kenji had survived, and she had lived to see their successes as well as their sorrows. How could she have ever known it was Mika's and Aki's deaths that would bring such grief? As Yoshio had always known, there was no way for her to protect them from life's misfortunes. But maybe now, after so much tragedy in both of their lives, her grandsons would find joy again. She smiled at the thought. Hiroshi might finally realize that his happiness sat right across from her, in his daughter and Haru-san, while Kenji would find his way in time, she was certain of it.

"Are you awake, *sosobo?*" Takara's voice rang out.

Fumiko opened her eyes slowly to the glare of the white lights, as she gradually focused on the face of her great-granddaughter watching her. She nodded and smiled, reached out to pull the child closer.

A DAY OF NO REGRETS

Hiroshi waited in the locker room to walk down the flower path to the *dohyo* for the last time. There, in the middle of the sumo ring, he would sit for his official *danpatsu-shiki,* the public haircutting ceremony that would signify his retirement at the age of thirty-seven. Hiroshi picked up the book of poetry by Basho that Kenji had given him and simply held it in his hands. His good-luck charm. He had memorized all the poems through the years to calm his nerves. But as he paced the length of the room, the weight of his white ceremonial belt tight around his waist, it was an old fable he remembered, and suddenly, he was a boy again listening to his grandmother. *". . . A very long time ago, a famous samurai, who came from a very poor family, had fought his way to the top, defending one of the richest landowners in Japan. But he still wasn't happy. While he was fighting and protecting his master all those years, a young woman from his village whom he'd always loved had married someone else. When he returned home a wealthy warrior, it was to find that life had passed him by."*

As a boy, Hiroshi couldn't understand why the samurai hadn't found perfect harmony. How could life have passed him by if he was a samurai? A warrior. Hiroshi took a deep breath and stopped pacing. What he hadn't understood as a boy, he now understood as a man. He struggled to remember the words his *ojichan* told them so long ago. "Every day of your lives, you must always be sure what you're fighting for." While he had sustained a nation in his quest to be champion, he couldn't save Aki.

Hiroshi walked down the flower aisle, the stadium filled to capacity, the roar of voices like a wave crashing. His retirement was being televised; everyone from city officials to sponsors and fans had come to see the great Yokozuna Takanoyama perform his final *dohyo-ri*. He marveled that most could see it at home in black-and-white. Tanaka-oyakata, Tokohashi, Sadao, the rest of his stable's wrestlers sat at ringside. His family watched from box seats.

The audience quieted as he stepped up to the *dohyo* to perform his last ring-entering ceremony, attended by Kobayashi and Wakahara, the only other *yokozuna*-ranked wrestlers. Dressed in their white ceremonial belts, he imagined the three of them were quite a spectacle framed within each small television. Hiroshi glanced up at the audience to let his grandmother know he was thinking of her. Then he moved through each step of the dance — the leg lifts and squats, his arms outstretched, each move bringing him closer to the finality of it — already memorizing the feel of the smooth, cool clay underfoot.

Afterward, Hiroshi changed into his formal *haori* jacket and a pair of pleated pants before he returned to sit in the middle of the *dohyo*. An attendant stood at his side with a pair of long, gold scissors on a tray. Assisted by the referee, Sadao and other selected *sekitori*-ranked wrestlers, sponsors, coaches, and Kenji each took their turns snipping off a few strands of his *chonmage*. Hiroshi sat stone-still under the hot lights of the stadium, his oiled hair glistening, his shirt wet against his back. Eventually, Tanaka-oyakata made the final cut of Hiroshi's topknot and severed the last threads that tied him to sumo, the sport he had loved since boyhood. Hiroshi was stunned by the thunderous clapping, an entire life ended with the cutting of his topknot. He could barely swallow. As he stood, his emotions lodged at the back of his throat.

Finally, both he and Tanaka-oyakata bowed respectfully to the audience, turning to each of the four sides of the arena. His unkempt hair fell across his forehead and covered his eyes so no one could see he was fighting back tears. He turned to his right and bowed again. Everything he had worked for came down to this final moment in time. Hanging from the ceiling, his large portrait had a place among all the other past champions and grand champions. He felt strangely distant from the *sumotori* who stared back at him, his nonsmiling gaze already a part of history.

Hiroshi turned and bowed again. He looked past the glare of lights to see the box seats where Kenji sat next to his smiling *obachan*, to see little Takara leaning forward and waving to him, to see Haru, always Haru, her hands no longer hidden, poised to grab his daughter if she should fall, if he should fall. And in the warm, thick air, he felt his *ojichan's* and Aki's spirits also there, watching.

Then at last Hiroshi faced the audience for the final time. He saw now that all the strength and control he commanded on the *dohyo* had little to do with the rest of the world. But unlike the samurai in his grandmother's tale, life wouldn't pass him by. It wasn't too late. Just outside the gates of the stadium, a new Japan prospered and grew; the ghosts of the past were put to rest as new generations moved forward into the world. And one step at a time, so would he.

ACKNOWLEDGMENTS

I'd like to thank Sally Richardson, George Witte, Hope Dellon, Joan Higgins, and all my countless friends at St. Martin's Press who have helped to bring this book to fruition. Also, thank you to Linda McFall and my agent, Linda Allen, and to the Ragdale Foundation for the gift of quiet and inspiration.

This book could not have been written without the support of family and friends. I'm especially grateful to my brother Tom through thick and thin. Thank you always to Catherine de Cuir, Cynthia Dorfman, Blair Moser, and Abby Pollak. And to those Wonder Women Dorothy Allison, Karen Joy Fowler, and Jane Hamilton.

Lastly, I'm particularly thankful for the following texts that helped me unravel the complexities of the Japanese culture: *Embracing Defeat* by John W. Dower, *Japan at War: An Oral History* by Haruko Taya Cook and Theodore F. Cook, *Japanese for Busy People* from Kodansha International, and *The Big Book of Sumo* by Mina Hall, given to me by Peter Goodman of Stone Bridge Press. Any mistakes are entirely my own.

ABOUT THE AUTHOR

Gail Tsukiyama is the bestselling author of five previous novels, including *Women of the Silk* and *The Samurai's Garden,* as well as a recipient of the Academy of American Poets Award and the PEN Oakland/Josephine Miles Literary Award. She divides her time between El Cerrito and Napa Valley, California.